PIP AND ESTELLA

The Estella Trilogy
Volume One

A sequel to Charles Dickens' *Great Expectations*

HUGH SOCKETT

Waterside Productions

Printed in the United States of America

First Printing, 2021

ISBN-13: 978-1-954968-33-2 print edition
ISBN-13: 978-1-954968-34-9 ebook edition

Waterside Productions
2055 Oxford Ave
Cardiff, CA 92007
www.waterside.com

ACKNOWLEDGMENTS

At the conclusion of *Great Expectations* Dickens leaves us with two puzzles: Did Pip and Estella ever marry, and what is to become of the three-year-old Pip, son of Joe and Biddy Gargery? As I reread the novel after watching the more recent of the movies, I tried out solutions to those puzzles first through a short story, then through a sequel novel which has eventually become the first book of *The Estella Trilogy*.

I am most grateful to two particular friends: Richard Hill, formerly of Penguin Books and founder of *Books for Keeps*, for his introduction to agents and his wise counsel. I owe a major debt to my friend John O'Connor, an English Literature Emeritus Professor at George Mason University, and a colleague for many years. John has been with these books since their inception, reading, commenting, making suggestions for sometimes quite radical changes. He has read every draft with care and kindness in his critical appraisals. His support has been invaluable.

I have been coached throughout the process of becoming an author of fiction by Mark Malatesta whose encouragement has never flagged. My thanks are also due to Bill Gladstone of Waterside Productions for his encouragement, but especially to Libby Sweeney who has proof-read the manuscript with great care and diligence.

This book is dedicated to my wife Ann who has tolerated the moody trials of a debut fiction writer with her usual grace, and to my immediate family: Justin, Stacey, Abigail and Jake; Victoria, Greg, Jack, Hanna and Megan; Jonathan and Victoria, and Nick, Terri and Jennifer.

TABLE OF CONTENTS

The frontispiece is a drawing titled *Estella and Pip* by Harry Furniss copied from page 456 of *Great Expectations* in the Charles Dickens Library, published by the *Educational Book Club of London*. The date is not specified, but probably circa 1910 the date given for Furniss' drawings of five hundred plates for the Charles Dickens Library.

I

A mile and a half from the village of All Hallows in the county of Kent, a gentleman was riding a well-known path to reacquaint himself with a lady whom he had known since childhood and whom he loved profoundly. Although he had once declared himself to her moments before she told him of her betrothal to another, he believed that she would never see him as a suitor, even though her husband had been killed by his horse.

Yet it was with a sense of unease that he was about to tell her that he was now engaged to be married to another, for she had never returned any hint of anything more than friendship to the signals of his passion, a legacy perhaps of her strange upbringing as the ward of a markedly eccentric guardian who had taught her to see every man as an object of derision, distrust and contempt.

His long-time friends in their cottage across the marshes had received the new intelligence of his engagement with unrestrained delight. Moreover, to their even greater satisfaction he confessed that the lady whom he was to marry was not she whom he was now intending to visit. On this solitary journey he walked his horse deliberately and carefully whilst he pondered the odd state of his mind about this lady that he had loved almost as long as he could remember.

It was a fine morning in June 1847. In his mind's eye was that lovely young woman of nineteen, a year or so older than he, nearly twenty years back. With her, he was—well, what exactly?

In love? Still infatuated? Thwarted?

Did he want her because he still loved her? He might agree with the judgment of his friends, that, because his passion for her developed when he was young, that first feeling of the turbulence of physical attraction and desire remained with him.

Did he want her because she didn't want him? Perhaps that simply enhanced the desire, as her guardian knew it would, yielding the incessant suffering of rejection.

Ought she to love him? That notion often crossed his mind as he had shown respectfully and carefully such devotion to her. Yet what, if anything, did she owe to him or he to her, then or now? The mere trifles of encouragement he was given on occasion had not deluded him. Sometimes what was possible seemed a little closer but then suddenly was out of reach.

Such thoughts about her tumbled through his mind as he approached her home. He contemplated this fact of human life: An initial explosion of desire eventually becomes a memory, but then, as that memory crosses the mind, so the remembrances of the turbulent passions surge again, if not in the loins, certainly in the heart.

For many months now he had tried not to see her through the prism of pity, distressed as she was, a widow after an unwanted short marriage, her brutal husband's neck broken by a kick from his horse with a sound like the crack of a walnut.

His recent travels abroad for years without contact seemed to have reconciled him to never getting closer to her than a somewhat languid friendship, the sort that acknowledges a common past, and renews pleasures when there are meetings, but little effort is made, on either side, to sustain them.

Getting married to his new love surely would squash any desire in him for her, finally and irrevocably. It would become the sort of friendship where, whatever the gaps of acquaintance, when meeting, both parties would say that it is as if we met only yesterday.

As he arrived at her home, he remembered that both the old house and the original brewery, the source of her guardian's wealth, were gone, demolished. She ordered this after that woman died an unspeakable death, her whole body burnt when she stood too near the log fire and her dress became an inferno. All that remained now was the small cottage, the gate lodge of the house, and he assumed she would be there living in cramped quarters to which she was certainly unaccustomed.

The sound of hooves on the gravel brought Estella out of the cottage.

"Estella," Pip called out as he dismounted, "how good to see you after all these years, but I have seen you look happier. Let me kiss your hand in greeting."

She smiled and took his arm as they sauntered together on the drive toward where the old house once stood.

"How very good to see you too, Pip. Back from your travels? It has been a long time.

"You deserted me by going abroad, not even saying goodbye. I only learned you had gone after I wrote to Herbert enquiring as to your whereabouts. You had been ill, which you also kept from me.

"I am still in such turmoil, living in this small cottage on my own, with only one maid. I get some solace in reading Miss Austen. But I know you are wise enough to provide me with some remedies."

He watched her carefully while listening, shocked that this strong woman seemed so incapable of gathering her life in her hands. Her long dark hair was coiled above her head, her startling blue eyes and skin like alabaster without the glow of yesteryear. She should be in the prime of her life, yet here she was, her beauty fading noticeably. At any rate, to him.

"Have you resigned yourself to this life, Estella? Does not the absence of these old buildings serve simply to enhance the memories, far from killing them? Or are you intent on self-immolation?" He said with a generous smile.

"Perhaps you can help me, though I doubt it. But first, how come you have decided to visit me?"

"I was here in Kent seeing Joe and Biddy at the cottage, and I wanted to know whether you were still here and if so, how you were."

"How nice of you. I hate this place, so much misery, so many bad memories.

"Not that the memories of you coming to play in the old house are bad, though throughout that time it was if I was under a witch's spell. I lived with this mad woman that I respected for what she had done for me, but I could not love a woman who controlled virtually everything I did. Since she died, and my dreadful marriage was done so quickly, I have not known what to do. "Am I to live in this cottage forever? Where else can I go? London?"

"Estella, my dear, you must put Miss Havisham and all that behind you for good.

"You must get away from this house. You need a new lease on life, a house and a home. Find or have a new house built somewhere nearby or perhaps far away. Take lodgings in London, too. She left you a substantial legacy, I am sure, and you can sell this ground. But consult Jaggers; he will give the best advice."

Estella's face brightened.

It was if a deep dark shadow had been lifted from her, and suddenly she was full of energy.

"Of course, Jaggers! Jaggers: The lawyer who brought me to my guardian.

"You have inspired me, Pip. Just what I needed. I must do that directly. Why did I not think of that? I can't just go on waiting for something to turn up, can I? In fact, my dear Pip, you have turned up. I must stop being lonely. Can I accompany you to London if you are getting the coach?"

"Yes indeed, but I came also to tell you that this summer I am to marry Beatrice, a Pocket cousin. She is twenty-five. I am very excited."

Estella's new brightness dimmed for a brief second, but she recovered herself. And with a somewhat hollow laugh, she asked:

"Marriage? At your age? I don't mean to mock you, my dear, but I thought we would be old bachelor and widow together. I know of

Beatrice, of course, and I am sure she will be everything you desire, but I have not met her.

"Oh, those Pockets were Miss Havisham's cousins; they get everywhere," she said impatiently, "but good fortune in your marriage, you will be a good husband and father, I know."

"I hope so, but let us get back to your situation."

"Come with me to the coach. Go to see Jaggers in the morning while I look for some temporary lodgings for you. I take it that I am right that you have no pecuniary difficulties?"

"That is right, dear Pip. Give me a short while to instruct my maid what to pack."

"I'll walk in the grounds till you are ready."

Pip wandered away toward the ruins of the brewery, stirred by his childhood memories of the place. Yet now that he had met Estella again, he realized he must come to terms with his feelings for her. He will have to wrestle with this eternal desire for her which will not abate, indeed has been rekindled with this brief meeting. Though she was seemingly depressed and out of sorts, even walking in the drive with her on his arm, the physical touch aroused that ever-smoldering emotion. The flame began to burn brightly once again.

"Ah, here you are. Let me help you into the trap."

As he took her hand, he had a vision of pulling her towards him and kissing her on the lips; her smile of thanks, however, was the old Estella, keeping him firmly at a distance.

"Thank you, Pip. I feel I am embarking on a new adventure and I am feeling quite giddy at the prospect."

It was an uneventful overnight ride to London from the Blue Boar Inn on the Rochester-Chatham Road, five miles from her home. Estella slept the night comfortably in a corner. Pip could not sleep but gazed at the woman opposite through the darkness and its fleeting shadows, imagining many different scenes and events in which they were ever to be together.

As the journey ended he began to see more clearly that when he married Beatrice, his love for Estella would always be on his conscience. Awash with speculations and conjectures, he dismounted at the coaching inn near the Tower of London tired and baffled. Estella meanwhile had slept well and was so cheerful they had a meal at the Inn before she set off for Little Britain whilst he hurried off to find her a place where she could stay in the city.

She was put down at the door to Mr. Jaggers' chambers in Little Britain and walked up the steps. In the hallway, double doors on her right shielded the lawyer's private office. In the hallway, Robert, the tall young clerk, sat at a high desk from which he descended to greet her.

"Begging your pardon, ma'am, can I be of assistance?"

"I need to see Mr. Jaggers, young man," she said with that characteristic haughtiness she had been brought up to project.

"Did you tell him you were coming to see him today?"

"No, but it is very urgent. Is he in court? Will he be back directly? I can wait for him in his office."

"He is in court this morning, though he should return soon. But I don't know what Mr. Wemmick would say, and he's out as well. Oh dear, I'll get into serious trouble if I let you into Mr. Jaggers' office."

"I will take the responsibility. Show me in."

"This makes me very nervous, ma'am."

"Stuff and nonsense. Do not fret, young man. I will tell him I forced you let me in so that I can sit comfortably in the inner sanctum. It's not Windsor Castle, you know."

"Well, I hope it'll be all right. You will tell Mr. Jaggers you told me to, won't you?"

"Of course. Here's a florin. Now run along."

Robert then opened the door for her, and she entered the lawyer's room with its walls of law reports with plaster casts atop them and a massive oak partner's desk, though Jaggers had no partner. It was a gloomy place indeed, she thought, like a gateway to the underworld. Though he had profoundly influenced her life, he always visited Miss Havisham when needed, not the other way around, so she knew him if only slightly.

A few minutes later, as she was gazing out of the window over toward the Temple, a side door opened behind the desk and a woman entered.

"I'm begging your pardon, ma'am, I didn't know anyone was here, I was just getting this glass," she said, pointing to an empty glass on the desk but standing still with her head down as if asking permission from this grand lady to fetch it.

This was Molly, Jaggers' servant in both home and office. She had a slightly disheveled appearance, of medium height, her greying hair in a bun, grey clothes and a white apron, shoes hid beneath a voluminous skirt. Approaching fifty years old, she still had a fine figure and blue eyes, which she raised very briefly to look at Estella, catching her glance. Surprised by the glance, Estella looked at her very carefully and then suddenly shocked, exclaimed:

"Here, come here, let me look at you. I know you, I know you, don't I? How do I know you?" her voice in crescendo as she peered at Molly.

"Who are you? Who are you?" at which Molly said in a whisper:

"I don't know, I don't know. It can't be you."

"Come here. Let me look at you with care," said Estella.

"I know your eyes. How do I know your eyes? Let me see your hands. Oh, oh, your scars, your scars, your terrible scars, I remember them from my childhood, the damage you did to them. And your hands are like mine!"

"How is this? How is this?" she shrieked loudly in a mixture of ecstasy and dismay. "What is this? What is this? I know you. I know you. Are you my mother?"

The two women fell into each other's arms, howling and embracing each other tightly. Mr. Jaggers had returned from court, and hearing the cries from his office, stealthily entered the room, remaining near the door, his head down, as yet unnoticed.

"You must be my daughter, my Ruth, my daughter, I gave you away, I gave you away. Oh, my God, I gave you away. He told me you would become a fine lady."

"But my name is Estella, not Ruth."

"I called you Ruth; you've been given another name."

Jaggers then coughed to indicate his presence:

"Please listen, both of you. Yes, Miss Havisham did change your name, Estella."

Estella looked at him blazing with anger and shouted:

"Mr. Jaggers, is this woman my mother?"

"Yes," replied Jaggers quietly, but with a shame-faced certainty in his tone. This tough, rather brutal lawyer known for his secrecy but also for his regard among the criminal poor, seemed knocked off balance in giving his answer.

But Estella's blood was up.

"How dare you? You have kept this from me for all these years, Mr. Jaggers. Shame on you! Have you no conscience? How dare you, how dare you?

"I was seven when I went to Miss Havisham. I am now over thirty years old. For over twenty years you have concealed my mother from me. You disgust me. I will take her away with me this instant."

"I had my reasons. Let me try to explain," Jaggers replied, quieter than his custom.

Molly was weeping, avoiding his gaze and looking in wonder at her long-lost daughter.

Still on fire with her anger, Estella shouted at him:

"I wish to know no more about it, what you got up to with my guardian. And she even changed my name, dear God!

"I remember my mother through a young child's eyes, watching her weeping, angry, assaulted. I remember being held with those scarred hands of hers.

"Now I must care for her, not you. So be quick, Mr. Jaggers, if you can explain this miraculous calamity. I will have her with me directly."

"I can't be quick, I fear, as it is a long story.

"Please, wait, please let me at least explain how this came about, so that you both are cognizant of my reasons. Molly, I have to tell you both the story, the circumstances and the reasons for Estella not continuing to live with you. Both of your stories will cause you great sadness, but you now have the opportunity to consign those circumstances to history and come together. I warn you both," he said grimly, "I will be telling you things that you won't know, and which may hurt you."

"Get on with it then," Estella cried, looking at him still with fire in her eyes.

"I will, I will. Put the case, Molly, that when I first met you I defended you on a charge of murder. You were living with your common law husband; he had a criminal background and a criminal's view of the world. He was Estella's father."

"Oh, my god-forsaken soul," says Estella, "I never knew this."

"Your husband, Molly, was a strong, powerful man, in fact with a sense of honor, especially among thieves as it happened. You loved him so deeply that your jealousy was like a tinder, only needing to be struck to burst into a flame of dangerous passion."

"Oh yes, sir, I loved the brute," said Molly through her tears.

"And that flame became an inferno. The man you loved was desired by another woman and he finally succumbed to her entreaties. You lured her to a barn, and you strangled her with those powerful hands of yours. That woman's husband was then about to be transported, and though it was some time ago, I have sheltered you here for fear of his return.

"Remember that—I was protecting you from that woman's husband. But I was able to have you acquitted of murder on grounds of passion, though you were always a wild untamable creature."

"Is this true, Mother?" Estella asks, beginning to weep herself.

"Yes, it's as he said."

"However, you had a little girl, about six years old at the time of your ignominy, so, now, she is able to remember you, your scars and your eyes, as she was not then a mere infant in a cot. Realize that I have seen children of your class, the desperate criminal poor, children hung or transported, destined to live lives of penury, disease and early death.

"You could be sheltered by me, or you could take your chances out there in the criminal world as a murderer, with a young child who might well have had no option but to whore herself."

"Yes, I gave you away, my Ruthie," said Molly, clinging to Estella's arm and burying her head in her shoulder.

"At the time I also had a wealthy unmarried client, Miss Havisham, who desired to bring up a girl, and I put the case to you then that her life would be infinitely better than anything you could provide. You agreed without talking to her father who, in any case, was on a prison hulk. In fact, he had secured an approach to me as a client when he heard that I had you acquitted and just before he was apprehended and later sentenced to be transported, met with him in jail.

"But I could do nothing for him then. He later contacted me on another matter. He was in despair, so he said, for his little girl. Now, Estella, you were the little girl I arranged for Miss Havisham to bring up, as you well know."

"And look what Miss Havisham has done to me, a gentlewoman with a rotten soul."

"I know, I know. I have often been assailed by doubts as to whether I should have followed this course. But, each time, each time, I examine the details, I believe I was correct in my judgment and I have hardened myself against my troubled conscience.

"You now may judge me; I hope kindly. I tried to act in both your interests. Estella, I have been wrong in not arranging for you to meet your father, but it was far too dangerous while he was alive."

Both women looked at Jaggers with surprise and said in unison: "Was he here then?"

"Indeed. He returned illegally from Australia a rich man, but he was being hunted by his enemies and the Law. And there is one more fact of which you should both be most conscious. Your husband you know, Molly. But, Estella, do you comprehend what I intimated, that your father was the convict, Abel Magwitch?"

"Was he not the benefactor Pip told me about?"

"Yes, indeed. In that faraway place he made a fortune, probably legally, and he was Pip's benefactor. Pip found out about this family soon after Miss Havisham's passing."

"Pip has never asked me or told me what he was doing."

"I am sure he was trying to protect you, and in any event, he was ill and then went on his travels. Before he left, Abel died in prison here, with Pip and Herbert Pocket tending to him and Pip told him of your existence and how you became a lady.

"It was a great comfort and he died with a smile on his face. I put the case that Abel's generosity to Pip was a way of having the pleasure of being a father, as a remembrance of the daughter he had lost and knew nothing of her fate."

"He were still a bleeding bastard," interjected Molly, who had so far been silent during these exchanges, "a right bleeding bastard."

"No doubt, Mother," said Estella, unnerved by this vulgar language.

She turned to Mr. Jaggers, and said:

"How strange that we are so tied together, Pip and I. How kind of him to help a wounded man. Extraordinary," she said quietly, almost to herself, "that he was Pip's benefactor."

"Indeed," said Jaggers, now addressing them both:

"You are mother and daughter, much older and wiser, and in Estella's case, much richer. While I will be sorry to lose Molly here both as my servant in this office and in my home, I anticipate your desire to live together. Am I right?"

"That's what I want if she'll have me, though Sir, beggin' your pardon, I am grateful for what you'se done for me, but now I've a daughter to care for, God help me."

"Then, Mother, we can collect your possessions from Mr. Jaggers' residence and then we will share lodgings. Pip should have found something for me by now.

"Oh, Mr. Jaggers, I came here this morning for advice on getting a house, now for both of us."

"I don't deal in trivialities. An easy process. Wemmick is the person to talk to. I assume you'll keep your lodging in town and find a place in Kent."

"Exactly. Good day to you. Mother, come with me."

As they were leaving, Robert told them that a Mr. Pip had left a message and she was to go to Cheapside near St. Paul's and there she would find her lodging. Estella thanked the clerk and ask him to call a cab and they set off holding hands.

Their continued silence in the cab was as much as either could bear, occasionally looking at each other and smiling, the only possible immediate outcome of what had happened. The hurt and the pain for both of them that had endured since their tear-filled parting all those years ago was there like a dark cloud beginning to evaporate, albeit slowly, as the sun burned away the vapors.

Yet whatever the bond of kinship, these were utterly different people. Molly was a convicted working-class criminal who had spent all these years as a servant, barely above a skivvy, to a man of fierce, even volatile temperament. Her speech was that of a Cockney, with no refinement, and she was illiterate. For years she had enjoyed no independence about anything. At this moment, however, she was filled with gratitude, longing and a certain fear of freedom.

Her reacquired daughter Estella, on the other hand, had a privileged education, comprising the usual accomplishments of a wealthy mid-century lady. As she looked at Molly, she was at first terrified at the thought of living permanently with her mother whom she knew only as a child living in abject poverty. But then, she thought, what could be worse than living with Miss Havisham?

Yet both of them had been deeply lonely; Molly as a servant, Estella as a widow.

Neither had friends, even acquaintances.

Alleviation of loneliness might bring blessings for both of them in their changing circumstances, especially perhaps in the glory of the English summer.

II

The redoubtable Mr. Jaggers sat slumped in his desk chair for some hours after the happenings with Estella and his servant, Molly. Wemmick came in and listened to the old lawyer unburdening his conscience.

"What damage I have been a party to?" He asked Wemmick.

"Was there no other course for Molly? I suffer from the tyranny of good intentions. Think of other such cases where I have intervened, directing individuals, usually poor, in direction I determined. I am becoming more than conscious of the limits of my wisdom, perhaps of my personality."

"If you will forgive me, Mr. Jaggers, I think a sense of remorse has been kindled by this reunion of mother and daughter."

"It has indeed. I'm in need of a rest and a period of reflection, and I think the Grand Hotel in Brighton will provide sufficient comfort and privacy for two weeks at least. I will depart forthwith," and, gathering some papers from his desk, he bid Wemmick good day and left..

Wemmick was startled by this sudden departure and told Robert, the junior clerk:

"Blow me down with a feather. I never knew him to take a holiday. I suppose that business with that mother and daughter has upset him as no other case has ever done."

"Well, Mr. Wemmick, stranger things happen at sea."

A man of pragmatic temperament, Wemmick immediately went into his small office and sat at the desk wondering how a refined rich lady like Estella would cope with mad Molly.

Mr. Jaggers' sojourn in Brighton lasted a month and he arrived back in Little Britain in early August, looking healthy and quite rested, though the weight of his remorse hung round his shoulders for half a year. However, four weeks or so went by in normal activity after his return before he called for Wemmick and shared his reflections with his colleague.

"Wemmick, I know I have been a hard man. I have taken decisions for people away from them, often under the guise of legal jeopardy. I must change my spots, still remaining a leopard in the court, but much more reflective rather than abrupt about the directions I give people.

"I was deeply shocked as I reflected on what had happened to Estella, Molly less so. For it was I, you know, who played a major part in leading Estella to marry that bounder Drummle. Indeed, I could easily pick out a dozen where what I advised had gone badly wrong."

"Mr. Jaggers, sir. First, I commend you wholeheartedly on your determination to examine your conscience on various cases, and I must say, if you will forgive me, that I have found your decisions in one or two instances quite difficult to fathom. But no crying over spilt milk. I am not a believer in fretting about matters that cannot be changed."

"Thank you for your consolation, Wemmick. I am resolved to change, but I have decided also that I need a partner. I am cogitating the possibility of offering to train Mr. Pip as my pupil. As you know, associations of lawyers have been talking since the Queen's Coronation about some system of legal education, but we cannot wait for that. Then I might apply to be a Queen's Counsel which seems more dignified than a sergeant-at-law. What do you think?"

"I am heartily pleased on both accounts," said Wemmick. "I had an inkling you might invite Mr. Pip. One must take care of one's legacy."

On New Year's Eve that year the Gargerys walked one evening from their home the two miles to the Three Jolly Bargemen, with their young son Pip, now almost ten years old, and with their longtime

14

friend, Mr. Pip himself, up for the holiday from London to cele-brate the turning of the year as was the custom for marsh people in this corner of the county of Kent.

"Emptied those spittoons yet, m'dear?" the landlord was calling out to his wife.

"Done last night afore we was in bed," was the reply.

"And polished, too?"

"Who do think I am, Joss? That brass has come up lovely."

"That's my Jezebel," said Josiah Steppings, the landlord of the Three Jolly Bargemen. "We'll need 'em tonight, my darlin', what with this north wind howling across the marshes, come from the North Pole, I shouldn't wonder. Gets into the chest, don't it? Maybe it'll keep some folks away, but it is New Year's Eve, so we must be clean and hope for good takings."

As the door opened Josiah broke off this conversation with his wife, turned around and proclaimed loudly:

"Well, well, well, if it isn't the Gargerys! Welcome!"

A public house used to be a place where a person kept a stock of ale and spirits for sale open to one and all to enjoy convivial times with their friends and neighbors. Sometime in the Early Middle Ages, such establishments in England were ordered to put a sign outside with a name which indicated it was a public house. Yet for many years local customers referred to such houses by the name of the owner rather than the name on the sign. So what would have been referred to Josiah Steppings' is by law the Three Jolly Bargemen. It was still a simple space, usually a large single room with a bar from which drinks were served, where smoke from clay pipes filled the air. There'd be several small tables and chairs, a couple of settles, a straw floor, a large log fire and two or three clean spittoons, always needed on a cold night.

"Biting cold out there, Joss," replied Joe Gargery, "but my wife would have her tipple."

"Shame on you, Joe Gargery," Biddy replied to mutual laughter, "you can get me a glass of ale then, and while you are on your feet and I rest my legs, get summat for our two Pips."

"Two Pips?" questioned Joss Steppings as Joe stood at the bar, "How come they got the same name?"

"Ah," said Joe, as if he were about to divulge a family secret, "Old Pip was my first wife's young brother who lived with us, see.

"But he 'came a gentlemun and then he went away on his travels. His sister had died, terrible that was too, so I was a widower, but later Biddy and I was wed, and we didn't know we'd ever see the dear old chap again, so we called our son Pip after him. Then up he turns like the bad penny after many a year, and oh, you would not believe, Joss, what a delight that was for Biddy and me.

"But nowadays, Biddy couldn't be calling out 'Pip' from the kitchen and they's both come running, so I says we call 'em Young Pip and Old Pip. Young Pip calls Old Pip his uncle too, though he's not his uncle, the dear old chap. They'se just best of friends."

"So that well-dressed fella with you is Old Pip? Well, well, well" said Joss, deploying his favorite expression. "I comes from Chatham where I was after I finished in the Navy only last year, but folks in the pub have gossiped about him a little, wondering what he were up to when he was off being a gentleman and on his travels."

"I don't rightly know where he were, Joss, maybe Araby, perhaps that country where Greek people live. But he had to be away, see, as he had a benefactor who died, so our dear old chap had no money.

But he'd become a proper gentlemun before that," Joe continued with a certain wistfulness, "and now he has a position in London, clerking or lawyering or summat. Yet, like he says, he's still a son of the marshes. See how the two Pips there talking to each other like they was man and boy. Too luvly to see."

Old Pip collected his ale, Young Pip his dandelion and burdock, and they sat down next to Joe and Biddy each with a glass of porter. Friends and neighbors were coming in and settling themselves down with ale, porter or occasionally some Kentish cider. Old Pip began to talk about how sun, moon and stars seem so different here in the marsh country from London, when Young Pip interrupted him.

"Can I ask you something, Uncle Pip?"

"Of course, dear boy, ask away. Not many secrets among best of friends, eh?"

"I'se wondering," he asked, "Why doesn't you talk like we do?"

At that, Old Pip spluttered into his beer, laughing loudly, splashing his overcoat, spilling more ale as he set his tankard down on the table, and said in a voice with a very loud Kentish accent, "Becos I'm a gentlemun, see?"

At which, most of the folks in the pub guffawed, and then burst into laughter as Young Pip tried to imitate Old Pip's gentleman's accent with a "Because I am a gentleman, see," equally as loud as his uncle's.

Laughter erupted from all sides of the pub, especially when the barmaid Beryl failed dreadfully at her imitation howling with laughter, at which the laughter redoubled. The merriment gradually died away after most folk, including Sam and Mary Friendly, Tom and Mary Butterworth and others had taken their turns at a gentleman's accent.

Joe and Biddy did not make the attempt, but Joe, as is his custom when there is gaiety and laughter, murmured to his wife, "What larks, eh, Biddy?"

"Our boys is funny ones, eh, Joe?" said Biddy quietly, clasping her man's solid blacksmith's hand with his gnarled knuckles and hardened skin on the palm and fingers, a legacy of years of laboring with iron, a thumb so tough it looked as though it could hammer in nails.

"You're such a handsome man," she whispered. "So tall and strong with your red curly hair."

"Now then, Biddy, I suppose I am tall, being almost six foot, and Old Pip is tall too."

Then he turned and smiled at her with that twinkle that thrilled her, grateful above all measure for sitting as close as he can to the woman who made him so happy and so calm after the belligerence of Old Pip's sister, his first wife, Georgiana.

"And I loves you too," he whispered.

Joe and Biddy also felt blessed with their son and she gazed at him with love and pride, a quiet powerful signal of mutual love which he returned with an open smile.

The youngster adored Old Pip, for whenever he visited, he could be seen watching his older namesake asleep in the leather chair in front of the fire after coming by the overnight coach from London, his face twitching as he dreamt. On such occasions, the boy would be like a cat waiting to be fed, silently urging his uncle to wake up to take a walk across the marshes with him.

General bawdy and country-like conversation resumed as the pub filled up, but Young Pip was eager to know how his older namesake became this gentleman with that accent. The raucous laughter started to subside and Young Pip said to his mother that Uncle Pip and he were going over to a quiet corner.

"Old Pip now, you be careful," Biddy exclaimed, "I don't want my son filled up with some nonsense."

Once settled in the corner, Old Pip said:

"Let's leave alone how I became a gentleman. I just want to say that I don't want you to grow up like me: I was a young man of great expectations. I want you to be a man of good expectations, with a conscience, always keen to do what is right. Do good in your life."

"I want to be like you, but still I think I knows what you'se saying."

"I'm sure you will in time. Tell me," he said, keen to change the subject, "do you watch your father at the forge?"

"I like watching my father shoe horses and he's going to teach me how to do it so I can become a farrier."

"Hmm," said Old Pip, as if reaching for a momentous decision.

"In that case, you'll need a horse of your own, won't you? I think, I think, yes, I am sure you're ready for your own horse. Shall we go to market tomorrow and get one?"

"Oh, thank you, thank you, thank you," said Young Pip, grasping his uncle's hands.

"I can think of nothing I want more. If not the market, my father often goes to Mr. Buzza at his stables."

"Right, tomorrow we sally forth in search of a nag for Young Pip."

A little while later, the pub's customers all rose to toast the arrival of 1847 with all the rituals rooted in the ancient customs and superstitions on the passing of the year.

By June 1847 Young Pip was using his new horse Boney with his father's cart to go to All Hallows Village, that same horse he had been given by his uncle at the New Year. The expedition this day was to buy provisions for the family. It was to change his life.

Boney was an attentive listener to his young master's ruminations on what was a lovely morning, his location of different birds on the small shrubs or hedges along the way such as the warbler, the blackbird, the chaffinch, even the occasional hoopoe with its black and white feathers and the projection like a stick from the middle of its head. Boney snorted his understanding of this nature lesson, the air billowing from his nostrils as he trotted along the track.

"Now, you'll help me remember what I must buy, won't you, dear horse o'mine?"

Ever complaisant, the horse gave a brief snort as Young Pip stood up in the cart to look inquisitively at a speaker with a commanding voice coming from across the Green. With a flip of the reins on his back, Boney began to canter along the track.

"Woah, old friend. I'm going to tie you to this post. I want to listen to that man talking. He's all dressed in black. Never seen anyone like that before. Is he selling summat? I must hear what he has to say."

He ran as fast as he could across the Green to where a small crowd was gathered. Standing on a box was a gaunt, tall man, about thirty years old, with a slight accent, as if he hailed from Shoreditch or Clerkenwell, a Cockney born within the sound of the church bells of St Mary-le-Bow. His voice was strong like a trumpet, resounding all the way across the Green, attracting not merely Young Pip's attention. This was Preacher Jeremiah Whitehouse.

"We are sinful, my brothers and sisters, and God saves us from our sins. It is so simple and so peaceful to feel the love of God. We go about our labors, but underneath are God's everlasting arms. Who can receive God's love? You and you and you, especially if you are poor, especially if you are a child."

He pointed to Young Pip now at the front.

"Yes, even you, young man. You can preach His word. So can your friends, so can your family," he says, his voice infused with fervor and tears.

"You can bear witness to God's love as a child, as a man, or as a woman. We can gather together anywhere under God's good heaven. All can preach, all can love, and all can learn the word of God. Why? God loves you and wants you to be good, to be perfect in word, in mind and in body. You who suffer, you who work in the fields, Jesus can save you. Love of God will sustain you."

As the crowd murmured Amen, Young Pip looked around with some astonishment at the crowd, seeing the hungry faces of the poor, disabled, filthy, wretched, men and women mostly field workers, perhaps twenty people altogether.

"We have seen the rioting, the fires and the village disturbances recently," the Preacher continued. "You may put these protestors into jail and upon the treadmill, but they will come out the same devils they went in. But if the Grace of God gets into their hearts it will change them. Everyone will be perfect. Nothing else can do it, Hallelujah!"

The crowd responded with its own gusty Hallelujahs, while the Preacher began his peroration.

"As a Primitive Methodist following in the steps of John Wesley, I seek my way to the heart of things, to bring men and women to a true relationship with God, and to pray that we may be good and do good…"

Bustling round the corner of the pub on his way from All Saints Church came the Vicar, the Reverend Claude Windnortham, in haste to deal with this interloper. He was a well-built man, tall, rather portly, with a frock coat, dog collar and gaiters, and a broad-brimmed hat, red-faced and full not merely of his breakfast, but of his own importance.

In the crowd were men and women he married and whose children he had christened and whose older and younger relatives he had buried. He commanded respects, if only for those conventional relationships with his flock.

Somewhat out of breath, standing next to Young Pip, he pointed at Preacher Whitehouse and, jabbing his finger, he asked:

"What are you doing, good sir? You are trespassing in my parish. You are preaching about our living and loving God, which is the responsibility of the ordained minister of God. I am a clerk in holy orders, within a church the Head of which is our glorious monarch Queen Victoria, Defender of the Faith, whom God preserves!"

"Your Reverend, sir," replied Preacher Whitehouse, "God wants His Word to be spread among all the people; for them to know they can be sinless and perfect."

Windnortham was not accustomed to being lectured about religion, as he had a degree in theology from the University of Cambridge so, as it were, he knew a religious thing or two. He bellowed his response:

"You so-called Preacher, are you one of those Primitive Methodists we hear about?"

"Yes, sir," replied Whitehouse quietly, "and proud of doing God's work in the steps of John Wesley."

"Fiddlesticks. That's as maybe. Young man, the Church of England carries the unique burden of God's word, not you vulgar itinerants without training, you dissenters, mere artisans, uneducated in the theology, philosophy and doctrines of God and His Church. It is our original sin we must confront, not some idea we can all be perfect. Begone, begone from my parish. You are no minister of God," at which the crowd murmured uneasily, in some deference to ecclesiastical authority.

Windnortham turned his back and strode away to his church, huffing as he went.

Young Pip was beside himself with excitement at witnessing this encounter. He remembered his errand and hurried to one of the little stalls, impatient to get the provisions and get home, while listening to villagers exchanging views about the rumpus.

He got what he needed, then reined Boney into a canter and they hurtled off down the mile and half to the cottage, passing a trap heading back on the way. Out of breath he rushed inside and there, sitting in the old leather chair, was Old Pip his uncle, still clad in his overcoat and holding his gloves from the overnight coach.

"Oh, it's Uncle Pip," and rushing over to stand by the chair, he continued: "I am so glad to see you, as I've been listening to a Preacher on the Green in the village. He talked about God and goodness and being perfect, sort of the things you've said to me."

"Wait, my dear young son," said Joe, standing near the kitchen door, "you can't come bolting in 'ere like Boney galumphing 'cross the marshes."

Words tumbled out of the boy in his excitement.

"Please, Father, I must tell Uncle Pip."

Grabbing the older man's coat at his arm, he exclaimed:

"This Preacher tells of those good expectations you told me to follow. I can't remember everything, but he spoke of God as loving and powerful, who wants us to be perfect, just like you've been telling me, though you never mentioned God. He talked of a different God from the one we used to hear about in church, when we used to go, who gets very angry when we make mistakes or are not as good as gold.

"I love this new God," he concluded looking up to the ceiling with a sense of awe.

"Hold it, hold it, dear chap. Old Pip is just come this minute from London and you'se going off like a chargin' lion."

Young Pip ignored his father and continued:

"The Preacher said us ordinary country folk can gather together and work at being good people, listening to the voice of God: We don't need the church. We can meet together in groups. But then the Vicar of the Church came by and there was a real rampage."

"That's sounds like a lark, eh, Old Pip?" said Joe, taking a chair at the table.

"I don't care who were right, all I know is that the Preacher spoke of goodness and good living and that's what Uncle Pip says I should do."

"Well, if the dear old chap says so, you do it, Young Pip."

"Oh dear, I am exhausted with your chattering, my son," said Biddy.

"That is no surprise," said Old Pip, laughing. "But who was this Preacher, Young Pip?" I've heard street preachers in London, and they often don't say which part of church they are attached to."

"He said he was Whitehouse and a follower of a man called John Wisley or Woozley or Wesley or something. Anyway, it began with a W, and he called himself a Medothist, no, wait a minute, a Methodist. I am so excited I get so confused. But he showed me God. Please Mother, come and hear him preach with me, You'll love him."

"Those Vicar folks are not for the likes of us," added Joe, "they'se gentlemun, see, always telling us how bad we are, but let it go now but yon Preacher seems more like us. So, we may come with 'ee, but awful dull I am, so your mother will tell me what to do."

"What do you think, Uncle Pip?" Asked the boy.

"Hang on, hang on, hang on, Young Pip, nuff of God. Old Pip had just arrived here when you came galumphing in. What news do you have, Old Pip?"

He got up slowly from the chair and said: "Oh, yes, I almost forgot in all this excitement about God. Our wedding is fixed for August."

Biddy rushed to him and threw her arms around Old Pip, saying: "Wonderful, dear Old Pip, I am so pleased it is not that Estella."

"Don't worry yourself about that," said Old Pip with a smile. "I am very fond of Estella, but marriage was never a possibility, whatever I might have wanted."

"Oh, a wedding," cried Joe, "what larks, eh, Biddy?"

"I am so very delighted I am with my Beatrice. She's a cousin of Herbert's. His wife Clara introduced us at a small gathering, and I think Clara thought as I was thirty I should be married, and she has been searching for the right person.

"As to her character, she has a strong will, is generous and open-hearted, and you will love her as I do. I am now doing well enough at Clarrickers, but I need something better. I have learnt a great deal there, much of it about the law on commerce."

"Tell me later what 'commus' is later, "said Joe. "Bring her to the Cottage, dear chap. Us want to meet her soon, don't we Biddy? Bring her here when she's fit and well."

"Oh, I will, I will, and I have wanted to bring her several times but she is a delicate woman, prone to illness, which is why we've not been traveling together, but my heart is full of her."

Joe and Biddy were overwhelmed with excitement at Old Pip's wedding and the prospect of grandchildren. Neither were strictly grandparents, but they would behave like them. But for Young Pip, this joyful announcement is a blow.

"Won't you come here so much, then, uncle, when you'se married?"

Old Pip put his arm around the boy to comfort him, realizing that he would not be coming so frequently, with his marital obligations.

"I'll always come if you want me, Young Pip, but I will have Beatrice to care for. But you are a good young man now, beginning to work with your father.

"Young Pip," and here he hesitated to get what he wanted to say very clear, "If you want to follow that religion, then do. For me, I wear religion on my sleeve, not being a good church attender, though I'll have to go there for my wedding."

"Now don't you take any notice of your Uncle on these church matters, my son," said Biddy now that Old Pip was well out of earshot. "He got some funny notions when he became a gentleman."

"I am very excited by this Preacher, mother. Promise me, both of you, that you'll come and hear the Preacher soon."

Biddy got up to get pies from her store in the kitchen and the four of them did them justice after the excitement at Old Pip's news had died down.

"Biddy," said Old Pip, "your pies are the envy of the neighborhood. Many folk would love the opportunity to enjoy them: apples, pears, blackberry, cherry, plums and rhubarb and the pie with strawberries is the best."

"That's as true as ever was," said Joe. "Now, there was a time when I was keen to tend to the two fruit trees at the back of the cottage, but the wind off the estuary usually blew off the blossom, so I stopped bothering."

"How fortunate we are," said Biddy. "My husband has a good trade since he inherited the Forge and this cottage from his lazy father whose apprentice he was. See, Old Pip, when his father died suddenly, that young Joe as he was then was left to carry on the Gargery tradition because it was in such a state no one else wanted it."

"Yes, and I'm such a lucky duck to have wed a good cook."

"Oh I marvel at it," said Old Pip, "there she is on a market day wrapping the fish and meat in muslin and putting it away in the larder cupboard."

"And I taught you some things too at my little school."

"You did, you did and I'll never forget that."

After feasting on the pies in celebration, Joe went to the Forge. Biddy and Old Pip went outside with Young Pip to sit on the bench and watch the birds, but soon Joe was back in the leather chair apologizing in his own way for his sleepiness, as the rain started.

That gave Old Pip the opportunity to signal to Young Pip and point to the upstairs with his index finger as the time had come to tell the youngster a little more about himself.

"Now my great expectations," he began, "came about because I gave some victuals to an old convict who was on the run from the prison hulks. None of that matters now, but I had a lot of money, and I spent too much and got into some odd company with supposed gentlemen, some of whom were very suspicious about my background as a country boy."

"Surely, you did something good with the money, didn't you?"

"Yes, only one thing. I used five hundred pounds to help Herbert get a position.

"But then the old convict came back when I was living in London and told me it was he who had given me the money. But he got caught by the police, another long story, and all his money was confiscated. But that's not what I wanted to tell you.

"My great expectations were very bad for me."

"Why? I don't understand. Why was it bad? You'd moved up from the cottage to London."

"Oh, it wasn't the loss of the money, though that hurt.

"My 'great expectations,' Young Pip, put up this barrier up between Joe and me, whereas before we had been best of friends. I then felt embarrassed to call him a friend with his country ways. I didn't want to associate with him and his pipe and manners.

"Listen to the dear chap snoring away downstairs. That's the man I deserted. The worst part was that Joe agreed.

"He decided too that my being a gentleman meant that I could not be friends with a country blacksmith like him: Just as he'd think my friend Herbert would not visit the cottage because he's a gentleman. That's what he seemed to say, but now, when I think about it, he just didn't want to force a friendship which I was breaking, not him.

"Yet, I was breaking it, throwing away the love and friendship of your father whom I had known since I could think. Worse still, I got very ill in London, and Joe came to look after me. When I got better, he was calling me 'sir' and he even paid my debts."

"Was it a lot of money?"

"Oh yes, it must have cost him dear, but you see what a true friend he was. Do you see how money got in the way, how it affected me for the worse? My loving friendship with Joe suffered, Young Pip, because I had now become a gentleman.

"Of course, I was only a gentleman in the sense that I had money once and some airs and graces Herbert had shown me. But I was no gentleman, young Pip, for a gentleman proper does not give up his friends, whatever their station."

"You must both have been so hurt, but now you'se best of friends again. But all that you tell me makes me so proud of my father."

"Me too, Young Pip, me too. And so it should. He is the best of men. But this really hurts me to tell you and it shows how bad I had become. It gets worse. Do you know, at one time, I even thought of paying him money not to come and see me? I didn't do it, but I thought about it."

"Oh he wouldn't have liked that."

"No, even now, when I am with Joe I am pained. I have always felt so ashamed, Young Pip, and I still feel it sometimes when I talk with dear Joe, how I had let him down. The comfort I should have derived from both of them, I thought I could never, never, never undo what I had done. But we had such good times before, and though now we are friends again, I think we are both still bruised."

"I think you are all best of friends now, whatever happened before. I am going to have to remember this all my life."

"I hope so, and that it is a lesson for you in what to avoid. Let's go down and wake the old man up."

The wooden stairs creaked as they came down to a dramatic symphony of snores from Joe who, hearing them coming, awoke with a waker's stare, a gathering of breath and a satisfied smile on his face.

"Morning, Father. Did you have a good rest?"

"It's a'ternoon, ain't it?"

"Yes," said Young Pip, laughing.

"Slept like a baby, I did, though I dreamt about you, Old Pip."

"Really?"

"You remember that old convict who became your benefactor?"

"Of course."

"I had this funny dream. You as a young lad helped him get a file from my forge to help him with his shackles. How could I dream that idea? That villain must have got in somehow and stole it from me, and it was one of my best files, too."

Pip laughed, somewhat guiltily: "I hid the truth from you. I did give him the file and some food and that was why he became my benefactor."

"Oh, I guessed that at the time," said Joe in a gale of laughter. "I was just testing' you!

"Now, I see your bag beside the door. Do you have to go back to London?"

"I must, old chap. It's been a wonderful day, but all good things come to an end. I've got the trap coming soon to take me to the overnight coach from the Blue Boar, so I'll sup there before we leave. I can see the trap on the track now."

"Now you wrap up warm," said Biddy, coming out from her kitchen. "I started to sit outside, but it's too cold. Still March, swallows not here yet. You'se to come back soon. Oh my, you look so smart, a proper gentleman with your topcoat and silk hat, gloves and your leather case. You take care."

"My young son will be miserable till you're back."

Young Pip grasped his uncle's hand as they walked to the trap, trying to hold back his tears.

"Look'ee, Young Pip. Come here. I need to tell you again before I go. I was a youth of great expectations of being a gentleman with money. I was misled by great expectations. I say again, you must live with 'good' expectations."

"Now I have heard about God from the Preacher, I will try, I will try."

III

After much careful thought Mr. Jaggers sent Robert to ask Mr. Pip at the Clarrickers Agency if he would kindly attend Mr. Jaggers at 11 o'clock the following day. Old Pip was put about by the invitation as he was embroiled in wedding matters, due the third Saturday in August, just two weeks away. He had constantly heard the story of the famous meeting and the reactions of Mr. Jaggers told with lively indiscretion by Estella, accompanied by coarse laughter from Molly. He anticipated this would be the topic for their conversation.

"Good morning, Mr. Jaggers," he said brusquely. "It is sometime since we met on the occasion of Estella's meeting her mother. I have heard from Estella several times about those conversations, and I understand Mr. Wemmick will assist them with the purchase of a house in the country."

"Yes, Mr. Pip. I hope it works out, as Molly is mentally unstable.

"Put all that aside. I have a proposition for you.

"I want you to become my pupil-apprentice as a lawyer and take over my Chambers here in Little Britain when I retire or I die, whichever comes first. As you know, formal legal training has yet to materialize, though there is much talk about it among lawyers. But I am getting old and I am tired of all this, the mess people make of their lives, and the mess I make of some of them. Will you join me?"

"Really? I thank you warmly for your kind invitation and, to be sure, my life in the Agency both here and abroad is now a mere convenience for keeping body and soul together. But I am getting long in the tooth, far too ancient to be trained to be a lawyer."

"Nonsense. I will train you. Put the case that you have extensive experience of the criminal mind through your benefactor. You have seen how criminals work, and, in Magwitch's case, you encountered that blackguard Compeyson whom Magwitch killed when you were trying to spirit him away to France.

"You have had experience in your travels of people in the larger world.

"You have seen eccentricity and the strangeness of human beings there and, for that matter in your dealings with that criminal from the marshes whose name I forget.

"You have grown to understand people. All that experience will make a good lawyer. You have had little schooling as such, but your education as a gentleman and your time at the agency are a quite sufficient background."

"I must confess I am intrigued."

"I hope you will contemplate the opportunity and the possibilities. My judgement about your abilities is not clouded by ignorance. I will pay you your present salary until I feel you are qualified, and we will have you called to the Bar. Then we will share the finances of our practice.

"Most important, Mr. Pip, you are now a man of exemplary character and can learn from me, and from reading cases and understanding the criminal law, in a few short years. Well, what say you?"

"I need to think about this very carefully and it is most generous."

"Of course."

"I am honored by your confidence in me, and your account of my qualifications. I will consult Beatrice, and, as I hope you will come to our wedding, I will let you know then. But we must undertake this adventure together."

"Oh, it's not a mere adventure, my dear Mr. Pip, it's a continuous earthquake, like living on the top of a volcano, not knowing whether there will be a next eruption, and if so which part of the volcano it is coming from, and what the temperature of the lava is.

"But let me stress finally that I will not expect you to purchase a partnership with me, but when I retire, you will have to live by your own wits."

"You are exceedingly generous. As I said, I will let you know at my wedding when I have talked with Beatrice."

"I will do my best to attend the ceremony, but I am unusually busy after a sojourn in Brighton. You will find that a lawyer has, in principle, freedom to work as and when he wishes. But volcanoes don't let you know when they are ready, and the same applies to the Courts of Justice, believe me."

"Thank you for this. I will now shake your hand and bid you good day, sir."

While Mr. Jaggers did need an assistant who might well become a partner, he saw in Old Pip one way of assuaging his guilt about Estella. His reputation for an utter lack of the sentimental would be sullied were he to admit this to anyone, least of all, Wemmick. Nevertheless he remained convinced that at some point Pip and Estella would be man and wife.

Englishmen have to be careful when talking about the bliss of the English summer day, lest they offend what a poet once called those of lesser climes. But it was such a day, when Philip Pirrip, groom, and Beatrice Mary Throgmorton Pocket, bride, were married at the church of St John, Hackney.

Indeed, that late summer of 1847 was lovely in the south of England, while in Ireland such glorious weather was rare and would mean little to thousands of men and women living under only what can be described as a tyranny. Beatrice's parents Algernon and Sybilla Pocket had a large house near the river Lea at Hackney, a rural area north and east of the city. The Pockets were a rambling sort of family with many branches, mostly gentry or aspiring to that class status and to gentility.

"I wonder, darling Beatrice, why your father got into this trade?" asked Pip as they were walking by the river the Sunday afternoon before their wedding.

"I am not sure, Pip. It was an adventure, I think. Yet different members of the family have reacted oddly, some with admiration, others with disdain.

"Because it was trade?"

"I suppose so, though my cousin Herbert was very much in approval. My mother had a modest dowry which had formed the basis for his adventures with timber, and she is very delighted that the profits enable her to ensure her daughter has a splendid wedding," she said, smiling broadly at him.

"So am I, dear."

"Of course, we will make some friends of our own, Pip, and I want to move in those circles to which my mother has aspired."

Pip flinched slightly at this remark but dismissed it as his bride seemed very cheerful and gay.

"Shall I accept Mr. Jaggers' offer, dearest?" He asked.

"Oh I think so. It is so appropriate for you to be a lawyer rather than just a clerk and it pleases me, too. You will be freed from keeping strictly to the daily grind, so you will be able to help me if I am in need."

"I am certainly of that same mind," he said.

"I am a little apprehensive about children, Pip, as I hope my constitution will not fail me."

"There is plenty of time to think about that," he replied, "but the Pocket tradition seems to indicate two although that will depend as much on money as on Nature."

Through his courtship of her, Old Pip had begun to understand the Pocket family, though he had such good friends in Herbert and Clara Pocket, so his choice of Herbert as his best man was obvious. While Clara had brought about the match with her usual vigor, Herbert remained uncertain about its viability.

The evening before the wedding, they sat discussing the couple over dinner.

"Our friend Pip is a lucky man," Clara began. "I know Beatrice herself had little literary education, though like most of the Pocket young women, she can sew, draw and play the flute, perhaps with drawing as her main accomplishment."

"Not much given to reading, certainly. I recall her saying she found Miss Edgeworth's *Helen* too difficult. Like all of us, she enjoys Miss Austen. You know, my dear, she is such a frail body by nature but also because her parents have constantly cosseted her without letting her into some of life's hardships."

"I do agree with that," said Clara. "She will deny that she is spoilt, but in fact her frailty always provides excuses for her general lassitude."

"She is a pretty woman, isn't she though, with her long golden hair and blue eyes."

"Yet I do find it a peculiar mannerism that when you talk with her she never seems to look at you. It is if her eyes flicker into the distance rather than focus on you. Strange indeed. Let us hope they are very happy in each other and I am sure they are very much in love."

"I hope so," said Herbert.

Indeed that Old Pip was in love with her was beyond doubt in every mind except perhaps his own. Confident in these Pocket friends, Old Pip felt a comfort in marrying her, as he did anticipate a steady life among a flock of children, thereby emulating the remainder of the Pocket family. His partnership with Jaggers might grow into something more remunerative, but problems in his financial future were not perspicuous or anticipated.

With this frailty and an uncertain dowry given her father's ventures, Beatrice was surprised by Old Pip's attentions at first, but she gradually grew over the months of their engagement into a profound affection and love for her suitor. She knew of Estella, of course, as Old Pip had revealed all his warts and scars to her early in their relationship, and she saw him as a husband of which she could be proud.

Above all, she saw him as a faithful man, trusting her instincts about him, her first and only suitor. She was fifteen years younger than he, so his maturity was another sign to her that this would be a splendid marriage and, perhaps, her health and demeanor would flourish under his tutelage.

Such was the preamble to her union with Philip Pirrip, whom everyone knew as Pip.

The bride's side of the church at the wedding was overflowing with Pockets of all descriptions and tastes. Beatrice had a pretty supporter and bridesmaid, one Cecilia Turnington, with Herbert supporting Old Pip. Joe and Biddy Gargery were prominent on the groom's much smaller side, Joe looking very uncomfortable, hatless, but in a suit and a velvet waistcoat.

Herbert's wife Clara and her children broke with the Pocket entourage by sitting on the groom's side of the aisle. Her two-year-old son made his presence felt, his cries sounding to him so wonderful as they ricocheted around the large building, until the organ announcing the bride's entry drowned them out. Mr. Wemmick was there with his wife, the former Miss Skiffins. Estella arrived quietly just before the bride, resplendent in the highest fashion as was Molly who accompanied her.

The service was unremarkable and solemn. The congregation then proceeded by carriage to Algernon and Sybilla's garden, a mere two miles away. The sun cooperated, roses were everywhere on trees and on lapels. Joe had been inveigled by Old Pip to propose the toast. The doctrine of 'best of friends' had triumphed.

Joe began.

"Well, I don't know, everybody. Who'd have thought this dear old chap would wed? I look at the luvly Beatrice and think 'who wouldn't?'"

At this there was much embarrassed laughter and some more generous applause. Was this a compliment to Beatrice or not? That was a puzzle for the elderly ladies in the Pocket entourage. Joe tried to clarify.

"No, I didn't mean that, I mean, Pip waited all this time for his woman. No, no, no, I mean his lady, him being such a gentleman. Oh dear, I am so awfull dull and I get so confused when I'm excited."

With that clarification on his quality and experience, the Pocket ladies were comforted that this countryman at least knew a lady when he saw one. There was much more joyous laughter at both the compliment and Joe's admission which those few there who loved him knew to be nonsense.

"Oh dear," he continued, "I have not had more than a drop and here I go, not getting it right."

The Pocket ladies now realized this bumpkin was in truth a drunk.

"I hope she allows Young Pip out, though, for me and Biddy need him; and that young lad would be mortified if he didn't appear."

And so, as a Pocket lady confided to her companion, this is a possessive drunk at that who does not realize the obligations of marriage.

Young Pip then called out: "I certainly will miss him. Indeed, I will."

"Goodness me, they can't even control their children," murmured the doyenne of the Pocket elderlies.

"But enough from me. Let us all drink to their health and happiness. God bless you both and may all your troubles be little ones!"

At this, the reservations of the elders of the Pocket clan were drowned in cheers and laughter. Sybilla's cat who heretofore had been a friendly nuisance now fled up an apple tree at the noise.

And so, to Old Pip.

"I have nothing much to say except that I am the luckiest man in the world with such a beautiful bride, and to be here is the company of such friends. Of course, I must thank" — and here he stumbled as he caught sight of Estella in the crowd looking at him proudly, even lovingly, and he was momentarily stunned by what he saw as her ravishing beauty — "I must thank as heartily as I can our wonderful hosts Mr. and Mrs. Pocket for their kindness and generosity in making this occasion so memorable."

As he sat down, he thought not so much about the woman who was now his wife, but how his commitment to her finished forever the possibility of a different relationship with Estella. No one seemed to have noticed his stumble, except Estella whose slight blushes remained unnoticed, and by Molly who gave her daughter a slight tap on the forearm.

With that he sat down next to Beatrice who was talking with her mother, and Old Pip turned to Joe:

"What larks, eh, Joe?"

"What larks, eh, Pip! Now, old chap, off you go and have lots of children for us to spoil and enjoy."

They both stood up holding their glasses as Estella and Molly approached. Old Pip was not mistaken; Estella looked ravishing. What had happened to the hard eyes, he wondered, which were now transformed and glistening with pleasure and delight. Joe introduced himself to Molly, leaving Estella with Pip.

"What a wonderful ceremony, dear Pip. Molly was just saying how fitting it was for you both to have such a magnificent day. Many congratulations, my dear."

"Estella, you look wonderful. The color suits you so well, and you look happier than I think I have ever seen you."

"Indeed, I am. To have rescued my mother from the clutches of Mr. Jaggers and to be able now to recover all those years lost is changing my life in ways I don't yet appreciate. But your Beatrice looks quite charming and I do wish you every happiness."

"We will not lose touch, will we, Estella?"

"Of course not, Pip. We both know we are bound by Fate to be dear friends. But I must not keep you from your guests."

She kisses him lightly on the cheek, as she would have done to her brother had she had one, but it sent ripples of desire down Old Pip's spine.

Beatrice was immediately by his side.

Estella turned to her:

"Beatrice, my dear, my love and congratulations. I have known this man since we were children and I am thrilled you are so well suited. We hope you will both visit with us soon. We have persuaded Mr. Wemmick to accompany us to see two houses soon, though the description of the one near All Hallows seems the likely choice."

"What will you call the house when it is yours?" asked Old Pip, "I recall the old one was Satis House."

"Satis House was oddly named. Satis is Latin for enough. So, I thought we'd call a new dwelling 'Numquam House' as in 'never again.'"

"Well done, then, and we will be excited to see it, will we not, Beatrice darling?"

"Oh, Pip, we will have many friends to enjoy," she replied with the implication that she did not want Pip to be too friendly with Estella, as she has obviously heard enough about her from him, and with a woman's intuition, cannot really believe that this is just a friendship. Men don't have women friends, she believed, they are either acquaintances or lovers. For women, a male friend is a sort of bliss, intimacy with no concomitant implications.

Molly was clearly overwhelmed by the munificence of the occasion but was also embarrassed to speak more than a greeting, remembering Estella's strict lessons in elocution to try to refine the coarse cockneyisms which formed Molly's vocabulary and tone.

Wemmick stealthily approached the bride and groom as their attention was demanded by so many of their friends. Eventually his turn came.

"My dear, this is Mr. John Wemmick who will be my companion in arms at Mr. Jaggers office."

"I am delighted to make your acquaintance, Mrs. Pip. Excuse me, but may I have a private word with your husband?"

Beatrice nodded her assent and turned to speak to Herbert who was nearby.

"You are coming to Little Britain then? I knew you would. I will help you. He needs support, you know. He's getting a bit fragile, even making a mistake now and then," and whispering in Old Pip's ear, "there is plenty of portable property to be acquired at the law, my friend.

"You must warn Miss Estella about Molly though; she is unstable. Her crime was hideous. Dare you talk with Estella about her?"

"At this moment, my dear Wemmick, the only woman I can think about is the one over there in white."

They laughed loudly, and Wemmick shook his hand, and pointed him to the garden door through which Jaggers had come, beckoning to Pip.

"I can't stay," he said, looking anxiously around but then relaxing when he saw Estella and Molly at some distance from him.

Old Pip interrupted him by raising his hand:

"On the matter we discussed, I would be delighted to have the privilege of working with you. I am both honored and grateful."

"How very satisfactory; I'll take you into court with me as soon as you are available. A very interesting case."

Jaggers left and Old Pip returned to talk with Biddy.

"Oh my, you look so smart, my dear," said Biddy, "You are more than a proper gentleman with your wedding topcoat and your beautiful silk hat. You take good care. You know," she said, drawing him to one side, "there was a time when I thought it would be you and me getting married."

"Now, come, come, Biddy. You're older than me."

"Yes," she said in a whisper, "but don't you remember that lovely day out on the marshes when we were children, just starting to grow as adults?"

"No, what was that?"

"You mean you've forgotten?

"Forgotten what?"

"We was lying on the grass behind the cottage, exhausted after running out on the marshes and you bent over and gave me a lovely kiss and said you'd marry me someday."

"I did? That must have been before I went to London."

"Yes, it was, and it stuck in my memory as a promise."

"Oh my dear Biddy, we were just two youngsters playing at becoming adults."

"I suppose so, but then you was away on your travels so long, I gave you up and settled for my Joe."

"I'd bet you've been happier with him than you'd ever have been with me."

"Probably, but I'll never forget that one kiss. It was my first."

"Hey, then, as it's my wedding day, let me give you another!"

"Good gracious no, Old Pip, in front of all your guests."

"All right, I'll wait till we are alone," he said laughing.

"You've become really cheeky, Old Pip, since you've got married."

He put his arms round this woman who had been so kind to him, taught him and fed him.

"I do love you, Biddy, you know."

"And I love you, my dear, and I do wish you every happiness."

"Thank you," he said looking at her carefully, as her young son sidled up to him.

"Here's my Young Pip," she said, "now he'll be miserable till you're back."

Young Pip came up and grasped his uncle's hand, trying to hold back his tears.

"Look'ee, Young Pip. Come over here. I need to tell you again before I go. Don't be misled by great expectations. You must live with 'good' expectations. I know I've said this before, but don't become a Pip like me. Follow your good conscience always. Just search for goodness and I am sure your expectations will be exceeded. Know that I will be watching and hoping."

"I will do my best. Please forgive me for saying this, but you do not need to tell me this every time we meet," he said laughing, "and I won't forget. Ever!"

"Remember, you'll still come and see us, won't you, or we will be on your conscience."

Old Pip laughed and put his arm around him.

"Bless you. I'll be there, but how long will you be there, eh?"

"I don't know, I really don't."

"Do you think they'll be as happy as we are?" asked Joe when Biddy approached. He was standing away from the crowd, puffing at his pipe which he knew many women could not abide.

"Yes, of course, now he's got that Estella out of his head."

"I wonder," said Joe sagely. "She's a changed woman since her mother came to live with her. Look at her. I mean, I've not seen her often but she's radiant, ain't she?"

"But he's married Beatrice," said Biddy with emphasis, "He won't break his vows."

"No, I agree. I was just thinking he might still think of her like he did when he was younger."

"I hopes not," said Biddy. "But just look at your lovely son over there watching him."

"Yes, what a fine son we have, eh, Biddy? He'll be a good man when he grows up, especially with Pip, the dear old chap, to advise him and his mother to help him when I'm gone.

"Don't you dare talk like that, Joe Gargery."

IV

Estella and Molly had settled into their lodging but they used Satis House occasionally, so it was not until June that their searches for the new house began in earnest. Part of the delay was that Estella had the idea that they should look beyond Kent, so the pair of them spent different weekends in counties within fifty miles of London. Numquam started to seem the right description, and the name for this illusory property.

After a while together, they had started to exchange small talk but often sat in silent contemplation, both of them wondering what on earth would happen next. But that soon changed as they got to know and like each other.

Estella told her mother that she did not want to know much more about her history than she knew already, and Molly was only too pleased to oblige given the vagaries of her past. One day, they agreed, would come a time for secrets.

"I'm still frightened those Compeysons might come after me after what I did. They'll know I don't have Jaggers for protection now."

"How can you be sure of that?"

"They's evil men, Ruthie."

"Put it behind you, my dear. I am proud of you and will be more so as you get used to living in this different refined fashion from what you have known."

"I'm doing well though, aren't I?"

"Indeed, you are, but you must stop using vulgar expressions. You must be more restrained and careful when you are with others.

You know what good manners are, you have seen them in the Jaggers household."

"Yes, I do, but since I came to you I threw all that away and became myself, not some gentleman's servant."

"I understand that: it must have been like throwing off shackles."

"I suppose so, but it was embracing you that was the real delight."

"Well, you were wonderful at Pip's wedding. Everyone was full of compliments."

"That's is because I didn't open my mouth," she said with a laugh.

By November Estella was no longer on the alert for Molly's indiscretions and Molly was no longer waiting to be admonished for something she thought quite trivial. Conversation between mother and daughter improved as they set about their newly acquired house with a will and Estella was astounded by Molly's natural good taste and sense of color.

Yet the most difficult initial aspect of their new life for Estella was Molly's way with men. Estella struggled to understand this, innocent as she was of the mores of sexual attraction that had engulfed her mother, and certainly never having dreamt of flirting with a man.

They had kept in touch with John Wemmick at Jaggers' suggestion. One afternoon shortly after Beatrice and Pip's wedding, they had come down to Kent on news of a large house which Estella had not really noticed before. As this seemed a serious possibility in the North Kent countryside, Wemmick came with them in the daytime coach. He was a personable man, about Molly's age and much attached to his wife.

The whole journey was a fraught experience for Estella, with Molly as cheerful a flirt as you could find in Shoreditch, behaving like a 'pert young hussy.' She didn't speak to Wemmick; she didn't need to. Rather she looked at him regularly during the journey with what can only be described as a 'come hither' look and her smiles and glances hinted to Wemmick her availability for whatever he might choose.

After an hour of this, Estella understood what was happening and was horrified, telling her mother to stop this silly nonsense. Wemmick bore it all with aplomb, given his belief that Molly was mad anyway. Estella then insisted that mother and daughter would stay a night or two at the Blue Boar, to enable Wemmick to ride the return coach without being eyed for hours as a potential bedfellow.

"What's wrong, Ruthie, it's just a bit of fun?" Asked Molly the following day after Estella had lectured her. "I've not had a man look at me for years, apart from old Jaggers."

"What *do* you mean?"

"Oh yes," said Molly, relapsing into her Cockney brogue, "he was very keen to get into my knickers at one time."

"Don't be disgusting, Mother, Jaggers would surely not do what you are implying."

"See, that's your trouble, Ruthie, You've never had a real man, have you, or it seems, even wanted one."

"But Jaggers? Tell me how that happened."

"I'd been there about a year and he started looking at me as if he wanted it, you know what I mean, don't you? Oh dear, maybe you don't. Then he pushed me in a corner and demanded it. Now he knew I were strong, so he wasn't going to force me now, was he?

"I said no unless he told me where my daughter was. He tried another time except I told him I'd also tell Wemmick. Then it was over, though he did not treat me very well, but I was fed and clothed, and work was not hard, so what more could I want?"

Yet, such incidents apart, Molly seemed content as training in the social graces, especially of speech, and the months passed quickly. This was not so much a matter of accent as the fact that Molly's vocabulary was so constrained. With improving that in mind, Estella read to her regularly each evening, the level of Molly's requests for meaning gradually subsiding as the months went by.

Molly found each tale fascinating as some were so far distant from her own experience. She often relapsed into her old linguistic formulations in describing characters.

Mr. Darcy was a 'stupid git', though she thought Lizzie 'a real trooper.'

Emma "didn't know her arse from her elbow," and her comments on Becky Sharp do not bear repetition.

As for *Oliver Twist,* to which she could easily relate, she was in tears almost entirely through Estella's reading of the book, fixated not just by Dodger whom she recognized as Abel as a youngster, but the plight of Nancy and the brutality of Sykes made her howl.

Estella meanwhile retained an austere stoicism in this education of her mother.

On a shopping excursion to Rochester, Estella was attracted to a little volume in a bookshop titled *Poems* and she thought it would be good for both of them to read some poetry. Thereafter they read one each night and Elizabeth Barrett Browning began to occupy a significant place in their hearts, the while softening the cruder edges of Molly's view of the world.

So it was that Satis House was finally abandoned and in the October of 1847 Estella bought Numquam House. Over the next couple of years, they reached a satisfying equilibrium and an intense devotion to each other. They rode over in Estella's carriage regularly to visit Joe and Biddy, whom Estella only knew through Old Pip's wedding, but who were glad to see them, Biddy's strong reservations about Estella notwithstanding. Neither of them rode a horse, a practice Estella had given up, and Molly rarely went near one. After each visit, Estella was mightily relieved that Molly passed the test of meeting the handsome Joe Gargery without so much as a wink or a nudge.

By the start of 1850 the sense of peace and calm was widely recognized.

Molly and Estella were settled in the country.

Old Pip and Beatrice had been married for three years. Sadly, they had suffered their first disappointment as Beatrice had miscarried in the December after their wedding, and again in late 1849.

Pip's training under Mr. Jaggers oversight was well under way, although the old lawyer was beginning to feel his age. John Wemmick was thoroughly delighted to have Old Pip as a colleague to whom he could talk easily and a strong friendship was developing.

Biddy and Joe Gargery were in thrall to Young Pip's enthusiasm and were now fully-fledged Primitive Methodists in regular attendance at the chapel in a house in Chatham which they reached in the cart pulled by Betsy, though for how long the old nag would be able to do this remained a matter of speculation.

Young Pip had become Joe's apprentice and was proving a workmanlike farrier, working with the horses he loved, though he saw his future more as a preacher than a farrier. Their ready cheerfulness as a devoted family was enhanced by their beliefs.

Mr. Jaggers had begun to feel the weight of his years and, in the absence of a wife, poured complaints about his condition on to his senior clerk.

Mid-morning on a grey but warm day in the early spring of 1850, Biddy came to the front door of the cottage, stepped outside and in a loud voice that God and the rabbits could hear, she cried:

"Biddy Gargery is my name,

England is my nation,

All Hallows is my dwelling place, and

Christ is my salvation, Hallelujah!"

From the Forge came the muffled cries of Hallelujah, where Joe and Young Pip were repairing the axle on a trap. They came out to Biddy, aglow in religious fervor, but she was stopped short by Young Pip's exclamation:

"Phew, I'm really hungry."

"And not a surprise, dear chap, you'se growing up so fast and you're always thinking preacher thoughts, so I can't keep up, can I, Biddy?"

"He's growing and needs feeding. I've got a luvly pork pie, Young Pip, and apple pie after. God is our provider, not me, so maybe we can be perfect for him."

"Thank'ee, dear Lord, for food and family," said Joe in a grace after they had sat down. We will try to be perfect for you, like Preacher says. God bless us, especially our dear Young Pip, but Old Pip as well, mustn't forget the dear old chap, and Beatrice."

"No, we can never forget Old Pip," added Young Pip to Joe's benediction. "He gave me Boney. I wonder, what are the horses like they use in the war, you know, with soldiers riding into battle? Horses get used, don't they, and they are so gentle."

Munching at the pork pie, he continued:

"Do they enjoy the fight? They must get killed too. But then men shouldn't be fighting anyway, should they?"

So captured were the family by their religious beliefs that these principles were embedded in all family conversation. It sharpened their questioning of the world around them, as they were always trying to set their lives against the goal of perfection and trying to understand what God would want of them. The world was no longer a place of a simple rhythm where everything was as it was.

Religion had enabled them to examine their lot and the lot of others. Primitive Methodism may have been an uncomplicated rudimentary theology, but one outcome, questioning whether God would like a particular behavior, led to a broadening of the mind. Conversations changed.

"Let me tell you, dear chap, when I was young, our country was fighting with that Boney man. He were from France, I think. Our hero was Lord Nelson. I was told that we won great battles between ships, but Nelson died when someone kissed him," at which Biddy and Young Pip exploded with laughter.

"No, no, no, you know what I meant. I meant he were dying, so they say, and he asked an officer to kiss him goodbye, though it were really 'good night.' He did a lot of kissing himself as he had that fancy woman, Hamilton were her name. He were a right scallywag like most of 'em Norfolk tikes.

"I were too young then, but sailors came around to our village, got one or two young men drunk and forced 'em into the navy. Never saw 'em again, and one was a cousin of mine."

"What would I do," mused young Pip, "if someone forced me into the navy? I'm old enough now. I'll be fifteen next month. Does God want us to kill other people?"

"Well, us not perfect if we'se dead, is we?"

There was a long pause while Biddy and Young Pip digested the import of Joe's theological insight.

"But," Biddy continued, "we'll protect you from gangs who search for you for the navy. No, I'm sure God does not want us to kill each other. But we'll ask Preacher Whitehouse."

"And not just other men, but the horses too. Boney is just like a person. Well, not quite, but near enough. I know he laughs, and he knows if I am upset."

"Horses are all right as long as they don't kick you. A blacksmith in a village yonder was badly hurt, lost the use of his arm, couldn't use a hammer at his anvil again. But Boney seems a good chap—for a horse."

Two miles or so away, Molly and Estella were sitting together on a bench in their picturesque and attractive garden. Molly struggled with crochet work as she sat enjoying the fragrances of the flowers and shrubs and relishing her good fortune.

"I feel like a real lady nowadays," she said.

"You are not dreaming, Mother, you are a lady. When Jaggers called the other day to discuss my will, he remarked how you had become a striking-looking woman of sound beliefs and good conversation."

"That's nice to know."

Estella had decided the time had come to explore her mother's secrets, after almost four years together. For too long it had seemed a taboo subject, best left alone.

"Mother," she began, "how you do like living here at Numquam?"

"My life has changed so much, dear Ruthie, and I am now a very contented woman. Did I tell you before how your father doted on you and he loved saying, 'Oh, my little Ruthie' as he held you up above his head when you were very small? You was always Ruth; I called you Ruth that day when we met in Jaggers' office, because I didn't know your new name."

"You've been calling me Ruth, which I like; it's for us. I don't want to change my legal name, far too complicated. But what else is there to know about you? Will you begin now to tell me your whole story? You know mine. Are you ashamed of it? Was it very brutal? I know you were saved from the gallows by Mr. Jaggers. Did he tell you that it was Miss Havisham I was going to?"

"No, he said I should forget you and never try to get in contact. I never knew your guardian's name till we met in the office. She seems even madder than me," and they both laughed.

Molly suddenly dissolved into tears, weeping at the memories.

"Oh, I must not weep again, Ruthie. Let me try to tell you everything, and I think I am ready to do that without raising all the old passions I felt. I am very ashamed, that's true, but I am glad we agreed not to discuss the past then until we were ready. I was frightened that you'd begin to hate me."

"Never, my dear. Whatever is in the past, I have found you. You are my mother."

In the beech tree near the house, a crow gave a loud squawk, as it had seen a cat nearby, and Molly jumped out of her chair, looking startled and frightened.

"Oh, I wish that bird would not make that awful noise. I hate sudden noises, I suppose, because I can't get rid of the idea that someone is coming to get me."

"It's only a silly old crow, Mother. You are perfectly safe here."

"Ah well, 'ere we go, as the earwig said when he fell off a cliff.

"When I was born, your grandfather Thomas Weaver was a prosperous shopkeeper and my father helped him before he died quite suddenly. So the business came to my father. My mother Nancy was a strong woman and she was taken suddenly when I was seven, though I was never certain whether she liked me and she definitely preferred my younger brother but he died earlier that same year."

"What did she die of?"

Molly could not conceal a slight blush as she said she does not know. Estella was puzzled but did not inquire further.

"My father then took heavily to the drink with wife and son dead. He had taken over my grandfather's business as I said which was hard work, selling groceries and such, but everything collapsed as the drink got to him. We was together in a debtors' prison for a while, then in the workhouse at Bethnal Green, my father and me, and a crowd of villains, young and old."

"What was he like before?"

"Very hardworking, very strict, loved my mother dearly, had a large moustache and beard on his chin, not the fashion, but he always shaved his face. Very strong indeed. He had blue eyes, too. I was fond of him. But he had a terrible temper in the drink, and I sometimes think my bad temper comes from him.

"But misery comes in threes. My mother dead, my brother dead, my father in debt, then he falls down steps at the workhouse, dead drunk and drunk dead. Oh dear, that's four."

They both giggled at her little joke.

"We had been moved before that to the Cleveland Street Workhouse, a gruesome place, little food, no real work, cruel wardens and a Beadle whom everyone hated. We'd worn the same clothes all this time, so, when you insist I have a new dress, I think back to those times and realize how poor I was and how rich I am now."

"I've heard about those places."

"Yes, he and I had to share a bed before he died. I was thirteen and on my own till fifteen, when I was thrown out after those years of misery."

"What on earth did you do?"

"My hatred for everything consumed me, as I hated everything in my life. But I loved my father and I liked men, in general. But as a young girl, I was the prey of every man in that hell of a place. One of them, whom I specially hated, cornered me one evening, and forced himself on me, so when he finished and was relaxing, I bit him on his face and ran."

"The rotten blackguard. Was he not punished?"

"Oh, no, men could get away with anything. That's why they threw me out straightaway, as they thought he might kill me."

"Oh my dear, dear Mother, how shocking, how terrible. What agony."

"I had nothing, only the clothes I stood up in, so I walked from there out of London to the north. I was lucky not to be having a baby then. I walked for days, through forests, but I must have been going in a circle, for I was soon back very near London. Each night, I had slept under bushes, out of doors in fields and villages. I begged for food. I had to shoo away foxes and one or two stray dogs."

"Upon my soul, what did you eat?"

"Plants, blackberries where I could find them. But I didn't steal anything. When I begged in the streets, some people were kind, others hated me. And I didn't go whoring or thieving either. It was a summer evening I met your father. Or rather he met me.

"He told me afterwards, he was on his way to rob a house just outside London, Southgate, I think, and he found me by the road-side, picked me up, took care of me, fed me and took me back to his very small lodging place, giving up the robbery for that night. He got clothes for me, and we became lovers. I must have been sixteen by then and he was, perhaps, five years older. He did love me a little, and he was a provider. Always."

"Where did you live?"

"We moved a lot around London to get away from the constables and his enemies. He was a kindly soul at heart, with a terrible childhood. He was a pickpocket at six years old and then 'in jail, out of jail, in jail' as he used to say.

"But I loved him passionately which was my undoing, and Abel made me very jealous. He had an eye for every woman, and one night he told me he was going to leave me for another woman, the wife of a man he knew, and I knew her too. I was beside myself. I hit him with a saucepan on the back, and could have murdered him, but he overpowered me, quieted me, went out the door, and I never saw him again."

"Never? Not even in the street?"

"Never, never. Except. I thought I heard him talking with Jaggers one day when I was working in the office kitchen, but I never went through into the office without being summoned. And, of course, I could never ask Mr. Jaggers."

"Oh, I think he must definitely have been there when you heard him. Jaggers admitted as much."

"But I knew who the woman was that he was going to. She was the wife of one of his friends who had turned into an enemy. Harry Compeyson was his name, as I recall."

"No wonder they were enemies. Abel was stealing his wife."

"My thirst for revenge overpowered me, though I knew it was wrong. I lured her to a barn near the Green and strangled her, but I was seen coming out of the barn, was sought by the constables and they found me at home with you. Abel had disappeared."

Molly paused and wiped tears from her eyes, but then her face hardened.

"That I killed her has been to my shame ever since. Sometimes, yes sometimes, I think I could easily do it again. She took everything away from me, the cow."

"I understand. I came quite close to killing my husband as he was such a brute. Might both of us have a tendency to murder?"

"Oh dear," Estella continued, "I must take a walk in the rose garden to calm myself after learning of those dreadful things."

"Perhaps I will go and rest for an hour too. There's more. But, Ruthie, I'd find a way to kill anyone who hurt you."

At that moment, the gardener walked by the French window.

"Hey, gardener," shouted Molly, "bring me one of those beautiful flowers to look at. What are they?"

In his rich country accent, the gardener replied: "Them's daffodils, ma'am."

"Yes, Mother, the most beautiful herald of spring, the flower that comes before the swallow dares."

After dinner that evening, Molly and Estella sat in their drawing room, enjoying a very small glass of whisky each with plenty of water. It was Molly who had urged Estella to obtain a stronger drink than the occasional wine, not least because she had been used to drinking gin, the main drink of the working class.

"Oh, isn't this lovely? I tell you, Ruth, between being sentenced to hang and meeting you, I had not wept once. I suppose I am now making up for it."

"Weep all you want, Mother."

"Anyways, let me continue with my secrets. I was arrested with you in my arms. Mr. Jaggers took up my case. He called it a case of passion, which it was, and I was released for him to look after me. I am still frightened at nights by the thought of that woman's husband tracking me down. That's why that old crow upset me."

"Now here's a coincidence. You told me about Compeyson earlier. I remember Pip telling me Compeyson was the name of the man who jilted Miss Havisham."

"I can't believe that they'se the same family, Ruthie, but it's not a common name, though. Maybe Pip got it wrong."

"Ask Jaggers. Jaggers would know. Jaggers knows everything. Not even God knows as much as Jaggers."

They laughed so much at her remark that Molly knocked the table where her glass had been placed, but she reached out like a cat to grab it before it spilled.

"Now I think about it, Pip also told me that Abel killed someone called Compeyson when Pip and Herbert were trying to get Abel to France. He didn't say his Christian name. That could be the husband of the woman you killed, wouldn't it?"

"Oh, I do hope that Abel killed the bastard. Oops, pardon my language, Ruthie. After I was sentenced, my dearest daughter, what could I do? I had to let you go, for your sake."

"Yes, I can now see why, and I don't blame you. You were not to know what kind of a woman Miss Havisham was. But I really wish I had all your passions."

"Listen, Ruthie, I've been watching you ever since we started to live together. You cannot go on despising men. From what you have told me, my great sadness for you is that you find it impossible to love a man.

"So, you are missing the excitement, the madness of ecstasy with a man.

"It's like there is an earthquake deep down in your belly, in the depths of your body. Then there's the longing for him which sits in your whole body and mind, your life. You don't think of anything else. Then you get this wonderful feeling of bliss when you lie in his arms afterwards. You want to be fondled all over.

"It is delicious, but it fast becomes a deadly poison if he does not return it, if he goes cold. Jealousy too will eat into your whole being.

"That must be what happened to Miss Havisham, I suppose, though I'd guess she was always a virgin."

"Probably," said Estella. "Miss Havisham was simply out for revenge on every man, and I suppose my lack of passion comes from her instruction, and it still seems to possess me now. I hated Drummle, the man I married.

"I tormented him, as Miss Havisham had shown me. I think, by showing my disgust whenever he wanted his way with me. He took his anger out on his beautiful white horse all the time, you know, using the horse as if it was me, or so I think. That was his downfall: for I was watching him one afternoon thrashing this gorgeous beast and it gave him a vicious kick with its rear leg. It broke his neck."

A brief silence followed, then Estella continued:

"To be frank, Mother, as we have no secrets, I was delighted. I watched him dying without feeling. But, you know, even with Pip, whom I like very much, I cannot get beyond just liking him. Pip is my friend. But I shudder at the idea of him touching me with desire. It simply repels me. Maybe because he is just a friend? I don't know."

"I want you to find a man you can love where, when he's not there, you think you're about to die and, when he's there, you just want to be handled and loved."

"Not likely, but not absolutely impossible, although I am changing since that mad woman died.

"Strange, I have never spoken to another woman about a relationship with a man, apart from the regular caustic instructions I received from her. I suppose, now I have had you to talk to about it, the more I think about my upbringing, the more surprised I am, that being your daughter with your passions, I did not act, leave, even kill the old woman. I don't know. But I just surrendered and became this strange creature."

"I think you must find out what God made you to be, not that I think God had much to do with it. Anyway, I'd like to see you properly warmed up by a man."

"Warmed up? I'm not an apple pie, you know."

"There is one thing that I remember from being a little girl, Ruthie. Every Sunday, I must have been about four years old, my mother would take me in the afternoon to the church at the end of our street. That's where I was christened, I was told. I remember being told stories about Jesus which, as a child, I enjoyed.

"Sometimes, when I was out foraging or lying in a ditch, I'd think of those stories and wish Jesus would come to me with a loaf or a fish, or a good Samaritan would pick me up which, I suppose, Abel was in a way. Then, of course, we was too poor to get you to a Sunday school.

"Abel went once or twice but he wasn't interested in God, only in the people there who looked rich. He'd then pick a man and his wife, follow them carefully to their house after and then choose his moment, usually during a Sunday when they were at church, to break into their houses, tying up the maids if they weren't at church. What a bastard, eh?"

"Language, Mother."

"I am sorry, but because of what he did, I can't think of anything else to call him."

"Blackguard will do. But when I was on my travels in Europe, I strayed into a church or two. One Christmas Eve, I was staying in a small town called *Garmisch Partenkirken* in the country of Austria, and I heard singing from a church called St Martin's. I slipped in through the main door and I was astonished at the beauty and the splendor, rich in statues and gold decorations and the choir singing like I suppose angels sing. I sat and listened, though I had no church upbringing.

"Along with everything, Miss Havisham despised religion, telling me Vicars and priests were typical of men, just out to rob you of everything, including your soul. But I still remember the wonderful sounds of those voices in that beautiful setting.

"But do those memories of your Sundays make you want to attend a church, Mother?"

"No, but do you think God will forgive me for being a murderer?"

"I can't speak for God, but I forgive you.

"Incidentally, in my letter I wrote to Pip saying that I was mortified that we had not seen Beatrice up here, and I think they will come soon. He replied that Beatrice had had a second miscarriage, but they would love to come. He also told me the Gargerys were now Primitive Methodists and I wonder how that has changed their lives."

V

The lives of the Gargery family had indeed begun to change in both a temporal and a spiritual way. The arrival of the spring was always an occasion for a celebration in the countryside, and 1851 was no different. The Three Jolly Bargemen hosted a scene of great gaiety one day with two dozen husbands and their wives and children, including the Gargerys and Young Pip, morose at Old Pip's absence and feeling guilty that he felt so glum.

The boy was growing up steadily, now well-equipped with letters and numbers from Biddy, but also developing the ability to read easily as Old Pip had always arrived with books which he invariably liked. His writing was not good, not least because he rarely had cause to do much other than spell his name. They decided he should try a Sunday School but that was abandoned when messages contravened their beliefs in Primitive Methodism.

He had become a tall young man, almost his father's height, but still not yet an adult, mere wisps of a beard appearing on his face. Yet he was strong, necessary to shoeing horses, and very agile.

The Gargerys had been sitting a while talking with the Friendlys and Mr. Buzza the ostler and saddler, when the pub door opened rather grandly and a stranger in naval uniform appeared.

"Good day, stranger, you are welcome on this festive occasion. My name is Josiah. Might I offer you a drink?"

"Thank you, no. I am at the Queen's service," said the stranger in a deep voice, "My name is Thomas Mistyfield. Landlord, tell me, are there smiths here?"

"Well, there's Joe Gargery over there, he's a blacksmith and with him is Sam Friendly who I think works with copper and more precious metals, though he lives a few miles off. Mr. Buzza there is a saddler and runs a stable."

"Thank you, I will talk with Mr. Gargery."

All the customers including the Gargery group had been eyeing this stranger, dressed in a naval uniform which did not betray his rank. Mistyfield had a military bearing and an impressive beard, and shoulders that looked as though he could carry a sheep, perhaps even an ox, without much difficulty. All in all, a very impressive presence.

"A very good afternoon, Mr. Gargery, I believe?" he said, addressing Joe.

"Indeed," said Joe, "that's me."

"My name is Thomas Mistyfield and I am the overseer at the Royal Dockyard at Chatham. I expect you go there sometimes; very pleasant town on the river."

"Yes, I went once as an adventure, but I got lost so I came home."

"Never been, never wanted to," interjected Biddy with a sour grimace.

"Now, see here, my good man, let me get straight to the purpose of my visitations across Kent. I am talking to every blacksmith I can find. It is the year of our Lord, 1851, and I am doing Her Gracious Majesty's work, looking for able-bodied men like yourself who are used to working with metal, particularly iron.

"For Captain Sir Thomas Bouchier has commanded me to find men who can help us build our new steamships. No longer hearts of oak, but skins of iron and steel. We have been using convict labor, bringing men from the hulks in the river. We still do, but they are rarely skilled and have no incentives to learn the great trade of which you are, I am sure, a master. Sir Thomas told me go out and seek all those loyal British subjects who work with iron across the County of Kent. 'Go find them, Mistyfield,' says he, 'Our country needs them.'"

"Go on, then, tell us more. We's very wantin' to know what you're up to."

"Sir Thomas has authorized me to invite you, as your patriotic duty to her Gracious Majesty, to come to Chatham to work to build what will be our finest steamship, Her Majesty's Ship *Majestic*, as she will be called. *Majestic* in name, in build and in power. It takes time to amass the skilled workmen we need so we will provide residence for your family and pay you a worthy sum each week for as long as the ship takes to build. Britannia must continue to rule the waves."

Turning quickly to Sam Friendly, Mistyfield said: "The landlord tells me, sir, that you work with copper. Our needs there are very limited, but I am sure you could contribute as you know metal."

"Thank'ee kindly, sir, but I'se too old a dog to learn new tricks. My family has been smithing copper, man and boy since the old King George's time, and we's not looking to change."

"I understand, Friendly, but now, Gargery, What say you?"

The customers in the pub were listening carefully to these exchanges, and now that Joe was being put on his mettle, there was virtual silence, apart from an infant moaning quietly on his mother's lap. All knew that he could earn significantly more each week than he could as a blacksmith. Such employment would be the desire of most men in that pub, who might have known how to plough a field, but had little knowledge of how to make one.

"I don't know about Britannia: what has she ever done for me?"

"Might I find work, too?" asked Young Pip.

"If my surmise is correct," said Mistyfield, drawing himself up to his full height, "you are your father's apprentice, so—of course."

"Yes, while I knows a bit about smithing, my real tasks are working with horses and shoeing them," at which Mistyfield realized that if he can offer work for the son, the father may well follow suit.

"I think you can serve your country well in that occupation in the dockyard where we have several stables and, if a cavalry regiment were to come to Chatham to embark, which I would deem possible, they would need many farriers."

Joe's hesitation began to crumble. He had still not quite recovered from paying Old Pip's debts all those years go, over one hundred pounds worth of his savings. He had now been feeding three mouths as well as providing some little monies to Young Pip for his work. He did not have the nest-egg he'd like to have. A good few months at this work would enable him to re-establish a pot of money for whatever might come along, death, injury, or catastrophes like a rise in the price of corn, making bread very expensive which he could recall from his youth.

Turning to Biddy, he said: "What an honor to be asked by a Captain, and from Her Majesty, too? What say you, Biddy; what say you, Young Pip?"

"I say we think about it; we have the Forge, the horse and much else to consider. Can we let you know, sir, in a month or so?"

"Time marches on, my good woman. How about a week? I will be coming back through this village again on my way back to Chatham, so leave a message with the landlord here. If you accept Her Majesty's invitation, I will send a boy to your dwelling with further instructions. For the present, I will bid you good evening."

So Thomas Mistyfield, overseer, left The Three Jolly Bargemen awash in self-congratulation and bearing himself as if he were about to meet the Queen, or perhaps an Admiral.

"How I hate soldiers," said Biddy. "They think they can lord it over people, using that Britannia nonsense and boys get sent to war and killed. I hate 'em."

"That I agree with," said Sam. "My brother was killed on some damn boat somewhere or other; press-ganged.

"Yet, a wise decision, Joe," Sam continued, "now you'se younger than me, see, and the Navy will pay you good. Chatham's not such a bad place, can be smelly and dirty and there's a few drunk sailors around. But he's giving you somewhere to live; it won't be a palace, but it won't be a dosshouse either."

The pub's conversation resumed with vigor as the Gargery's decision was discussed. Sid Brownlow said he wouldn't work in Chatham if they paid him. Enoch Middlemiss said it would be exciting to live in a town. The women in the circle were of one mind: If you are comfortable, stick to it, don't take a risk, and don't let your children go to war. Young Pip pushed on to the settle between his parents.

"Let me sit close to you both. Now, would God want us to work on ships that go to war? If we didn't, someone else would, though p'raps that's not a reason. Let us ask the Preacher what he thinks God would want. He is coming to see us any day now, isn't he?

"Mother, did he not say on Sunday he'd like to visit?"

"That's right, and I'd expect him any way as he said he'd be heading out toward Rochester to preach in the villages on the way."

Two days past, and the Gargerys were anxiously waiting for the Preacher's call because they had to make a decision. They need not have worried, for on the third morning, a cantering horse could be heard coming down the track to the cottage.

Preacher Whitehouse was all in black and with what Young Pip saw was really a fine horse which made him wonder how a preacher got money, whether it was his own or did the chapels give it to him? When I'm a preacher, I'll have a horse like that, he thought.

"Greetings to you all in God's name. Mrs. Gargery told me you would like to talk with me, and as I am bound to Rochester, I thought I'd call on you."

"You are most welcome, ain't he, Young Pip? Come out here with us, Biddy."

Biddy curtsied to the Preacher, a rare gesture for her, who said: "All who come in God's name are welcome here. Gather round."

"Let us begin with a hymn. God bless this family and make us perfect for Him."

"Amen," said everyone in unison, Joe's powerful voice being the dominant.

"Let us sing a hymn of praise," said the preacher and he started off on a well-loved hymn in which all joined, Joe being slightly discordant, Biddy in a pretty soprano and Young Pip still experimenting with his broken voice.

"O For a thousand tongues to sing

My dear Redeemer's praise
The glories of my God and King,
The triumphs of His grace."

"That is the best start to our talking, family. Now what can I help with?"

"You tell him, Young Pip, you're good with thoughts and words."

"Preacher, sir, an overseer from Chatham Dockyard has asked my father, and me as well, and my mother can come too as we will have lodging, to work there as we know iron-work and they want to build war ships nowadays with iron and steel and less wood.

"This overseer, Mistyfull I think his name was, said he had come from the Queen and the Captain and that it was our duty. But we don't think God wants us to kill other people or help other people to do it, like sailors in the Navy."

"War and bloodshed are contrary to God's teaching. But, sometimes, there is such evil that we must fight. We Methodists believe in peace; we are peaceful people, we are peace-loving, and we want all Earth's people to love peace more than war and to seek perfection in God's name."

"H'mm," said Joe thoughtfully. "So, God would not have liked all that terrible fighting against Boney when I was young. I must have been twenty years old when he was caught by that general, the Iron Duke. I liked a Duke of Iron."

"This is where we must be careful as Methodists. For the Church of England always supports the Queen. We can't be unpatriotic as we won't gain respect. Do you see?"

"So, let me think," said Biddy, "Do you think God would want Joe and Young Pip to go to work on warships in Chatham?"

"Pray for guidance. But I think He would not object," said the Preacher, avoiding Biddy's direct question with some discomfort. "The ships might never be used for fighting.

"However, there we have a small growing community there, and, Biddy, we also have a woman preacher, Alice LeBone. I know you will like her, and you can help extend our little community. But now I must leave if I am to get to Rochester before nightfall."

"Let me help you on your horse, Preacher," said Joe. "You've given me much to think about, and Biddy will help me."

"Pray, my friends, pray. Thank you all, God bless."

As the Preacher cantered off, Joe sat back in the old leather chair and with a grumble said:

"I'm awfull dull, Biddy. God does not want us to fight. Britannia tells us we have to. Preacher says we must pray. Who should we follow?"

"We must do as Preacher says and pray for guidance."

"But I think we should follow Britannia," said Young Pip. "We's not going to kill anyone, are we? I think it would be a lark to go to Chatham. I wonder what it's like there, living in a town. If we don't like it, we just come back, eh, Mother?"

"I can see you two want an adventure. I'm going to have to talk with this preacher woman, Alice, and make friends with her."

With some trepidation the Gargery family moved to Chatham. Arrangements were made for Betsy and Boney to live with Mr. Buzza at the stables, and he also brought his cart along to help them take what they needed. Joe shut down the Forge and Biddy packed up her kitchen. Buzza rode up front with Joe, with Biddy and Young Pip facing backwards. He was both excited and timorous, as he knew only family home and forge, the village and the marshland. They had been told that their tenement residence had plenty of furniture and Biddy surmised it will only be a few months while that boat was out at sea.

Buzza knew Chatham well so he acted as a guide.

"Who lives in them big houses?" asked Young Pip.

"Very important people," said Mr. Buzza.

"Those there are for Master Shipwrights, Master Ropemakers. Over there are the houses for the Captains and Admirals."

"See, when you'se an admiral," said Joe, "you'll get a big place like that."

"Not me, Father, I'll be a preacher."

"What a lot of buildings," said Biddy.

"There has to be warehouses for the Navy. Then there's bar-racks for the seamen and some for workers like you Gargerys. Here we are now," he said as they approached through an archway with two floors above it like all the buildings made of bricks fashioned in Kent over the centuries.

Inside the arch there was an office of sorts where Hector Bristle, the caretaker and gatekeeper of the building, lived. He was a mild man of a friendly temperament, and not especially proud of his position, but obviously hard of hearing, putting his right hand to his ear when listening such that repetition was fre-quently needed.

His left arm seemed damaged, perhaps from a wound, so it hung slackly through the arm of a lowly naval uniform. He was slim, well groomed, clean-shaven, balding, with dark hair going grey. He greeted them warmly but, as with all new tenants, with some cau-tion, though these folk seemed sensible enough to him.

"Let me see," he said, as the cart stopped inside the arch and he came down the short stone stairs from his office, "who have we here?"

"We's the Gargerys," said Joe. "This 'ere is my wife, Biddy, and that's our boy, Young Pip. Mr. Buzza who's kindly driven us over 'ere will not be stopping."

"I'm Mr. Bristle, the caretaker and gatekeeper. Is this your cart?"

"No, like I said, this 'ere is my friend Mr. Buzza who has kindly brung us from All Hallows, and he is not stopping."

"So you won't have a cart here. Oh well, welcome to the Dockyard. I s'pose you'se bin recruited by Mistyfield."

"That's right, and a fine gentlemun he is too."

"Oh, is he? That's news. Seems more like a drunken sailor to me. But I jest. You are all in number 27. Go along the square at the far end, up the stairs to 27. It's a nice place, view of the river.

"And, young man," he said, addressing Young Pip," I want no rowdiness or drunkenness here."

This stern admonition took Young Pip by surprise as neither rowdiness nor drink were within his compass.

"Well, thank'ee, Mr. Bustle."

"Bristle, please. And here is your key."

"My apologies Mr. Bristle," said Joe without embarrassment.

Moving from the familiar cottage to a two-room tenement was a shock. The rooms were small and the windows especially were badly in need of a clean which made the place seem gloomier. The furniture had not been used in a while, and the kitchen had a bad smell as if a rat or a mouse had departed this life under the sink.

Buzza helped moved their possessions and then, wishing them luck on their new venture, and thankful he was not a man of iron, departed quickly with a wave to Mr. Bristle as he drove his cart under the arch and back toward the calm of All Hallows.

Biddy rolled up her sleeves, and with Joe's help, made the rooms habitable enough. Even the sun shone brightly through the windows. The dead mouse was removed. Food and clothing were unpacked. Rooms were assigned.

"We can always go back for anything we need," Biddy said wistfully, "we's in Chatham, not America."

"That's right, Biddy," said Joe heaving a bed into position.

Young Pip went down the stairs and out into the square, walking around, nodding to a few people in greeting. It was mid-afternoon when they were ready to explore the seaport of Chatham.

"Young Pip, you'll be off by yourself I know, but do take care."

"I will, Mother. I'll catch up with you."

The noise of the town was deafening on ears that were used to the clanging of an anvil in a place with only the sounds of nature and the human voice as accompaniment. Walking along what seemed the main thoroughfare, Joe said:

"We's going to need those muffler things for ears in this town, Biddy, you know, like we have in snow," at which Biddy smiled and replied, but Joe could not hear her for the racket.

Young Pip was wandering behind them, astonished at such a place, so crammed with human beings. Something touched his arm and he turned to see a very pretty young woman, her plump breasts almost wholly visible above a shabby dress and shawl. Her eyes were a startling blue and her hair a dirty blonde. Her looks betrayed a world of what would be called 'hard knocks,' but Young Pip was far too innocent to see that far into her world.

"Come with me, young fella," she said, in a strong Cockney accent which Young Pip recognized as somewhat similar to the way Preacher Whitehouse talked. "I've got things to show you never saw before, you'll love to feel them, so soft for your strong hands. What's your name?"

"My name is Pip, and I'm to be a farrier in the dockyard yonder. We just came here."

"Stone the crows, what's a farrier?"

"Oh, I work with horses, shoeing them and brushing them."

"There, see, I knew you liked to use your hands. Give me your hand, feel my tit. See, that's nice and soft too and ooh, it feels so good, do you like the feel?"

"I do," said Young Pip, his face puce with embarrassment, "but I don't think I should do that."

"If you like it and I like it, what's wrong with it?"

"Come on, Pip, don't deny it, you liked it. Just like when you wash and stroke your horse. Does your horse get hot and wet sometimes? You liked it, didn't you?" she said, pulling his head down to kiss him hard.

"There, now come with me just around the corner there and I can give you lots more to feel, only it'll be much hotter."

"I don't know, I have to catch up with my family up the street. We've just arrived, and we want to see the town."

"Oh, come on, just a quick one. I'll let you have it for two shillings."

"I haven't got two shillings."

"Gorblimey, what do you take me for?" she said loudly, "I don't do nuffin' without money. Oh, my gawd, you ain't done it before, 'av yer?"

"Done what?"

At this, she burst out laughing.

"Tell yer wot," she said, still giggling, "Find me after you've been in the dockyard for a month. The lads there will tell you 'what.' By then you'll be gaspin' for it. And you'll have two bob to give me. I'm off."

Aghast at this reaction, Young Pip shouted after her:

"Two shillings for what and what's your name?"

"Nellie," cried the young whore as she disappeared down an alley.

"What did she want?" mused Young Pip, shaking his head, "bit of loving perhaps? Where are my family?" And he hurried up the street to call out to Joe, "Hey, Father!"

"There you are, my son. We was wonderin' where you were. Biddy, I need to get some better boots than these if I'm going to be working on ships."

"Yes, Joe, there's a stall, see what that cobbler's got."

"What might I do for you, sir?" asked the cobbler.

"Well, I ain't really a sir, likewise, but I need some boots."

"These should fit, try 'em on. I suppose you've come to work in the dockyard?"

"You are right, friend, and we have found out God's word in village of All Hallows."

"Oh dear, is you a religious fella, eh? From what I hear you'll need God's help there."

The cobbler guffawed and wagged his finger at Joe and said, "They're using the roughest of the rough, convicts mainly. I wouldn't let on you're a religious man, if I were you. That will be seven shillings."

"Now I'm very confused, but God will protect me, I am sure. Here's the money."

He walked off toward Biddy who was listening to a woman preaching, standing on a box.

"As I finish, good people," said the preacher, "just remember: God is watching you. God is with you. Hear the word of the Lord who has come to help us be perfect, perfect in His love," at which the Gargerys lead the small crowd in Hallelujahs.

"Do you know Preacher Whitehouse?" Joe asks the Preacher.

"Oh, of course she does, Joe: This must be Alice LeBone, our Preacher."

"And you must be the Gargery family. Welcome to you all. Preacher Whitehouse told me you would be coming to join our little community. You can come to my home on a Sunday. That's serves as our chapel."

"Thank the Lord, my dears," says Biddy, "we have found Alice in this terrible place. I'm off to our rooms now to make your supper. You two look around and find out about your jobs."

"Young Pip," instructed Joe, "you go up to the stables and make yourself known as a Gargery should. I'll go to the dockyard and you'se come back here next to the cobbler's stand in two hours. That should give us time. Take care, my dear chap. God be with you."

Young Pip walked up the street and found a large building with horses neighing and stomping their hooves. It was by no means full, as he assumed that meant the cavalry were not in town.

"Hallo," said a young man of Pip's age standing in front of him. "I'm Horatio Fletcher, named after Lord Nelson, but everyone calls me Fletcher or Fletch. It's good work here, especially since I love horses."

"Hallo, I'm Pip, just arrived from All Hallows, come to work in Chatham with my family. I love horses too, and I worked with my father at his Forge in the village. It's very noisy here in the town. It makes my head sore.

"Fletch, can I ask you something?"

"Oh yes, Pip, when we's working together, we'se going to have lots of talking, I know."

"I expect you know the ways of this town, but after I came along the street earlier, a girl came up to me in the street, lots of her bosoms showing, and asked me to do something around the corner, but she wanted two shilling for whatever it were. I didn't have any money and then she ran off saying I hadn't done it yet. What did she mean?"

"You? A country boy?" he said with peals of laughter, "and you don't know what she was offering? That must have been Nellie. Ah well, I don't s'pose you get many whores in the country."

"No, I don't know what a whore is."

"Blimey, I've never met anyone, leastwise a young man, who did not know what a whore is. Now, look'ee here. You know how babies are made, don't you?"

"Yes."

"She will let you do that to her if you give her money, and she'll make sure she doesn't have babies, so she doesn't come around telling you you're a father. She's very popular with some of the men here, usually the older ones, some married, most not. But two shilling is really cheap, she must have taken a fancy to you. She likes a good time, too. I must get to her myself afore we sail, if we do."

"This is what goes on in towns, I s'pose. I don't think God would like it."

Fletch was now consumed with laughter.

"No, I don't suppose He would! But we're going to be working together on our beasts of burden, so let's be friends, and I'll give you advice about how to avoid the perils of the flesh. And, who knows, maybe, we will get to work on cavalry horses, big brutes they are."

"Good to meet you, Fletch. Now I must find my father. He's going to work in the dockyard."

"Oh, I pity him as it can be really nasty there. The laborers are convicts mostly, very rough and some very violent. But see what your father says. See you tomorrow."

"Goodbye," said Young Pip as he walked back down the street to the cobbler's stall, trying to take in the sights and sounds of the town and the coarse character of life, what with drunks and whores and the like.

"Father, Father!"

"Oh, there you are, Young Pip. We must be getting home."

As they walked up the stairs to number 27, they could smell Biddy's cooking. She asked how they fared, as she was getting worried.

"I have a new friend, bit older than me, I think. Oh, and I found out what a whore is."

"Shh, Young Pip," says Joe firmly. "We don't want your mother to hear about that. It's not right for a good woman to hear."

They entered the living space, drab as it was compared to the comfort of their cottage.

"Biddy, my dear, I didn't like the dockyard. I didn't like the men, specially the convicts. I don't know how long I can stay there. There was so much cussing and blaspheming, taking the name of the Lord in vain.

"I told one or two of the men about how God wants us to be perfect, and they laughed at me and pushed me around, but I'se bigger and stronger than most of 'em, not being locked up in a hulk but working hard at my anvil, so I didn't get any rough stuff."

"Now, look'ee here, Joe Gargery. You are not to get into any fights."

"Oh, no. Not me. But I think, yes, I think God would want us to feel sorry for them convicts, such poor creatures, working in shackles, however bad they are."

"But them's still God's children," she continued. "Anyway, let's see how it works out. We can't go back to the Forge now till that ship of yours is built, can we? I'm feeling lucky as I am sure I will be friends with Alice. You two will be tested and will find strength, with God's help."

"I am troubled by the work, too. What has my country ever done for me? Oh, dear, that sounds selfish, don't it?"

"Pray for guidance, Young Pip," said his father. "Now here's the vittels Biddy has given us, so let me give thanks to the Lord afore we eat. That *Majestic* is going to take some time, a year so. We start laying the hull soon. Maybe it'll be done in a year or two."

"Here that long? You said months, not years," said Biddy , exasperated.

"No, no, my love. That's what I thought. There'll soon come a time when I won't be needed, and we'll be back at the Forge," though his face revealed uncertainty about that claim.

VI

In July of 1852 Beatrice said she would like to visit Estella and Molly, though she was pregnant again and a little weak after her miscarriages. Old Pip was starting to blame himself for them, even speculating to himself that it was a divine judgement on him for his love for Estella, though he was delighted that, once again, she was pregnant.

Yet learning the law was a continuing hard task. Jaggers was in the last stage of his instruction on such matters as tort, contract, administrative law, the latter in its infancy, but with a heavy concentration on the wilderness of the criminal law, punctuated by long discussions on how to make punishments fit crimes. Proposals for more formal legal education were still meandering through committees of varying kinds, so *ad hoc* training meant that those who entered the law could come from a variety of backgrounds, not merely university cloisters.

They joined the Chatham coach at the Bull and Mouth Inn near Aldgate for the eight-hour journey, some thirty miles with one change of horses. They were put down at the Blue Boar Inn near All Hallows on the Rochester-Chatham road, an old building with low beams, log fires and comfortable rooms. The landlord was Jonah, the younger brother of Josiah landlord at the Bargemen, who served them a hot meal of duck cooked in cider. Beatrice needed her rest and went directly to bed.

Old Pip was finishing his dessert when two men entered that part of the Inn where the bar was located. They seemed to be brothers, without beards, but not clean-shaven, and their expressions were furtive, though candlelight made it difficult to see them properly.

There were three other couples, one with a boisterous young child who was sent to his room for the various iniquities he could not comprehend.

The two men captured his attention because, as a lawyer, he had met criminals of various descriptions in London in the course of his training. The men looked around at the company with some care and then, as they contemplated each couple, whispered to each other, always behind hands, quietly. They rebuffed Jonah's attempts at conversation and left, allowing Old Pip to retire to bed with a sense of apprehension that the two were up to no good.

Old Pip arose at dawn and went for a short walk, sniffing the country air with remembered delight. The road was deserted but the dawn chorus and the morning cocks were in full throat. Mid-morning after a long breakfast he returned to the room to find that Beatrice had dressed and had a light breakfast in their room.

Looking out of the window, he saw Estella's trap waiting for them. Beatrice adjusted her bonnet, holding his arm as they mounted the trap and Old Pip pulled a rug over his wife's knees. The driver veered off the track after a mile and new vistas opened up across open country before he turned into the track which led directly to Numquam House.

Estella came out of the house at the sound of the returning trap and went immediately to Beatrice as she dismounted:

"Oh, my dear, how d'ye do, you look tired after your long journey yesterday. Rest awhile here in the garden and we will serve some tea. Let me see, you are a cousin of Herbert's, am I right, but on his father's side?"

"How d'ye do, Estella. Yes, my father Algernon was Herbert's father's youngest brother."

She faltered slightly in her step and Estella showed her to a chaise-longue which, with two raffia chairs and an old oak table, made up the garden furniture under a sweet chestnut tree.

"But I will rest, if you allow me, dear Estella. Pip has told me so much about you, I feel I know you. But I have continuous apprehensions about my condition, as I have lost two babies since we married. I have not been pregnant for almost a year, so I hope my body is refreshed for this one."

"Your loss grieves me intensely. Pip will be a wonderful father, I am sure. So, you must rest to ensure this baby is born. We will meet often after that and get to know each other."

"Pip darling," said Beatrice, "I am quite put about even by our journey from the Inn. Perhaps a little sleep will help."

Old Pip pulled up her pillows, making sure the rug covers her body, as Molly emerged from the house clutching her crochet work. Though just over sixty, she appeared very confident, composed and really quite beautiful. Estella looked at her walking towards them with pride, lovingly, but also with a sense of triumph. Her hair was newly prepared, her clothes were in fashion. Old Pip had only seen her occasionally at Jaggers' office, so he was utterly surprised by the transformation.

"Goodness, Molly, you are quite changed. I would not have known you."

"Ah, Mr. Pip, but I could not have known happiness until my beloved daughter found me. She has helped me abandon my old ways and manners over these few years, and I like my conversion to a new woman."

"Ah," said Estella, "I don't think Pygmalion could have done better."

"And who's he?" asked Molly, a question shared by Old Pip and Beatrice.

"He is a famous character in Greek mythology who created a beautiful statue of a woman which he loved as his finest creation, and the goddess Venus turned the statue into a real woman with whom he fell in love."

"But I ain't no bleeding statue," cried Molly laughing, relapsing into her Cockney style and sitting in a chair near Beatrice.

"No, my dear, it was just a flight of my fancy.

"But enough, isn't Beatrice lovely? Quite wonderful and a treasure for Pip," she said staring at Beatrice, almost as if she could not take her eyes off her and quite unnecessarily adjusted the woolen rug over her. Old Pip looked at the two of them, delighted at how solicitous Estella was for his pregnant wife.

"Thank you so much, Estella, I am so grateful. But you seem wonderfully settled here as you are, I presume, in your London lodgings."

"We are. Now Mother and I are making up for lost time. She especially loves the garden, don't you, dear?"

Molly nodded approvingly while engrossed again in her crochet work.

"She arises at dawn, or so it seems, and goes for a constitutional, smelling the roses, admiring the delphiniums, checking on the dahlias and so is often up listening to the dawn chorus. She loves the experience of the country, the garden, its walks and lawns, not forgetting the orchard, where we had so much fruit last year. Each day I have to call her in to breakfast and that sometimes will take a quarter-hour."

"Well I must say, living together suits you both," said Old Pip. "I have never seen you look so calm and relaxed too, Estella. Come now, show me around this spectacular garden."

Molly continued her crochet work, looking over frequently at Beatrice who was now fast asleep. Estella took Pip's arm. The gardener was tending a rose arbor and touched his forelock as they passed and the deference was lightly acknowledged.

"Poor Beatrice; she was never a strong woman but trying to bear children has been such a trial for us. She has miscarried twice, as she told you, and I am hoping against hope she can carry this child to its full term. I do my best for her, and I am making my way with Jaggers but that will take time."

"Let me help you, Pip. I have some money, you know. I will make you my personal lawyer too, though I hope not to use you too often."

"No, my dear, I would not dream of trespassing on your generosity, though I'd be delighted to offer legal advice as needed, not least as you now have Molly to care for and to give her new life in the time that God has in mind for her."

"That is rather gloomy, isn't?"

"Of course, but both Jaggers and Wemmick think that her earlier sufferings in life remain with her, and that they may have left a wound in her mind which might re-open at any time."

"Stuff and nonsense. I will hear no more of this, Pip. You have seen her. She is calm and relaxed, thoughtful and kind, and we have talked together about our pasts, so there are no secrets between us, and she has confided in me without reserve. Mind you, she can be startled by nothing: The loud caw of a crow behind her in the garden made her start recently.

"I surmise that, buried deep in her mind, is the worry that the husband or children of the woman she killed might be intent on revenge. But she is surely quite safe here, perhaps less so in London. She has also been teaching me about myself, too."

They turned the corner into a second rose garden which cannot be seen from the house.

He was silent for a moment, then said: "My dear, are you sure you should not employ someone to protect you both? It would not be difficult to find someone, even posing as an additional gardener."

"No, and again no. I'll hear no more about it. After all, we have been about in London before we came here but experienced no trouble, no one calling without invitation and no one following us. Why would anyone follow her down here to the wilds of Kent?"

"Maybe, but can you be sure of that? My growing experience of villains is that they do not tell you in advance what will happen."

"I am grateful, Pip, but you are worrying too much. But I must tell you what Mother said about Jaggers recently—he has more answers than God."

They laughed again heartily, looked into each other's eyes for a long moment and came slightly closer as they faced each other.

"Oh, Pip, dear Pip," she said, moving to him and stroking the lapels on his velvet morning coat with her hands. "I do hope you will be so very happy with Beatrice. You so deserve it. I think fatherhood will suit you well. And you are such a handsome man, you know."

He smiled broadly. She then clasped his arm tightly, as if to walk on, but still looking at him carefully.

"Beatrice and I will be happy, I am sure. I'd like to live in the country again if it were not for my occupation."

"Now, you see, that's where I could help."

"My dear, please do not raise that subject again, or we might stop being friends."

"Impossible, I cannot imagine life without your friendship, dear Pip, whatever has gone between us in the past. We share so much. You really are the only friend I have."

They were still standing close to each other, looking into each other's eyes again, then each turned away after a sudden smile of recognition that for the very first time, they have together crossed a barrier of sexual distance typical of adulthood into a realm of sexual possibility.

These mere glances went through Old Pip like a rapier, thinking how she had never ever looked into his eyes quite like that.

Was Estella really available to him?

Just a few yards away lay his sleeping wife and here he was wanting desperately to hold this enchanting woman to him.

Estella in her turn was shocked at her own spontaneous forwardness but more still at the kind of thrill she had never really experienced before, a fluttering in her heart and breasts.

Could this really be halted, could they deny themselves?

Was there really no possibility with her/his dear friend and now her/his possible lover?

Thoughts like these raced around in both their minds like snow in a blizzard. They walked back slowly to Molly and Beatrice in a subdued, not an ordinary silence; a silence of the kind in which conversation was rushing along, too hasty to be articulated.

The others were talking gaily about babies. Beatrice seemed rested, so they went in for lunch.

After lunch, Estella accompanied Old Pip and Beatrice to her trap.

"Thank you for a delightful lunch. I really do feel rested."

"Then that was alone worth your visit, Beatrice."

"But please excuse us, I am sure I will take to my bed after the journey back to the Inn."

"It has been quite delightful," said Old Pip, "we will return tomorrow on our way to see Joe and Biddy." After a profligacy of goodbyes, they rode in Estella's trap to the Inn.

Sitting at their dining table after dinner Estella and Molly continued their evening talking about Old Pip and Beatrice.

"Isn't she beautiful, Ruthie?

"Oh, indeed, she is. I am quite surprised that Pip found her attractive enough to marry. He is such an active creature and she seems so passive."

"I expect that is just because she has been pregnant almost since marriage. That will make you tired, certainly. Does their happiness make you a little bit envious, Ruthie? I saw you looking at her very closely."

"I must confess to being a little confused. I looked at him when we walked in the garden with different eyes and began to feel the stirrings in me that you have described. In fact these were new eyes, but I am strong enough to control my passions, if they emerge as they seem to be doing."

"I am not surprised, my dear. If I were much younger, I could find him very desirable."

"Mother," she said, laughing indignantly. "You must not say such things."

"I will not talk of it ever again. But if not Pip, we must go out in London and try to find someone who stirs your heart and your loins."

"Enough, enough!" she cried, "I am off to bed."

At the Inn, Old Pip and Beatrice had taken an early supper and retired and lay in each other's arms. Beatrice commented on how comfortable the room was, with its low ceilings, four-poster bed, and thick hanging curtains shielding small windows.

"That was an excellent supper, my dear, but you didn't eat much, nor at lunch."

"I am so sorry, Pip. This baby does not want to let me eat but I must eat more, for his or her health, too. I am so fortunate that I have you as my protector, Pip darling; I am so anxious to give you a child. I know you will be a wonderful father. What more can I do to make sure our baby is born and lives?"

"We must just take good care of you and not exert you too much."

"Yes; I am not nearly as strong as Estella or Molly. I find their story so very strange, indeed quite outside my understanding. Think about it. A criminal mother gives away her child who is then brought up by a mad woman to be in an upper class. Mother and daughter meet by a complete accident many years later, and now they are obliged to live with each other. Do you think Estella really wanted it?"

"Oh, yes. You see, my dear, she was extraordinarily lonely. No relatives, no friends, living in the depths of the country after a brutal marriage. Anyone to cure this loneliness would be a godsend."

"Even you?" asked Beatrice quietly, a comment which was like a thunderbolt in Pip's confused state of mind.

"I have told you, my dear, about Estella and me. It is a long and tortuous story and I have come to feel that she is more like a sister to me, or perhaps a cousin."

"Are you sure about that, Pip? I saw her looking at you at lunch and she did not look sisterly."

"After all these years, I can hardly think she is likely to change and I am sure her mother will not influence her, even though she has a checkered past."

"Ah well, I care not. I've got you now, not her," she said, laughing. "Oh, Pip, I miss you so desperately when you are doing your lawyering all day."

"I know, but we will be much better off financially. But you must take care. I should not have urged you to come with me as the journey was very difficult, as will be our return. I think your continuous rest will serve all three of us."

"Indeed, I pray there may be three."

"When we go back to London, the airs of the capital will be especially noxious in the summer heat. I will ask Wemmick if we can go to Walworth to stay, and he and I can walk across the bridge to work each day."

"That would be wonderful," she said sleepily.

Old Pip laid awake, lying on his back, contemplating his life silently. Beatrice had sensed Estella's response to me.

Damn female intuition!

Damn whoever invented conscience!

She was almost loving in the garden today, touching my lapels and looking into my eyes differently. I cannot help myself responding to her affection, but I must control myself: In all conscience I cannot be unfaithful to Beatrice, even in my thoughts and desires. Yet Estella is invading my private thoughts yet again just when I thought I had put her completely behind me.

Perhaps we should not see her for a long time; she is happy with Molly and does not need me to look after her. Yes, that's it. I won't see her. But then if Beatrice does give us a baby, she will want to show her our baby. If we have one. Come on sleep, knit up the raveled sleeve of care.

At Numquam House next morning, the sun was scarcely above the horizon as Molly lit her candle and got out of bed, yawning. At the same moment, two men, one with a scar on his face, had climbed through the privet hedge surrounding Numquam and were standing behind a large beech hedge which shielded the rose garden from the orchard.

The first man said quietly to his companion: "Keep dead still when she appears, Jack. I think this old barndoor hinge should do it; she's old."

"We'll have an hour to get away, won't we, Billy? Morning coach from Chatham?"

"Yes, we'll run back to the cart in fifteen minutes, so shouldn't be a problem."

"Wait, here she comes now. Remember, not a whisper or any noise."

Innocent of this looming catastrophe, Molly was talking to herself about her wonderful life:

"Another gorgeous morning, I am so lucky. I am so happy, wandering around our beautiful garden in the morning. Ruthie told me always to wear my straw hat as there are lots of flying insects in the early morning, and they are pestering me already."

She stopped to admire the peonies ready to bloom. She was full of good humor and peace, wandering across the lawn and through the two rose gardens, pausing as she did to admire the blooms not yet open but ready to release their seductive smells. She sat awhile on a bench looking at a rhododendron bush, its ravishing purple flowers now on the turn.

"I must remember to ask Ruthie to teach me the names of the birds. I know what a sparrow is, at least, and a pigeon, though they are cleaner here than in London. And of course the crow, but its these little prettier birds I don't know. This is strange, such a lovely morning, so why aren't the birds singing? Why are they so quiet?"

She got up from the bench and passed through the arbor at the other end of the rose garden from the house, noticing how wet the roses were, thinking she would ask the gardener to cut some for her room.

At that instant, an iron hinge wielded by a man of great strength came crashing down on the back of her head, crushing her straw hat into her brain, blood spurting from her head, trapped by the hat as it gushed from her broken skull.

"That should have done for her, she never saw what was coming, did she, Billy?"

"Come on, now, Jack, let's get to the fence afore anyone sees her."

"She is dead, isn't she, Billy?"

"Well, if she ain't, Jack, she's going to have a big headache."

"Don't throw that barn hinge away here, we'll chuck it in the river."

"Take that, you bitch, for killing our mother," he said, looking with utter venom at Molly's body, lying face down on the grass, the blood seeping into the grass from her hat.

"Yes, back to London now. Oh, Jack my brother, revenge is so sweet I can taste it."

Time passed. The birds returned to singing, conscious perhaps that strange events have passed. Somewhere along the track, a cart drove away fast. A crow landed near the body, then flew away cawing hysterically.

Estella appeared at the door of the house and called her mother to breakfast. She then went back to her table and waited. Ten minutes passed and Molly did not appear. Estella went to the door and shouted:

"Mother, where are you? Come to breakfast." She noticed the gardener emerging from the shed where he lived, scratching his head and yawning, obviously newly awake.

"Mother, come on."

Fifteen minutes passed. She became seriously agitated that her mother may be ill, or have fallen, or strayed down the lane, so she started to walk as quickly as she could along Molly's familiar route, surveying the garden as she went. She crossed the rose gardens, turned through the arbor and screamed with such volume that birds within a half-mile took off.

The gardener heard her shrieks and rushed across the garden looking for her.

"Who did this?" Estella howled, lying down, grasping her mother's body.

"Get a message to the Blue Boar for Pip to come."

The gardener hastened away, harnessed the pony in the trap and drove off, leaving Estella howling with grief.

At the Inn, Pip turned over in his sleep, then awoke as the sun streamed in and his first thoughts were of Estella the previous afternoon. He smiled to himself and got up. There was a loud hammering at the bedroom door, waking Beatrice up suddenly.

"Mr. Pip, Mr. Pip, it's Jonah, there is a call for you to go to Numquam House immediately; there has been a terrible attack."

"What is it, what is it?"

"Terrible news. Miss Molly has been attacked. Miss Estella's gardener is here for you to take you there immediately."

Old Pip dressed hastily, then grabbed a cloak, hat and stick.

"Go, my dear, go. I will stay here in bed and come later if you send for me."

The trap was driven wildly to Numquam House. Old Pip sat silent with a face full of worry and concern, asking no questions of the gardener in his grief for Estella. The trap arrived and Pip jumped down and ran over to Estella in the garden, sitting on a bench, away from the body, weeping hysterically. She took his hand and they walked to Molly's body. The blood had stopped flowing. The gardener approached but stood some way off.

"Oh, Pip, my dear Pip, I called out to her to come in for breakfast. She didn't come, and then I found her, like ... this. Who did this? Who did this? Who did this?"

Old Pip took control. He called the gardener over and embraced Estella to comfort her.

"We need to move her into the house; the kitchen table will be best. Pick her up carefully, gardener, and with me let us take her into the house."

They took Molly's body carefully into the kitchen and laid her on the table, while Estella walked away, sobbing and crying out in agony. Blood was seeping from the wound and neither man had managed to avoid it fouling their clothes, the gardener with more of a problem than Old Pip, who quickly grabbed a sheet of paper from the sideboard.

"Gardener, find Miss Estella's driver, and have him take this note for a courier to go post-haste to London on the next coach, and then find a constable. Here is a guinea which should cover the cost." He grabbed a sheet from a drawer and wrote:

"*June 25 '51, To Messrs. Jaggers and Wemmick:*

Gentlemen, Molly has been murdered. Please to come to Numquam House immediately if possible. In haste, P."

Estella had gone into the house and was sitting in a chair in her drawing room weeping, looking around with wild eyes, where Pip found her:

"We will stay with you, if you will, for a while."

"Oh, my poor, poor dearest mother, how right she was to be frightened. What a terrible end to such a sorrow-filled life. We had such a wonderful day yesterday with you and we talked into the evening. She was so happy, so content, so changed from that scrag of a woman I saw not five years ago."

"Wemmick and Jaggers will know how to find the man, or men. I saw two such villainous looking fellows at the Inn, one with a scar on his left cheek. This must be connected to the woman she murdered. Why else would anyone want to kill her?"

Estella screamed: "How can I survive this?"

Old Pip put his arms around her again which she warmly welcomed—but without any of the sexual tension of their last meeting.

"Find some rest now. I must return to Beatrice. But I will be back to look after you."

She smiled weakly and he left her. On his way out he signaled to her maid who hovered around like a frightened sparrow.

"Just look after her."

VII

After three days of hectic confusion with constables, funeral arrangements, and the dark bric-a-brac rituals of death, Molly's coffin was interred in the All Hallows churchyard. Old Pip escorted Estella, and Jaggers and Wemmick attended with Joe, Biddy and Young Pip. Beatrice was not physically or emotionally strong enough to be there.

Biddy was sobbing, though she had never met Molly, but she felt for Estella's grief and, with her own new religious convictions, was verging toward forgiveness to Estella after what she felt long ago was her treatment of Old Pip. Joe and Young Pip were very solemn, the father's arm around his son's shoulders as they contemplated the evils that could run in poor and criminal minds.

After Molly's body was lowered into the grave, stones and dirt were thrown and then finally Estella launched a large clutch of roses from the Numquam garden into the grave. The Vicar, whom Young Pip recognized from the altercation with the Preacher, said the final blessing and shook hands with the company, expressing his condolences.

Estella went to the vestry to collect the death certificate. The Vicar expressed his concern at the presence of criminals in the village. Estella nodded sympathetically, murmuring a thank you. It was difficult for her to contemplate Molly's abrupt removal from their time together, but who could possibly share her grief?

Meanwhile Jaggers and Wemmick talked quietly to those remaining mourners as they walked slowly toward the church from the grave.

"This is indeed the most terrible misfortune and tragedy," said Jaggers. 'Wemmick, make inquiries among your informants and we will bring this villain to justice."

"Indeed," said Wemmick, nodding his head vigorously.

"I have some inklings, and Mr. Pip will help me with descriptions of the men he saw at the Inn."

There was a pause as Estella returned and Jaggers sought to control the situation.

"You need rest, Estella. You may return to the house in my carriage now, and then Wemmick and I will return to London. Mr. Pip will no doubt want to be with his wife.

"Meantime, I will inquire in the neighborhood for someone in addition to your maid to come to protect you. I think we can be certain the villains have completed their dreadful task, and do not remain in the area but we need to take precautions."

"Thank you, Mr. Jaggers. Forgive me, but I would now like to be alone.

"This house has so many happy memories; I am loath to give it up, but I will now be living with some ghastly memories too. Thank everyone for me, and I hope I can bear this terrible grief. It's the first time I have lost someone I loved. I did not regret the passing of my husband, or, for that matter, Miss Havisham. Thank you for being here, too. I know Molly would have appreciated it."

"Oh, my dear Estella, my heart truly grieves for you," said Jaggers, as they walked from the churchyard.

"This is perhaps not the time to say this, but I must do so now. I am still immensely troubled by the saga of both of your lives and my part in it, and I am hoping to learn from it even at my age. I have been trying to fathom why I thought only about Miss Havisham and little or nothing about you. I should have thought much more carefully of your interests above hers.

"Had I cared to look, I could have found many a family able and willing to foster a child, but all I thought of was satisfying this wealthy client. Well, not entirely, I suppose. It was a year after her failed wedding, and she was already well into this pathetic pattern of grief. I suppose I thought then that caring for a child might bring her out of it, but that was to use you as a pawn for another's needs. Yet once you had formed some kind of relationship with her, I could not legally intervene."

"Gracious me, Mr. Jaggers, I appreciate this unveiling of your conscience. I suppose Molly's sins were compounded by your lack of judgment, rooted in your arrogance in determining people's lives.

"Is it too much to say that you have been a disastrous influence in my life?"

"Chastising me is your right. I beg your forgiveness. But also for putting the man Drummle in your way, but there, I confess, I was myself deluded. However, I am now trying to find space in my life for putting the demands of the law behind the demands of my conscience. I am taking the waters on regular visits to Brighton to reflect on all my doings and to harness my regrets."

"I do forgive you, for what it is worth, at this distance from your decisions. I do hope you will find a way to become a better man, even at your advanced age."

"I hope so too, but I also hope to have the pleasure of your company at some appropriate juncture after you have completed your mourning."

"Well, perhaps, Mr. Jaggers, perhaps. Good day to you now."

Wemmick and Old Pip watched them both sadly, out of earshot, and Old Pip remarked:

"Estella is on my conscience, Wemmick. I must care for her."

"Of course, I am sure Mr. Jaggers will understand."

"Understand what?" asked Jaggers, approaching them.

"Oh, just that I am sorry to have been so diverted that I have not been able to attend at your office to learn from you, and now what am I to do? Estella is on my conscience. I must care for her."

"I perfectly understand, Mr. Pip. I have made terrible mistakes with Estella and with Molly, and I have just told her so, unable any longer not to beg for her forgiveness. Why, in God's name, did I not put her interests first above those of Miss Havisham? Why was I so blind?

"I simply failed to think beyond the legions of children I witnessed in distress when given the opportunity to treat one little girl as precious. I have become aghast at my own failures, having been, as Estella has just told me, an arrogant self-satisfied inadequate human being. But enough of my tribulations.

"You have a lifelong relationship with Estella, Mr. Pip, and long may it continue now that she has lost her mother. You must return to the Law once you manage to resolve the contradictions of caring for her but, more important, for your young wife.

"Burdens descend upon you, it seems, like sorrows, in battalions."

Jaggers wandered off to view the gardens, murmuring "how distressing," leaving Wemmick and Pip alone.

"We miss you at Little Britain, you know; but we do understand your predicament."

"May I ask you something, John, and I put you under no obligation whatsoever as I ask this, and, as it is a personal not a professional matter, I trust I am at liberty to call you John."

"Understood, Pip."

"Might Beatrice and I come to Walworth for the next months? London is so dirty, the air is so thick, and I would like Beatrice to be free of it at this time. She should be there during the day, of course, resting.

"She will get a bit stronger and nearer her confinement, anticipated next March, and we would return to our lodgings well before that. I am going to have to see Estella more than usual for a while and it would be a great solace to know Beatrice would be protected behind your moat, though no responsibility to care for her would fall on your dear wife. Or yourself."

"My dear Pip, it would be an honor indeed. I must first consult my partner, of course, but I am sure she would share my delight. Indeed, since Aged P passed on three years ago, there is adequate accommodation for you both."

"How can I thank you, John? I know Beatrice will be enormously happy at this, not least because she is lonely when I am at work."

❧   ❧   ❧

"I have been giving some thought to the identity of the killer," said Wemmick as they approached the office in Little Britain about a month after the murder. "It is assured that he was not after portable property, but only anxious to dispose of the lady. The murder does not seem random, especially as you saw the two villainous individuals at the Inn, but that possibility should not be discounted.

"It also seems to me a comfort to conjecture that Molly knew nothing of it. Simply, someone stole up behind her silently and gave her a monstrous crack on the head with some kind of blunt instrument. If she had been aware of her attacker, her body would not have been face down, and I noticed no signs of any kind of struggle. I am sure that, given her character, she would have been a worthy adversary for this villain."

"You are right, John. I learnt nothing from the Landlord. They were not staying at the Inn. They had a mug of ale each evening, kept to themselves, and then left."

"Knowing the criminal mind as I do, it is important to be confident about the answer to this question: By murdering Miss Molly, was there another person on whom revenge was being sought, other than the victim herself?' I have thought about this but put the question to one side. Yet as carefully as we consider the case, we must not also put out of our minds any individual with access to Miss Estella's property—the gardener, for example."

"The gardener? He seemed innocuous enough and he stayed at the house. Estella told me that he looked as though he had just got up from bed when she saw him in her search for Molly. He drove me in silence to the house and helped me move her body. That surmise seems unlikely, though possible. But I do not know whether Estella knew him or not before she hired him. He could be an informant to the killer, able to relate Molly's movements and habits to another. I will ask Estella about this fellow again with all speed."

"Ah, Mr. Pip, in our business it is important to recognize every possibility. Never, ever discount our inklings. Inklings are everything. Meantime, I will contact some of my informants and see what comes up."

Such daily conversations as the two men crossed the river from the peaceful streets of the village at Walworth to the hurly-burly of the Great Wen were part of Old Pip's learning the law. Among the legal fraternity, considerable concern was gathering about transportation and the treatment of the poor, but Old Pip gained so much insight into the vagaries of the law during these encounters such that Wemmick's observations were as valuable to a new lawyer as his senior's.

On the way home one late August evening, they were discussing the full details of the sad news of the sinking of HMS *Birkenhead* a few months earlier in February 1852 on the rocks off the Western Cape with the loss of over six hundred lives, news of which had just arrived in London.

Knowledge of the disaster had arrived in London but what actually happened was not properly understood. With British pride, the talk was more of those sailors and soldiers who cried 'women and children first' into the lifeboats, some two hundred being saved, but as a result many men drowned.

"I suppose the ship's captain must have given the order?"

"I assume so," said Wemmick.

"But what if you were a woman watching the ship sink from afar with your husband still on it?"

"All would have to be very brave, I suppose, and a sacrifice for both parties. But, you know, Pip, I wonder whether it was as good an idea as is thought."

"What do you mean?"

"Well," said Wemmick. "It would surely have saved more lives if the able-bodied men had got into the lifeboats first. Though it sounds callous, if you think the important thing is the numbers of lives to be saved, then 'women and children first' is foolish.

"It means just a lot of dithering and fussing around, children screaming, time spent as the ship was sinking in helping the weak, whereas all the men would have been in the lifeboats before you could say knife."

"My goodness, Wemmick," Pip replied, "how do we judge the alternatives? Support for the weak against the numbers of lives? What an interesting dilemma."

"Now, I don't mean 'every man for hisself,' you know. I am thinking about what the ship's captain might order. Even so, I find my thought quite shocking. If the captain said to himself, I mean from the safety of dry land, 'How might I get the overall greatest amount of happiness if my ship floundered?' he would have to take into account the number, would he not?"

"What a conundrum," said Pip, "I'm glad I'm not a ship's captain," and they laughed heartily as they approached the house.

The search for Molly's murderer was badly in need of a conclusion, and Wemmick's informants had been hard at work with only a fluttering of interest from the constables. Gradually a picture of the killers was beginning to emerge. Wemmick finally thought he had found the perpetrator and he began the discussion in the office.

"Gentlemen," said Wemmick, addressing Mr. Jaggers and Old Pip, "I have had great regrets that we have not tracked down the killer or killers, but my inklings seem to be bearing fruit. I have been working to discover the real identity of the gardener first. Miss Estella was too trusting when she hired him. My informants worked hard to discover his identity, as he seems to be an important part of the plot, not least because he volunteered his services, but then removed himself immediately after the crime."

"That is certainly odd," said Jaggers, "as it seemed inevitable that that would be a cause for suspicion, don't you think, Mr. Pip?"

"I do. But might his leaving Numquam House not indicate his complicity in the murder? For someone might just have asked him in the Three Jolly Bargemen who was in fact living at Numquam.

People always gossip about wealthy people and their houses. Or, of course, perhaps it was the man in the lane who asked?"

"Who is this man, Mr. Pip? I have not heard of him."

"Estella mentioned to me recently, Mr. Jaggers, that Molly told her she had seen the gardener talking with a man in the lane.

"In any event," said Wemmick, "I put it about through my informants that the gardener need not be afraid, if he was innocent of any part in this plot, and that he should come to meet with us. He came to see me a few days ago, and I asked him to call today. We will see if he does."

There is a knock on the office door.

"What is it, Robert?" cried Jaggers testily.

"There's a Mr. Thistlewood to see Mr. Wemmick, sir."

"That must be him," said Wemmick. "Call him in."

Thistlewood entered, dressed in old clothes, dirty with age and soil, and a cap which he held nervously in his hands. Old Pip immediately recognized him from his visits to Numquam House at the time of Molly's murder.

"Ah, Mr. Thistlewood," Old Pip said. "We have met before, have we not, and you were the gardener for Miss Estella and her mother, Miss Molly, am I right?"

"Yes, sir. I heard from some people I know that suspicion might fall on me after the Numquam tragedy. So, I thought I should come and meet with you gentlemen, as I do not wish to be under suspicion."

"Thank you for coming. Mr. Jaggers here is my senior and we are both lawyers, so you must anticipate some questions. Start at the beginning. Why did you choose Numquam House as the house to which you would offer your services?"

"It was chance. I'd been laboring on a farm near Rochester and I left."

"Or were you dismissed?"

"Well, I did get into trouble there, but it was not my fault."

"No, it never is. Was it a fight, or were you just lazy?"

"I did have a disagreement, but I was surprised when he hit me, so I hit him back. I was about to pull my knife, when the overseer came over and told both of us to go."

"Do you always carry a knife for protection?"

"I was attacked in London once, but a friend helped me and told me always to carry a knife in future."

"Who was this friend?"

"He was a friend at the time, but we fell out recently."

"And the cause?"

"He had lent me some money and I couldn't pay it back, so he attacked me, and said he must have it within a month."

"So you were in debt. By how much?"

"Fifty pounds. I know that's a lot, but it kind of built up, must have been over a year he helped me. But I was paying him back little by little as I was working at Numquam."

"Fifty pounds; a princely sum. So, when you were out of work in Rochester, he was lending you money all the time. When you paid him back, where did the transaction take place?"

"I'd arrange a time with him to meet in the pub at All Hallows."

"Always in the pub?"

"No, he'd come to Numquam House sometimes; well, never into the house or garden, as I'd meet him in the lane, usually just after I'd been paid. See, I lived in the shed, and Miss Estella fed me, and what she paid me every Friday regular as clockwork, I'd be giving most of it to him."

"So he knew to be in the lane sometimes of a Friday. Now, when you went to the pub, did you talk about the house and its inhabitants? How much did you tell him?"

"He was always very keen to know everything, I suppose. Now I shouldn't have told him this, but I overheard Miss Estella and Miss Molly talking in the garden, and I was surprised to hear Miss Molly saying something about how her husband had been a criminal. Or something of the sort. He was very interested in that, and when I told him their names, he laughed and said: 'What a great piece of luck.' I asked him why, but he didn't say."

"Look here, Thistlewood," Old Pip said, raising his voice in anger. "Who was he?"

"I am sworn not to tell anyone my friend's name."

"Was there more than one?

"Yes."

"That's not surprising," said Wemmick. "I don't suppose the name of your friends is Compeyson by any chance? And one of them has a scar on his face, does he not?"

Thistlewood was very shocked, but answered quietly:

"Yes, my friend is Jack Compeyson. I don't know his brother. How did you know that?"

Old Pip returned to the examination:

"It is none of your business how we know. You will help Wemmick find him and once he is located, we will have constables bring him in, then you must give evidence at his trial on the charge of murdering Miss Molly.

"But one last thing. In your meetings with Compeyson, did you ever mention Miss Molly's love for the garden or that she had a morning constitutional?"

"I think I may have mentioned it in one of our talks, because I was suspicious of her always walking around the garden in the morning when I hadn't started work, checking out the flower beds so she could report me to Miss Estella."

"You are not merely a knave but a fool," said Wemmick, "she was simply enjoying being outdoors after a life of living in the city. She gave not a tinker's cuss about you."

"Excellent," Jaggers intervened, "we have our man. You must understand, Thistlewood, that, were you to refuse to give evidence, and given what you have told us, you would be charged with being an accessory to murder."

Putting his head in his hands, he said: "Oh God, oh God, all right, I have to tell you, I suppose. I do know what happened to them brothers. They both went to sea to Jamaica right after the murder of the lady. But they'd booked on that boat that floundered, the *Capricorn* was her name. If they went, they's both dead.

"Now I don't exactly know it was Jack who did Miss Molly in, but I don't know who else it could be. But them brothers, they was terrible villains, but he was the leader, and I don't know why they were after Miss Molly."

"Oh," said Jaggers, "simple. She murdered their mother."

"What?" said an incredulous Thistlewood, "that explains everything. They was always on about their mother, saying what a lovely lady she was and how she'd run away with a big fella called Abel."

"And this is correct, too, which is why Molly murdered her."

"Dear oh dear, what a sorry mess."

"I am sure we can have the passenger list examined. For your sake Thistlewood, I hope you are not making this up," says Old Pip, "as the penalties for the obstruction of justice are very serious indeed."

"No, sir, God's truth. Honest. I tell you all I know."

"Well, you could have gone to Miss Estella and Molly's killer could have been apprehended, right?"

"I'll have it on my conscience the rest of my days, sir."

"Well," says Jaggers, "that won't be much of a burden for it is plain that you have none. You, sir, are the scum of the earth! Get out! Get out! Get out!"

Thistlewood left hurriedly, dropping his cap and banging his leg on the door as he went.

"Very well executed, everybody, especially you, Mr. Pip," Jaggers concluded. "He did not realize the character of the garden path up which he was being led which is a crucial move in examining a witness. So that, as they say, is that."

"Excellent, but a sad sequence of events," said Old Pip. "I will acquaint Estella of this outcome soon."

A knowing smile passed between Jaggers and Wemmick, unnoticed by Old Pip who left for home.

Five months after the meeting with Thistlewood, on a quiet Sunday morning in February, Beatrice suddenly went into labor. Given her two previous miscarriages, Old Pip was beside himself with anxiety and the Wemmicks were also very troubled— Mrs. W. perhaps more by the inconvenience than the prospect of dire alternatives to a straightforward birth.

Wemmick himself hurried along the street to fetch a midwife to help Beatrice. She was a large helpful Cockney lady called Ethel, who bossed everyone around, ordering Old Pip out of the room to fetch towels. Thereafter, Old Pip and Wemmick walked to and fro in the sitting room in silence, and then in the garden. Old Pip was outside the house when he heard the cries of the newborn.

He rushed back to Aged P's rooms, and there was Beatrice with a boy in her arms. He was overwhelmed with affection, joy and pride.

"At last, at last! Oh, my dearest, such a lovely little boy, and this time, you succeeded. Now I must care for you both unfailingly."

Very softly, Beatrice murmurs:

"At last indeed. I am so thrilled I have given you what we have for so long hoped for. What shall we call him?"

"I thought we might call him after the Prince, and perhaps add Joe as well?"

"How lovely. If he were Albert, we can nickname him Bertie. I think there is a Pocket relation called Bertie, but I don't know his whole name."

Old Pip kissed her fondly, gave Albert to the midwife and made his way to Wemmick's parlor.

"Well, that's a surprise, my dear," said Wemmick.

"Yes," said Mrs. Wemmick icily, "and I expect Pip and Beatrice will want to take their new little treasure home soon, won't they?"

Old Pip entered the room, overwhelmed with delight.

"My dear friends, we did not intend, of course, for Albert to be born here at your lovely home, but our profound thanks are due to you for your gracious hospitality. As soon as Beatrice can get up, we will have a carriage take us back to our lodgings. We will be eternally grateful, and I will remind Albert for as long as I can of his birthplace."

"Thank you, Pip, thank you. Wemmick and I want you to be sure you don't leave too early. You must both be careful indeed after this excitement," said Mrs. Wemmick, her tone greatly softened by Pip's enthusiasm and thanks.

"I saw that a children's hospital has just been opened at Great Ormond Street," said Wemmick, "should there be any need."

Thus Old Pip, Beatrice and baby Albert later returned delighted and proud to their London lodgings. Messages were sent out to all and sundry. The baby seemed very strong and healthy and was the apple of his parents' eyes. Beatrice was very frail post-partum and a wet nurse, oddly named Wisteria, was engaged for Albert, but Old Pip could not get out of his head Wemmick's little joke that the wet nurse so named might cling to the baby.

VIII

Becoming a parent at last had thrilled Old Pip, and he began to work to complete his training with even greater diligence dawn to dusk in Jaggers' office, impressing his senior with his grasp and his guile. Now back in his London lodgings, Pip was missing his walks and conversations with Wemmick, and early in the day before Mr. Jaggers arrived, they had turned once again to shipwrecks, especially that of the *Birkenhead*, which they gnawed over like a puppy at a bone. Both agreed that maritime insurance is a game for the brave and irresolute, not for the patient investor.

Heads were nodding sagely when Robert opened the office door and announced a Mr. Unworthy, a swarthy large blond young man, very well dressed, though looking also uncomfortable in his frock coat and cravat. He carried a top hat and gloves, though clearly unfamiliar with both. He spoke with an Australian accent, one not familiar to the gentlemen he had come to see.

Indeed, Old Pip looked amused and Wemmick stared as if he was seeing a very strange animal.

"Gooday. I am Ezekiel Unworthy from Queensland in the great land of Australia."

"A very good morning to you, sir." They shook hands.

"I am Mr. Wemmick, senior clerk to this practice. This is Mr. Pip, partner to Mr. Jaggers, who is detained in court."

Pip and Unworthy shook hands.

"What precise ways may we be of assistance to you, sir," asked Mr. Pip, "as it seems you have come a very long way to greet us this morning? So, it is the Antipodes from which you hail?"

"No, as I said, I am from Australia," at which Wemmick raised his eyebrows at Old Pip.

"Ah yes, Mr. Unworthy, Mr. Pip at your service. Won't you sit down?"

"Thanks, but, oh dear, I need to wash the soot out of my body. London stinks, y'know. So much smoke. I live in the outdoors, you see, Mr. Pip."

"I would assume so. What brings you to Little Britain, Ezekiel?"

"I am looking for my father, though he was not married to my dear mother, old Sal."

"London is a large place as Mr. Pip and I know, and unlike what I assume is the case in what I believe you call the outback, we do not know everyone."

"No indeed," said Ezekiel, laughing. "But my mother found a scrap of paper with this address on it and I immediately decided to search for my father. This was the only thing she could find of his apart from some old clothes in the shack he built."

"Very well, but pray do not hold us any longer in suspense, who is your father?"

"Well, this probably won't mean anything to you, but his name is Abel Magwitch."

To say that Old Pip and Wemmick looked thunderstruck at this news underestimated the volcanic power of Ezekiel's statement.

"I'd guess he is living somewhere in the hereabouts, as he had this address."

There was what used to be called a pregnant silence for a minute or two while Ezekiel looked quizzically at them both, from one to the other.

"Well, please, do you know him? It seems you do, do you not, Mr. Pip?"

"We have a long story to tell you about Abel. But let me say first that he is dead these few years. Let us hear of your paternity, and then we can explain."

Ezekiel laughed again, partly from nerves but also because of the strangeness of these members of the legal fraternity, their manner of speaking and their dress. He was brought up in what within a generation was being transformed from a wilderness into sheep country. An itinerant tutor had taught him as well as could be expected following his mother's early introduction to the literacy.

But a liberal education was farthest from anyone's expectations in the outback. His education was one of experience, of herding sheep, washing them, trimming them, packing the wool and getting the best price at auction. He thus presented himself in Little Britain as a rough diamond, though whether his character matched that of the priceless stone was waiting to be discovered.

"Well, I never met my father, so while I am sorry to hear that, I am not as mortified as I might be had I known him."

Again his staccato laughter engulfed the room, leading Wemmick to smile with the utmost condescension.

"You never knew him?"

"I fear not, Mr. Pip. But, of course, I did not make this journey solely to find my father. As you seem a pair of good blokes, as we say of good people in Australia these days, I have some idea about investing some money here as well as in the home country. See, I may not be a hifalutin' educated Pommie, as we call you English, but I have money."

"I was a broker before I became a lawyer, so I am sure I can help. But please do relate the story of your paternity."

"Right, right. Where to begin? Abel Magwitch was transported to Australia as I presume you know some years ago, I am not sure when, but he was sent to the new Moreton Bay Settlement, founded in 1825 or thereabouts."

"We didn't know that detail."

"Life was very challenging for convicts in their penal colonies, though Moreton Bay allowed them to roam a bit. Convicts usually stick together in small towns or villages partly because the regular settlers sometimes used them, sometimes not. Others take their chances, knowing that they'd be unlucky if caught, and distances are so great, no constable in his right mind is going to chase off into open country pursuing a convict.

"Old Sal says Magwitch was a loner, and her husband, John Unworthy was an adventurous man. He had a friend, John Oxley, who found the site for Moreton Bay and he wrote to John advising him of the opportunities there. So John and my mother came from England, Norfolk I think, to Queensland shortly thereafter, again probably in the 1820s."

"He must have been a very brave man,"

"Not to mention his wife," Wemmick adds.

"My mother, old Sal? Oh yes, she is like a living legend. Of course, I never knew John, but they laid claim to five hundred acres near Redcliffe raising sheep and it was granted, probably through his connection with Oxley, a very powerful man in those parts. That was a lot of land for a claim in those days, especially near the Brisbane River so he had water. John was a real pioneer. One afternoon, Abel, almost starving, came to the door offering help."

"Did Unworthy know he was a convict?"

"That was my impression, though Mother is never clear about that, perhaps because of what she did later. But John put him to work and fed him. Together they worked dawn to dusk, and the farm went so well, the money rolled in, and Abel had worked so hard, John let him use two hundred acres for himself, provided he did not give up working with John. John, you see, was a devout Christian as is old Sal. You know, forgiveness and all that."

Old Pip smiled knowingly, remembering his conversations with Young Pip.

"It was a gentleman's agreement, of course, for convicts serving a life sentence could not own that land at that time. John and Abel trusted each other, at least with regard to work."

"How unusual and how generous. Did John and Sally have no children?"

"None. But this was the beginning of the boom in wool which good old Macarthur had started. So both John and Abel were getting very prosperous. It must have been John who was unable to father a child or how did I get here?"

Another bout of Unworthy's raucous laughter followed, at which Wemmick cringed but recovered himself and said nicely:

"How unfortunate to go all that way and have no children to carry on your work, or indeed help."

"Right, and that must have been partly why he engaged Abel so easily. Christian or not, he could see that money was leaping out of the land in the form of a sheep. Time went by and both John and Abel continued to prosper, working all the hours God sent.

"One day, not sure when, as Mother tells it, poor old John was repairing a fence a mile or so from the homestead, when he was bitten by the venomous Eastern Brown Snake, a real danger in those parts. When he did not return for his tucker, I mean for his supper, she rode out to search for him. He had died in great agony, but she could do nothing for him. So she left the body and rode away to find Abel to help her, as her young maid in the farm, another released convict, would not have been able to lift him."

"So, Abel comes back with her, puts the body on his horse, takes him to the farm, and lays him out. The nearest preacher was fifty miles away and, in the heat, he needed to be buried. Abel dug his grave, and he, Mother, and the maid said some prayers. Old Sal told him to copy an epitaph, and he made a beautiful cross with John's name engraved on it which said: 'Here lies John Unworthy, a Christian gentleman.'"

"What an extraordinary tale, but Magwitch could be very generous, so I am not surprised."

"You knew him, then?"

"To be sure we did, did we not, Wemmick?"

"All too well, but pray sir, finish your story."

"Quite simple really. One evening, Abel told her he was going back to England, at which she got up and said she would miss him, and the rest is history. Here am I, their love-child. Abel Magwitch was the father I never knew, but from what I know, the most generous, hardworking and passionate man whom, through my mother, I admire. I am sorry not to have met him. How did he die? Do you know?"

"Presumably then, Ezekiel, he never knew of the outcome of his affair with your mother as she did not write or seek him out. However, I will be brief."

"Long ago when I was a child living in marsh country down in Kent, your father Abel, then a young man and a convict, grabbed me in a cemetery one evening near the hulk from which he had escaped. I gave Abel food and a file for his shackles from the Forge and the cottage where I lived. I was only nine years old and terrified of him. He was captured and transported. Without my knowing it, he became my benefactor, showering me with his wealth even from Australia, so that I could become a gentleman, just because I had brought him food that evening."

Ezekiel appeared a mix of mystified and alarmed as Pip's story unwound.

"I did not know it was he. Suddenly several years later, he appeared in my lodgings, presumably the end of his journey after his, how shall I say, his sojourn with your mother. But he had real enemies here and he would also have been hanged for returning from Australia. So, with a friend, I arranged an escape to France, but he was confronted by his worst enemy, whom he killed. I watched him do it. He was then captured and died in prison before he could be taken to the gallows. His money was confiscated."

"Did he have any children?"

Old Pip looked steadily at Wemmick and said to Unworthy: "I am afraid I am not at liberty to disclose that to you."

"So he does have other children, my half-brothers or half-sisters?"

"That is not what I said, Ezekiel.

"I said I cannot disclose whether or not he had children. If there were any children, they would be illegitimate as he never married, at least not to my knowledge, and it is not within my responsibility as a lawyer to disclose such factors, if indeed they exist."

Wemmick whispered quietly to Old Pip: "You get more like Jaggers every day."

"I like you, Mr. Pip, completely discreet. I trust you. As you can see I am still a young man, only eighteen, but my mother has handed over the farm to me. First, I think we should invest in shipping as it is a lifeline for Australia. This is a note for one thousand pounds and there's more if we are successful. I would like you to become my investment agent.

"Second, old Sal tells me I must find myself an English bride while I am here. There're not many pickings where I come from. I will return to Australia, as soon as I have found a bride to show off to my mother."

He again laughs his raucous laugh.

"I am not looking for some fashionable genteel woman," he continues, "but for a farmer's daughter who can pick up a sheep and give me a dozen children. I want to found an Unworthy dynasty, or should it be a Magwitch dynasty. My lawyer will help me on that, won't you Mr. Pip?"

Old Pip laughs and says, "I won't find you a wife, but I will manage your legal affairs."

"But now I must bid you 'Gooday' as we say in Australia and begin my search. I am told South Wales would be a good place to start."

They all shook hands and Ezekiel left.

"Was I right, Wemmick?"

"About what?"

"Not telling him of Estella's existence. I thought I would tell her of his existence first, but I am unsure about that, maybe because my personal inclinations are getting in the way of my duty."

Wemmick raised a quizzical eyebrow and looked surprised by this covert admission, though he couldn't decide what the 'personal inclinations' were.

"Well, there is the question of whether portable property might come her way, I suppose, if she were to meet the gentleman. But I have an inkling that Mr. Unworthy may live up to his name."

"Yes, I think so too. You are right, as always, Wemmick. Portable property is indeed a frequent source of many a matter of conscience. In fact, my life seems these days to be ruled by my conscience which I suppose makes it omnipotent."

"And a good thing, too. I wish Mr. Jaggers had had more of that in his prime."

In celebration mode, Mr. Jaggers invited Old Pip and Mr. Wemmick to lunch at The Cheshire Cheese near Temple Bar. The purpose of the lunch was, ostensibly, to recognize Old Pip's being called to the Bar. Against the continuous sounds of men drinking well and eating as well, Jaggers began by saying:

"By Jove, Wemmick, I have been thinking on what you said on the way here, that we should have searched for the Compeysons, not of course, Miss Havisham's *in absentia* bridegroom, but that other gang. Your inkling was right that he who was transported had hired another villain to do his work."

"I am glad for Estella's sake we found the men."

"An admirable sentiment, Mr. Pip, but my congratulations once again. Jugged hare and claret suit you?" and he called the waiter for a flagon.

"Wemmick and I were serious about Molly's sanity, you know, Mr. Pip. No one must know what I will now tell you and certainly not Estella, but its telling will continue to fill your stock of information on the criminal mind."

"Then, the reasons for your concerns were not simply related to her known criminal past, then?"

"Not to the criminal past of which you are aware. I tell you this as an absolute secret. She confessed to me all her sins when I got her. She had always from as long as she could remember been a child of intense emotions, difficult to control. She admitted that she was responsible for her young brother's death and in a most cruel way."

"Great heavens!"

"Indeed, Mr. Pip, she hated the attention he got soon after he was born, an early sign of her madness, and when her mother was out and she was looking after him one freezing winter day, she shut the poor child, then four years old, outside in a shed."

"Did he die there?"

"No. She told him she would kill him if he called out or if he told anyone afterwards. She let him out just before her mother returned, almost frozen with cold."

"In God's name, why would she do that?"

There was a pause while a waiter in a ragged apron put three large tumblers and a tankard on the table and another brought large pewter platters of meat and various vegetables.

"Let me continue. Her mother was exceedingly angry and distressed when she heard what had happened, and the tie of kin that existed between mother and daughter was snapped," he said, snapping his fingers, "that very evening. Needless to say, Mr. Pip, the poor child died of pneumonia shortly thereafter."

"You will now appreciate our concern, eh, Mr. Pip?" said Wemmick judiciously.

"More than that," said Jaggers with a belch. "Pardon me, dash it, this hare is good, and the claret is really splendid. Why don't we grow vines in Kent?"

"Too cold," said Old Pip.

"More's the pity," said Jaggers.

"Anyway, Molly told me, the son's death so affected her mother that the poor woman was soon dead of a broken heart. Not merely at the loss of a son, of course, but, as the mother put it, at raising a she-devil for a daughter. So her father lost a son and a wife in short order, became a drunk, lost his business and was soon dead.

"Waiter, bring a platter of cheese and another flagon of this delightful claret."

He apologized again for another belch, which Wemmick and Old Pip greeted with a smile.

"Goodness gracious me, I have never heard of anything so evil. How could anyone, even a child, wreak such havoc on their loved ones?"

"Oh dear me, wait till you are fully in practice. Ask Wemmick for some instances," at which the older men laughed uproariously.

"Who knows, Mr. Pip, when she might have flown off the handle? Of course, when Estella and her mother met, causing me such distress, and I explained their respective fates to them, I could not mention her other victim. The woman was quite mad which was why I held her on so short a leash as my servant. Just thinking about it demands another fill of claret."

He then took the flagon, splashing spots on the oak table and added almost a beakerful to his tumbler.

"I am astonished at this grave and terrible information," said Old Pip. "But when Beatrice and I met Molly, she seemed an utterly changed woman, calm and relaxed and totally content, but now does Estella not have a right to know?"

"I think not, though men of goodwill may disagree on this point. Life is full of secrets and much damage can be done by revealing them. I dare not count the number of secrets I have. I am simply glad Estella did not have to confront any of Molly's madness. I'm afraid responsibility for a large part of her distressing life can be laid at my door, and I am humbled to realize how badly I treated her."

"Maybe, that is for your conscience, Mr. Jaggers," said Old Pip with a grin, "but you are right."

"A different topic. Now you are qualified, I hope you will come to court with me shortly so that I can introduce you as my apprentice advocate, if you are able to get away from your familial duties. It is now almost five years that you have been my pupil and I think the time has come for you to join an Inn of Court and debut at the Bar.

"Welcome, Mr. Pip, to the community of lawyers," he said raising his glass somewhat unsteadily.

"Now," he continued, "you will not need to hear the case, though there are several coming up on the docket when you are ready."

"That was a splendid lunch, Mr. Jaggers. Next time, Wemmick and I will dig deep to foot the bill."

Later that week, when Jaggers was in court, the topic turned once again to the old lawyer.

"He seems to be a different man, these days, " said Wemmick.

"I've not known him as long as you have, John, but to me he seems milder, calmer and older. I think he started to think very seriously about his responsibility for who Estella had become and what she had experienced."

"That's true. Through all the lofty sentiments and the somewhat brutal behavior, there is a heart beating for the unfortunate. But he seems to have convinced himself that he is no longer Solomon."

"Think about Estella," said Wemmick. "He took this poor little girl, daughter of a mad woman and handed her over to another mad woman. That would make you think you'd made a mistake, wouldn't it? But he just wanted Miss Havisham's good graces because she was rich. When he organized Estella to go to her, the woman was already crazy. No wonder he is reflecting on his works. I should have protested, but I was young."

"I wonder what he will do now. I found my pupillage with him very interesting, important and full of, oh dear, I have to be careful here as I was about to say—great expectations.' Let me just say promise."

"Now, see here, Pip. I am about to speak my mind, which is a duty, not a pleasure. You are going to be a good, maybe even a great lawyer. Nothing to be ashamed of there. But I know of your life, and I would say without knowing you intimately, and forgive me if this seems impertinent.

"You talk about your conscience too much and don't follow its dictates. Since you took that file from your father for Abel and then were puzzled about it, there is a constant problem in your life about your choices which affect your conscience. Please don't be a hypocrite.

"You are playing fast and loose with your obligations to Estella and to your wife, to the Gargerys and to Mr. Jaggers. He is tolerant because he has known you since you were a boy. But you cannot juggle all those interests together without seeming two-faced—Oh dear, I sound very pompous."

"Not at all," said Old Pip. "You seem very wise to me, though I need to think about it."

106

"Put it this way. If you had to put each of these obligations in order of importance, which would be first? Jaggers, Beatrice, Estella or the Gargerys?"

"Obviously, that's straightforward. Beatrice because she is my wife, Jaggers because he is my employer, the Gargerys because I owe them so much, and last Estella, my long-term friend."

"That is what you are saying, Pip, but is not Estella the real priority?"

"That is a terrible indictment, John."

"Deny it if you will. If that makes sense to you, then the challenge will be how you cope with it. Nothing is private. All our preferences are common knowledge. Anyway, my friend, think on these matters."

"I certainly will. Your judgments are always wise."

Down in Kent, Biddy had reconciled with the time it was taking for the ship to be completed. Joe had not been sent away on completion of his work as the quality of his contribution was such that the ship builder was not of a mind to see him depart.

Biddy therefore made a good friend in Alice LeBone, the preacher, and she got used to Chatham, a place of intense historical pride in a dockyard stretching back to King Henry VIII and an equally strong contemporary parochial pride in the successful launching of the HMS *Majestic* that June, one of a long line of ships launched there, as Overseer Mistyfield pointed out.

It was April 1853. The ship was being fitted out and various rumors were circulating about her future, awaiting whatever Admiralty House determined. Joe had earned good money and replenished his nest-egg, so he was very anxious to get back home.

Young Pip loved working with horses in the dockyard stables, and his friendship with Fletcher was growing, though the topic of what to do with Nellie had not re-emerged. Biddy and Joe were concerned that Young Pip would have to go to war, even as a farrier, but they both want their normal lives resumed.

"Tell me, Alice," said Biddy as she walked with Alice to her usual preaching location, "do you think God wants us to fight each other?"

"We cannot try to be perfect and then hurt each other, Biddy, or we are not in the image of God. There have been riots between Catholics and Protestants in a town called Stockport, not fortunately involving any of our religious community. They fight, though I don't think there was any killing. I think God will be very disappointed."

"I had not heard of that," said Biddy. "How sad. I am terrible worried that Young Pip will be dragged into a war, if there is one, but he did say he would go if he could just look after the cavalry horses and not as a soldier."

"God will protect him, Biddy."

"But perhaps God is busy protecting our enemies too? Ain't he too busy or summat to protect everyone, for many thousands of Christians have died fighting?"

"Now that is something we will need to talk about in our little community. Oh dear, our faith does present us with so many difficult thoughts, but that is why we must have faith. But now I must speak the word of God." She set up her box and began to preach.

Far up the street two strong young men, Young Pip and Fletcher, were working on a gray mare outside the dockyard stables at the far end of the street, checking hooves, brushing coat, combing mane. Both were nigh on sixteen years of age. Fletch was a true song-bird, explaining to Young Pip that his mother was always singing. Together they sang the old song "Our Goodman' as it told of a man who mistook a cow for a horse, though they don't remember many of the lines except the first verse:

'Our goodman came hame at e'en,
And hame came he:
And there he saw a saddle horse,
Where nae a horse should be.'

They stopped their singing and put down their brushes when a Recruiting Sergeant in full dress uniform of the Fourth Light Dragoons walked by with a corporal in tow. He stopped and came across to them:

"Young men, I am Sergeant Enoch Whistler, and this 'ere is Corporal Jack Dereham. Your country needs you. I have it on the greatest authority that our country is already involved in a struggle with Russia in an area of Asia Minor and the disintegrating Ottoman Empire, and the fleet is being prepared to carry our troops to the likely battle area."

"Beg your pardon, sir," says Fletcher, "I not met no Ottoman, though I saw a Chinaman once."

"Ah, young man, think of the life your country provides for you. Think about how you should help it to get justice from its enemies. Think of your duty to our Queen."

"My family and I thought about just such an invitation, sir," said Young Pip, "and me and my friend Fletcher 'ere are prepared to help, but not to kill as we are under God's Law."

"But I see you are farriers, not cavalry or infantry. Your work will be essential as horses are cavalry and mules are also needed in supply, and, after years in India, I have never seen such farriers as yourself fighting in the heat of a battle. I will walk up the street, recruiting others, and when I come back I will need your clear answer."

"Isn't this exciting, Pip? Travelling the seas to fight the Ottomen or the Ruskies, what a task, eh, looking after all those horses. Where will the anvils be, I wonder, so we can shoe them?"

"I hope it turns out as much of a lark as it sounds, Fletch."

"Will you'se get a uniform? Where do we go for them in Chatham?"

"Why do we need a uniform, spending our days mucking out horses?"

Fletcher was indignant. "You can't go to a war without a uniform, Pip. Look out, he's coming back."

"So, young men have you decided to support your Queen or languish here in the fleshpots of Chatham?"

"We will join, sir, as farriers. Farriers only."

"On those terms, young men, will you now take the Queen's shilling, so that you can acquire your uniforms as farriers. I assume you are both at least sixteen years of age. You are assigned to the Fourth Light Dragoons."

In unison, Fletcher and Young Pip said: "We will."

The Sergeant handed them each a shilling.

"You are now almost under Her Majesty's command from this date, October 5, 1853. Give your names to Corporal Dereham here. He will instruct you to attest before the magistrate tomorrow, at which time you will receive a bounty. Report as soon as you have attested and purchased your uniform to the Dragoons' cavalry officer. You will work in their stables, and sail on the *Majestic* probably in mid-March. Welcome to her Majesty's service."

"I must now go and explain to my mother and father, Fletch, after I have attested and got my uniform. My Bible will be my real guide."

"I have to get to Rochester to see my folks, Pip. I'll ask for a horse from the stables, then I can buy my uniform here later with this lovely shilling."

He tossed it in the air with delight and walked away singing.

IX

As Biddy said later, everything happened so quickly. Joe and she had given up Chatham and come back to the cottage, with Young Pip staying in the stables where he slept.

Before you could say 'knife,' the *Majestic* was launched and was off on her maiden voyage for a week so that by March 1854 was readied and loaded up to sail.

Then Young Pip was back in the cottage for only a night or two to say goodbye, and in the 'twinkle of an eye,' as Joe expressed it later, the *Majestic* had departed with Young Pip and Fletch on board.

So fast! Joe and Biddy returned from Chatham after a tearful afternoon watching the *Majestic* set sail bearing their precious son. They prayed very hard that night, not just for his safe return, but for all involved in the war. Methodism was a very generous faith.

By June 1854 HMS *Majestic* was anchored off Malta for the undertaking of a war which was outside the concerns of the couple with their young child in their London lodgings. The baby Albert was eighteen months old and had become a strong child with his mother's complexion and his father's jaw; or so visitors said. Beatrice appeared to have recovered from Albert's birth quite quickly. Old Pip gazed at her lovingly as he tickled Albert under the chin and held his hands.

"I could stay here all day watching my two darlings, but Mr. Jaggers is in court yet again today, and though I have been with him on many occasions in the past months, I hope soon I will get the chance to address the court."

"I hope so too, Pip, but I must tell you, Pip, I am now certain I have another baby inside me."

A delighted Old Pip bent down to hug and kiss her and then his son.

"That is so exciting: I'd love to have a daughter. Remember, you have had a successful birth and there is no reason for you not to have another. I firmly believe we have passed the stage of losing babies. Be confident, my dear. But you truly must rest, as I am also concerned about you being pregnant again so soon after Albert. That was, of course, my responsibility."

"Oh, no, my darling, I love our intimacy. One of my Pocket cousins had a baby every year for four years each November. I will do my best to be careful, though I fear some discomfort inside today."

She rubbed her stomach and told him to go.

"And I do hope you will get the chance to speak in court sometime soon, dear Pip. I don't like you spending your time there just watching Mr. Jaggers."

"Watching and learning, my dear. This lawyering is a way I can help the poor, even if they are criminals."

"That is a lovely idea, though most of the time these criminals are just that, a class of people who have no morals, no religion and see other people as things to be plundered and hurt."

"No, my dear Beatrice, there are certainly some, I am sure, who are born to criminal families, and then grow up as criminals and have children who are criminals. I am not sure that it is in their blood, in their nature, or whether it is that the circumstances of their upbringing are so harsh that the criminal life is the only path open to them. They never get a chance."

"That is so like you, my dear, you seem to be able to find good in everyone. Why is that?"

"I am never clear about it myself. As I have told you, I became a person I did not like, that is, I became a gentleman, though I was really a country boy with country ways at heart. I do not think that there are people who are born evil.

"Think of Miss Havisham. As far as we know, she was a good upright young woman. She had everything she desired—and her world fell apart. At that very instant, she became a vengeful, even wicked woman, who got worse with age. But that is what she chose to do; she had the chance not to. And she turned it down."

"But you are surely not comparing my relation to a criminal?"

"Why not? Look at the damage she has done to Estella, for all her wealth. I will ignore what pain she inflicted on me."

"Of course. You, my husband, will always know better than me," she replied with as much sarcasm as she could muster.

"Not so, my dear. I will always value your opinion and I will always listen to you, but never by merely accepting what you think because it is you who think it.

"And now I must get over to the Bailey."

He grabbed his barrister's white wig and gown and hurried out. He quietly and cautiously entered the court, which as usual was somber and dark, the judge high up in a full-bottomed wig and gown and again, as usual, an elderly man. In the dock was a small boy age twelve who was charged with theft and conspiracy as a member of a gang of thieves. He was probably about four-foot tall and had to stand on a large box to be seen by the court. Old Pip sat down next to Jaggers, as was his custom. The prosecution was making its final address to the jury.

Jaggers looked drawn and unwell, and whispered to Old Pip:

"Good to see you in court at last, Mr. Pip. I am not too well this morning. Before I conclude on this case, I will present you to the judge. So be prepared to recognize the court."

"This is the case we spoke of, am I correct, and you are going to ask for the jury and the court's mercy, am I right? I look forward immensely to hearing you."

The prosecution barrister was a middle-aged portly man, grey-wigged, who managed to convey a sense of utter boredom as he spoke.

"And so, gentlemen of the jury, I rest my case and trust you will find this young criminal guilty and deserving of transportation at the least. Harsh sentence it may be, but such laws protect all God-fearing, Christian people from such vagabonds and villains as the individual standing in the dock."

He sat down and Jaggers rose to address the court.

"M'lud, before I respond to my learned friend, I wish to introduce to you my junior Mr. Pirrip, known to all as Mr. Pip, who has been unable to attend your Lordship's court before, due to domestic difficulties which the court need not be apprised of. M'lud, Mr. Pirrip is becoming a lawyer of whom we have great expectations."

Old Pip rose and bowed, though looking a little crossly at Jaggers for his use of the phrase that haunted his life.

"He has experience of the criminal mind, as an observer, I should say. He is of the utmost integrity and I am sure..." Jaggers coughed and spluttered over his words, "he will soon be an adornment to this court and a lawyer of consequence in the times in which we live."

Jaggers still stood uncertainly. The judge saw he was unwell.

"Thank you, Mr. Jaggers and welcome to the Bar, Mr. Pirrip. This court has known Mr. Jaggers and his excellent advocacy for some years. I have no reason to doubt his judgment about your prowess. But are you quite well, Mr. Jaggers? Can you continue with your summing up?"

"I'm afraid, m'lud, I am unable to continue..." His voice faltered and he collapsed into his seat, "... I have not been at my best for some time."

"Do you desire an adjournment, Mr. Jaggers?"

Jaggers was silent but conscious, murmuring. Old Pip rose to address the court.

"If your lordship pleases, I am well-briefed on this case and I will gladly take my senior's position and address the jury."

"This is somewhat unusual, but we need to bring this case to a conclusion as there are many other cases on the docket. But, as you are new, and the evidence is not challenged, your summary to the jury is merely a formality, I suppose. Continue then, Mr. Pirrip, if the prosecuting counsel has no objection."

The barrister waved his hand condescendingly: "No objection, m'lud."

Jaggers looked up at Old Pip and nodded from his semi-recumbent seat. Old Pip began:

"Gentlemen of the jury, you have heard the circumstances in which I now find myself, and should I breach any of the etiquette appropriate to His Lordship's court, please ascribe that to my position as a junior and a novice, and I will stand corrected."

"I have studied this case in detail, as part of my initiation into my senior's practice. Here we have a boy, no more than a child, who, the prosecution has shown, is guilty of both thievery and conspiracy as a member of what, in modern parlance, is called a gang."

"Let us examine the child's background together, for child he is indeed."

He paused and looked at the jury closely, though he had been surprised at hearing his voice echo around the court.

"I expect some of you will have boys of his age, and how different, how very different is the upbringing of a child of yours compared to his. I am right, am I not?"

One or two jurors shifted uneasily in their seats.

"His mother, I am told, died when he was very young. His father was transported for criminal activities when this boy was a mere three years old. The boy was supposed to go along with his father but he was kidnapped by criminals and taken from his father's care. He was thus an orphan struggling to live in the cesspools of iniquity that are, regrettably, to be found in parts of this noble and ancient city.

"He was then prey to all the villains and whore-mongers out in those streets. He is of puny build as you can see, so hardly able to defend himself from the attacks of those better physically endowed. Did he, gentlemen of the jury, have any choices to make, or is it not most likely that he was a mere pawn, thrown hither and thither in the hurly-burly of the criminal world?"

Murmurings of agreement arose from the gallery, though the members of the jury remained stone-faced.

"I put it to you, gentlemen," Old Pip continued, "that while we are treating him before this court as a villain, he is in truth, a victim. He has been used by all those who have conspired—yes conspired—to use him for their own unspeakable ends. We should be searching for ways to prevent such devilry as consigns a young boy to this kind of fate. Once again, gentlemen of the jury, think of your own children in this regard.

"I should inform you also, gentlemen, that my learned senior has contacts which will enable him to be cared for by a family that is willing to support and help him recover from all that has been done to him.

"Gentlemen, on the evidence you have no option but to find him guilty. But you can recommend mercy to the court with all the power that a jury can muster. Mercy, gentlemen, mercy.

"God never gave this boy a chance. Will you?"

Old Pip sat down. Jaggers took Old Pip by the hand and smiled. Mild applause in the gallery was silenced by the Judge.

"A fine start, Mr. Pip," whispered Jaggers. "I apologize for my incapacity, but you did better than I could have done. My congratulations, sir. You will adorn the Bar for many a year. Please come to see me tomorrow."

The following morning Jaggers was sitting in his chair, looking unwell and once again morose, gloomy and troubled.

"In our business, Mr. Pip, we always face problems of making difficult decisions and choosing the right course of action. I am convinced I was right not to mention to them Molly's brother's murder at her hand, and Estella must never know of that. But here is a related problem on my conscience which I have delayed confronting for far too long."

Old Pip grins: "You mean, there is more?"

"This is no laughing matter, Mr. Pip. For me, at any rate. When your benefactor came first to this office to discover your whereabouts, he also gave me one thousand pounds to give to his former wife, Molly. He did not know, and I did not tell him, that she was in the next room. I took the money and promised him I would give it to her at the right time: Then he left.

"As you know, I thought Molly was mad. Giving her the money would enable her to live outside my care and protection. On the other hand, giving her that money could have enabled her to establish herself in a different town or village and live a quiet life.

"I was not oblivious, of course, to my own convenience to have her working for me. I have been recently thinking that, as their relationship progressed so well and, from all reports, she seemed settled, I would transfer the money to her, but I have been cowardly, given my great difficulty in telling them their story anyway.

"And now, of course, suddenly, she is dead. What shall I do with the money? Thinking as a lawyer now, Mr. Pip, who is the legal owner?"

"May I speak frankly, Mr. Jaggers?"

"Pray do."

"On the case at hand, the money is clearly not rightly the property of him who is its holder. Nor in my view does it fall under rules of confiscation of assets from criminals as it was entrusted and thus alienated before the criminal's apprehension. It is known that the donor was a certain lady's father.

"Put the case, as you say, that without countenancing any guilt and conscience the holder might have about the deceased lady's mother, it is incumbent on the holder to transfer the money to any surviving relative of the deceased for his or her sole use.

"It was not the intention of the benefactor that the money should be transferred immediately to her for whom it was intended, and therefore the discretion of the holder is of major account. Nor is the status of the relationship between the deceased pair of any consequence.

"I would further advise that the holder of the money has no obligation to add any interest that might have accrued while the money was in that holder's possession, because of the money's status as a gift. That is my advice on the legal position. I also think it is right."

Jaggers smiled broadly. "You put the case as clearly as I might have done myself, Mr. Pip. Whether it would pass muster before a judge of Queen's Bench is quite another matter. Will you take the note to Miss Estella?"

"I will gladly do so and go directly to her lodgings."

Old Pip left the office, scribbled a note to Beatrice and asked the clerk to see it was delivered to her immediately. He walked hurriedly to Estella's new lodgings, still near St Paul's in Cheapside, but not in the buildings where she had lived with Molly.

Estella was dressed in black and welcomed him warmly. They went into the living room and sat in opposite chairs.

"Oh, Pip, in my distress, I could not have wished to see any other person but you. Thank you for your note about young Albert's arrival. How are they both? I must send him a gift."

"They are well indeed. But I come on business, bringing you some good news.

"Oh, how I need good news," cried Estella.

"This will please you, I am sure. Mr. Jaggers has entrusted me with bringing to you a note for one thousand pounds which your father left with him for your mother's use."

Estella immediately bristled with anger.

"How dare he have done this?

"No, wait," she said quietly. "I have resolved since this tragedy to remain calm, the calmness she and I felt together."

She burst into tears. Old Pip got up to comfort her, but she stayed him with her hand and composed herself.

"Think, Pip, how pleased my mother would have been to think that Abel had thought about her. Is Jaggers really so inhuman? Surely, he could see what a pleasure it would have been to her."

"He said that if he had given her the money before she was reconciled to you, she would have left him and disappeared."

"What a selfish fellow: so he kept the money so he could keep Molly in his service."

"I think he convinced himself it was in her best interests."

"I am aghast at such perfidy, Pip. He thinks he knows all the answers, like God, as Mother once said. Yet why did he not do this after we had begun to live together?"

"I really don't know. Maybe guilt of some kind?"

"It baffles me but it also upsets me exceedingly."

"Oh, Estella, you know how sorry I am for your loss, as your lonely life had become a miracle of reconciliation and love, only to be dashed by that foul villainy.

"I will return soon, but now must hurry home to my wife."

"Of course, of course, but don't leave me too long."

Old Pip said his goodbyes and promised to see her again soon.

As she watched him go, Estella sits alone with her thoughts.

Looking out of the window, she could just see the dome of the Cathedral. She was beginning to feel the kind of turmoil at his absence that Molly had promised her when she found herself in love with a man. Now she was waking up feeling like a young girl, even approaching fifty years of age, desperate to be wooed and loved—sensations which for years she had sublimated, and with Molly's advice had navigated *la ménépausie*. Images of intimacy cascaded through her mind and body which left her puzzled as how to get relief.

But she had to entertain whether she would ever experience that kind of loving. The image in her mind of a lover was always that of Pip, his hands, his lips, his body entwined with hers.

Yet, just as she had told Molly she might find herself able to murder someone, so she struggled to put the thought of killing Beatrice right out of her mind, should it be poison, perhaps hiring someone to do it, or just pushing her off a cliff. Such dreadful thoughts she was always ashamed of, but it was as if, like her mother, she could not stand the idea of another woman having what she thought was hers, a classic case of jealousy.

She had grown up, she knew now, with a constrained conscience, as she had been given a carapace of mild evil by Miss Havisham, so that she could capture a man only to Frustrate him endlessly with her unattainable beauty.

Yet now, the closeness of her relationship with her mother had softened that infamous upbringing completely. Murdering Beatrice was just a wild fantasy. Maybe. Yet with only those five adult years shared, she recognized that her mother was the first person she had deeply loved.

That love, she thought, had taught her how to be fully aware of another's feelings. Before Molly, she had never thought much about any other person and how they felt, except to tease and frustrate them, as she had with Pip. Gradually, she changed in those five years, from being hard, brittle and beautiful to being soft, warm and beautiful.

She now faced the ultimate dilemma of the lover—did she want his happiness more than she desired him?

That she loved him was not in doubt, but to love someone was to want their flourishing, even if it could not be shared. This was the exact moment at which she finally put behind her the old self-centered Estella who would have cared nothing for the possible damage and wreckage that might ensue just as long as she could wrap her arms around him in ecstasy. That was gone.

"I must tell him that I love him," she concluded out loud, partly to convince herself she could do it.

Beatrice was sitting in a chair in their living room and she greeted Old Pip on his return from Little Britain very wearily, moaning slightly. A maid hurried to bring him a glass of wine and to take care of two-year-old Albert now walking and talking.

"I'm afraid I am very unwell: My stomach hurts."

"Just rest, my darling. I will fetch a doctor directly. I have been reflecting on my recent court appearance. Now I am, as you know, a rather reserved man. But as I began, I found this passion welling up in me. I thought of our own young boy, our precious Albert, and how different that poor child's upbringing must have been.

"Think of it, my dear, imagine it was poor Albert at three years old, prey to all the worst elements in London. Anyway, when I sat down, there was great applause which annoyed the judge, but the jury did as I pleaded and recommended mercy for the child, which the judge accepted. So that was a very good beginning. But you must now rest, my dear."

"Oh, I am so pleased for you, Pip. I was thinking about getting out of London as it is such a dirty place. We had such a good time in Walworth when Albert was born, but we cannot ask John Wemmick again, can we?"

"That could be a very good idea, darling. Let me see. Young Pip has left for the war, but I am sure Biddy and Joe would be delighted to have you to look after. It will take their mind off Young Pip. I will send a message this afternoon to say I will be coming up for a quick visit, and when you feel a little better, we will go to the Cottage, if they agree, as I am sure they will."

The Saturday of that week, Old Pip took the coach and then a trap to the Cottage. As he rode up, Joe appeared with a shovel in his hand, sweating profusely, and Biddy not far behind, in similar condition.

"Old Pip, what a treat, old chap; I was just saying to Biddy what a feast we will have when Beatrice and young Albert visit us, dear old chap. We'se been gardening. There'll be beans and peas and carrots and cabbages, not forgetting potatoes. God and Nature will help us."

The three sat on a bench outside the Cottage.

"I have to be quick, my dears, as I must get the night coach back to London. As you know, Beatrice is an admirable soul, and we think she is having another baby which is rather soon after Albert. She is weak, at the moment, and you'll remember how helpful it was to her to go to Walworth with John Wemmick. Now I think it will be six months or more before she delivers, but…"

Biddy interrupted: "Of course we'll look after her, Pip. She's family now. The air here is very clean and pure. The sun is shining this June. We'll love looking after Albert the baby, too, won't we Joe?"

"My dear old chap, it will be a great pleasure. You bring her here just as soon as maybe; we'll be ready."

Beatrice's sojourn with Joe and Biddy that summer soon became a real delight for her. She got to know just what loving and generous folk they both were, and Albert flourished, too. Old Pip was a regular visitor, and his time was in such demand that he went only once in a trap with Beatrice and the baby to visit Estella. Beatrice was concerned after that visit that he seemed morose which she attributed to her not being with him on a regular basis, a misunderstanding which concealed potential difficulties.

Although Beatrice still had fits of ague, and some stomach pains, the fresh air and excellent food, and her relief at not having to run a home made her improve mentally and physically, much to Old Pip's delight. A new baby, hopefully a daughter, was everyone's expectations. Old Pip was now comfortable in every way that a man could expect, with his successful advocacy in court and his lovely family, except for the confusion he felt about Estella, which was, as usual, a matter for his conscience.

And, of course, for hers.

After visiting Beatrice and Albert several times, Old Pip felt he must see how Estella was faring and coping with Molly's death after his visit in September. It was now long since her murder. He was feeling very clear about his relationship with Estella. He had put his love for her quite out of sight. She opened the door to him, and she had obviously been weeping.

"Do come in, dear Pip," and she sat down trying to compose herself. He sat down and there was a brief silence, after which Estella wiped her eyes, sat up and looked up at Old Pip with a very serious but friendly look on her face.

"Pip, my dear man, my tears were for my mother. I may as well tell you straightaway that I have a confession to make. We met all those years ago, and I have lived long with the blight with which Miss Havisham infected me, my inability to respect, let alone love, a man. My mother opened my eyes to my body, to what I had refused to feel. She has several times described to me in rich detail, almost too rich, what I have lost in being so blighted.

"But I am growing out of those terrible inhibitions. Unfortunately, you are now married," here she hesitated, "and this is my confession." She paused again, then very shyly, "my new-found feelings are directed at you, my oldest friend and confidant."

Old Pip looked at her very closely as she said: "I want you to know that, if I understand myself aright, I love you."

"But I am married, Estella," he cried. "Are you saying this to torment me further as you have done all our lives? You know I have loved you, more or less, since I was a child. Why this declaration now?"

"This is what makes me so unutterably sad. Had I had my mother's love, for all her faults, I would have known what desire was: I would have seen her loving someone, watching them, caring for them, touching them, hearing their voices together, even though any cross words that might have passed between them.

"I would have witnessed a man and a woman living close to each other, fondling each other's hands and bodies, seeing the look of desire in their eyes. I could have expected to feel like them. Of such matters, I have no memories, no recollections, as I was never a witness to them."

Estella then raised her voice almost to the point of anger.

"When I told my mother about my guardian, she asked why could the woman not realize her great good fortune in not being trapped into marriage with such a blackguard? That had not occurred to me. That wicked woman stopped up my sensibilities and passions, making me the instrument of her own revenge, moreover for a man who was a nasty villain. She just constructed a nightmare and wove me into it. But, oh dear, I must be calm."

Then, confidently and closely,

"So, Pip dearest, I cannot stay silent.

"I know you have loved me all the while.

"I also know that we cannot pursue our relationship as one of love and passion, but I cannot bear for you not to know my newly found and deepest desire."

Old Pip gazed at her, barely hearing what she was saying.

"That said, my most profound wish is that we will continue to be friends, and that you have a long and happy marriage.

"I want your happiness because I love you. I am sure we can live with this secret and even, as I expect, I go to my grave with my love for you not fulfilled, I can now still live my life with the delight of thoughts that might have been, and still enjoy your company, and watch you become a husband and a father whom I adore.

"Believe me, dear Pip, I know from my mother's experience the importance of keeping my emotions in check.

"I will not ever be a threat to your marriage, ever. I promise."

"Estella, my dearest," he said very quietly and slowly, emerging from this prolonged confession of love, "I have borne my love for you these many years. Knowing you in fact do love me is both an immense delight but it will also be a more serious and unremitting burden on my damn conscience than it ever was."

They got up from their chairs and moved towards each other. They embraced, wrapping their arms around each other. He kissed her on the lips. She responded and shuddered with delight. Then she put her finger on his lips and smiled broadly, saying:

"That was a quite delicious first and last time. And now you must go. Who knows what the future may bring?"

"That's all very well, but my head is spinning, my heart is aching, my body is alive with desire."

"Shh, my dear. Just look after you wife and son. They need you more than me."

"You are right. I will see you anon, but I will write as I cannot lose touch with you. I will see you too each time I visit the Gargerys."

With that, he kissed her again, and rushed out of the house to get to the coach for London.

X

Old Pip might have quibbled then with the details but not with the tenor of Wemmick's criticism. When all is said and done a friend has a license to be frank, and yet Old Pip's history gives Wemmick, let alone us, little confidence that he will resist Estella. Few can attain the ambition of trying to be a loving friend but not a lover, especially when one has a conscience suddenly confronted with the surprise of her declaration. He was confounded too by the realization that Beatrice had spotted the threat that her husband's friend of a lifetime could indeed become more than a friend.

Estella's love for her mother had changed her as a woman. Her conscience was awakened as she considered the needs of others, whereas heretofore such matters had been outside her ken. That consideration extended to Beatrice but more so to Old Pip. She was wary, but as confident as always that she could handle herself and her love for the married man she loved.

Mr. Jaggers was moving into old age in a redemptive mood, given to reflection on matters from a busy and complicated life. His concern also now seemed to be with his conscience, though his frailties were apparent to Wemmick, who was beginning to regard him with compassion, a lonely elderly man. Yet Jaggers had not become sentimental, as his attitude to the gardener Thistlewood displayed, or less cautious in his judgments on the lives of others.

Joe Gargery was in a somber mood not typical of this jovial good-hearted man. Earlier in the year, as preparations for the War in the Crimea got under way, the iron clipper RMS *Tayleur* ran aground off Ireland on her maiden voyage out of Liverpool with the loss of three hundred lives out of the six hundred and fifty on board.

This disaster for a technologically advanced ship alarmed everyone associated with ship-building. The humble Joe Gargery was haunted by the possibility that some mistake of his, as with the *Tayleur*, might sink the ship on which his son was sailing, let alone by the absence of news of his son Young Pip.

However, Beatrice's pregnancy kept the Gargery household on tiptoe.

She was handled sensitively and carefully by Joe and Biddy as the date of her confinement drew closer, the stress growing daily. Albert was a great joy to Old Pip and he came to the Cottage six weeks before her due date with a promise to return to Little Britain office if needed.

Although Biddy was probably competent, Gladys, a midwife from All Hallows, had been engaged and was on the alert. She had visited Beatrice, and once or twice putting her ear to the mother's stomach, identified the sounds of a baby's beating heart.

This brought great comfort to Old Pip, Joe, and Biddy and not least to Beatrice, a person for whom any pregnancy would be life-threatening. She had talked about her possible death in her conversations with Biddy who tried in her own way to comfort her with God's grace.

One February afternoon, the heavily pregnant Beatrice seemed in good health. She had walked slowly down the track for a few yards with Old Pip and she suggested that they ride over to Numquam in the trap Old Pip had commissioned for her while she was at the cottage. He was nervous about a meeting with Estella, but he could not easily refuse.

They arrived mid-morning to Estella's great surprise and she immediately arranged for lunch, which passed off amicably, Estella and Old Pip sustaining a difficult distance from each other. Once again, this made Old Pip somewhat morose, for which Beatrice upbraided him as they started home, a condition which, he told his wife, was due to his profound anxiety about the forthcoming baby which satisfied her as an explanation of his mood.

On the way back to the cottage, however, a fox chasing a rabbit rushed in front of the trap. The horse reared up suddenly, then lurched heavily to one side, almost throwing Old Pip out. It then broke into a gallop. Beatrice was tossed around like a leaf in the wind. She immediately went into labor. They got back to the cottage much more quickly than anticipated, as Old Pip had to struggle to bring the animal under control. He then carried his wife up to the bedroom, alerting Joe and Biddy to the event and to her condition.

Coming downstairs hurriedly, he ran the horse and trap as fast as he could to fetch Gladys while Joe and Biddy, anxious to help but not knowing quite what to do for the best, looked on with immense concern. Gladys came, examined Beatrice and expressed surprise at how quickly Beatrice was progressing with the birth: She had just heard the baby's heartbeat, so all was well on that account.

Two hours later, however, as the pains developed, Beatrice began to slip in and out of consciousness and a fever seemed to be developing. Suddenly she began to give birth, as it were spontaneously, a mere four hours after first going into labor in the trap. Gladys and Biddy were alone in the room, with Joe, Old Pip and Albert downstairs.

Beatrice let out a sudden howl and the baby emerged. Furious attempts by Gladys to bring breath into the little one's lungs failed.

The baby, a daughter, was dead.

Beatrice was shrieking in pain at the delivery and continued to do so until she was fully relieved of what was in her womb. Gladys and Biddy tried in vain to comfort this sad, distressed mother. Old Pip could stand it no longer and rushed up the stairs.

The Cottage was suddenly transformed from a delight of anticipation into one of disappointment, engulfed with a profound sadness. Gladys explained to Old Pip and Biddy that she had seen it once before, where a baby had died immediately before or whilst emerging into the world, some kind of shock, she said, though no one understood why. Joe had hurried off to find a doctor, but it was too late.

Beatrice slipped gradually into unconsciousness, the fever continuing, and she passed away a couple of afternoons later with Old Pip lying on the bed beside her. The midwife had helped Biddy wrap the dead child in a shroud and laid her in a cot by her mother's bed, a sad but beautiful little corpse. As Beatrice was dying, Old Pip spoke to her quietly:

"Beatrice, Beatrice, my darling. How can this be? My fault, my fault once again."

As she passed away, he folded her tiny hands over her breast. Joe and Biddy came into the room with Albert, weeping. Biddy handed Albert to Old Pip who held him close, murmuring:

"Your mother is gone, my dear child, she is gone."

"Where?" said Albert, now crying loudly.

"I wish I knew."

The next day, Old Pip travelled with his dead wife and daughter in a hired carriage to their lodgings near St. Botolph's in the City of London. That Saturday, the cortege and mourners went up the hill to the cemetery at Highgate, open since 1840. The men went first, as was the custom, led by Old Pip carrying Albert, then Joe, Herbert, Jaggers, Wemmick, Algernon Pocket, two clerks from Little Britain, followed by the women: Biddy, Clara, Mrs. Wemmick, and a gaggle of female Pockets. The coffin was covered with masses of flowers, and one or two wreaths, increasingly a fashion.

After the committal, the cortege and the Pockets departed. Most of the mourners left. Jaggers and Wemmick shook Old Pip's hands in condolence, excusing themselves in the belief that they should leave him with his family. Biddy held on to Albert, sobbing gently. Joe wept quietly. Estella was standing alone, watching, but Old Pip brought her into a group with Joe and Biddy.

"Joe, Biddy, my dears," said Old Pip, putting his arms around them. "Since Beatrice died, I have been thinking on how I can care for my son. I do not wish some other person to care for Albert if it can be avoided. I'd like him to grow up within my family. Dare I ask if you would both continue to care for him at the Cottage for a while?"

"Best of friends, old chap. I think we might, might we, Biddy?" Joe said, smiling.

"The sadness of your dear Beatrice dying when she was trying to bring you a sister to young Albert here is almost too great for us all to bear, especially you, dear Pip. I know you'll be coming to visit, oftener than you have been."

"Indeed I will."

"It will be a comfort 'aving 'im, Pip. Young Pip is off at war as a farrier. Albert has been as easy as pie while they were both with us, and he knows us."

"I have always been in debt to you both as my family. Come back to my lodgings now before you go back to Kent tomorrow, stay the night, and the maid will sort out more of Albert's things. But before we go, I need to speak privately with Estella."

Joe and Biddy took Albert to a patch of grass under a large ash tree at the edge of the cemetery, but they kept a keen eye on Old Pip and Estella.

Biddy murmured to Joe that she wants to know what that lady is up to.

"I will not even try to say how sad I am at this tragedy, my dear Pip," said Estella as they walked. "Remembering what I confessed to you, I have to speak my mind to you, now, I hope, without invading your grief. At our last meeting, we ventured into a space we had not previously occupied. I was, and am, thrilled by that. But I am anxious that we avoid any idle gossip and take our time. You must know Beatrice's death was, for me as well, a thunderbolt, something I never wished for or envisaged. I know it was of more than equal sadness for you."

"I share your sentiment, my dear, and we can be quite frank with each other now. I would not have married Beatrice if I had thought at any time that you and I might have married.

"I have a variety of matters on my conscience about Beatrice, but her death was not something to which I was a party. It was easy to convince myself that I could continue to love you whilst married to Beatrice.

"After our recent meeting, things changed. I tried not to think about you at all, to enable me to care only for Beatrice and Albert, hoping that my love for you would always be there, quiet and undisturbed, as we agreed. But, frankly, I doubted that could happen."

"Oh, please, dear Pip, will you please stop giving me reasons to love you. However, I am determined that we should not meet for a while, certainly well into the autumn. I have decided to revisit some of those places in Europe that Miss Havisham sent me to long ago. Venice seems an appropriate place for unrequited love. Let us see what is between us when I return, though I am already eager to be back. That will give you time, too, to think about Albert's care and his future."

"I will miss you desperately, Estella, but I am grateful indeed. My emotions and are too awry now for me to think straight. The arrangement for Albert is good, especially as I also anticipate hard work, now that Jaggers is slowing down. I would kiss you on the lips, my dearest, were not the Gargerys over there, but," he said putting his arms around Estella affectionately, "'safe travels,' darling; write when you can. Promise."

"A message, occasionally, to let you know where I am."

They walked back to the Gargerys. Estella said goodbye and walked off to her carriage.

"Estella was consoling me as an old friend, Biddy. She was very fond of Beatrice, but she was also consulting me because of my life abroad. She has been planning to do some travelling on the Continent for some time and will now be away for a month or two at least.

"My dears, I will need you both even more as I grieve for my dear Beatrice."

Biddy smiled broadly and said: "Well now, you always have us for company."

"I don't know, Old Pip, dear old chap, what God was thinking about when He took your Beatrice. I'll have to ask Preacher Whitehouse if he knows."

"Wait in the carriage both of you and we will go to my lodgings. I will follow momentarily. Forgive me, I must talk with Beatrice first."

He went back to the grave, now filled in, whilst Joe and Biddy took Albert by his hands so that he could swing along, and they walked away from the cemetery to the carriage.

"Beatrice my darling, Albert will be cared for: Joe and Biddy are good people and his living in the country will be good for his health, out of London. I…am…so…sorry."

He wept copiously on his knees for several minutes, his mind whirring with his real distress and sadness at losing the mother of his child. That done, he went to Albert, hugging him and putting him on his knee next to the Gargerys waiting in the trap, unable to stop talking once more about their son, Young Pip, and his fate.

Following this terrible event, by October 1854 Albert became quite settled at the cottage, occasionally asking for his mother when his father was there. Without news of Young Pip, Joe was banging out his frustrations by singing a hymn, punctuated by the hammer blows on the anvil which eighteen-month-old Albert was watching and enjoying. Biddy was almost in tears as she peeled potatoes. Joe stopped singing and wandered into the kitchen.

"I don't know, Biddy my love, 'bout our Young Pip in the war. Only that one letter."

He pointed to the letter on the mantelpiece over the brick fireplace and asked:

"Read it to me agin."

They went into the living room and Biddy picked up the letter and read:

'*This Bit of Papper cost me a Shilling and a verrey ard job to get it atorl it would give me much pledger to wright to you as awfen as I could. I will wright to you as soon as you write to me if you will please to send me some papper and stamps so I can wright to you again.*'

"Now," said Biddy, "that was back in April. He obviously wrote in a hurry as he's forgotten how to write his words properly. I 'spose he just has no money or is just too busy. But we would have heard if he had been hurt, wouldn't we?"

"Lor' bless us, I should hope so. We've prayed enough for him, the dear old chap, he will come back to us, I feel it in my bones."

"Oh, Joe dear, I wish I could feel like you. At least he wasn't supposed to be fighting. We'll talk with Old Pip; he wrote to say he'd come today so as he can have good time with young Albert, didn't he?"

"Oh, talk of an angel."

The noise of a trap could be heard outside.

Old Pip dismounted, crying out "All Hallows Eve soon, so ghosts will be about" and, making faces at young Albert. He picked him up and swung around him, then rubbed noses, the child squealing at his father's kisses.

He embraced Biddy, had a long handshake and hugged Joe.

"Best of friends, eh, Old Pip?"

"Best of friends, my dears," said Joe, "but we are so worried about the young 'un. Biddy just read me again the one letter only in nine months."

"You must not worry . There have been several important battles as is reported in London. Remember, Young Pip is a farrier, not a cavalry man or in the infantry. A mortal danger is disease and illness, from which no one is excluded."

"God bless 'im, I hope he's safe. I wish I knew where he were."

"Dear Joe, he is in the Crimea. Biddy, come here and I will explain it to you both."

Old Pip then sat down at the kitchen table, Albert on his knee, and, using various pieces of cutlery and pots, he produced a crude if largely accurate montage of Western Europe.

"This pepper pot is England, and Young Pip went on board at Southampton. This big spoon is the *Majestic*, sailing down France which is this bowl, and Spain, this other bowl, and Gibraltar the salt pot, which stands at the entrance to Mediterranean Sea. That sea is all this part of the table, and he drew an imaginary line on the table. "I'll put this little boot of Albert's to mark Italy, south of which is an island called Malta, the mustard pot, which is where he first got off the ship."

"This grography is very confusin', ain't it Biddy?"

"It's geography, Joe."

"It's still confusin'."

Old Pip continued: "Now we can move the big spoon, the *Majestic,* there to Malta. The Crimea where all the fighting is happening is right across the table and inside the Black Sea, this saucer. If I put a dab of butter on this part of the saucer, that is where the Crimea is. Ships going into the Black Sea have to sail through the Dardanelles, this little fork, and everywhere there will be ships and ports and soldiers and whatnot."

"So that's a long way past Holland, ain't it, Biddy?"

"Oh yes, Joe, that's many miles away. Joe and I pray all the time for his return, Pip, and we have young Albert learning his prayers too, we hope you don't mind."

"While he is in your care, I am pleased for you to do what you think right. Prayers may give him a conscience. Anyway, let's have some fun today and some walks. I am gradually getting used to being without Beatrice, though it is very hard.

"I must return to London tomorrow for a week to prepare as the courts will be opening in January, but I'll be back for the holiday season.

"Now, I just want time with my two best friends and my darling son here. I'm sure we will hear from Young Pip soon. After lunch, I'll just go over to Numquam as Estella sent me a note saying she was back from her travels, and plans to be there for a long stay, so I won't see her in London."

"Three months, is it?" asks Biddy. "Good lord, has our Beatrice been gone that long?"

"You ride over on Boney, old chap. Young Pip would be glad for him to be ridden. But you'll be back for supper and to see Albert afore you goes to London, won't you?"

"Of course."

On his ride over to Numquam, Old Pip was considering Albert's future. He was sure that Biddy would be more conscious of his worries by talking to Albert regularly about him and, for instance, whenever she read to him, would say such things as 'your father gave you this book.' Joe would be much less aware of the possible confusions in the child's mind, but, on the other hand, his loving care for Albert overrode Old Pip's concerns. As he approached the house, he knew he must be more conscientious in coming to see his son and be significant in his growing up.

Arriving at the door, he started to tremble in anticipation. As he knocked, Estella threw it open and flung herself into his arms: "Oh, how I have longed for this moment."

They embraced and kissed deeply. Old Pip held her, then broke off the kiss to look at her.

"Oh, darling, if I could only count the number of times I have imagined this."

They kissed again. She started to unravel his cravat.

"Say you will stay here at least tonight and then forever."

"I have to go back to the Gargerys for supper and then on to London by the night coach."

"Then we have no time to lose."

She took his hand and pulled him hurriedly up the stairs to her bedroom. Two hours later, they were lying naked on her bed, in each other's arms, her head on his shoulder.

She stroked his face and, looking deeply into his eyes, said: "I know your body, I know your lips. I know your mouth. I don't even care about anything but the present. Just love me like that again and again and again. For the first time in my life, I am feeling whole."

She lifted herself over him and kissed him, lips, neck, body.

"Do you know I once told Molly I loved you as a friend, but the thought of your lust or desire repelled me? How ignorant I was. For years, all this has been waiting for me."

He smiled, and stroked her hair dangling over his face.

"Now, my whole being feels as though it has been wakened from a long dark night. I cannot stop quivering with delight and ecstasy."

Old Pip pushed her gently on to her back, stroking her:

"All my life, it seems, I have been waiting to run my hands over your body. When I first met you all those years ago and you were this haughty rich child, your body was growing to be a woman and I used to dream of your nakedness, though I did not then know why or what for. Now here I am fondling you and feeling the luxury of having had your inner warmth around me, and everything is lovelier than I imagined it to be."

They kissed again sensuously without a break before Estella pulled back and said:

"Let me try to explain. I suffered so long from Miss Havisham's curse. It was not just the distrust and indifference to men in general, but the idea that I could taunt men, and get them to believe they would be unable to satisfy their physical desire for me.

"The core of the curse goes beyond that. It not only put me in the frame of mind where I could say what I did to Molly about you, but it shackled my own desires, made my feeling for my own body warped, unable to grow, to give or to surrender. It was not as though I was ashamed of my body—indeed I was proud of my looks, but I simply had a revulsion to physical desire such that the very idea of a man, any man, sweating and grunting over me, was utterly distasteful."

"Oh, goodness gracious, how could anyone feel like that?"

"By being raised by Miss Havisham. As I think I told you before, I never saw any two people in love with each other. I knew nothing of it. But I now realize this has been most disturbing for me. I simply had been trapped into ignorance, not knowing or desiring what I was missing. My attitude became my habit."

"But what happened to bring about this change in you, darling?"

"Do you remember my showing you the garden when you first came here with Beatrice?"

"How could I forget? Our meeting haunted me for days."

"Beatrice lay there resting, quiet, lovely, and I suddenly had this image in my mind of the two of you naked and in fulsome passion, I suppose, like what we have just enjoyed. I imagined her ecstasy as she felt you inside her. Molly had hectored me to put aside the Havisham curse, and I had willed myself to do it. Mere will was not enough.

"For suddenly, in that instant of gazing at her, this vision of you both was so exciting that my revulsion fell away, and my whole being was hit by an earthquake of desire. I wanted what she had. My mouth went dry, my breasts started to tingle, I felt a warmth coursing through my body I had never ever felt before.

"I wanted you; I craved you as Beatrice must have wanted you. I went to bed that night and I dreamt and dreamt of us, our love and the greed with which we have just taken each other. As I told you, darling, it was not a desire for any man but for you, and you alone, my dear, dear Pip."

"Oh, my dear…"

"Why you? Because I have known you for so long. I have never known you to do anything to hurt anyone. You are a good man, but I have known you intimately only in the conventional sense. My desire for you is thus rooted in my emerging understanding that I was incomplete and that our friendship was incomplete.

"I have known almost since we first met that you were in love with me, though I was also unable to understand what that might mean. I must have hurt you terribly that time long ago when you told me you loved me and I responded by saying I was going to marry Drummle. How dreadful that must have been. Then suddenly, last year and before Molly died, I knew I was in love with you too. I then knew it was not to be. And then Beatrice died."

Old Pip was stunned by this outpouring of love.

"Darling Estella, that was a great shock for me, but then not a surprise at all. Her frailty presaged an early death. Your presence was always around me, my thinking about what you were doing, who you were with. Travelling abroad as I did for those years didn't put you behind me. Marrying and having a child didn't do it. I confess again, that I would not have married her, had you been, so to speak, freed of the Havisham curse."

"Thank you, thank you for that; so we have only truly thought of ourselves as lovers since we had that first kiss."

"Yes, apart from my youthful imaginings, that is true. My marriage was not rooted in passion. It was conventional. We had children because that was required of a married man and woman. We could both accommodate ourselves to each other. Your vivid imagination did not match the reality of our coupling.

"Did I love her? Yes, so far and it would have been far enough: but I knew, and perhaps she knew, it could never be and never was the full-throated passion we now have. My love for you is not just a kind of nostalgia."

"Oh, Pip, dearest, loveliest man. I am so longing to spend the rest of my life with you."

"That is my earnest desire, too. Though I must also confess that I am not as healthy as I would like to be, unlike you who is the very epitome of beauty and good health."

"Pip, darling, we are both fifty years old, or thereabouts. We do not have much time in this life."

"Shall we marry, then?"

"Need we?"

They helped each other out of bed, stood naked in full embrace, kissing each other, and then dressed, fondling each other like the first-time lovers that they were. They dressed and decided to go to London together in a day or two and then return for Christmas. Old Pip would have to decide how he would tell Joe and Biddy that he intended to stay with his lover while in Kent. Meantime, he needed to get back for supper.

XI

1854 was fraught with gloom and worry in the Gargery family. Joe and Biddy had been told that Old Pip was staying with Estella, apparently to keep her company in the festive season which heightened their suspicions. They too pondered the fate of the boy they thought of as their grandson. Christmas lanterns on the cottage walls had been taken down as the New Year began.

Old Pip told them of battles in which Young Pip might have been involved and in particular about the Charge of the Light Brigade which had occurred the previous October. This day he had ridden over from Numquam to see them and tell of how Estella and he took Albert with them to London to see his Hackney grandparents, but the boy's grandmother, truth to tell, seemed to be uninterested for all the fuss the family made of the child.

Puffing at his pipe outside that January day, Joe had no immediate commission to fulfil, though he had expectations. He stood gazing into the distance at the front door where he saw the figure of a man hobbling down the path leaning on a stick.

"Biddy, my dear, come 'ere. I can't tell with my eyes, but I think there's someone up the track."

"Now who could that be at this time of day?"

She came to the door next to Joe, wiping her hands on a towel and peered up the track.

"Wait! What?" She screamed, and started running, "It can't be. I think it's Young Pip. He's got a stick, maybe he's hurt."

Joe followed Biddy and they set off at a run to the figure on the track, leaving Old Pip to follow, and Albert coming to the door to see what the fuss was about.

Joe got to him first. "Oh, my dear son 'ere, 'ere what's the matter?"

Biddy rushed up and engulfed both of them.

"Oh, Mother, Father, I am hurt, in my leg."

He dropped his stick and fainted. Joe picked him up and carried him to the cottage.

"Oh, my goodness, Joe. He is wounded; look at his ankle. The poor boy."

The ankle seemed very badly broken and his leggings were thoroughly stained on his left leg with the blood congealed well up his calf and down into his boot. Young Pip shivered violently as Joe carried him to the cottage and he drifted into unconsciousness. Joe and Old Pip then carried him as gently as they could upstairs to his bed, both surprised how light he was after his travails.

Biddy came with a bowl of hot water and a scissors and cut off his leggings to reveal a poisoned ankle with a clear hole where a bullet had struck, though no sign of the bullet. She carefully washed the gaping wound and then cut off the uniform trousers completely on his left leg. There were other scratches on his knee and thigh, and she washed those carefully. The stench of his filthy clothes and his wound was overpowering.

Young Pip seemed to be drifting into a coma, which left his parents feeling helpless.

"Joe, Biddy, do you have honey?" asked Old Pip. "I once heard that the ancients used to fill a wound like this with honey, and, as we have nothing else, why not try it?"

Joe rushed downstairs and returned with a jar of honey and a spoon.

"Biddy let's try the honey. We have to do summat."

"You're right, Joe. Pour it into the wound, Biddy, and seal it tight."

"You'll need to do that every day, wash out the honey, and pour more in. I think I can be of most help by trying to find some other potions. I know some have used maggots to drink up the poison, but I'd not be sure of that. Estella might have some honey, and I'll ride past there anyway. Can I get some in the village?"

"Mr. Buzza keeps bees," said Joe. "He'd have some. Funny isn't it, a Mr. Buzza keeping bees." He laughed, but only for a moment, at his own joke.

"I'll then get straight up to London, find an apothecary and tell Jaggers I am needed here. I'll visit Buzza on the way back. The wound requires cleaning and dressing every few hours, so we'll needs lots of honey."

Joe then preoccupied himself with Young Pip, but murmured: "You do all that, Old Pip. God bless."

Old Pip rode over first to Estella at Numquam with the dreadful news about Young Pip. They decided to travel overnight together to Old Pip's lodgings where he once lived with Beatrice. He got out of bed at sunrise next day and drew the curtains to bring in the murky London sunshine.

"I must get to Jaggers directly and then go back to Kent, my darling. I will tell Joe and Biddy that we plan to live together quite soon."

"I understand, but hurry back, please."

The brief meeting with Jaggers was done in a rush, and Old Pip visited an apothecary near the Tower which Wemmick recommended, and then got a cab to the Bull and Mouth Inn for the Chatham coach. He flopped into the coach, exhausted, hurried to pick up some honey on the way from Mr. Buzza in All Hallows, but was in a quandary about what to say to Joe and Biddy about Estella. He arrived at the Cottage and was greeted very warmly by Albert and by Joe:

"How is he, how is he?"

"He woke yesterday, the dear old chap, without a fever, and he has had a cup or two of broth and he smiles his old smile. But that leg is orful, though the honey has helped him and he's very weak."

"I've brought some potions and honey from Mr. Buzza. Is Biddy with him? Can I see him?"

"Oh, I am sure you can, old chap. You'll mek him healthy again, I know."

Old Pip carried Albert upstairs. He embraced Biddy, who was sitting on the bed. Young Pip's face was thin and drawn. A small stool was on the bed on which his leg rested with a huge bandage around it.

"We just popped in to see how you're faring."

"Oh, Uncle Pip," he said very quietly, "how good to see you and your lovely son. I can't tell you how much I have missed you."

"And all of us have missed you more than we can say. But I just came to see you, and I am sure you need continuous rest. Biddy's told you about Beatrice, I'm sure.

"Yes,"

"Sometime soon you'll be able to tell us all about your adventures."

"Yes, but I do need to get out of bed and get this leg of mine on the ground again or I will just get weaker lying here."

"Now don't you go rushing yourself, young man."

"No, Mother."

He fell asleep and Old Pip and Albert followed Biddy downstairs where Joe was waiting.

"What news? What's to become of him if he's lame like a horse? He won't be shoeing them, that I know."

"We'll see, Pip," said Biddy. "First things first is getting well. He has the spirit to heal quickly and he will find a way in life."

There was a noise from upstairs. Biddy rushed up to find Young Pip standing out of bed. Joe followed.

"I don't want to sleep now Uncle Pip is here. I am ready to come downstairs as I'd like him to hear of my adventures."

"Are you sure you can make it, me darlin'? Pip, come and help."

"Let's get the dear chap down the stairs," said Joe, "then set him in that old leather chair near the fire and with rugs to keep him warm, and the stool for his gammy leg. Old Pip and I will get him down some way."

The two men went up the stairs together and they struggled, but with great care, to get Young Pip down the stairs without hurting him further. He was clearly still in great pain but was put in the main chair with his leg on a stool. Biddy put Albert on her knee, and Joe spoke first:

"We must start with a prayer to God for delivering our dear son home to us. Thank you, dear God, but us thanks can never be enough for this miracle of healing."

"Amen."

"It is so strange to see this room after this long while," said Young Pip says after recovering from the journey down the stairs. "Nine months away and we hardly came here when we were in Chatham. But God has seen me right. You want to know all about my adventure? We'll go a bit at a time as I remember it.

"Here we go! Fletcher and I waved to you as the *Majestic* sailed. She sailed well, probably because my father had worked on her," which elicited a loud cheer from Joe. "Calm sea and we was soon loaded to the brim with men, more horses and provisions sailing out from Southampton. The Farrier Major, Mr. Turner, talked to us about handling horses on ships which we'd never done before. We would try to get them on deck in turns, so they got some fresh air. But, oh dear me, the smell!"

"What was your regiment? Were they all on the ship?"

"No, the Fourth Light Dragoons regiment was on its way back from India. Not what we were told by the Recruiting Sergeant. Below deck we farriers all worked together, and I got used to the gentle sea, so did the horses. Overnight we passed the Rock and we was soon in Malta."

"I can't make nor head nor tail of this grogaphy—no, geography," said Joe. "Where's this Rock? I must be awful dull."

"Joe, that's where the salt pot was. The Rock of Gibraltar. Do you remember?"

"Oh, yes, of course the salt pot, not the mustard, dear chap. That was Malta."

Young Pip continued: "We led all the horses on land, though there was not a lot of green grass there. Every day there seemed to be more ships, more officers, horses and more men. We farriers cleaned out the *Majestic*'s hold, throwing the muck into the harbor and then loading on fresh straw brought from England. Fletcher and I became friends with three other farriers: Willis, Hardy and Freeman, all from the north of England.

"We were in Malta for ages, and April turned very hot and kept on getting hotter in mid-May and then June. That's when I wrote to you. It was all so busy and hectic, there was no time, apart from no paper as so many soldiers wanted it. Late June it got so hot soldiers were fainting in their wool uniforms. Nobody cared much how us farriers dressed, so we went around bare-chested. Then our skin burnt which was very painful. We threw buckets of water over the horses or led 'em to the beach to walk in the sea. The island got so crowded and so hot we was glad to sail again for a port called Scutari, but everyone talked about the Crimea which was further away still. And that was when terrible things began to happen. Can we rest awhile afore I tell you of that?"

"Of course, dear old chap, why not have a little sleep? Old Pip and I will have a walk with Albert for an hour and when you wake, we'll go on if you'se ready."

Young Pip was soon asleep. Biddy went to the kitchen to prepare a meal. Joe and Pip walked down the track towards the Battery which they could see in the far distance. Albert was put in his perambulator and pushed alternatively by Pip or Joe and he too fell asleep quickly.

"You are right, my dear Joe, it is a miracle he is back with us. I have been reading of the disease, the loss of life and everything that makes a war so terrible for a man."

"Well, dear Old Pip, I have not had the pleasure of fighting for our Queen. But some of those men I worked with at the dockyard had, and their tales made my skin crawl, and made me very frightened for my dear son."

"But what is he going to do when he is back to health?"

"Ah. A very good question. Maybe he'd go off and be a gentleman like you, Pip? Maybe even a preacher as before he went away he was very friendly with God."

"Well," said Old Pip, "any friend of God's is a friend of mine."

"Me too," said Joe, laughing so loudly that Albert stirred.

"God forbid he become a gentleman, certainly not one like me. I have told him so."

"You has done what?"

"Joe, old chap, don't you remember? Becoming a gentleman broke our friendship. I was so foolish about it, and you thought a blacksmith couldn't be friends with a gentleman, didn't you?"

"Well, Pip, you was a different person, wasn't you?"

"I know and that was the trouble," he said, with tears in his eyes. "I felt as though I lost you, you whom I loved more than anyone else."

Putting his arm round his dear friend, Old Pip said, "I often think of how you helped me when I was ill. I remembered the larks and my sister's Ram-Pages, but at that time wanted to forget it all."

"Oh, my dear old chap, we was never going to lose our friendship."

"I am not so sure, Joe. Sometimes I think meeting Miss Havisham was a curse, and being a gentleman an even bigger curse, but the biggest curse was that convict interfering in my life with you."

"No, Pip, these curses were all part of your edication. Life is the only teacher and now you are the fine fella we all knew you would become."

"Oh, my dear Joe, my thanks. You are so wise. I must tell you too that Estella and I are forming a new relationship. I will stay at her house tonight again and will do so always while I am here. You have enough to handle with Young Pip and with Albert."

"Oh, well, I s'pose it matter not, dear old chap. She's back from her travels, then?"

"Yes, and she has much to tell but I think we are now very close as we have not been before."

"Like what?"

"I will tell you both by and by, but not yet as I need to see how it works out, though I am sure it will. Truth to tell, I am in a slight daze."

"Well, bless me, my dear old chap. Losing Beatrice like that was so terrible. I'm sure you'se very lonely. I was when Georgiana died. A man needs a woman in his life and in his bed. You deserve the love of a good woman, and from all accounts Miss Estella has turned over a new leaf."

"And I was under it? " Old Pip asked, and they both laughed heartily.

"Let's go see if yon farrier is awake."

On their return they saw Biddy on the bench with Young Pip, who was eating a pie and drinking beer from a large mug.

"Are we ready to listen to our hero, then?"

"No hero, Old Pip, if you'd seen what I've seen—terrible, terrible. The ship was crammed as we sailed east carrying more than double what was intended. Soldiers, lying on deck. Horses, cheek b' jowl in the hold. And the sun; I never thought I'd see a day when I wished it would rain. Three days into the journey, both men and horses started to get sick.

"Let's go in so I can get comfortable in the chair."

He put his wounded leg on a stool and continued. "The horses were tightly packed in and hated the heat, though we used pumps with water from the sea to cool them down. Third day out of Malta it was, soldiers cried out from below deck. The ship's doctor was called, and word ran around the ship that two men had the blue death."

"What's that, son, a blue death?"

"Biddy, that is the most frightful disease; its proper name is cholera. It is called the blue death because when its victims die, their skin turns blue—well, blueish."

"When that rumor spread, I spent as much time as I could with the horses, but I got up in the hot fresh air then as much as possible. But then soldiers started to die."

"What do they do with a body on a ship?" asked Joe, "nowhere to bury them?"

"They were thrown overboard, Father, seemed like dozens and dozens of them. Heat made their bodies rot. Then it was the horses. Then a frightening storm, like we've never seen in Kent. Lightning and thunder non-stop. The sea got very angry, too. The five of us were below deck with the horses for an hour or so as the storm raged. When it finally subsided, we could see that several horses had collapsed. Dead. We pulled them out from the other horses to get the carcasses up on deck to throw them overboard. After that we usually had two or three horses die each day."

"We has seen some bad things, Old Pip, old chap, ain't we, but this is the devil's work."

"But things just get worse. Once we sailed into port, Scutari it was called, those of us who weren't sick got up on deck to see land where we so badly wanted to put ourselves down. But the sea inside the harbor was full of floating bodies of horses and men, drifting in from the sea after the storm. Fearsome sight."

Young Pip stops there, tearful, looking into the middle distance.

"Don't go on, now, dear boy."

"No, let me go on. We were now worse off than when we were at sea. For the wind then blew like a gale for four days and the ship was not docked, as the port was not big enough. Smaller boats vessels were used to get us from ship to shore."

"Now, Uncle Pip, you are a gentleman. How could officers who are gentlemen be so, well, rather stupid?"

"What do you mean?"

"There was officers demanding we get their horses ashore, impossible with the wind and the sea. We tried: and I saw at least six lovely animals, cavalry horses, drown as they were pitched off the vessels by the sea, and I had to help try to rescue them which was impossible. It was far too rough for them. Imagine! Trying to load a beautiful animal just gone through that terrible journey, without exercise for days, on to a small boat which is rocking fiercely. I didn't understand it."

"Common sense is not evenly distributed in the population, among officers no less."

"Oh, I saw that. Then we landed, but immediately the five of us were transferred to a group called the Light Brigade."

"Why Light Brigade; were the horses small?" asked Joe.

"No, the Heavy Brigade carried more armor, almost like the knights of old."

"Now I must rest again. More tomorrow."

Old Pip came back from Numquam House the next day to take Albert for a walk. He knew his conversation with Joe would have been relayed to Biddy, so he did not need to hide his love of Estella. He knew, however, that Estella and he were going to have a conversation soon about Albert, and he was in two minds whether Albert should be with them in London. On balance, he thought, leave things as they are, and we will come to see him often.

Joe was in the Forge, Biddy doing her chores. This was a picture of family life, except for the son of the household, waking up, grabbing a stick by his bed, hobbling to the bedroom and getting himself down the stairs.

Joe heard the noise and hurried inside to the stairs, where Old Pip was sitting with Albert.

"There you are, my son. You came down all by yourself, too?

"Yes, I am better. But now, let me get this story over. We landed in early July at this port called Scutari and later that month we were shipped to a place called Balaklava. This was a dirty town, full of all manner of villains and whores mixing with a vast numbers of soldiers and horses, but we were camped outside the town. It was mid-October, and getting very cold at night, and the tents weren't good. Us farriers lived with the horses, of course, and the Dragoons had arrived from India and they joined the Brigade. Their farriers spoke of an excellent journey, without any disease. They was lucky."

"How many cavalry were now in the Brigade?"

"I suppose we looked after six hundred or so horses, Uncle Pip, as I counted them one quiet afternoon. It was a wonderful sight to see such beautiful animals. Of course, some of them were new to cavalry work as so many died on the voyage. But let me tell you what happened.

"The Light Brigade was assembling and the five of us farriers was walking toward the assembly. Riding past us was a man on the most beautiful horse I have ever seen. He, not the horse, had a huge mustachio and a hat with a large feather sticking out of it, obviously a commander as he was being followed by three others senior officers. He passed us, but then turned around and bellowed: 'Who the devil are you lot?'

"At that point Major Turner replied: 'these men are farriers to the Brigade, my Lord.'

"Truth to tell, I didn't know it was Lord Cardigan, the Brigade Commander. It could have been the Archbishop of Canterbury for all I knew," at which Joe howled with laughter.

"That afternoon, we were all at the top of a valley, and all of us five were fussing with the horses readying them as the officers wanted. We had been checking their shoes all the time as cavalry horses can't ride unshod."

"The noise all the time was ear-blowing. Big guns going off, men shouting—then there was a silence, followed by a bugle and the Brigade rode off to the top of a valley a mile from where we were. What a sight they were as they disappeared to the top of the valley. More shouting, and another few bugle calls and we could hear the Brigade riding down the valley. By the sound of the hooves, they was breaking into a full gallop, sounding like far away thunder.

"That much we could hear, but then the boom of guns, but us could not see from where we were waiting for the Brigade to return so we could clean up the horses. The noise of the horses galloping was growing less intense but there was more boom, boom of guns, from the enemy, I supposed. And it was so. We waited and waited. Then up from the valley and over to us came several frantic rider-less horses, followed by a number of the cavalry officers, some with wounds. I saw one lying over his horse as it cantered back to us. We were running around catching the horses and tying them up as best we could."

"Then Major Turner told us to bring our pole-axes and our tools and we ran with him up the top and then down into the valley, more than a mile. It was a dreadful sight. We could see the killing as we ran down the valley. Officers were screaming, horses were limping around, many were dead. I saw one officer pull his pistol and shoot hisself."

Biddy and Joe both started to weep as they looked at Young Pip with admiration and love.

"It was terrible, terrible."

He paused with tears in his eyes, "but we had work to do.

"Major Turner was walking round with his sword and his pistol killing horses that were dying. The five of us were ordered to take the shoes off the dead horses, as they would be needed, and put them in stacks. It was all confusion, what with the smoke of the guns still in the valley and the smell—oh, the smell of dead men and horses.

"I was de-shoeing one horse that was still alive but with wounds on his neck and an officer came up to me and told me to cut off the hoof of his dead horse nearby, a strange custom. So, I got my Pole-axe and with one blow severed the hoof and the officer wandered away with it.

"But then it happened. I don't really remember this, but Fletcher was very close to me working on another horse, so what I tell you now is really his story of what happened.

"I was working on the hind hoofs of a brown horse, de-shoeing it. That I remember. Major Turner came up to finish the animal off and was pointing his pistol at its head. I remember that too. That moment, the horse kicked, I was flung in the air, Major Turner was knocked down, his pistol went off and the bullet from his pistol went right into my ankle. The pain was so great I fainted."

Biddy howled in anguish. Albert shrieked at her noise and Old Pip comforted him.

"Oh my dear boy, what a terrible thing."

"At least you're alive," said Joe, "and that's the miracle."

"I was alive then, but only just. I fainted twice, but Fletcher carried me back up the hill. I don't know what happened to my axe. He saved my life. Doctors there attended to the officers, most of whom were far worse off than me. I was given some grog, and some bandages after they pulled the bullet out as they patched up my ankle. Fletcher came by when I recovered; that was when he told me what happened.

"Later that evening, Major Turner came to me, lying in a tent, and told me I'd be no good any more for the work, that I had done a good job there, and he handed me some papers saying I was discharged, and that I should get myself on a boat going back to England.

"Just like that. My war was over.

"I got on a cart full of wounded officers going to the port at Balaklava. I was in terrible pain. I was allowed on a ship returning home with the wounded men, of whom there were hundreds from all the different battles, officers, infantry, everyone. I was given some help on the ship.

"They changed the bandage once, but to try to stop it getting infected, a doctor poured whisky into it. I thought I'd die: the pain was as bad as when I got shot. But I got off at Southampton where there were what seemed like hundreds of vessels, what with the war and so on, and luckily, I was told of one returning to Chatham. With my uniform and my wound to help, I was given rides from there, though I walked as best I could from All Hallows."

"Who would have thought we would have such a brave Gargery, a hero," said Joe

"No, Father, I am not a hero, once again. I am just very fortunate to get home to my family when I think of all the dead men I have seen—cholera, battle, and other diseases. I don't know what Hell is really like, but war must be as close as we get on earth. God must have protected me, and I intend to serve him as a preacher."

"Whatever you choose, my son, I think God will be very pleased to have you alive."

XII

Old Pip spent as much time with Estella as he could, sometimes disingenuously telling Jaggers of his need to support Young Pip and his son Albert, though he was in fact seeking time to get back to Kent. One Monday in early February he arrived in the office, wishing Mr. Jaggers a very hearty good day to which the old lawyer replied that he doubted whether he would find any health or happiness this year.

"You look tired after your long excursion, " he added with a slight grin.

"Oh really? I've had a wonderful time with my son Albert down in Kent, all the while helping my family cope with a severely wounded Young Pip. He is very weak and has been discharged from the service of Her Majesty, not that he was a deserter. A bullet clearly struck him in the ankle, and little medical help was available on the battlefield, according to Russell's reports in *The Times*. I do need to visit an apothecary to take potions to him in Kent, if I can have your permission."

"Punishments for deserters are very severe of course, but I am glad he does not fit into that category. At least this is not a matter for your troubled conscience, Mr. Pip," said Jaggers, with a continuing smirk.

The wily old lawyer had long conjectured that Old Pip wanted to be with Estella, much to Old Pip's confusion. To try to cover his embarrassment, Pip raised questions about the abolition of transportation, the use of prisons for incarcerating criminals, some of the uses of transported individuals becoming pioneers, and the significant question about how to get prison punishments to fit the crime. That long diversion done, he asked:

"Have I your permission to get to Kent with potions for the wounded young man?"

"Of course, my dear Mr. Pip," he said, grinning from ear to ear, "I will keep the pot boiling."

Old Pip could not contain himself.

"Mr. Jaggers, may I take you into my confidence? Estella and I will probably marry in the next few weeks. I'll say no more about how our relationship has changed. But I would like you to know of this eventuality."

"Why probably?" he said without the least hint of surprise. "Surely you have been destined for each other *tempore quo non extat memoria,* or as we would in English, from time immemorial?"

Repetitive reminiscence is one of the properties of lovers who, through memory, indulge it and renew the excitement of their love. Such was the case when he told Estella of Jaggers' remark, a recollection he was to repeat regularly to her great delight.

When he returned home, Old Pip said:

"I told him you and I would be living together, but he said marriage seemed perhaps unnecessary at our age. So our secret is out. He warned me about the legal side of marriage, by concluding the discussion with thoughts like these, as I remember them, but in this manner."

Old Pip continued, imitating Jaggers:

"'Marriage certainly seems to me over-rated, my dear Mr. Pip, myself having never married or been tempted to do so. But bear closely in mind the legal rights conveyed by marriage. Put the case that the state of matrimony is hedged about by many laws. The body politic cares not a jot nor tittle as to whether married people love each other. It is interested solely in the property rights marriage entails which are not guaranteed to those who are mere partners.'"

As this imitative account continued, Estella could scarcely contain her mirth.

"Marriage, Mr. Pip, does offer protections likewise. Nevertheless, after a lifetime of courtship, there or thereabouts, you should be very happy. Give Mrs. Pirrip my best wishes for your marriage, if she is still on speaking terms with me," at which the pair of them collapsed with laughter on the settee.

The idea of defying convention reflected the wild unruliness of their passion. However, they married quietly in St Bride's, Fleet Street on February 14th, 1855, without family or friends, with only John Wemmick as a witness. They celebrated by going to the opera that night to see a performance in London of Verdi's *Il Trovatore*, and the fierceness of Leonora's love brought tears to Estella's eyes, though Old Pip was more dispassionate, except at the Anvil Chorus which stirred him, as he knew how much Joe would have loved it. Their life became full of energy throughout the year.

They erected a small memorial to Molly in the garden with the legend around it 'Molly Magwitch' and the date of her murder.

They took the packet-boat to Dieppe for a week, a town which, as the guidebook suggests, was a meeting place for people of distinction.

They attended lectures and thus talked with interesting people afterwards, such as John Ruskin and his support for the Pre-Raphaelite Brotherhood, and decided to consider seriously having Millais paint Estella's portrait. There were concerts, too. Estella read voraciously, especially George Eliot, wondering how a man can write with such sensitivity.

They tried to hear John Stuart Mill when they could. Old Pip was beginning to be regarded as more than just 'up and coming' after his dramatic debut. He was beset from time to time by the 'hope-not' situation in which Jaggers finally retires or dies, but he was also taking some civil law cases, particularly in a brief for Charles Bradley, a tobacco manufacturer.

They did not neglect the family, especially Albert, though whether he should come to live with them was constantly left unaddressed.

✤   ✤   ✤

All that year Young Pip had begun to recover. By the autumn, the shattered bone had finally welded itself into some sort of shape, by the end of 1855 he was walking with a stick and an odd gait. Joe took him to Chatham to tell Preacher Whitehouse he was ready for training, and arrangements were made for him to start when he felt comfortable with riding.

After a solid lunch one Saturday, with Old Pip calling over from Numquam, Joe announced his decision:

"The overseer from the dockyard left a message at the Bargemen. He said they'se were recruitin' for men to work on a new ship. They'se building something new with new tools, too. Biddy agrees and I'll start in the New Year. Young Pip 'ere don't need me now."

"Well, good for you," said Old Pip. "You'll have to learn new ways of work, I expect."

"Me too. What larks, eh?"

Biddy seemed reluctant but wanted to support her husband.

"My Joe is now sixty years old, but very strong and eager to work," she said to Old Pip that afternoon. "He liked the challenge of the work, you know."

"I could see that. He's not a sentimental soul, though capable of great love, and our religion has taught him to look at every person as one of God's children and, in a straightforward way, he tries hard to practice what he believed to be true. It's lovely."

"Yes," said Biddy. "He tells me of his conversations with fellow convict workers, and he tried to conceal how horrified he is at the tales he hears of violence and anger and brutality."

"I am sure he feels God's blessing on his skills too."

"I love him for all that, though his aches and pains are terrible at times. His knees have begun to creak, his feet get sore easily, and his memory gets worse."

"I tell you, Biddy, his employers are lucky to have him because he is a calming influence in a turbulent place of work, I'd be bound."

"He seems to love riding to Chatham each day, too."

"We'll see whether he likes it or not," confirmed Biddy. "We'll get another horse, I think, so he won't need to stay overnight."

Not that Joe had any intention of staying overnight, his main luxury in life being to snuggle up to his wife before they slept— after they prayed, of course, kneeling on those aging knees at the bedside.

After that conversation, Old Pip wanted to put forward an idea to his namesake now coming to the end of his long convalescence.

"I feel like some fresh air after that lunch. Young Pip, let's get out again: It's a fine day, but we won't go a long distance."

"Let me pick up my coat and my stick, uncle, too."

As they began their walk, Young Pip was exultant over both walking out and enjoying the marsh countryside. He would always be lame, not the best physical condition for an itinerant preacher, but he was a determined young man and, once again, he reveled in God's willingness to save his life at Balaklava for what he believed would be His purposes, so he never complained about his injuries.

"I am very glad," said Young Pip, "that I don't live in countries on the Mediterranean. I got hotter than I had ever been there, sweat pouring off me, and how the soldiers managed in their red uniforms is beyond me."

"Ah, you had the misfortune to see the Mediterranean from that awful ship. Estella and I have both travelled there, to Venice and Naples, not together I might add, and I was once in Athens. Some day you must visit them in April and September when the climate is excellent for an Englishman."

"I hope so. But now I just think of my good fortune and God's grace. I have been doing some training as an Exhorter in this area of Kent. I will be accepted as a Preacher as soon as that is done. I'll be nineteen soon and I'm ready."

"What is an Exhorter?"

"It is more like practice preaching. I tell the audience, so far just my companions in the Circuit, of the perils of sin and the joy I have felt in knowing God and Jesus His Son. It is quite difficult. How can poor people believe in God when they are starving or being persecuted by a bailiff or a landlord? But I am learning, though I follow Preacher Whitehouse's script, but I listen to Alice LeBone too.

Young Pip continued. "It makes no sense that women are so demeaned; they have souls like men. Alice manages to speak to women in a thoughtful special way which makes me somewhat envious. For it is no use just getting up and speaking, you have to persuade and exhort."

"That is true in the law too. If I am in court, I have to persuade a jury, and I exhort them too, usually to find a person, adult or child, not guilty."

"Learning to preach God's word will be an important stepping-stone in my life, now I am no more able to be a farrier. I've been riding to Chatham regularly and to the villages in Kent, West Malling, and Wateringbury to the west, Hollingbourne and Harrietsham to the east, more as a listener than a preacher. I hear of some of the problems the poor laborers on the farms are having and I am getting to know those and managing to avoid issues of rick-burning."

"Of course," reminisced Old Pip. "I heard all about that rick-burning which started with riots said to be led by a Captain Swing. My own father might have been involved and perhaps transported, or perhaps hung. Joe never knew what happened to him, or he would have told me, but south-east Kent where he had lived was the center of it.

"I know of your commitments to preaching, of course, but I must still make you a proposition: That you come and work in our legal practice, before you finally commit to preaching. Jaggers is getting old, and I need a junior partner, someone I know and trust. I know Jaggers will accept you. I will pay for your training and support you."

"Oh, Uncle Pip, how wonderful and how generous. But it is an opportunity I cannot consider in line with the conscience you once stirred in me and what I now believe was my experience of conversion when I first heard the Preacher.

"Why don't you believe?"

Conversation paused, as the two men then quietly sat on an old boat where Old Pip started to whittle a stick as he used to do on their walks years ago.

"Most of the people I met when I was a young gentleman were believers only in name, just so as they could then get married or be buried by the Church," he said, laughing.

"I think the Church was also rather oppressive and on the side of the rich. I admire your sense of direction toward the poor, which I try to help in a different way. I did not grow up in a religious climate, so I am surprised, now, when Joe says grace before we eat. I have never really encountered religion."

"There is always time. Oddly, in the Crimea, my beliefs were sorely tested by the death and destruction of men and animals and I could not believe God would want that, but He leaves us to our own fates, so belief in Him must be sincere and voluntary."

"True. A year or so ago, I asked a lawyer acquaintance why he believed in God. He replied that if it isn't true, it doesn't matter; and if it is true then I will have got into Heaven."

"That's too crude, funny though it is. What is so wonderful about the simplicity of my beliefs. God wants us to be perfect. God has good expectations of us, not just you."

Putting his arm on Old Pip, Young Pip continued: "You should listen to a Methodist preacher. But in my life's work, I want to save souls, not just keep them out of goal."

"That is an interesting way to put it—you sound like a lawyer. But while I think you see it as your religious duty to help the poor, I hope as you get older you will find more practical ways to do that than preaching. I just want you to think about your life in terms of the good expectations I urged on you, but not to be hemmed in. Joe may need help at some time."

"That also does depend on you, Old Pip, I suppose. Albert is now three years old and, if he stays at the Forge, then Joe will have an apprentice. If he comes to live with Estella and you, now that you are married, then I may have to help Joe. But God's will be done."

"Estella and I have been thinking about Albert for some time now. Should I take the young boy out of his life now for a life that would be very different? But we are going to have to decide. I even worry about taking him away from Joe and Biddy as he seems to be the apple of their eye, but they have each other, of course. Look, the rains are coming on, we must get back."

They hurried back to the house along the marsh track. The older man took the young man's arm on his right side, away from the damaged left leg, but together they reached the cottage door, soaked from the pouring rain.

The day after this conversation, Young Pip went to Chatham and was told that reports from the villages in northern Kent were excellent and that he could begin a career as a preacher, whilst continuing to learn the Scriptures.

A few months later on a Sunday in April 1856 Young Pip preached in All Hallows. The life of an itinerant preacher in Kent proved quite exhausting for him, but Boney, still his faithful companion, eased the journeys by making him feel as comfortable in the saddle as a horse can. A large dog ran across his path one afternoon, and many a horse would have shied and tossed its rider into the ditch. Not Boney. The incident brought back the memories of Old Pip's account of coming back to the cottage from Numquam with Beatrice.

Many of the villagers that Sunday were out walking, watching the ducks perform their rituals or the children playing with a hoop. Joe and Biddy came to hear their son and the audience was growing apace. Perhaps fifty souls were there. The Vicar was nowhere to be seen. Young Pip set up his box.

He was not an original preacher, yet, having like many a preacher, he had developed a formulaic address, emphasizing or repeating phrases, dependent on audience responses. Crowd participation depended on exhortation and persuasion. Young Pip had not yet held an audience in the palm of his hand. His voice carried well, but it was not the trumpet of John Wesley. Yet.

"I bring you the word of God." he began, leaning on his stick, standing on a box and letting his voice go full bore.

"Amen," replied the gathering crowd. Josiah Steppings' voice rung out above all others with his Amen, no doubt in anticipation that many of those in the crowd had not yet decided whether to take a drink with him, but, hearing his voice, they might've.

"God loves all his people, especially those in need. Let me tell you how I came to know the Lord Jesus. I heard Preacher Whitehouse here when I was but a few years old. I held no religious beliefs, but the warmth and love of God penetrated my soul, such that I rushed home to my family bearing the good news. You can do the same. Bring His word to His people, my friends.

"But, make no bones about it, we are all sinful, my brothers and sisters, but God will save us from our sins before we meet him in the angelic hereafter. We can be perfect through His love. It is so simple and so calming, just to feel the love of God.

"Do you feel it now, brethren, just give your soul up to Him. We all go about our labors, sometimes frightened, sometimes worried, sometimes hungry, sometimes unhappy; but, my brothers and sisters, underneath are His everlasting arms."

A chorus of Hallelujahs broke out from the crowd.

"Believe me, I have seen unhappiness in its worst form, in war. Men broken, dismembered, shocked beyond recall, but His everlasting arms are always there. Who can receive God's love? Is it just for the halt, the lame and the blind, or is it just for the rich man or the Queen of England? No, my friends, no, God's love is for everyone, especially you and you and you, adult or child, man or woman," and he made his point by thrusting his finger at individuals.

The chorus of Hallelujahs developed as a crescendo of noise such that additional passers-by or folks on the Green came across to hear what was being said.

"And who can preach His word? Not just vicars and bishops and archbishops, but you and you and you. We can all bear witness to God's love as a child, man, or woman.

"All can preach, all can love, and all can learn the word of God. You suffer, you who work in the fields. Jesus can save you. Love of God will sustain you. He is our Master, our Christ, and all we are brethren. We have seen rioting, fires and the disturbances in the villages, all within living memory. You may have put these rick-burners into jail and upon the treadmill, but they will come out the same devils they went in!"

"But, my friends. But!" he shouted in a loud voice, "but, if the Grace of God gets into their hearts it will change them. Nothing else can do it," he said, deliberately enunciating each word, and then, *sotto voce*:

"Nothing else can do it."

The audience cheered: "Well spoken, Preacher," said Tom Friendly, amid general murmurs of assent.

With voice raised, he continued: "All sorts and conditions of men are listening to its message with gladness of heart. I can hear your hearts beating with it. Our message has won its way among the people because it speaks to our deepest human instincts.

"Throughout my short ministry, I seek my way to the heart of things, to bring men and women to a true relationship with God. In Kent we are going to succeed. Amen, Amen."

The crowd shouted its Amens, and an alarmed dog barked from a cottage garden, and across the village other dogs joined him in a cacophony of barking sympathy.

An excited audience then swirled around Young Pip, congratulating him, asking whether he will be holding services and prayers.

Josiah shouted: "Three cheers for our hero-preacher Hip! Hip!" and most of the audience responded.

"You must be a soldier hero with that gammy leg," said Enoch Middlemiss.

"I am no hero," said Young Pip, "though I was at Balaklava."

"Oh, my dear son," said Biddy. "Tears in my eyes. To think, a son o' mine up there preachin."

"I am so pleased you have now heard me properly, my dears, but it's not original, you know. Oh, and I have had a message earlier to meet with Preacher Whitehouse to discuss my progress so I must now go to Chatham directly. But first, Father, how are you enjoying the new work? You've been there for a few weeks now."

"I am awfull dull, as you know, but these new tools and ideas, they excite me. I'll tell you all about it later."

"Very good, Father, I will see you tonight at supper."

While Young Pip was exhorting the faithful, Old Pip was walking to Little Britain when Wemmick called him from behind him. They went together into the office where they found Jaggers, looking very weak, slumped in his desk chair with a mountain of briefs in front of him.

"Good heavens, Mr. Jaggers, where did all these come from?"

"Now I have a competent partner, Mr. Pip, I have instructed Wemmick, as he well knows, to refuse nothing. I am sure you'll manage most of these, though there is one case I want to take on. It's an interesting story, as it mixes the criminal with the civil and may involve different courts.

"Six months ago, Lord Binding, an obscure Anglo-Irish peer, came to England with his third son on their way to Cambridge where the youth was to study theology. Both were walking down King's Parade when an elderly don, Dr. Horace Dingleberry, approached him, asking if he was Lord Binding.

"On receiving an affirmative answer, the don assaulted the said Lord with a walking stick, resulting in injuries to my lord's left elbow which, as he was left-handed, meant that he was unable to undertake many of the pursuits that are the privilege of the well-bred and well-endowed.

"The assailant, however, was Lady Binding's much older brother, she whom, let it be said in Gath if not in Ashkelon, had suffered severe mental and physical ill-treatment at the hands of the said Lord for many years. However, the son, The Honorable Marmaduke Binding, a rather repellent youth in my estimation, then snatched the walking stick and began to beat the elderly don about his person, not knowing of course, that this was, in fact, his uncle.

"For Uncle Dingleberry was at least twelve years older than his sister, Lady Binding. He had refused to go to their wedding as Lord Binding's reputation as a blackguard reached even the denizens of King's Parade who, as we know, walk up and down daily, exchanging gossip about all and sundry, especially the University Chancellor, presently the Prince Consort. Binding had often been a topic there, though he was far away in his bogs in Ireland.

"Dingleberry had received only pleading letters from his sister about her ill-treatment which, because he was a don and not a man of means, was unable to do anything about it, and in any case thought that perhaps she was making a mountain out of a molehill.

"What a tale! So where's the litigation here?"

"First, there are charges and counter-charges on assault and battery against the Honorable Marmaduke and Dr. Dingleberry. I am retained in the learned doctor's interest, for there is also the civil complaint by the noble Lord that Dingleberry's stick prevented him from riding to hounds on Michaelmas Day, the only day of importance in the selfsame Lord's calendar.

"But Dingleberry has entered a civil complaint against Lord Binding's treatment of his wife and wants me to call the three sons as a witnesses. Dingleberry, of course, has no money, so I will be acting pro-bono. I am happy to be so engaged as I regard the Irish peers as primarily responsible for the Irish condition, which is a blot on civilization. So, Mr. Pip, as time goes by, you too will take cases where you feel obligated to act without payment.

"You may ask what motives I have for taking this particular case. I have referred to the Irish peers' responsibility for the troubles that beset that country.

"But I am also dismayed and disgusted by what I hear of Binding's treatment of his wife, something which, if the gossip in my club is true, is also the case of the Duke of Monmouth who treats his wife like a horse, demanding her obedience. There is one case, as I recall, in Ireland, where a man locked his wife in her bedchamber for seven years before he died. I suppose I am trying in some small way to assuage the guilt I still feel about Estella and how she suffered at the hands of her husband.

"This domination of men over their wives has to be stopped. Though not married, I can see just how uncivilized and barbaric it is. There must eventually be laws which enable a woman to have command of her own property: If that were the case, she could act independently, and these male brutes would not be able to dictate to wives according to their every whim.

"Of course," he continued, "I don't really expect to win much for the learned doctor, but Binding will pay through the nose for his counsel and, with a bit of luck, I will find grounds for an appeal and I will then make it difficult for him to settle without crippling damages, so he will have to continue to throw his money at his lawyers. The publicity will force him to do so. So, though my motives are both pure and impure, my conscience is as clear as a summer morning.

"I anticipate the bankruptcy of Lord Binding with the greatest pleasure."

"Wemmick, I think our senior is becoming quite a radical, though we always knew he had a touch of the rascal in him, did we not?"

"Enough of that, Mr. Pip. Enough too of Binding v. Dingleberry, and Dingleberry v. Binding. I think we can say, can we not, Wemmick, that Mr. Pip has proved an excellent addition to our practice and on this day:

"I propose to make him a full partner with me to share in the gains and losses of our work."

Wemmick applauded loudly, and Old Pip, somewhat shamefaced, said: "After all my comings and goings, I am delighted that you place such trust in me, Mr. Jaggers. I am, of course, thrilled to accept and I know this will please my wife immensely."

"It is my great pleasure," replied Jaggers, "to know that this particular ship will be well manned, but age will out, and I have been losing some of my previous skill and for that matter my enthusiasm for this work. I do hope to retire soon at some convenient point as yet to be determined. But I of a mind to search for another young lawyer who can in the longer term become a partner. What say you, Mr. Pip? This new legal training assures me that such a man will be well versed in cases and the law but lack any real experience in dealing with the kinds of unfortunates around whom we have based our practice."

"I have had some words about this possibility with Young Pip whom you may have met but don't know. Unfortunately he is entranced with Primitive Methodism, as he was before and after his Crimea experience, and is already a preacher. He can therefore be ruled out."

"Rightly so," said Jaggers, "one Mr. Pip is quite enough for any practice," and they laughed quietly at his comment.

"Yet the problem remains. Our practice continues to grow, especially as Mr. Pip's advocacy is earning a name for himself. I suggest that we all search our contacts and see if we can find anyone suitable. I know my personal lawyer, Mr. Courtisone, will have an extensive list of lawyers he knows, and I think he has been involved in giving advice on legal education. I suggest that we gather together some names and conduct interviews when and if we have any possibilities. I don't feel to be in any great hurry on this matter."

XIII

The wheels of the law grind slowly and the Binding-Dingleberry had been making very slow progress through the courts, which seemed to Old Pip and Wemmick to be an indication that the old lawyer wanted to delay his retirement, unable to tear himself away from a splendid career. Meantime, after a year or so on the road, Young Pip had an urgent note from Chatham in early February 1857, which spurred him to go quickly to the preacher's base where plans for a chapel were well advanced.

"Welcome, friend in Christ," said Whitehouse. "First, my reports of your preaching are overwhelmingly satisfactory, as they were when you were a mere exhorter, and we are brothers, not a hierarchy, so I want to give you advice rather than orders, as is the practice in Romanism, I believe.

"I want you to consider carefully an approach I have had from our chapel in a town called Salford, an industrial center in the north-west of our country. I gather there is terrible poverty there with these new factories bringing in people from the country to lives to which they are unaccustomed. But they have asked me whether I can nominate a colleague to come and share the Lord's work there, someone who would value or would need a different experience.

"I firmly believe, my friend, that you would benefit from a few years in that situation, after which you could come back here to Kent, experienced in preaching the word to people who are distressed. I ask you to consider this because you are not married, will be twenty years of age soon, and you have built a strong reputation here. I think the time has come to pick up a different challenge.

"I myself anticipate moving elsewhere but will serve wherever the Lord wishes."

"That is most exciting, and my inclination is to accept immediately. When will this be?"

"Take time for travel and to part with your friends and relations. Trains are in the offing, but I suspect the coach would be satisfactory. The Chapel there expects you, hopefully by the beginning of February."

"I am at God's service. Anno Domini 1857 is clearly providing new challenges. I will leave as soon as I can. You know, of course, that I have been recovering from my injuries in the Crimea, so my family is constantly worried about my health and general demeanor. Salford is far away and it will be difficult for me to see them frequently, and, of course, they are not getting any younger."

"I understand, and may God be with you. Let me know as soon as you have decided."

"That will be quite soon, I assure you."

Young Pip hastened to the cottage after his meeting with Preacher Whitehouse. He realized when he arrived and dismounted that the faithful Boney was now quite old, and she had just carried him around Kentish towns and villages for a few months, but he would not need her in Salford. Without dismounting he surveyed the cottage and the surroundings with a look of great pleasure, riding around to feed his nostalgia. Biddy came out to greet him. Albert was inside drawing.

"Oh my darling boy, how good to see you again after all this time. You'se a wonderful preacher."

"Well, thank you, my dear."

He dismounted and hugged her, saying, "Oh, I love hugging you, but is my father here, as I have news and I want to tell you both?"

"Can it wait? As you know, he's been back in Chatham working on the ships. I hope he gives it up soon. He's getting too old for that hard work, you know."

"Oh, but that's him riding down the track, isn't it? Oh, and a new horse."

"Yes, poor Betsy died, and he now has a lively young mare he calls Josephine, after Boney's wife, that emperor not your horse, so he says. I'd know him anywhere, he is such a good man, your father."

Joe dismounted hurriedly and asked: "Is everything all right? I didn't know we'd see you. I thought you'd be off for a year. So, what's the news? There must be news, or you wouldn't be 'ere."

As they walk into the cottage, Young Pip on Biddy's arm, he said:

"The Preacher wants me to go to Salford; that's up north with those new factories and the like with very poor people, worse than our field laborers here, I shouldn't wonder. I can't refuse, and, in any case, I am sure this is God's will."

"But not a for a day or two, eh, Young Pip? That will mean we don't see you so much, but then we got used to that when you was in that war.

"But let me tell you about Chatham. They wanted me back there, as you know, just for this new ship they're building. Biddy and I thought about it. They said to just come, but we didn't want to live in Chatham as we remember the last time."

"He's doing it for the money, of course. I'm not moving to that Chatham again either, so we got Josephine so Joe can ride to work every day. Takes a couple of hours, of course."

"Excellent name for her. How is it going, father?"

"I so enjoys the ride, 'cept when it rains. I can really enjoy the countryside before getting into the hammer and tongs of the ship-yard. Mind you, they've got some very powerful machines and those new tools. It'll make short work of the ship building. We'll have her afloat in two shakes of a lamb's tail, you see."

"Well now, Joe, we have the rest of today, because they don't want you Saturdays. We'll go to chapel tomorrow, though we haven't built it yet. Alice's front room is large enough for our little community. We'll have a feast Sunday night afore you'll go to work Monday, and Young Pip leaves."

"That's wonderful, my dear Biddy. You'se such a good wife. I do like the work so much. I'se seen so many new things since we did the *Majestic*. New cranes pulling up large sheets of steel, new kinds of tools—very 'citing. I'd love to work wi'em. Us both having new adventures, right, Young Pip?"

Sunday dawned and Josephine was hitched to the trap and the family drove off to All Hallows for the service. Preacher Whitehouse was apologetic about Young Pip going so far away, but God's will must triumph over personal predilections. On Monday, Joe saddled up Josephine and took Young Pip before dawn to the Blue Boar Inn for the coach to London.

Young Pip had a good journey to London watching the fields before crossing Tower Bridge to the Bull and Mouth where he was to get a coach to Birmingham. From there he would get a coach to Manchester, though he hoped steam trains might soon be available at a reasonable cost. The journey to Birmingham was uneventful. After mounting the train for the Manchester part of the journey, he began a conversation with a lady he found most attractive.

"Greetings," he said after spending a while wondering whether he should begin a conversation. "My name is Philip Pirrip, but everyone calls me Pip and I am on the way to Salford to begin a ministry."

"How nice to meet you. I am Harriet Middleham on a visit to my grandmother in Manchester."

Harriet was a factory owner's daughter from Birmingham. She was tall and elegantly dressed with a fashionable bonnet, a lively countenance, but surprisingly travelling without a chaperone. After they had exchanged these pleasantries and began talking, a plump well-dressed young man seated near them offered to change seats so that they could converse more easily for which they were both grateful.

"How kind of you, sir," said Young Pip. "Now, Miss Middleham, tell me more about you."

"Harriet, please. I am a free spirit, I suppose, and much less disciplined than a preacher."

Young Pip gradually became both disturbed and exhilarated by the conversation, not least as he was unused to talking with a woman, except in his work as a preacher. He felt stimulated by the warmth of her body seated next to him which he tried to avoid but which the train necessitated.

He was shortly overcome with his ineffectiveness as a conversationalist and the narrowness of his perspective on life.

"How come you walk with a stick?" she asked.

So after he had rehearsed the story of his injury, she began to talk about political issues, of the country's relationships with Russia and Turkey such that he was quite swept away by her informed comments, about which he knew little or nothing.

"My goodness," he said, "are you a diplomat?"

"Good heavens, no, but I am interested in politics, especially in terms of women's rights. I supported the Chartists, and of course, they were assaulted in Manchester on a peaceful protest. Have you read Mary Wollstonecraft's essay on how poor women were treated and how important it was to vindicate their rights?"

"I fear not. Should I?"

"I think so, as you will meet some distressed women in your work, I am sure."

His head began to reel with this blizzard of knowledge and experience, ranging from Jane Austen to Trollope's recent novel, and he realized he was in fact uneducated.

He asked what she planned to do and was startled when told that she was certainly not going to get married and that she was contemplating starting a broadsheet for women. She was obviously a woman of independent means. After a diatribe about men, and how weak too many of the women in Jane Austen's work were, she was almost whispering in his ear so that their travelling companions would not hear, she turned to religion. There, at last, he was on surer footing only to find that she had abandoned the official church and was interested in John Wesley, but also in what she called Unitarianism which Young Pip had never heard of.

So she instructed him about problems with the divinity of Jesus and how she had attended Cross Street Chapel in Manchester at the initiation of this set of beliefs. He felt simply dumb in the face of this literate, passionate and beautiful woman and to whom he felt a strong attraction.

He descended from the train in Manchester first and she held his hand as she got down.

"So," said Harriet. "Your chapel is in Queen Street, Salford. I will try to come down to hear you preach one of these Sundays. My grandmother has a house on the Oxford Road here, and I am sure I could use our carriage."

She then shook his hand firmly and walked from the station to where a carriage was waiting. It would be too much to say that young Pip was smitten by her, more in awe and totally astonished that a woman, yes, a woman, could be so articulate and how ashamed he was that she talked about ideas and politics about which he knew so little.

Meantime, Young Pip met with the elders in his chapel. They prayed together and talked about their work with the poor people who left the country to bring their labor in the factories. Young Pip was allotted a quiet room in a house near the Chapel which was private and furnished well enough for his needs.

The owner was Septimus Parsonage, a devout widower, not a Methodist, but who was rich enough to allow the Chapel to use its rooms as he had bought a house in northern Cheshire at the pretty village of Northenden with its impressive ancient Elizabethan church. Young Pip was invited for lunch and before he left the village he walked to the church which he thought admirable with its extensive graveyard where the graves indicated that it was the local church of the wealthy landed Tatton family who lived at nearby Wythenshawe Hall. That visit made him wish that his austere religion could have at least something of beauty woven into its dogmas and practices.

However, this desirable arrangement for his accommodation meant that he ate in the common room of the chapel. As yet he was the sole occupant of the widower's house, more preachers being anticipated.

The following Sunday Harriet was in Young Pip's small congregation and she talked with him afterwards.

"I have told my grandmother of this interesting young preacher I met on the train and I am bidden to ask you to meet her if your pastoral duties allow. Perhaps we can go now, and I can bring you back before your lunch. She is interested in your ideas about God."

"I would like that very much," said Young Pip, and they set off in her carriage.

Harriet was polite enough in the carriage to ask more about his life, not just his injury, and she heard all about the Kentish marshlands, the cottage, his uncle and his family. She appeared fascinated, but then asked about the people he was meeting in Salford, and she interrupted him to bristle with anger once again at the treatment of the poor women in the factories.

However, the meeting with Harriet's grandmother did not go well. The old lady was not interested in his ideas at all but was a truculent and passionate defender of the Church of England, its historical role since the Reformation, and its significant place as an established church to which, she argued, every person owed loyalty. On these topics she lectured Young Pip severely.

He listened but decided not to engage in religious argument with this elderly rich opinionated woman, anymore, he thought, than he could talk with the Vicar of All Hallows. He was very polite, but felt disengaged, looking at Harriet from time to time to try to gauge her reactions. But the lively Harriet he had found so interesting became quite dumb. When the grandmother was done, Young Pip thanked her profusely. No further conversation would develop, so he took his leave and Harriet rode with him back to Salford.

The return journey to Salford with Harriet in her carriage was one that Young Pip regularly looked back later in life with unbounded astonishment, in terms of the topic and its aftermath. Harriet immediately began talking about women's rights in much the same way as Mary Wollstonecraft the author had apparently done, ignoring the conversations with her grandmother. Then, she asked:

"How old are you, Pip?"

"Just twenty."

"I am twenty-two. Have you ever been in love, Pip?"

"No, I have not as yet met the woman I wish to marry."

"Ah, marriage is a prison for a woman, and why should a woman suffer so?

"She has to do everything at her husband's behest; he commands any property she brings to a marriage and while a man may have a dalliance with another woman while married, it is unthinkable for a woman to do so. I will never marry."

"That would be a pity," said Young Pip, fascinated but anxious to shy away from the topic. "I see what you mean, and I do understand it. I've been lucky that my parents were partners in everything."

"Let me be frank, as I suspect you are a man of intellect not bound by outdated assumptions," Harriet continued.

"You are an attractive, handsome man and I am a woman capable of passion in my own way. What conventions are there that hinder the two of us from enjoying a union?

"I would very much like to spend the rest of this afternoon in a bed with you simply enjoying ourselves without any pretense that we will have a long-lasting relationship, merely an encounter in which desires of the flesh are satisfied.

"Miss Wollstonecraft and others have advocated what is called "free love," and I agree with them. I want to enjoy my body with a man but not in a marriage-bed."

Young Pip fell completely silent, simply unable to grasp such a radical notion which went against all his assumptions about relationships between men and woman which, he had assumed, were part of civilized behavior, whether held religiously or not. He could comprehend this not as an extreme hypothesis but as an actual invitation, and he felt a stirring in his body that he had not previously enjoyed.

She continued:

"You see, Pip, my guess is that you have not yet experienced that special close relationship with any woman, being of a religious bent. I would have thought God would have wanted us to enjoy our bodies as his creation. If I am not mistaken, behind that mask of propriety you have, I see a man humming with desire which you do not see how to combat.

"But that is as natural as any other feature of human life, to love and be loved, not in the romantic sense, but just as a fascinating bodily activity exemplifying freedom. Put your religious conscience to sleep for a while and take me to your lodging.

"I will teach you to enjoy a woman without there being any commitment to each other."

The carriage was rattling across the cobbled streets of Salford. Young Pip suddenly allowed himself to imagine being in bed with Harriet. His knowledge had been enriched by his life with sailors and soldiers in all manner of crude ways which he found both distasteful and, at once, desirable. He had seen plenty of whores on the streets in Balaklava and knew that his fellow men had indulged themselves. He had not, but not because he did not desire them. He turned to look at her, his body starting to respond eagerly to the possibilities.

"Would you like to see where I live?" he asked gently.

"Oh yes," she said with a smile, "and where you sleep, I hope?"

"It is just along the street here. When we get out of the carriage, would you tell your driver to go somewhere else and return say, in an hour?'

"Macintosh," she said to the driver, "you will put us down shortly, and we want to continue our religious discussions in private, so please take the carriage to the park and return to the house in two hours."

"Yes, Miss."

"Two hours, remember."

And they went upstairs.

Back in Kent at Numquam House that June, everything had been prepared for lunch with the Gargery family. Joe and Biddy had never seen Estella's home with its sad past, but it was now enlivened by her marriage to Old Pip. On arrival, Joe asked to see the memorial to Molly which had fascinated him when he first heard of it. He had not been acquainted with Molly but was surprised by her elegant looks at Young Pip's wedding, and he wondered simply how it was possible for a woman of such low birth to emerge like a butterfly from a caterpillar.

But then he thought of how Old Pip had become such a butterfly as he moved from being a blacksmith's apprentice to being a gentleman. Not so surprising after all. So they all went to admire the simple stone put there at the place where she died.

"How tragic," said Biddy, "but what a beautiful tribute."

Joe touched the stone in awe.

"Yes," said Estella. "I suppose it is a heartfelt tribute to what she did for me, not just a remembrance."

As they sat down to lunch, Old Pip decided it was time to take the bull by the horns.

"Albert," he said, as the others listened, "I am your father. You are five years old. Since your dear mother died, you have been living with our dearest friends here, and I have been visiting you regularly. But now Estella and I have this house and lodgings in London. How would you feel about making some changes whereby you come to live with us, but, just as I have been doing with visiting the cottage, you could come and visit Joe and Biddy regularly."

"That's very hard for me, Father," and he began to weep quietly.

"Look'ee here, my dear young chap," said Joe. "We love having you with us and we will never not want to see you up with us having some larks. No hurry, is there, Old Pip; we will be ever so pleased with whatever decision you and your father come to."

"No hurry at all, just so as we think about it."

Now that the topic was broached, everyone was relieved. Joe and Biddy were thrilled to have him but knew there was no long-term future for Albert with them, and they also knew he needed an education, which was nigh impossible in All Hallows. Old Pip no longer had any concerns about Estella's thoughts on the matter. She liked Albert and would want to have him with her, thinking of arranging tutors for him. But no one thought a decision should be hurried.

"Have you heard from Young Pip?" asked Estella, changing the subject.

"He had a very interesting journey, he said, though he didn't say why, did he, Joe?"

"No, it was just a short note, saying he'd arrived, and he had a room in a house near the Chapel. I s'pose he's starting with his preaching too. I 'spect they speak different up there, so I hopes they understand him."

"Oh Joe," said Biddy, "the word of God can be understood by everyone."

"No, I meant the way he talked with his, what's it called—oh yes, his accent. His accent might be a problem for the dear old chap. I met some convicts who I s'pose were speaking English, but I didn't understand a word."

"Well, he will be away for a long time, though not as long as he was at the war, I hope."

"Now, how's you getting on with your lawyering, Old Pip?"

"Well, I had that case I told you about when I was first in court. Since then, my stock has improved, I think, as I find people coming specially to me. At first, I was puzzled how they found me, but then I realized that people come in droves to the courts to watch. Many are simply excited by the details of cases which are often terrible. Others don't have anything else to do, so I suppose the reputation of a lawyer gets around.

"The important thing is that Jaggers is very pleased with me and we are on the lookout for a young lawyer to join us, and who might eventually become a partner. Jaggers is looking around among his lawyer friends for such a person."

"And I would like to think he can find someone quickly," said Estella, "so that my dear husband can get more help. He is working too hard and I sometimes fear for his health."

"Yes," said Old Pip, "I do feel the stress of the work, and I get various aches and pains from the stress."

"Now, look'ee here, Old Pip," said Biddy. "You take care. You're not as young as you were."

"That is true, of course, by necessity." They all laughed.

After another walk in the garden, the Gargerys headed home in the cart to leave Old Pip and Estella able to take an afternoon nap which had become a staple of their lives together.

Meantime the room at the widower's house in Salford had witnessed a coupling of two very passionate people, one a novice, the other an established practitioner in the arts of making love all through the summer. They would always lay together for a while afterward and Young Pip was bemused by how much she had praised him and how satisfied she was with him as a lover.

Certainly, he felt a tremendous sense of relief that he had now experienced making love with a person who was both sensitive to his inexperience and enjoyable as a woman. She did not over-power him, or simply await his interventions, but led him through it as though they were partners, her caresses of his body being as delightful to him as his feelings he had when he fondled her.

"I could sleep a long while now," said Harriet one afternoon, "and most people say it is the man who goes to sleep immediately afterwards."

"I feel like talking to you, Harriet," said Young Pip.

"Go ahead, but whatever you do, don't say thank you, or I will feel like a whore expecting a payment. It is a natural expression for us both to enjoy freely. It really is fun, you know."

"I know. It is wonderful and each time, it is more delightful than before. All right, I won't say thank you, but I must say how much I have learnt about myself. It is like waking from a long sleep, for I have put my desires out of mind as I thought they were not appropriate for a preacher. I now don't see why, though I am sure I would be castigated by an Elder, were I to mention it. But when we were in the coach coming north I was very surprised by how much you talked about of which I was ignorant. I do need to learn from you."

"What sorts of things?'

"You have mentioned Miss Austen and Mr. Dickens and I would like to read their work, but you are also well versed in politics, are you not? I have been blinded by my preacher training and think only in religious phrases. My life has been bound by growing up in a country family, and while I have spent a year in a series of tragic events too horrible to talk about, I am not educated."

"Why so horrible?"

"Do you like horses, Harriet?"

"Yes indeed, I ride my horse Brodie each morning when I am in Birmingham."

"Ah," he said, raising himself up on his elbows and looking into her eyes. "I mentioned this briefly in the coach, but not the detail. I was on the battlefield after the Charge of the Light Brigade where three hundred and seventy horses died.

"As a farrier, I was instructed to take the shoes of the dead ones so they could be used again. I lopped the foot off one horse with a pole-axe as a souvenir for the officer who owned it. And when we arrived at the port earlier, the water was full of dead horses and men, brought in by the tide. We threw dead horses off the ship in twos and threes when the journey proved too much for them."

"Oh, please Pip, say no more, how terrible," and she threw back the bed clothes and moved down the bed to kiss and caress his wounded ankle, stroking it lovingly.

"Your body is so beautiful, you know. I must find a place where we are completely unaware of others. Here I am, half-expecting your Elder to come in any moment. I will certainly see you often for us to talk politics and literature and it can be in a tea house or walking in the park, not every time in bed.

"I want you to be careful, though. If you feel you are falling in love with me, then you must tell me so that we can end our love-making, though we could continue to be friends. I must be free and totally unencumbered to enjoy my body when and where I feel."

"I understand that, Harriet, but let us meet in the tea-house across from the Chapel in Queen Street, say, next Tuesday? My meeting with the Elders are on Mondays and I am preaching again each day."

"I won't come and listen to you there, but I will see you next week. My carriage will be here directly, so I must dress and go downstairs."

XIV

A bowl of cherries adorned the table of one of England's most ruthless monarchs, famous for his six wives, and for the breach with the Pope which created the Church of England. Eating them, the King commented that they must come from the Garden of England. The Gargerys did not hail from Kent's lush valleys to the south that became famous for their fruit growing, but they came from its northern marshes. Unlike Kent, the countryside in the north of England had been emptying its population into towns. In 1781, the Scottish engineer James Watt had invented a steam engine powered by coal which changed the world. In their thousands, people moved to the new factories, located near mines where coal could be drawn from the ground.

By 1860, however, Young Pip had lived with the trials and tribulations of urban life in Salford for almost three years, and he felt satisfied he was doing good. Disease was rife: Smallpox and scarlet fever carried off children and adults in large numbers. Poverty was a perennial challenge. Conditions in these towns were far, far worse than what he had experienced in Chatham, not just because families lived cheek by jowl in these concentrations of houses, but because the factories emitted the effluents of coal, filling the air with sulfur and other poisonous fumes, especially dangerous to human life when fog from a river kept the muck from rising into the sky.

Salford was no exception. People lost their independence when they moved from the country. They could not grow their own food, or even get their own water. Their lives were controlled by others, the wealthy factory or mine owners. Dark satanic mills dominated the landscape where he valiantly tried to pursue his mission. In a dirty slum near the Emmens factory children ran around naked, sewage littered the street, men and women lay drunk, with a couple of men obviously dying on the pavement.

They met for lunch and he described those conditions to Harriet, who rapidly changed the subject.

"Let me look at you, my sweetheart," she said. "I suspect you are like your father, tall with reddish hair and beautiful blue eyes, such a splendid and adorable creature."

"Thank you, darling. I have to put all this poverty behind me. I am reading ferociously and am awash with questions I need to have answered from the novels or such political essays that impress me."

"For my part, I am thrilled to have a pupil so eager and so intense about the plots, especially those which addressed problems of the poor. I have found an appropriate place for our bedtime available at any time in the home of my widowed friend Cecilia, yet we have reached a wonderful equilibrium where we are both anxious not to overdo our passion."

"And that makes our union the more delightful."

"I think I am coming to see you with more intense desire than I expected."

"Me too. I would marry you if you wanted children."

"But without my having religious beliefs?"

"I am convinced that religion is a glue that would hold a marriage together, and I am very much in love with you. I suppose, at almost twenty-four years old, I am also now relishing my work and I am now a more important and senior member of the Circuit of Primitive Methodists there."

"Ah well, let us enjoy each other while we can."

One Sunday morning, Pip was preaching outside a factory owned by Messrs. Emmens and Engels. The audience was responsive and getting off his box he greeted a foreign-looking gentleman in a frock coat:

"Did you enjoy my preaching, sir? May I know your name?"

"I am Friedrich Engels. You speak vell, I tink. But such matters do not interest me. *Auf Wiedersehen.*"

Young Pip wondered why this German man had stopped to listen, but assumed he was the owner of the factory, trying to find out whether he was saying anything seditious. As a preacher, Young Pip often talked with beggars, drunks or prostitutes.

A woman beggar accosted him one afternoon, as she sat at the corner of Queen Street near the Chapel. Her condition was terrible, with torn clothes, and smelling of dirt and vomit and much else. Being a preacher, he could not afford to give much, very little other than a farthing here or there. He stopped and asked her for her name.

"Annie Smith," she replied.

"Tell me, Annie, how come you to be in this condition and to be begging?"

"Oh, sir we's in a terrible plight. We used to rent a lovely cottage at Sharston Farm down near Northenden from Squire Tatton, where my Cyril worked the plough. But time was hard, and friends in the village were coming to work in the new factories and Cyril and my two boys thought we should try it.

"We was shocked when we came as the house was awful, the water from the pump was filthy. Now my husband could work horses on a plough as good as any man, but these new machines frightened him, and then, a month ago, he made a mistake and the machine cut off the top half of his middle fingers on both his hands, so he could no longer work, and he was dismissed.

"Of course he couldn't pay for a doctor and his wounds got very bad.

"Did you try using honey? When I got this leg, that helped."

"He dipped them in honey, but we only had a little and no money to spend on it. His hands swelled up something terrible and the poison went up his arm. I could not find work, even in the factory, as we can't leave the boys for long. So I started to beg. But then he got very sick and he died last week, I suppose from the poison. I'm trying to avoid the workhouse as they'se terrible places. All I can do is go on begging and I manage to collect just enough to buy a bit of food. What will happen to us when winter comes? "

"Come with me, Annie, and we'll get you some food and some clothes."

Although this was only one person, Young Pip saw it was a symbol of women's distress. He took her to his lodgings, brought out his small box for his money, and found two shillings, making her promise to get food for her children. He was so stirred by this experience, though it was not the first, that he decided to press the Elder to see how they might start on relieving these intolerable burdens on the poor, rather than just giving them the Word.

A month or so later, he had finished preaching and saw a very pretty Irish girl standing as if waiting for him.

"Young lady, how might I help you? I was glad to see you in the audience again."

They look at each other with an amused sexual interest.

"What is your name?"

"My name is Magdalena Burns," she said in an accent familiar to those in the south of Ireland.

"My family came from County Cork last year as we were starving, and I want to know about everything here in England. I work in the factory yonder, with my three brothers and my father. I'm the youngest at nineteen."

Young Pip looked at her and found her dancing green eyes and her translucent skin enchanting. "Well, now, it's a fine day for Salford, so perhaps we can take a walk together along the Irwell here and you can teach me about Ireland and its troubles."

Young Pip was now a man of sexual experience, so he viewed women like Maggie with a vivid imagination.

"I'd like that, and I went to Mass earlier."

"Do you go every day?"

"Well, you know, you just get into the habit. When I was younger I thought of being a nun, really to get away from home. I had this holy period when I was ten but as soon as I discovered boys, that was over. But are you one of those dissenter people?"

"Yes, I suppose so. People call me Preacher, but my name is Pip. But, you know, while I value my beliefs very strongly, I want people to come to God in their own way. So, call me Pip."

"Now that is strange, to call a priest by his Christian name. Jesus, Joseph and Mary, I'd be run out of town if I called my priest Francis, which is his Christian name. We are very, very strict in our religion."

"Tell me about it, because I really don't know. I know you worship Jesus' mother and that your church is ruled by the Pope, apart from that not much."

They were now walking by the river, but it was no romantic spot. Fish had long since left its murky waters, now more like oil than water. The smell was noxious but then, people had long since gotten used to it. Dead cats or dogs were regularly seen floating down the Irwell which was, in truth, an open sewer.

"Well, I can tell you, Pip, I don't like this confession. I am happy to tell God of my sins in a prayer or two, but I don't like sharing them with my priest. If I think unholy thoughts, I keep them to myself. God knows about them, so why tell the priest?"

"Surely, you don't have any unholy thoughts. You are too young and, if I might say so, too pure."

"Ach, not at all at all. I think some unholy thoughts when I watch you a-preaching."

"Now then, don't embarrass me. Tell me more about confession."

"I go to church and into a special booth: There is a screen between me and Father O'Grady. He asks me about my sins and what I want to confess. So, I think back on my week and of all the things I think are my sins, and he listens. You'd be surprised by the number of sins I collect in a week, calling someone names, arguing with my father, lots of things. Sometimes he will give me advice, but then he cleanses me of my sins and tells me to say prayers, like twenty 'Hail Mary's.' But the priest wants to get into your thoughts, not just what you do."

"Confession sounds like an inquisition."

"Oh it is. I talked with my friend Patty last week about it. She doesn't tell the priest about anything that he might think unholy, me neither.

"You see, Pip," she said, stopping to look at him, "I am having these unholy thoughts about you at this moment, but I am not going to tell the priest. I love coming to watch you speaking."

"I am having thoughts about you too, Maggie, but I would call them delightful and pleasant, not unholy. If either of us were married, then it would be a great sin. But just feeling attracted to someone, I don't think that's sinful."

"The way I've been taught, I feel so guilty about admiring you or, as we say in Ireland, fancying you. You have beautiful eyes, you know. Oh, I should not have said that. And I'm even more guilty because you're not a Catholic."

"Maggie, we know there is no future for us, but let us enjoy each other's company and walk together like this sometime."

"We will, but it must be very secret. My father would kill me if he knew if I was walking out with a Protestant. And I'll try and keep it from the priest. He's supposed to keep what he is told secret, but he'd blab to my Da, I know."

A clock struck five.

"Oh, my God, I'll really will get killed," she said, running off.

Two days later, Young Pip was out walking along the river towpath and met Maggie on her way home from work under a bridge. It was dusk.

"Maggie, how wonderful to see you again so soon. Oh my, you look so lovely, so, if I may so, so desirable."

"I hate you! I hate you!"

"What DO you mean? We hardly know each other."

"I hate you because, oh, Mary, Mother of God, I love you."

Young Pip put his arms around her to give her some comfort and she kissed him with passion.

"You don't know, do you? I have been watching you from a long way off. I once followed you home, thinking I would ask to come in.

Then I decided I had to speak to you to see what sort of a man you really were. I only meet young men from Ireland; a few are all right, but many are drunks.

"You looked to me like a man sent from Heaven for me. Sweet, strong, gentle, lovely hands for stroking me, and," she chuckles, "very desirable indeed."

"My dear, dear Maggie, that is such a compliment. You are so desirable but that is not possible for you, is it?"

"No," she said, "Don't go on. I so desire you, but it cannot be. Neither my family, nor my church, nor my country will let me love you. When I talked to you first, I thought, it will be all right because he will turn out to be a nasty fella, but you weren't. You are now everything I would want but cannot have. This is the end."

Suddenly, Maggie let out a shriek. "Watch out, Pip, Run! Run! They're after you. God bless you. I love you."

She ran away from the three men running along the towpath toward him. Pip started to move quickly, but his leg prevented him from running. So he stopped, turned toward the men, starting to explain, but father and brothers landed blows to his head and stomach.

"You dirty Prod, you think you can have our Maggie, eh?" A hard blow felled Young Pip, and they all began to kick him on the ground.

"Stand up and fight, you bastard English."

"He's not going to fight. He's a weakling, he's a preacher. Look at him and he's only got one leg. Leave him be, the peg-leg."

"Now, see here, preacher boy. You ever so much as look at my daughter again. You see that river there? That's where they'll find you, along with the cats and dogs, maybe sewn up in a bag if we have the time."

They walked away, glancing over their shoulders at him. Young Pip got up, checked himself, brushed himself down and hobbled slowly to his lodgings, thinking of Maggie's beautiful face and breasts, realizing that he must soon find himself a wife.

At their next meeting he told Harriet about these encounters, so the topic soon turned to the treatment of women.

"Do you not see, Pip, how this Annie has been having to bear the burden of her family? She says her husband was the one who wanted to try out coming to the factory, but why would he do that? We don't know precisely what their conditions were as a worker on a landed estate, but I'd surmise that if he was a good worker, the landowner would look after him."

"That's a bit harsh," said Young Pip. "Wasn't the husband just trying to better their lot?"

"Yes, but I am sure women put their family before themselves and that means they put up with their husbands making all the decisions. I decided when I was quite small, maybe around the age of ten that I would never marry.

"Now, about your Irish flirt. She was trying to find her own life, free from family and church. I admire her. But don't be shocked at this, once she kissed you like that you should have taken her straight home to your bed as your mutual desire was clear to you both.

"I am sure you imagined that didn't you? That would be the ideal, would it not? Intense passion? Exploring each other's lusts and wants? But then, of course, social customs make that impossible and she could become pregnant with all that implies."

"Certainly, I desired her but she was too vulnerable, a nineteen-year-old child."

"Fiddlesticks, Pip. You see how women are defined? 'Vulnerable,' my foot.

"She just wants your body. She wants you to have your way with her. She told you so. What was it you said she said, 'very desirable'? But as a man you think that she should be restricted as you have at the back of your mind some nonsense about preserving herself for her marriage to some drunken Irish lout which will probably be a dreadful experience."

"I stand corrected," he says laughing, "I do understand your point of view, my dear Harriet, and it would have been nice, but quite out of the question.

"But tell me, how does your mother's life fit into your free love perspective?"

"My mother, bless her soul, was ruled by my father. No independence. After I was born, thank God she could have no more children, or she would have died of exhaustion. Their marriage was empty, so unlike your parents. No common pursuits, except those that he wanted to do. She did all the usual things, needlework, playing the piano and so on. I thought she would die of boredom. She read a little but was not really interested in novels or in politics, maybe just because he was. Nor is she now, poor dear."

"Tell me more about your family. How did you handle your father if he was such a tyrant?"

"It was not easy, but as I was his only child he doted on me, especially as I was a daughter. He had no interest in finding me a husband as he liked having me at home. I realized that if I married, I would be trapped like my mother, so I was very pleased that I did not to have to deal with young men.

"But, when I was about eighteen, I became aware that he was looking at me as though he wanted to possess me. He never actually tried, thank goodness, but I hinted to my mother that he seemed to have more than a fatherly interest in me. I think their bed life had been over, possibly since after I was born.

"After I told her she made very strong efforts to seduce him to get him away from me. It succeeded as they seemed much more affectionate afterwards. But think of it, Pip, how a man, my father in this case, can so warp the natural affections simply because he has the power to do so."

"So, how did this all change?"

"He fell very ill. I went into his study one afternoon and he was sitting his chair, unable to speak. He could not get up; he was paralyzed. That lasted several months before he finally died, and we found out he was quite rich. It was too late for my mother, but I was then nineteen without any entanglements. He left me well-to-do. So, Pip dear, I am a free woman, slightly self-indulgent. You are teaching me to be more active, more practical, in pursuit of my beliefs."

�֎   �֎   ✷

Although Young Pip's ministry was progressing well in the terrible conditions he encountered, his relationship with Harriet was now so deep they might have felt like marriage, for all their different protestations. He for religious reasons: She to be free. For the New Year 1861, Harriet said she needed to visit her mother in Birmingham and Young Pip went to Kent, though he waited until Christmas was over.

In the marshlands of Kent, Sunday feasts in the cottage had been saddened by Young Pip's absence, but there he was now, once again with the family.

"He seems different; very confident somehow though I can't put a finger on it," said Biddy.

"I suspect he's been seeing a woman, but don't ask him," said Joe, "he'll tell us when he's ready."

That possibility loomed in the background over the celebrations, especially as Young Pip was so joyful. He took strongly to Albert and they walked and talked and played, and Albert was thrilled, given his father's absence.

After a splendid Sunday of laughter and games and walks, Joe had left for the Chatham dockyard early the following morning by the time Biddy, Albert and Young Pip were having breakfast. Young Pip was very uneasy that morning for reasons he could not fathom, perhaps because he had not said goodbye to his father properly, or, because he had to get back to Salford very soon.

He took Albert out on the marshes, looking for tadpoles. When they got back, Young Pip sat with Biddy on the bench together when a stranger appeared in the distance galloping toward them. The stranger arrived, slightly breathless, and dismounted.

"Are you Mrs. Gargery?" said the stranger.

"Yes, sir, what can I do for you?"

"I am the dockyard manager. I fear I have very bad news. Your husband, Mr. Joe Gargery is dead."

Biddy and Young Pip looked at him in total disbelief. Biddy's face began to crumple, then she broke into an unearthly howl of dismay and disbelief. Young Pip staggered to his feet, grabbing hold of Biddy.

"How so?" He asked.

"I did not see the accident as I manage the dock office. But he was learning how to work on the huge steel plates brought to the new ship's side when a plate got loose off the crane and fell right on top of him. He was killed instantly."

Tears were now engulfing Biddy: "Oh, my poor lovely Joe, my best of men, my heart, my joy, my friend, how did you let this happen? Why did you have to go back to that filthy work?"

"It was no fault of Mr. Gargery's, and we are going to have to look carefully at those cranes. A plate fell the other day, but no one was underneath it."

"What?" cried an exasperated Young Pip. "You mean you had a major incident and did not examine whether it would be repeated? How irresponsible can you be? Why to goodness did you not find out about that before continuing?"

"We thought that was just a rare occurrence. We do our best to protect our labor."

"Clearly not enough."

Albert had rushed out of the cottage to Biddy, crying in sympathy and howling a child's cry when he was told the news.

"Isn't Joe coming back, then?"

Biddy picked Albert up and held him tight. Both were weeping. Young Pip was now more composed.

"Mother, my dear, this must be God's will."

Turning to the Manager, he said, "My friend, I realize this was not your responsibility. I am a preacher. My father Joe was the best of men. If I did not believe this was God's will, I would be exceedingly upset, angry even. How, pray, are we to recover my father's body?"

"Can I have a private word, sir?"

They walked away from Biddy and Albert.

"I have arranged for your father's body to be brought here immediately and I expect it within the hour, but it is not in a condition which you or his wife would want to see. These plates are very, very heavy; need I say more? I have given instructions for the remains of his watch and other light possessions to be packed separately. His horse will be attached to the cart bringing him."

"I understand and will try to convey the matter to my mother. I must try to be brave for her and trust in God."

"You have my very deepest sympathies and apologies. The dock owners have asked me to give you five guineas to help with the funeral."

"Thank you, sir, but that offer disgusts me. We are not yet dependent on charity. I bid you good day."

He looked up the track at the Manager riding away, unable for the moment to grasp what they have been told.

A cart approached bearing Joe's body with Josephine tied to the cart and walking behind. Biddy and Young Pip stood with Albert, all of them scarcely able to believe what they were witnessing. It was only yesterday he was here, large as life. The body was in a plain sealed wooden coffin which two men carried reverently into the house. Young Pip pointed to the table and they place the coffin reverently on it and departed.

"I want to see him."

"No, Mother; let's just remember him as he was, beautiful, loving and the best of men."

Young Pip and his mother held hands. Albert's hand was on Pip's right shoulder, and they each placed their hands on the coffin, while Young Pip said a prayer of redemption.

"Now he is perfect. We commend him to you, God. He's a really good chap, he loved You, and we think You'll like him."

At All Hallows Churchyard, two days later, the Vicar led the cortege to the grave. Biddy and Young Pip both want him buried in consecrated ground, and Methodists have no graveyards of their own. Old Pip and Estella acted as hosts and had invited guests to a wake at the Three Jolly Bargemen.

The crowd was large, consisting of some dock workers, Joe's customers, Herbert and Clara Pocket, Biddy's old pupils, people following Young Pip's preaching, and of course the lawyers, Jaggers and Wemmick and his wife who had never met the dead man, but knew how attached Old Pip was to him. Preacher Whitehouse and Alice Lebone from the Primitive Methodist fraternity in Chatham, which Joe and Biddy had come to enjoy so much, were there. It was a solemn, immensely sad occasion, as Joe was much loved and without an enemy in the world, except once or twice, himself. Leaving the churchyard the mourners assembled on the Green.

Young Pip spoke to the company:

"I never thought I would see this day. My father seemed immortal. I never knew him be ill. God has called him home, him being such a good man."

A loud Amen emerged from some of the audience.

Jaggers frowned.

Old Pip raised his eyebrows at his beloved wife next to him before speaking:

"All of us who were lucky enough to know him knew his qualities. He was always willing to put himself down, yet he was a person of very keen intelligence, and an excellent smith. Above all, he was capable of immense love. His love knew no bounds. But I must stop now, as my heart is faint at our loss."

There was a long moment of silence as each mourner thought about the dead man.

He then continued in a quiet, almost lonely voice: "Joe brought me up, and as he would say 'we was always best of friends.' He was steady as a rock in friendship, especially when I was very unsteady in it. I don't know how I will contemplate the world without knowing Joe is there, puffing at his pipe, hammering away at the anvil, or just being there, joyous, full of life and always ready for larks."

Murmurs of acknowledgment rose from the audience and then Young Pip concluded:

"You will all appreciate, I know, how difficult a time this has been, so we will leave you now and no doubt meet with many of you soon. I should have left on Monday to go to preach in the north, but I have sought permission not to leave till tomorrow, but my mother and I want to spend this evening together."

Later, in the Three Jolly Bargemen, Jaggers and Wemmick, Herbert and Clara gathered round Old Pip and Estella. Biddy returned home with Albert to grieve on her own.

Impeccably dressed for mourning though unknown to most people there, Mr. Jaggers then stood to say: "I am stunned by yet another tragedy; Molly, Beatrice and now Joe. As I get older, they become more difficult to bear. I particularly recall, Mr. Pip, when I came to inform you of your benefactor. The way Joe looked at me, and I caught his glance more than once, was intelligent and penetrating. I vividly recall his refusal to accept any money from the benefactor: Losing a child, he said, is not to be calculated in terms of money. But I don't think anyone else there quite saw, as I did, the steel in his character."

Herbert added his own eulogy: "Do you remember, Pip, when he came to our lodgings all those years ago? He had it ingrained in him somehow that he was inferior to everyone else, yet his good nature made him far superior."

"So what will happen to your son now, Mr. Pip?" asked Wemmick.

"A difficult question, John. Estella and I have been wrestling with this long and hard, haven't we, my dear? Now Biddy has lost Joe, to lose Albert too may well be devastating for her as she loves Albert like a mother. Then, of course, we are not sure how we might help Albert adapt to our lives. Once again, in the old phrase, our conscience makes cowards of us all."

"Pip, dear, it is whatever you want."

"But I don't know what I want," he said in an exasperated tone.

"Might the Bar be in his future?" said Jaggers quietly.

"Possibly, Mr. Jaggers, as long as he does not get saddled with great expectations, I am sure we can work out a way forward. But for the moment, he stays with Biddy to whom he will be a great comfort. Perhaps it is also up to her? Like Joe, I am feeling 'awful dull' about it."

XV

L eaving Albert in Biddy's care, Young Pip traveled back to Salford on the Tuesday with great sadness at the death of his beloved father. It was a bitterly cold month which deepened his low spirits. He had been chastened by his experiences as a preacher, especially with the two women. Annie Smith had shown him the weakness in his work, trying to save souls but being unable to offer practical hope. His distress at the state of the poor he encountered grew ever more profound. And now the loss of his father. He thought how empty Whitehouse's advice was when he urged the family long ago to pray for guidance. Against that, Harriet's radical views were constantly in reverberating in his mind.

The year moved on, but Young Pip remained critical on what preaching was achieving, if anything, and the topic was constant in his life with Harriet. However, at a meeting in the November of 1861, when the season brought extraordinary bouts of public intoxication with Christmas approaching, the three preachers himself included were sitting at a round table praying in silence. The elder then stood to speak:

"My fellow preachers. We are still witnessing the degradation of human beings, especially the poor through their consumption of strong drink. We in this Circuit have been preaching the word of God, urging our audiences toward perfection and holiness as a very high level of how we conduct ourselves. Many of our forebears, especially John Wesley, our founder, urged upon us the importance of sanctification, the use of our bodies and minds as God's vessel. We have spoken for many a year about temperance and how strong drink should be taken in moderation: yet, its evils persist.

"As our companion preachers in this north of England have done, the time has come, to campaign through our preaching for total abstinence. To put aside entirely strong drink as it undermines our quest for perfection, sanctification and holiness. I urge you now to preach in your Chapels and in the streets the vital significance of avoiding any drink. In God's name."

He had not seen Harriet since his return and was very excited as she had sent him a note asking him to meet in the tea house before his preaching.

"Oh my darling," he said with as much fervor as he was capable of, "your eyes sparkle, your face is as beautiful as Aphrodite's."

She smiled at him, touching his hand as he sat down. He bent to kiss her on the lips, the glares of the customers notwithstanding. She looked at him closely, and said quietly:

"I need you badly."

They took a cab to their meeting place and released their tensions with a fury they had not known before, their love blazing like a wildfire, for him releasing the emotion of his father's death and with which he had still to come to terms.

Young Pip had selected the big public house on The Crescent on a street with the same name in the temperance quest. He had the Elder's approval, and later that day he stood on the pavement outside the building on his usual box, equipped with pamphlets which he thrust on passers-by. A crowd gathered, and he looked at Harriet at the edge of the crowd, her smell in his nostrils, amid the dozen or so women who had stopped to listen.

"My friends, you cannot attain the perfection God wants for you if you drown yourself in the evil drink. Do not allow drink to lull you into a sense of well-being when your spiritual life beckons. My belief…" but he was cut short, as the door of the Crescent crashed open and two very drunk well-dressed gentlemen arm in arm cannoned into the street, belching and laughing, frightening Young Pip's audience. Both spoke English with heavy German accents.

"You see, my friends," Young Pip said, pointing at the men, "how terrible is the state aroused in you by these evil potions. I say to you …"

He was immediately interrupted by Engels and his companion Karl Marx, both very drunk.

"Achtung, Karl, here is der young preacher I spoke of."

"*Gott in Himmel*, but he is so young."

They both laughed uproariously and staggered around Young Pip.

"Now *mein liebling*, of what do you preach? The evils of capitalism?

"No, of the evils of strong drink."

Marx and Engels laughed long and noisily, attracting the attention of other passers-by.

"Good luck with that, *mein leibling*. Just remember that all of us in this very corrupt world, especially if you are poor, find an outlet for our misery in *Trinke, Trinke, Trinke*!

"But solace is to be found in God's love."

Marx came close to Young Pip and wagged his finger in his face. "Opium, opium, opium is what you are peddling to the poor. You think it is religion but what your preaching does is to get them satisfied with their lot. Excuse me," and he turned away to belch loudly.

"You talk of abstaining from strong drink when you give them the religion drug. One way or other, they can forget their deep troubles eh?"

"God's love is not a drug," Young Pip replied angrily.

Engels intervened, "Tell me, Preacher, how did you get your leg in that condition?"

"What has that got to do with God's love?" Young Pip answered, fuming as his anger built.

More soberly, Engels asked: "Be still, my friend. Was it in a factory accident, I'd guess, or on a farm with rotten equipment. Are you a victim of factory owners or landlords?"

"No, my friend," said Young Pip caustically, "I was wounded in the Crimea. I was a farrier and there was an accident just after the

Charge of the Light Brigade, and I was shot in the ankle which took five years to heal properly."

Marx guffawed.

Harriet stepped forward, jabbing Marx in the chest.

"Who do you think you are, sir, behaving like a drunken sailor?"

"This your woman, Preacher? " asked Marx.

"Don't be so foolish," said Harriet, "this preacher is a war hero, and don't you dare treat me as anyone's property."

Marx sobered up a little: "I apologize. I am drunk. Let me see some of your pamphlets, and in return I will give you mine," said Marx, searching in his overcoat pocket from which he finally extracted out a battered copy of *The Communist Manifesto*. They exchanged pamphlets. Marx and Engels walked drunkenly down the street arm in arm shouting, "Workers of all Countries, Unite."

Young Pip sighed, looked at the first page of the Manifesto and said to himself:

"This looks interesting," and to Harriet, "We must look at this together."

Two weeks later Young Pip was preaching, with Harriet again in the crowd outside the Crescent early on a sunny morning, and he spotted Engels and Marx as they walked toward the pub. To a small audience, he concluded:

"May God bless you all: remember, total abstinence is God's watchword."

He got off his box, and dropped his stick, which Engels picked up and handed to him.

"Thank you, sir, and a very good morning to you. I have been reading your pamphlet. It is challenging, and Harriet and I don't agree with much of it, but I believe in broadening my mind. So, my thanks to you and, I am sorry, I forget your names."

"Friedrich Engels. *Guten morgen*, Preacher. This is Karl Marx, my philosopher friend. And you are?"

"Just call me Preacher, or Pip which is my nickname, and everyone uses that name."

"And your lady?"

"This is Harriet Middleham."

"And a fine English beauty she is," said Engels at which Harriet got extremely angry:

"How dare you comment on my looks, or is this because I am a woman to be treated like an interesting piece of property as your friend did the other day?"

"My most humble apologies, Miss Harriet," said Engels, taken aback by the vehemence of her attack.

"I should think so too," said Young Pip, "yet I read the first part of your Manifesto. Very interesting. I don't understand much of it as I am not nearly as educated as you two."

"Mr. Pip, *mein liebling*," said Marx, "perhaps we can discuss it over a drink? Ah, but as you do not drink, would you both care to join us in the establishment over there which I think will serve us a cup of tea, or, if your religion will allow, a cup of coffee?"

"That would be a pleasure."

"Now don't take much notice of Marx, Herr Pip," said Engels, "He is always proselytizing."

"I may be a preacher, but I am always interested in new ideas, especially if they concern the poor. But be careful, Harriet is a scholar of some breadth."

The small coffee shop was run by a man who looked foreign to Harriet, and Marx established that he used to be a seaman, with origins in Constantinople, but evidently no longer with any faith in Allah or Mohammed.

"Oh, this is wonderful," said Marx. "Friedrich, do you remember that shop near the Bois de Boulogne where they sold coffee made in the Turkish style? I love it, and it is even better when you have had too much to drink. It battles with your stomach and your head. Have you tasted Turkish coffee, Mr. Pip?"

"Not that I am aware, as I don't drink coffee often; it is too expensive."

"I found coffee to be less bitter in Constantinople than in Paris," said Harriet, making it plain to the two Germans that here was a woman of parts who would be a likely foil for their arguments, whatever they might say.

"Really," said Marx, "I have not been to Asia Minor, but we must all have a cup and I will pay."

"Accept that," said Engels, "before he changes his mind.

"But let me explain some things to you. You know, don't you, that I, with others, own that factory where you preach. Some years ago, I became fascinated with what is now called the Industrial Revolution, how people had come from their country life to work in factories and in mines. My father allowed me to come and this factory and, while doing so, I wrote a book…"

"You wrote a book?"

"Yes, yes, about the conditions poor people live in here in Manchester."

"Let me know the title later," Harriet said. "I'd like to read it."

"I will bring a copy for you, Miss Harriet. However, I was utterly shocked, for the conditions were much worse than they had experienced in the country and they were dependent on the rich for everything. What I had thought in theory was worse in practice. A little later, I went to Paris and met Karl, whose work I had heard of, and we became good friends, in drinking as in our politics and our philosophy.

"That document you now have is written by both of us. People would call us scholars because we write long and often. We are both German; I am a Prussian and Karl is a Prussian Jew but we want to see revolution in all countries."

"Ah, so this is the message of your Manifesto. I read pamphlets but, the Bible apart, I used to read no books. But my dear friend Harriet has been teaching me and we are planning to read a political work, what is it called, Harriet?"

"*Du Contrat Social*," she adds.

Engels raised his eyebrows at this, but Marx picked up the conversation.

"I do not wish at this moment to get into argument with Rousseau or his followers. Allow me, please, allow me to try to explain to you as you both seem thoughtful people what we are thinking. All the time we are developing our thinking, of course, and I will soon publish a large book about our thoughts. I realize you are quite new to these lines of thought, so stop me if you don't understand."

"We'd like to hear your thoughts," said Young Pip, with a certain guardedness in his voice.

"First," said Marx, "throughout history, the greatest men are those who have worked for the common good. That would include some religious people, like Jesus of Nazareth. The greatest men are never the people who worked for themselves."

"Who defines what is great?" asked Harriet innocently. "I mean is Charlemagne greater than Caesar Augustus or do we take their word for it that they are working for others?"

Young Pip nodded his agreement about the problematic definition.

"Well, let us postpone what counts as a great for the moment."

At this point Engels was looking carefully at Harriet given her probing question.

"Now, religion," Marx continued, "expresses real suffering and is a protest against real suffering. Your audiences are all suffering from something; partaking of religion is the sign of an oppressed creature."

"Well, I certainly agree that people in my audiences are in pain which God's word seeks to remedy."

"But some people believe in God because it is fashionable, not because they are in pain," chimed in Harriet, "or are you saying that pain is necessary for religious belief without examining why people believe?"

Marx was slightly flustered by these interventions and since he rarely talked to a woman, apart from his wife, he was not sure how to keep his temper.

"All right, there are exceptions. Not just your audience. Most people are oppressed. But also, and this is very important to understand. We do not realize that we are all creatures of the social conditions in which we live. We do not determine our own consciousness, what we think and feel."

"You mean we do not have the free will that God has given us? I am not sure I understand that," said Young Pip.

"Put it like this. You grow up, shaped by everything around you. You think about things in the way you are raised. So, for example, if you convert to religion, which is a public form of consciousness, so now you think in religious terms. It is you as a member of a society, with all its faults, strengths, and so on, that make you what you are."

"But we all have choices, don't we?" asked Harriet. "I mean I decided to sit down with you three together. Was this not a matter of free will?"

"Yes and no. You only sat down with us because you are interested in our ideas and are able to contribute to them. Were you an outstanding fox hunter, Harriet, you would not be here."

"As a matter of fact, I do ride to hounds when I am at my Birmingham home, but I agree I am not an outstanding hunter. People can hunt and read, you know."

Engels was now getting fascinated by this woman, images of her on horseback swimming through his mind.

"Yes," said Marx uncomfortably, "but let me continue with a different thought.

"A person who has property usually seeks to satisfy their own selfish needs by getting power over others. Think of the rich man at a stall bargaining with the poorer shopkeeper. Who has the power? This social consciousness is based in the economic relations between people."

"I think I see that, though it is surely not true of relationships within families," argued Young Pip.

"No, it makes no difference, family or not, for a father will decide how his money is to be distributed and his sons and daughters will act in terms of that father's power. They may love each other, or may not, but at the root of the relationship is the economic, not the ties of kith and kin, as you say in English.

"Property is at one level objects, money, farms, factories, but it also indicates relationships of power. The workers in Friedrich's factory must work to live and he pays them just enough for them to live; no more, no less. That worker is selling his labor to Friedrich and others like him. Owners, like the rich man at the stall have financial resources we call capital which enables this kind of power they have, so capital may not be merely money, but homes, farms or factories."

"But what about my dead father Joe, a blacksmith who did not work for anyone but himself? He was not in power over anyone, working at his anvil?"

"Oh, but he was. When a man comes to have his horse shod, who has the power in that relationship? Joe, as he sets the price. But if a rich man comes along Joe may lose his power, if Joe needs the business, he might accept a lower price than he would charge most people. So, how they deal with each other is economic but, generally, your father has the power."

"We use a French word to describe your father Joe the blacksmith. He is *bourgeois*: That is, he has his own capital, his property, and while he seems to be at the bottom of the financial pile, he still has capital in his tools, his workshop and so on. Shopkeepers the same, all *bourgeois*."

"Why all these fancy terms?" asked Harriet.

The coffee arrived and Young Pip sipped it and made a face but did not protest. Marx drunk his in one gulp and ordered another. Engels tapped his cup handle as he watched Harriet.

"It is a way of conveying what we mean to an international audience," Marx replied sharply.

"But," he continued, "compare Joe to the worker in Friedrich's factory. I expect you know a few of them. The worker has no power at all, unlike Joe. The house he lives in is owned by the factory owner and he and his children can be thrown on the street at any time, especially if he is injured and cannot work. Even worse, look at Ireland, where families can be evicted at the whim of the landlord, the man with the capital.

"You see that man does not own the tools he works with, unlike your father, Joe. Joe is different from that factory worker who, again a French word, that worker is not bourgeois but *proletarian*."

"I can see the difference between the two, certainly. For a start, my father has much more freedom and independence, even if he is relatively poor, though he is not poor like the agricultural laborers I met in Kent who, like the woman's husband and family, are at the mercy of the landowners. Or take the case of Annie Smith whom I met recently, whose husband lost his fingers in a machine and as he could not get a doctor, he died as the poison ravaged his body. But you both seem to talk about the system, not individual people, like Annie."

"Correct. You are getting to see the problem," said Engels, "we think it goes like this. Take this country. The *proletarian*, another new term, does not own the tools he works with; the bourgeois man does. They are his capital, but then there is the capitalist who not only owns his business but can use the wealth he gains to get more and more wealthy.

"And each of these are classes of people. There are numerous proletarians, fewer bourgeois and still fewer capitalists. That is not an accident: for the capitalists have much more power, the power in fact to have the poor starve. In Ireland, during the Famine, there was no delay in the shipment of foods to England and France though millions were starving."

Marx now was getting very excited, his words tumbling out in his enthusiasm as he sensed that Pip, if not Harriet, was responding to the argument. He continued:

"If we are right about these three classes, the relationships between these classes constantly change. Why? Because new ways of producing goods are developed, the cotton gin, gaslight, the steam engine, or electricity. What would Joe do if machines could shoe horses? And who owns those means of production?

"The rich capitalist of course, but Joe does not have the same interests as Friedrich, the factory owner or Alice's dismissed husband. The interests of each class are not the same. Of course, a country may try to make people think they are all one, but that is a false form of consciousness, being a patriot."

"Well, now these are interesting thoughts," said Harriet, finally falling a little under Marx's spell and his argument.

Young Pip agreed: "I don't mean to say the other ideas are not. I had a real struggle when I went to the Crimea as a farrier which is where I got my gammy leg, and Joe and I had long discussions about whether our patriotism was more important than our pacifism. Are you saying I am a member of one of your classes, and that's who I am, whether I like it or not, then to be a patriot is misleading?"

"Yes, just as religion misleads."

"And how do women fit into all this?" asked Harriet.

"On equal footing with men," Engels replied.

"Let me finish our basic thoughts," said Marx, trying to keep his patience.

"This struggle between classes will demand revolution, if all the social ills obvious in factory work are to be solved. It is the proletariat who must rule as dictators, and the power of the other two, the capitalist and bourgeois must be destroyed. Classes will then be abolished. But the proletariat workers must be organized.

"Do you like art, Pip? You must see a painting by *Hansenclever* that I saw in Dusseldorf. *Arbeiter vom der Magistrat,* which shows workers arguing with the City Council while an orator outside the window is exhorting the crowd. He captures the start of the revolution so well."

"Oh, yes, I have seen that painting," said Harriet, to Marx's immense surprise. "I am not sure that you are right. It struck me as a piece of propaganda; but then you clearly agree with its message."

"Is that not true of all art?"

Engels intervened at this juncture: "Revolutions, Pip, Harriet, are the engines of history. Think about that. The Christian takeover of the Roman Empire was a revolution. Think of all those Christians who died in the arenas killed by wild animals. They were true revolutionaries – and they succeeded.

"Great social revolutions are impossible without feminine ferment, as women, while they cannot be considered a class, are the most oppressed of all whose status in society can only be solved by revolution."

At which Harriet smiled at him and they exchanged interested looks. "So, Mr. Engels, for you there is no real divide between men and women?"

"No," he replied with a slight smirk, "men and women should be completely unified." Harriet immediately grasped his sexual inference, but it passed by both Marx and Young Pip. However, Young Pip retrieved the conversation.

"I can understand the general direction of what you call Communism, but you will never convince me revolution is needed. It's fine for you with your theories. But I have seen war and bloodshed and appalling human misery at close hand and I would not wish that on anyone. I will work throughout my life to prevent it.

"Annie Smith needs help, not revolution. We must seek to remedy these social ills gradually, not through civil war."

Marx sighed, almost with condescension. "We will have that discussion another time. But if these ideas spread, I prophesy that substantial bloodshed is inevitable."

"That would be unfortunate to say the least," concluded Young Pip.

"Thank'ee, gentlemen for your interesting ideas, and of course, for the coffee. I do agree on one matter. I do think people who are, what did you call them, proletarians, should organize themselves to make lives better. Maybe that is something I could help with as a preacher. I don't know."

He got up and finished his coffee, which had left him a little more energized.

"I very much enjoyed the coffee: It is a taste to be acquired. Come, Harriet."

"A moment, Pip, must you hurry off? I'd like to discuss the issue of women further."

"I fear I must attend to my duties, but tomorrow in the teahouse, right?"

"Of course, my dear," she said with a grand smile.

He walked to the shop door, waved goodbye and moved up the street toward the Chapel, turning over the conversation in his mind, while Engels whispered to Marx.

"Karl, here is a man sympathetic to our ideas. Yet he balks at revolution. Are we really sure a gradual approach won't work?"

"I just don't see how it could. I feel like a much stronger drink."

"You go to the Crescent. I'll talk further with Harriet about women and be there shortly." Marx left and crossed the road.

"Now, dear Harriet," said Engels, looking at her lustfully. "I have marveled at your intellect. You are gifted, intelligent and beautiful, and I want so badly to make love to you. Come with me, please," he begged her.

"Do not be in so much of a hurry."

"All right, what is the relationship you have with this Pip?"

"We are close friends and lovers. So I will discuss with him first whether I will couple with you. I will not marry because I believe in free love as people call it. We have been lovers for some time now. You are an attractive possibility to me, and I am sure you would be an excellent lover.

"But were a dalliance with you to destroy my friendship with Pip, I will not countenance it. I don't know what he feels about our future, but I would be happy to live with him, though not married, so that we could retain our independence. But believing in free love does not imply playing fast and loose with the feelings of others with whom we are close. We have to be honest. Be assured, I am not asking his permission."

"You will make a poor communist, I fear, as you have too strong a moral sense about you. I will bring my book to your home if you tell me where it is."

"Oh, no, not yet. Just bring it with you and give it to Pip. I'll get it from him."

"Thank you, no doubt we will see each other again."

XVI

By mid-summer of 1864 Mr. Jaggers was coming to the office rarely and was not looking at all well, almost as if he had some wasting disease. He had postponed his retirement, indeed both Wemmick and Old Pip felt he was clinging on, as if he could not bear to leave, certainly not before the end of the Binding v. Dingleberry case. One morning in late June, he arrived at Little Britain only to slump in his chair with uncertain breathing.

"Mr. Jaggers, sir, you should be at home in bed. Can I help at all?"

"No, Wemmick. I think I am not far short of meeting my Maker, if He can spare the time for an unbeliever. Where is Mr. Pip today, by the way? I'd like to see him if he is available."

"He was at the Bailey earlier on the Clerkenwell case, so I expect he will call in shortly. Ah, here he is," as Old Pip entered the room, "and I will leave you two to converse."

Wemmick grimaced at Old Pip as he left, conveying his concern at the old man's health.

Pip tossed his wig and gown on a chair but stood by Jaggers' desk, watching him closely.

"How was your case, today, Mr. Pip? You don't seem your usual self."

"Oh, it is nothing, I am sure, but I get these pains in my back and stomach."

"T'was ever thus. However, I wanted to see you on a strictly personal matter which I anticipate coming to fruition in the next few days. I am pleased that Lord Binding is now on his last legs, legally and financially, so I can retire completely. The case has dragged on and on, with appeals and counter-appeals but my initial objective has been achieved, I think."

"That must be satisfying, but what was the personal matter?"

"Ah yes, I am talking of my death and subsequently my will."

"This is most distressing, sir; you have been a friend to me for many years. The very thought of your passing is a great sorrow, no doubt as great as the event of its occurrence."

"Now, Pip, and I will refrain from calling you Mr. Pip today, for I am speaking more as a friend than a partner lawyer. My life has been solitary, except for those acquaintances I have made through the Law. I am also by nature, if not judgment, a parsimonious man. I have kept my private affairs private, and my will has been drawn up by my friend Mr. Courtisone. In discussions with my bankers a month or so ago, however, I find that I am much wealthier than I had envisaged. When all is said and done, my estate will be valued at the sum of eighty thousand pounds or thereabouts."

"Great Heavens, how on earth did you amass this fortune?"

"I did inherit a useful sum from my esteemed father, a doyen of the East India Company, which proved essential to my practice. I have been fortunate also in my brokers. I have also had some profitable engagements as a lawyer outside the practice at Chancery."

"And you have no family or relatives?"

"None whatsoever. At least, I assume that is the case. My maiden aunt, Martha Jaggers died early this century when she was a relatively young woman. She left me some investments and a house in trust. But my father, whose older sister she was, once hinted that there was more to Martha than met the eye. He once inferred that Martha, when quite a young woman, had had to go away to the Continent.

"We could put the case that she went there to bear a child, but, if so, such a child would have been adopted wherever she visited. We might have one of Wemmick's inklings and suppose that such a child grew up, married, had children of his or her own and they would be my first cousins. But it certainly appears that thereafter,

Martha lived a quiet life in the village of Wargrave in Berkshire. Were the child legally adopted then, in law, there would be no claim on my estate anyway.

"None of that speculation should affect the dispositions of your wealth and property."

"I suppose not, but you see what happens when an old dying lawyer conjures imaginings out of his declining brain. I met you through Magwitch and began to keep an avuncular eye on you, and of course everything that has happened since. Estella, Molly, Joe, and you have made me regard all of you as my family. The will's contents affect you in a particular way, so I want you to have knowledge of it. I do not want you to make any decisions immediately which might later be complicated or indeed be made redundant by this bequest.

"Estella and you have a house in Kent, but you need a house here in town for your practice if it is to grow and thrive and for you to entertain. So, I will be leaving my Soho house and furniture to you and your wife. You may wish to keep my driver and servants. For the remainder, you must await hearing from Courtisone."

"My dear Jaggers, this is such a munificent gift for Estella and I, and your hints suggest your will is a boon for my family as well. You are extraordinarily generous, my friend and partner. You have anticipated our thoughts very well. We have been looking at various properties and not found anything yet."

"How comforting. Now I have not had the house decorated or improved in the last forty years, but I suspect Estella is a woman of taste and will have great delight in transforming it."

"My friend, I hope your demise is not as imminent as you anticipate."

"I have had enough, Pip. I have much enjoyed watching you grow into this work. I have yet another confession to make. After we discussed the matter sometime last year, I completely forgot that I had a note from Courtisone at the time saying that a Scottish friend of his suggested a young man by the name of Hamish Macdonald. I do apologize, but such faux pas indicate the need for me to hand up my wig. You may not wish to follow that up yet. That will depend on the briefs coming in. If you do, get Wemmick to arrange it.

"The time has now come. I told Wemmick this morning that I am retiring from my practice this very day. I will go home and await my demise. I want to control my own death as I have controlled my life. Ergo, I must now go home to die. Have the clerk call me a cab now, please, Pip."

Old Pip opened the door and did as he was bid. He watched in astonished silence as Jaggers put on his coat, picked up his silk hat and silver-topped stick and walked slowly out of the room, not turning to take a last glance at a room in which he had lived a major part of his life and then he realized neither of them had said goodbye. He sighed and went immediately to Wemmick's office to rehearse the departure of the old lawyer.

"I have given up trying to explain the man," said Wemmick, "but recently I had an inkling he was done with work, indeed with life. But time and tide wait for no man, so let us discuss this potential partner he forgot about. I took the liberty of consulting Mr. Courtisone's senior clerk this morning. Of course, Mr. Jaggers should have followed this up some months ago."

"I don't see any immediate urgency, John, unless we get drowned in briefs."

"Don't leave it too long, Pip."

Throughout the remainder of 1864 Old Pip had occasional bouts of pain, so Estella got him away to Numquam House when needed. He told no one but her about the visits he had made to the doctor concerned with these stomach pains. Now it became clear to him that the practice would suffer financially if they did not find a new lawyer.

It was the Feast of St. Valentine, 1865, when they took the trap over to the Cottage, though Old Pip had been calling regularly since Albert moved there to ensure that the boy knew his father well.

"What brings you two here, this fine morning?" asked Biddy.

They all embraced. Albert shook hands with Estella at which she bent down and kissed him. Old Pip picked him up:

"Goodness me, you are now a big, strong boy. It is splendid."

"I'd like to go on a train, Father, but I am enjoying old Boney."

"Ah, my favorite. He must be a very old horse by now."

"Yes," says Albert giggling, "that's why he farts a lot, sleeps a lot and we don't go far."

"That sounds like me."

"I hope you'se hungry," said Biddy, "I've been making some pies and desserts as I have a visitor coming tomorrow."

"Who's that then?"

Biddy blushes deeply and said: "Nobody you'd know, just a gentleman friend."

"It's Harry Shoreham," Albert chimed in, "lives in the village. We meet him when we are at Chapel."

Old Pip and Albert exchanged sly smiles.

After lunch Biddy and Estella stayed at the table, and Old Pip took Albert out for a walk.

"You have been so wonderful taking care of Albert all these years, Biddy. After Joe died, we all thought it best for Albert to stay with you and you thought so too, I'm sure. You'll remember we discussed it a year so ago, but now we wonder whether the time has come for a change."

"You mean you want him to come and live with you?"

"We are not sure. We certainly don't want Albert to come if he would be unhappy or miserable. But you are still a young woman and you don't want to be a widow all your life, do you? You need a man in your home, and in your bed."

Biddy blushed again: "Yes, that is true. I do get lonely for a man. I think this Harry is very nice, about my age, also a widower, no children, and a Primitive Methodist who goes to our Chapel. Joe and

I knew him from chapel when his wife was alive. Oh, I don't know. My Joe is irreplaceable."

"But if he has a mind to marry you, I am sure he is wondering whether Albert comes with you, which would be different were Albert your own child."

"Yes, I know he might not want that. Like Beatrice, Eleanor his wife died in childbirth and that was a long time ago. He loved her deeply and still misses her after all these years, but he don't know what it's like to have children. And I'm too old for more of that malarkey."

Old Pip and Albert then walked in, hand in hand.

"Albert and I have been talking. I explained to him my wanting to get to know him as a father should know his only son. He said he knew life here would be very different if Biddy and Harry were to decide to marry. So, he and I have decided he will come to live with us for six months, and we will see how we all get along. We will find a tutor for his education. I don't think he should go to school in London, not yet, as it is too much of a leap from a quiet country life to the hurly-burly of a school classroom."

"Come 'ere, my darling boy." Biddy said, putting her arms around Albert. "You knows I love you, but your father wants to get to know you properly and there's not much of a future for you here, is there? The Forge is closed, and you'd have to go somewhere to be an apprentice. Maybe if you go to school in London, you'll become a lad of great expectations, like your father was. Anyway, it would be an adventure, wouldn't it?"

"I will do my very best to make you as happy as I can, Albert, and I want you to call me Estella, if you are comfortable with that. Biddy my friend, Pip and I will come to Numquam quite often and will make sure we bring him to you. We are staying there tonight, so shall we pick Albert up tomorrow before Harry arrives?"

"I'll have his things together ready."

Estella turned for the door and invited Albert to go with her. Old Pip embraced Biddy and whispered in her ear:

"Haven't we come a long way since my sister died?"

"Wouldn't have missed it for the world. But I do miss Joe."

"Me too."

Albert rushed back from Estella and went over to Biddy:

"I do love you, Biddy. I hope I can like Estella too, but she will never be like you."

"You will get to love her. She is charming and loving. When you are older, she will share her shocking history with you. But your father is the same good man I've known for years and he will take care of you."

It had been a considerable time since Courtisone's original recommendation for Hamish Macdonald had reached Jaggers. Wemmick found out that the young man was still available and very interested in a London practice, so a date for interviewing Mr. Macdonald was arranged for late in February .

"As you will see," said Wemmick, "the proposed gentleman comes with a splendid review of his potential. He is apparently staying with friends in Surrey for a short vacation from Edinburgh, at Richmond-on-Thames, I believe, so we must get him here this week and with relative ease on his part, rather than having him come from north of the border."

"Please arrange it promptly, John, and be with me when we talk. We need another lawyer urgently, not least because I too am not feeling too well these days, though I cannot identify the cause."

"It's been a hard year. You'll be better when the weather changes."

Fortunately Mr. Hamish Macdonald was indeed a young man, tall with the familiar ginger hair of the lowland Scot, fresh-faced and very personable. It was a long interview, and Old Pip was impressed with his experience so far and with his mastery of legal nuances.

Old Pip asked him to wait in the outer office for a moment. Wemmick and he agreed Macdonald would be a fine catch and that

Courtisone's work obviated any need to go further with enquiries as to his suitability. Macdonald was called in and invited to join the practice. He would be on probation for a calendar year at which point his salary would increase. He accepted immediately and Wemmick would discuss the financial details. His tenure started on March 1st, 1865.

"Eminently satisfactory," said Wemmick. "I had an inkling Courtisone would find us the man."

"Indeed, we will start him devilling immediately."

Preacher Whitehouse had been moved to London, so the year also saw Young Pip's life in Salford ending as he had been asked to take on the Preacher's responsibilities in Chatham. This news he promptly shared with Harriet.

"My dear," said Harriet one afternoon when they were resting together, "I know you need to move on, but what will your future be? You have sounded occasionally as though you would gladly give up preaching for practical activity on behalf of the poor. But now, you are going to be the leader at a chapel which is clearly growing apace."

"This invitation has started to clarify matters for me," said Young Pip. "I will accept the position as it will be a good place to see how I might take up some of those communist ideas about organizing the poor. But I have come to realize something else which I must share with you.

"I always enjoyed immensely my time with young Albert, my uncle Old Pip's son, who is now ten years old. I realize that I do want children of my own. I feel my life would be incomplete without a family. So I am not the free spirit that you are. I am going to have to marry if I am to start a family."

"Oh my dear, dear Pip. I care for you very much, maybe I am in love with you. Let me tell you this. You are a magnificent lover; I will never forget how your hands are on my body so that I am already envious of your future bride, whoever she may be. She will be amazed at her good fortune when you lie together."

"Shh, my darling. You are expressing the joy and excitement I have had with you, for while you have been my only lover, you have taught me how to express my love. I am certainly in love with you."

"I knew this moment would come," she said, "because I am simply not interested in raising a child. I would gladly live with you forever, but this is the end. When I have been with you, I have never been tempted to go with someone else. That German factory-owner invited me, but I was afraid that it would spoil our friendship and frankly he was a bore. Our time together has been exactly what I mean by free love; that is, just loving without social obligation, only the loving friendship of two people."

"I know of no one at the moment that I could marry, except of course, you. But I know just how determined you are to preserve your total independence which perhaps I could give you, but maybe the risk is too great. Being with you has been a wonderful time for me and I will always treasure your love. Perhaps we will find each other when we are old. But I will need to leave as soon as possible, but, before I do..."

"Just once more, my darling Pip."

Both Old Pip and Wemmick were disturbed by the absence of any word from Mr. Jaggers since he left nine months ago. No one had heard or seen anything of him since he left the office that June morning. Then, early in April, Mary, the house servant who succeeded Molly, appeared in Little Britain with tears in her eyes to say that her Master was dead. Old Pip asked when the funeral would be, but Mary said it had already happened, that her deceased master wanted no one except Courtisone to ensure it was indeed his corpse being buried. He had also requested that a month passed after his funeral before anyone was informed.

"Enigmatic to the last," said Wemmick to Old Pip, though quite what the enigma was Wemmick did not share.

"Rather weird, I think," added Old Pip.

His will was keenly awaited as those who knew him suspected that he was a man of means. But Mr. Courtisone had left immediately to take the waters in Leamington Spa and some legal ends had to be tied up, so knowledge of the will, like knowledge of the author's death, was also delayed.

Young Pip had begun his duties in Chatham two weeks before, and he went to see Biddy for the first time since coming south. There he learnt that Jaggers had died later and that the reading of the will had been delayed but would be read shortly. He went promptly to London, sending a note to Old Pip and Estella as he knew they would gladly accommodate him.

The brass plate at the street entrance read *Courtisone and Courtisone* with no indication of their profession as lawyers or doctors. They were the premier lawyers in the city with a line going back through to the end of the 17th Century when a young man, the son of a French courtesan, rumored to be yet another bastard son of King Charles II, established himself as a lawyer with the name Courtisone.

Old Pip and Wemmick were chatting as they arrived at these dour buildings.

"He was a remarkable man, 80 years old, you know. I've worked with him for forty of them."

"Really, so long, and him working till the last. An admirable man, tough but the sort that makes you proud to be British, though a very odd ending to a full life."

Inside the main door, Estella and Young Pip were waiting. Mary, Jaggers' house servant, was also in attendance, along with Sam, his driver. Old Pip embraced Estella and then Young Pip.

"Young Pip, I am so delighted to see you."

"I am back in All Hallows, Uncle. Rather sudden. Preacher Whitehouse has been promoted to a circuit in London. However, you sent a message to Biddy saying that Jaggers had died, so I thought I should pay my respects."

A clerk appeared and showed them all into an inner office door, and then to yet another door that opened to a cathedral-sized room where, at the far end, sat an imposing man with a shock of white hair and piercing blue eyes. He was dressed perfectly, his tailor obviously being a man of great skill. Several chairs were placed in front of the great man's desk which, had it been a dinner table, would have sat fourteen people comfortably and all those in attendance took a seat.

"It is my duty," Courtisone began, "to read the will of Nathaniel Arbuthnot William Ponsonby Jaggers, and I would like you to remain silent until I have finished."

Old Pip smiled at Wemmick, who raised his eyebrows.

"This will not take long:

"'I, Nathaniel Arbuthnot William Ponsonby Jaggers, being of sound mind, do declare this to be my final will and testament, dated this fifth day of May in the year of our Lord, 1862.

"I direct that my house, its furniture and all its accoutrements become the property of my friend and partner Philip Pirrip and his wife, Estella Pirrip of Numquam House, All Hallows in the County of Kent and that they receive ten thousand pounds.'"

"Oh, how generous of him," said Estella, slightly aghast at the figure.

"Pray let me continue without interruption."

"'From my estate, I direct that five thousand pounds shall be given to my loyal clerk, John Norman Wemmick of Walworth in the County of Middlesex.'"

Not able to contain himself, Wemmick murmured: "I don't believe it. I don't believe it. I had no inkling of it." He smiled and patted Old Pip on the back.

Courtisone looked up and frowned.

"'I direct that one thousand pounds be given to Philip Pirrip, the younger.'"

"But I don't deserve such largesse, do I? Praise be to God!"

"'I would be most grateful if you would each abide with my earlier instruction to keep silent, so that we may complete the reading with all due speed. Conversation will come later."

"My dear chap," Old Pip whispered, "he did not see much of you but admired your dedication."

"Please, ladies and gentlemen," getting as angry as a mild-mannered lawyer would allow, "let me finish."

"'I direct that one thousand pounds be given to Mrs. Biddy Gargery of the Cottage, Next All Hallows in the County of Kent.'"

"Oh, she will be thrilled indeed," said Young Pip to Estella quietly. "Now she will be in comfort all her days."

"'I direct that five hundred pounds be given to Mary Smith, my house servant and there now resident, and two hundred and fifty pounds to my carriage driver for many years, Samuel Waterfall, of the same address.'"

"Oh, my master, how kind," said Mary bursting into tears.

"Now please listen carefully.

"'I direct that the residue of my estate shall be invested in a Trust for the Relief and Education of the Poor, to be administered by a Board of Directors comprising of Mr. Philip and Mrs. Estella Pirrip, Mr. Philip Gargery, and Mr. John Wemmick. In the event of Philip Gargery taking a wife, that lady shall become a member of this Board.'

"Attached are details of the Trust. I would advise you again that the terms of the Trust cannot be executed before Probate is declared. Months, maybe a year."

"That, ladies and gentlemen is all. However, I should tell you that the residue of the estate is at current value sixty thousand and nine hundred pounds. The interest from such a large sum will approach five thousand pounds per annum, so the work of the Board should begin as soon as Probate is declared in several months; then the directors can convene."

After that statement Courtisone did not have to call for silence. It was sustained, as if each person had received a profound shock, such as the death of the Queen or, say, the sinking of a passenger ship which would promote great sorrow, but few tears. Looks and gasps of astonishment were the reactions among the beneficiaries.

Stunned described this silence, broken by Old Pip:

"Excuse me, Mr. Courtisone, how much?"

"Five thousand pounds per annum. I would judge at a conservative amount of interest accrued on capital, and, as I will retain responsibility for the legal and other affairs of the trust, I anticipate the funds will gradually increase. I suggest you name it The Jaggers Trust."

"I am sure we would want to do that," says Old Pip.

The others nodded in agreement, apart from Mary, who got up and moved to another part of the room to weep with gratitude.

"But think, my friends and colleagues on the Trust, what we will be able to do with such funds."

Young Pip found his voice:

"Mr. Courtisone, would the terms of the will allow us to spend part of its capital, for instance, to build a school?"

"Yes, the provision is that not more than ten per cent of the whole may be used for a capital project in any ten-year period, but it may not be used for a religious building, consonant with Nathaniel's wishes. As you have heard, my dear friend Nathaniel was a clever and thrifty man from whose perspicacity you are all beneficiaries."

"Good day to you all," and he retired from his cathedral into an inner domain. Those attending got up silently and filed out of the room.

"Let us all go to what is now my office in Little Britain and celebrate the life of this great man," said Old Pip, holding Estella's arm and leading the way.

Walking back, Estella said, "Pip, dear, a letter arrived by a courier from your office this morning. It asked that you receive it immediately and, as you were not there, the clerk sent it around. It was from Australia of all places to judge by the markings."

"If it is from who I think it is from, then my conscience bleeds once again."

"Why dear?"

"Several years ago, before Molly died and before we finally did what we should have done when we were young and twenty, a man walked into our office by the name of Ezekiel Unworthy."

He then told Estella and Young Pip the story of Ezekiel as they walked to Little Britain.

"So this Ezekiel is my half-brother. I would have been angry with you once for not telling me earlier, but never again. Let's see him if he were to come to London."

"He may not be coming, of course, just writing with investment instructions."

"I look forward to meeting him. I wonder if we share any of my good looks."

"No, my dear, you are an exquisite original."

"That is certainly true," ventured Young Pip. "Yet my mind is full of ways in which we can use the Trust money to help the poor. I will have to reconsider eventually my position as a Preacher and, perhaps, work for the poor in different ways. Chatham will be very different for me.

"But I will confide in you both, rather than my mother," he said laughing. "I have enjoyed in Salford an intimate friendship with a wonderful woman, Harriet Middleham. We have been very close, but she is a radical, determined not to marry and is certainly unwilling to have children.

"While we are still good friends, I really am looking to get married and the sooner the better. I just need a bride. Now I have only been preaching for four Sundays at our chapel, but I am strongly attracted to a young woman who attends regularly. Our eyes meet from time to time which evokes a smile from both of us."

"Now that, as your father would say, is the best news today, my dear old chap."

"My dear Young Pip," said Estella, genuinely shocked, "did you really have an intimate relationship with her without being married all that time and when you were a preacher?"

"I confess I did, and it was incredible, exciting, magnificent, ecstatic and long-lasting."

"How thrilling! For my part," Estella continued, "I am delighted. There is nothing, absolutely nothing in this world to match the bodily intimacy of a man and a woman. Or so I have discovered. But waste not another minute to find yourself a bride. Finding someone you love and being with them is really the most marvelous experience a man or a woman can have. I waited too long to find mine.

XVII

Courtisone allowed the Pirrip family access to the Soho property in October 1865 before probate had been declared, knowing that the Gerrard Street house would need extensive work. Estella visited it once or twice, and Courtisone denied any responsibility for the delay in probate being granted, which they presumed was a matter of gathering together all the details of the old lawyer's assets. Mary and Sam showed her around, and both of them decided to stay on until they decided where they will live, for which Estella was particularly grateful.

However, following Jaggers' death Old Pip was extremely busy getting to grips with new and numerous briefs with Macdonald which suddenly descended on the practice, so that his attention to the new property was irregular. The project was thus stalled for some months, until as Old Pip put it rather oddly, he could surface from the mountains of paperwork under which he was buried.

Yet although throughout the summer the briefs were brought under control, there was a swirl of problems yielding conversation topics in their household which Estella and Pip agreed to lay out one evening at dinner.

"Pip, darling, we need to decide on Albert's education, don't we Albert?"

"Yes please," said Albert, "and I would very much like to have some tuition in painting."

"That can certainly be arranged and we will arrange for tuition in other subjects too."

"Do you think we should keep the Jaggers house, my dear?" asked Pip. "It's very gloomy. Might we sell it and find somewhere more to our liking rather than go to the trouble of decoration and improvement?"

"I think we should decorate it to our taste and then see, for it is so convenient to have a house in Soho. It will be much more valuable once the decoration is complete."

"Perhaps, and by the way, I am uncertain as to how we will treat your half-brother, that Unworthy fellow, if they do return?"

"I am not of a mind to pay him much attention, I must say. He seemed a bit of a rascal to me."

"I heartily agree on that score. Oh my goodness, we have not really solved any of these matters."

"I know, Pip, but we will, we will. I am more than a little interested in a certain gentleman of our acquaintance who is in search of a wife, although unlike my Australian half-brother as I recall, being able to carry a sheep was not a criterion."

By October 1865 probate had been declared and Albert came with them to Gerrard Street for a serious examination of the property and the need to come to a decision.

"Go around the house again, Albert, see what you can find."

"Thank you, Father."

"Estella, I remember this house and a dreadful dinner party for men only which Jaggers gave. Herbert came too. Jaggers took a considerable interest in that Bentley Drummle character you were married to for a while, and I was never clear why."

"Say no more about him, my dear, the man was a blackguard.

"Goodness me," Old Pip continued, "this house is a confounded mess. It is still not stripped of the books or the old furniture but I think we could make this our own, at a price."

"It is very gloomy," said Albert returning from his explorations. "I suppose we have got so used to strong light living in the country, even when the sky is grey, but I would like it all to be white as white can be."

"I agree," said Old Pip. "Changing it seems to be a matter of decoration. The glass in the windows does not look as if it had been cleaned recently. Is that not part of Mary's tasks? But it is so dark with these oak panels, this dingy staircase and those dark brown rooms up here. So dismal. It all needs lightening up for, as Albert said, we were also outside so much in the marshes, we had light all the time."

"Being brought up with Miss Havisham, I am used to gloom, but I will banish it from this house. I think I will dedicate the money Jaggers kept from Molly to its restoration. It would be good to have just a trace of both my parents here.

"Here are some new possibilities too for me to investigate: Lamps lit by gas to replace the candles, new ways to get water into the house too, especially for a water closet. This will be very challenging. But what do you think, my dear, shall we create the most interesting house in London? I have heard mention of a company called Morris, Marshall and Faulkner, based in Red Lion Square and with a good reputation for modern design. Perhaps we can consult them?"

"This should be your project, Estella. I am still having a difficult time keeping up with my work, though it will be easier now Hamish Macdonald is with us. You must meet him soon. I need to watch my health, too, as I have this recurring pain in my abdomen. Fortunately, today it is abeyance. Why don't you talk with Mr. Morris and have done what you like? I know I would delight in any outcome you had masterminded, and the use of Molly's money as a start is an excellent idea. Give it a romantic feel."

Estella smiled broadly, walked slowly toward Old Pip and they kissed and put their arms around each other. They held on to each and looked deeply into each other's eyes. Then Old Pip drew Albert into their embrace which pleased him greatly.

"This house needs a new name, though, if we are to make it our own."

"Yes it does. If 'Numquam' means "Never" with respect to my dreadful childhood, perhaps we can call it 'Semper'—always—to celebrate us three."

"That's Latin, isn't it? Will I have a Latin tutor?" asks Albert.

"Of course, of course. But Semper House it is."

"Will we keep Numquam as well?"

"To be sure, Albert, we must have a place out of London," said Estella, "and we certainly need somewhere near Biddy, don't we? Yes, let us be committed to this house. We can't sell it now."

As they walked down the broad staircase, Albert was in the middle holding hands with both his parents.

Young Pip's ministry at Chatham was proving a great success and a new building was finally opened as membership and subscriptions had risen rapidly in 1866. The scenes following the Sunday service at the newly built Chatham Primitive Methodist chapel would be of interest to those who knew the times when Preacher Whitehouse converted Young Pip.

Preacher Alice mentioned the changes to Biddy when they met one Sunday.

"Have you seen? The chapel is getting fuller, and there's a different class of people coming."

"I noticed that," said Biddy. "When Preacher Whitehouse was here, you wouldn't see these fancy hats."

"I wonder why these richer people are coming. Even the men with their frock coats and top hats. Perhaps they have found Vicar Windnortham a strain compared to Young Pip, or even Preacher Whitehouse."

"I am worried though, Biddy. I don't want our Primitive Methodism to become fashionable. That would destroy its ambition."

"Well, I think I agree. We'll have to see what my preacher son makes of it all."

Young Pip was in much improved clerical garb, as befitting a Methodist preacher. He stood at the door, greeting his flock by name as they left: the Bumbershoot family, the Horniman brothers and their pretty young wives, and the Favershams, Maud and Hortense, rich spinsters and others.

He reserved a very warm greeting for a young woman of striking good looks, who was the last to leave, purposefully he hoped. His insides started to tremble slightly as she approached, for this could be the young lady he had been waiting for, even though he still thought lovingly about Harriet.

"It is such a pleasure to see you in Chapel so regularly," he began. "I should have asked your name before this, but now let us share a greeting."

"Indeed, I am Susanna Urchadan, an old Scottish name, and as you can hear, I come from north of the border, good Presbyterian stock, a Lowland Scot without that Highland burr."

"What a fascinating name, on both counts. I do not think I have ever met an Urchadan. But a Susanna? Hmm. Do you know the story in the Book of Daniel about the beautiful young woman, called Susanna, who refused to be seduced by two judges, so they lied about her being intimate with a young man? And how Daniel questioned them separately and proved they were liars? I hope you have not had such an experience, Susanna," he said with a broad smile and a twinkle in his eye.

"Not yet," she replied, laughing.

"I do not wish to be impertinent, Susanna, but I wondered if we might take a walk together sometime."

"I would like that," said Susanna, blushing slightly, "and thank you for your pretty comment about my name, though I fear my knowledge of the Old Testament is not as good as it should be. My carriage will not be here for a half hour, so perhaps we can walk now?"

"Oh, indeed. Will you take my arm, if that is not too forward?"

"I would like that too. Tell me about yourself. How did you get that limp?"

They walked down the street from the chapel toward the Medway River, the day a February grey.

"I was a farrier at the Battle of Balaklava and was accidentally shot in the ankle which took five years to heal so that I could not get about easily. But, believe me, I was no hero, and I will always walk with a stick."

"I believe an uncle of mine died in the Charge of the Light Brigade. I will find out; perhaps you knew him."

"I doubt it. We lower class farriers didn't know any officers, I'm afraid, except seeing how they treated their horses."

"Very badly, I expect. Far too many gentlemen officers treat their horses as they do their ladies, in my experience."

"What do you mean?"

"Let me confess. My cousin has introduced me to a few young men she thinks I might marry, but those who are not simply after my dowry have no, what I would call, depth to them. They are superficial. Intellect or culture does not interest them.

"You are, I think, the first intelligent man I have met, putting aside my cousin's husband who is very intelligent and writes serials; Sir Charles Dickens. Do you know of his work?"

"I do. I used to read quite boring religious pamphlets and, of course, John Bunyan's wonderful *Pilgrim's Progress*. I had a friend in my previous ministry who introduced me to a world I had not known, including Dickens, Miss Austen, Mr. Thackeray, the poets and others. But I am constantly astonished not to find more intelligence among the upper classes.

"I could tell you many a story about gentlemen officers who seemed to me either ignorant or stupid, though it was difficult to tell which, especially in the treatment of their horses."

They both laughed heartily and walked more closely together.

"Now, tell me more about yourself, Pip; may I call you Pip, rather than Preacher Gargery?"

"Of course. I would like that very much. Little to tell, really. I was converted as a child by Preacher Whitehouse. My father was a blacksmith and later a shipbuilder here in Chatham, but he had a forge at All Hallows where I spent my childhood, After I recovered from my wound, I went around the county as an itinerant preacher and then went to the north where there were many factories."

"Always working with the poor, I suppose."

"Oh yes, a great challenge. But I met there two interesting German scholars there, Friedrich and Karl. I forget their other names. Friedrich owned a factory, but Karl was a philosopher, working in Paris and they met and became friends there. His family is quite rich, I think. But I met them when I was preaching abstinence outside a pub and they both came out drunk as lords.

"Yet those two people are brim full of ideas. They are really revolutionaries, too, and while I don't agree with that as a solution to anything, I was very impressed with their ideas. But that is for another time. We must return for your carriage."

"I'll look forward to that. Can I tell you how much I enjoy your preaching and now your company? I've been coming to chapel for some time. I used to sit at the back, but then one day, our eyes met, so I moved nearer the front, and I earnestly look forward to being in your chapel every Sunday. Oh dear, have I been too forward?"

They looked at each other very warmly and retraced their steps.

"Not at all. I must confess to looking at my congregation each Sunday to see if you are there."

There was a pause after that exchange, but Young Pip then resumed:

"I can't express how much I have enjoyed our walk. Dare I ask? Might we meet somewhere else during the week? I have a sense that we will get on very well together."

"I am living at my cousin's house at Gads Hill. I am on my own for the moment with only the servants there for this month. Can I send my carriage for you on Wednesday? We can have a private lunch, and perhaps another walk, this time in the grounds of the house if the weather is clement."

"That would be such a delight. I know we will get to know each other much better."

They walked back to the Chapel and the carriage arrived: Young Pip escorted her to it, opening the door. They held hands, looking thoughtfully at each other.

"The carriage will be here Wednesday at noon. The house is only a half-hour away."

She waved and he followed, gazing at the carriage till it was out of sight, and sighed.

Young Pip stood still, as if tied to the spot. "What a beautiful woman. I love her."

Susanna smiled to herself as the carriage trundled along to Gads Hill, "At last, a man I could marry."

On Wednesday morning, Young Pip arrived in Susanna's carriage at Gads Hill. On the way, he thought deeply about Susanna. He believed he was infatuated with her, but not casually. After all, he told himself, he is now thirty-one, well past an age when most men would be married. She shared his religious beliefs and, interestingly, seemed to value his interest in ideas and in action to help the poor.

That she is the most beautiful woman he has ever set eyes on, he confesses to himself, is more than an important factor in their relationship. He wonders what Harriet would feel about her. But, above all, he could easily see a life with her and, while it is somewhat sudden, he felt the urge to get on with it.

Susanna meantime had been alone in the house with no one to share her most profound feelings for Young Pip. Her maid was dressing her on the morning he was due, while she thought about him as so noble, very handsome and strong, and the legacy of his wound inspired her love for him, heroic as it obviously was, and she loved him for denying it.

Although she thought she was much younger than him, a mere twenty-two years old, she has had opportunities for attachments numerous times since she was sixteen, and she has never felt the fluttering in her heart, or the potential for passion coursing through her body as she thought of him.

Above all, he was so good to talk to and she could see them building a life together, even given how much and how little they already share. But also, even if he had not watched her, she had been observing him weekly and, as she says to herself, 'this is my man, I am sure of it.'

She walked down the four steps at the front of the house hurriedly to Welcome him. It was an impressive home, not grand in the style of a castle, but a large comfortable home with all the appointments a large family would need.

"What a lovely house. Who owns it, your cousin's husband?"

"She is my second cousin, but she has always taken an interest in me since my parents died. She is Lady Dickens, of the Hogarth family, and the wife of Sir Charles Dickens, though they are estranged, as I understand it, even though her sister Miss Hogarth manages his affairs. But my second cousin continues to use the house, as does her husband on occasion.

"I did not tell you, I think, that my dear parents were killed in Sicily in one of the rarest weather events there ever. As I was fifteen and at school, they decided to go on a grand tour together. As a family we had been to France and Germany for vacations, but they wanted to see regions of southern Italy. Although he was a careful banker, they loved adventures together. I was fortunate to live with parents utterly devoted to each other.

"They were staying in the town of Castellamara and two terrible tornadoes struck the island. It took two months before we were able to bury them in the family plot in Edinburgh. The devastation there was like an apocalypse. However, Pip, thereafter, I lived with this cousin for a time, and later with my dear maiden aunt to whom I was greatly attached, my father's sister, and she gave me a large inheritance. When she died, and while I kept a small place of my own on the outskirts of Edinburgh, I spend much of my time here."

"Oh, my dear, what a terrible story. My father was killed in a shipyard accident but being taken away by a freak of Nature makes me ponder divine intervention, though not now."

Tears came to his eyes, so he rapidly changed the subject.

"When we last met, I mentioned the Manifesto the German scholars gave me which is challenging to read and to think about."

"You shall tell me all about it at lunch."

They went into a spacious dining room with modern furniture, as if the Dickens were the first owners and had bought it recently. Lunch was served.

"My conversion to my faith," he began, "rested on the idea of perfection linked to my helping the poor in whatever way I could. Frankly the Germans have not rocked my faith in God, but they have shifted the way I think about the world. Before we talk further about the German people, I want to share with you two matters that have been eating at my conscience. We must have no secrets from each other if we are to progress, don't you think?"

"Of course. But see," she said with delight, "as I told you the other day, I have never met a man whom my cousin thinks eligible who would ever discuss their conscience, perhaps because they do not have one."

They both laughed and he reached out to hold her hand, at which she smiled broadly and gripped it hard.

"That is so very kind of you. But now here I am with my first worry: I am preacher at this beautiful little chapel in Chatham, but who attends? The congregation has increasingly fewer poor people and many more well-to-do people. We seem to be stealing our congregation from the churches. As a result, the poorer folk are too embarrassed to attend. It is as if my chapel has become fashionable. What do you think?"

"I appreciate your discomfort and your confidence in telling me about it. You are right: It has become fashionable, but you clearly do not know why, do you?

"I fear not; enlighten me."

"It is you, my dear," she said, stroking his hand. "The men come because their wives insist. Half of the ladies are in love with you and the other half are just anxious to be part of the fashion. I mean, if you have to be saved, you might as well have a handsome preacher to show you the way."

"How awful! Then I must give up the Chapel and go back to itinerant preaching. The only good that comes out of it being the fashion is that I collect money which I then give to the poor. There are times when I wish my uncle had never mentioned my conscience."

"Oh, I am so sorry to have spoken so directly, but I know you would want to know what I think, though I could have been more tactful. What is the other matter?"

"More personal. This is difficult to say, so I will just speak it, as we are the outset of our relationship. When I was in Salford, I had an intimate relationship with a woman, Harriet Middleham. It was never one in which I could consider marrying her because she was a free spirit, a believer in free love, a follower of Mary Woolstencraft, and absolutely determined not to have children.

"It lasted for the years I was there, and before I left, we parted on good terms as friends. I don't think I was ever quite in love with her, but we were frequently intimate. I need to tell you this, once again, as I feel our relationship is going to become very important to us."

"It is marvelous to have such frankness, Pip. I have read Woolstencraft too, but I suppose I am still too young or not brave enough to venture down the road that your friend has done. I do understand how and why women feel like her. I suppose my conventional upbringing counts as a barrier to my experimenting with men. At least yet."

They laughed gently.

"I am not in the least upset by your telling me. I am sure that, in that miserable context, being with an interesting woman was a godsend, but I want children; lots of them."

"So do I, which was why we parted, but it was she who introduced me to novels, politics and poetry."

"Ah, I see. I should say that I regard your telling me this as yet another reason for me to admire you. Putting out of the way of our growing relationship what later might have been a major obstacle is an important sign that you, like me, see a future for us. Or why would you tell me this at this juncture?

"Odd, really, but I have never really thought about whether it would matter to me that a man I was in love with had had previous intimate experience. Now I know it does not."

"How wonderfully generous of you, Susanna, to understand my past. I should add I told her I might invite her to my wedding if I were to marry."

"Wait, Pip, let me think on that for reasons I don't yet understand. But we are not yet at that stage, are we? On the other hand, perhaps we are."

They left the table and went through French doors into the gardens and walked across a lawn, arm in arm. Young Pip stopped and looked at her.

"Susanna," he says with a smile, "if, as you say, the women in my congregation are divided between those in love with me and those into fashion, into which half do you fall? For, I hope this does not come as too much of a surprise to you," he said slowly, deliberately and shyly, "I have long admired your beauty in the Chapel, and I feel already I know you intimately. I wonder whether you think we might have any grounds for a permanent relationship?"

Susanna responded with a mock protest. "Preacher Pip, we have only had these two meetings apart from the weeks of looking at each other in Chapel.

"But I think," she now said with love in her eyes, "that is quite long enough. I don't think I am being forward, dear Pip, but are you asking me to marry you?"

"Yes, I suppose I am. No, I certainly am. I know this is very sudden, but from whom do I need permission?"

"No one. I am my own mistress. Oh Pip, I need to savor this very moment as I have dreamt about it often enough recently, but, yes, Preacher Pip, I would be thrilled to marry you. I am not impulsive, believe it or not, but life is too short for long engagements and we are certainly not young, though perhaps I am.

"But I have wanted you as my husband when I heard you preach about the evil practices in factories you had seen. We can get to know each other later. But my marriage condition is that you give up being a Preacher and that we continue your work together using my large dowry."

"That is two conditions: I am minded right now to say "yes" to both because I love you. But can we agree to marry anyway and work at both conditions? Or are the two conditions separate? If I did not give up preaching, which I have said I will do, you will not marry me?"

"Oh no, I would be in despair if we did not marry. Please give up preaching and but let us work on the other condition which, I gather, will mean working on your conscience. And now, please kiss me and hold me as I hope we will do for years to come."

"How wonderful," he said as they embraced each other.

"Condition one is already satisfied, Susanna. It has been suggested that I become the manager of a newly formed Trust which can dispense over five thousand pounds each year for the relief and education of the poor. I am on the Board with my uncle and his wife. The Trust rests on a munificent bequest, but much more of that later.

"As to my German scholar friends, they have impressed me with two observations, not that I understood much of their argument. First, we need to see the world; yes, the world, as having three classes of people. There are those who own the wealth, those with capital. Then there are people like my father, who own small businesses and are their own masters. Finally, there are what they call the proletarians, a French word. These people do not own the tools they work with—in factories or on farms."

"That makes sense to me as I dislike the greed of the well-to-do of which, of course, I am one. Tell me more."

"Obviously my target as a preacher has been these poor people, and I have tried to save their souls. I had an awful encounter in Salford with a woman begging on the street. Her husband had his fingers severed by a machine, so he could not work and was dismissed. They had no money for a doctor, the wounds were poisoned and he died.

"But in this world what good would that do for the woman to save her soul or tell her she should seek perfection? I feel as though

I have achieved nothing. I have given them a religion to help ease their oppression, as Karl would say."

"No, my dear, you have been a source of great comfort to many people, I am sure."

"But that just helps them accept their station in life. For the second idea Karl and Friedrich put to me was that the proletarian class needed organization as a class. They need to be more conscious of their class, of their assigned position in life."

"Although they were hardly an organization, the agricultural laborers in this county and elsewhere burnt ricks."

"But that is just a short protest. Needed is fundamental organization with a list of things to be achieved. And I think that can only be done through politics. But Karl and Friedrich thinks politics won't change the class system with wealth distributed as it is. They think revolution is needed, and the proletarians should rule."

"I see, but revolution cannot be peaceful, can it, and it can be disastrous, as in France."

"Enough of politics," he cried. "There is one matter we have not discussed, the date for our wedding."

"You have a public position, my dear, which I regret to say means that we should be conventional without any pressure."

"I agree, but our courtship has been so rapid that while we can spend as much time as possible together, perhaps we should think about next Spring rather than this summer."

"That will be excellent, as I will have to go to Scotland for at least a month to finalize aspects of my affairs and to see all those who will not be able to make the journey for our wedding."

"The months will pass quickly, I know," and they embraced with tenderness and great love.

XVII

Throughout the autumn of 1866, Estella and Albert were engaged with William Morris viewing wallpapers and paints for Semper House. Albert was excited by the whole venture, a vivid contrast to life in Kent. Morris was keen to introduce Estella to the Pre-Raphaelite Brotherhood, though she had heard them lecture on various occasions, but hints about her background suggested to him that she was not bound by social conventions.

He made no attempt to hide his fascination for Estella, even at her age. She sensed this intrusion and was flattered and amused but fiercely loyal to her husband, so she ignored his quizzical looks as he sought to hold her glance. Artists were such bounders, she thought. At the end of a long morning, they brought a set of sample wallpapers back to the lodgings to share with Old Pip.

"How is the work on the house proceeding, Estella?"

"Well, I think. You know, this young man Albert has real talent for color and style. Morris likes the challenge and was very impressed by some of Albert's comments. He encouraged him to draw and to paint."

"Biddy was always getting me to draw in between reading and doing numbers. I should read more now, but I did draw scenes on the marshes— birds, sometimes.

"Father," he asked, "did my mother draw?"

"She did, a little, and she did love fine art. She studied drawing as part of her education. Sadly she was always too frail to be able to spend time on it."

"Father, I'd like you to tell me all about her soon. I think I am now ready to know."

"My dear boy," said Old Pip, "I have wondered when that time would come; let us do that soon. As to drawing lessons, maybe Estella would like to take part and perhaps we should engage a painting tutor? You could both learn together, but let's discuss Semper House first. What are our choices?"

Estella fetched the samples from the table in a small corridor where she left them. They were all in a hurry to move to Semper House, as their lodgings were cramped with Albert now there.

"Morris and I like these," she said, opening up the sample book on the table. "The wallpaper names are exotic, but I think Meadow Sweet for our bedroom, Purple Pimpernel for Albert's room, Lily Leaf for the drawing-room and Arbutus for the dining room."

"Good Heavens, very interesting choices, you know. But don't forget that we want everything to be light as the house is so dark. These are a little dark but if doors, windows and whatnot are all white, it will look very impressive. You will have the painter cover every door and piece of wood in the house white, won't you?"

"Yes. Morris agrees on white. I have letters to write, so I'll leave you two now."

Old Pip called Albert over: "Come and sit with me. I promised to tell you more about your mother some time ago, and for some reason we have not done that yet, probably because I am too busy. First, is there anything particular you want to know?"

"Yes, am I like her in looks or how I am, or am I more like you, or even like Joe or Biddy? I have led a very happy life but there are lots of parents around."

"Understood. You have your mother's color and her tempera-ment. I have a small locket upstairs with her portrait which I will show you. However, you're not an excitable young man, always rush-ing around; and your country upbringing may have helped make that temperament settled. Your talent for drawing comes from your mother, too. She certainly had an eye for color. You will also be very handsome. Your hands are more like mine, show me."

They looked at each other's hands, with their long fingers and small palms.

"How did you meet my mother?"

"Oh, Clara Pocket was always trying to find me a bride; and when I met your mother, I was smitten. She was a distant cousin of Clara's. But your mother was very frail. You know that she lost two babies before you arrived to our great delight, and in Wemmick's house. We had some good times together but losing two babies and then your little sister's death was a severe blow to us."

"How did she die? I remember a commotion but did not understand."

"On the way back to the cottage from Numquam, the horse leading the trap shied and took off in a gallop such that your mother started to give birth. The midwife could hear the baby's heartbeat, so she was alive. But the poor baby died as she was being born. I never had such a terrible time in all my life, for your mother was so distressed at the loss of the baby that she could not stand the strain.

"That was why you stayed with Joe and Biddy for the next few years. I could not look after you on my own and I wanted you to live with family. Poor dear Beatrice; perhaps she died of a broken heart."

Albert got up and stood on the chair next to his father, putting his arms round his neck and crying softly, both of them weeping.

"Let us take a cab up to Highgate Cemetery after lunch, Albert, and visit their grave."

"I would like that a lot," said Albert. "Since my mother died so early in my life, when I say I love her, it is the right thing to say, but it isn't felt. By that, I mean, I don't spend my nights weeping and thinking of her. I never really knew her but visiting her grave will put me in touch with her."

Later that afternoon, Old Pip and Albert were standing in front of the stone monument to Beatrice and her daughter. They had bought flowers at the cemetery gate and laid them down carefully.

"Now I do have somewhere to go when I think about her, Father. I do remember how warm she was when I sat on her knee."

"I do so regret her passing, Albert, and I would dearly loved to have had a daughter and a sister for you. But, you know, it was always apparent that with her poor health and general weakness she might not have a long life. And so it proved."

When they got back to the house, Estella could see that this had been an emotional and important experience for them both. She embraced both of them and said nothing, except that their dinner would soon be on the table and that they should think about the first meeting of the Trust tomorrow.

Semper House was not ready for Christmas celebration in 1866, so family and friends gathered at Numquam.

The first meeting of The Jaggers Trust for the Relief and Education of the Poor was held at Courtisone's offices on February 1, 1867. Courtisone briefed them on their responsibilities and his relationship to the Trust and they signed document establishing its existence.

That done, the directors appointed Old Pip to be their chairman and acknowledged Susanna Urchadan, soon to be Gargery, as a member the Board. Old Pip had invited Hamish Macdonald to attend and proposed that he be Secretary to the Trust, but not a director. So the Board comprised of Mr. Pip, Mr. Pip the younger and the wives of both, together with John Wemmick. Young Pip was formally appointed Manager of the Trust at a handsome salary, previously vetted by Courtisone. The understanding was that he would continue his preaching in Chatham until a replacement could be found. The party then adjourned to The Cheshire Cheese for lunch, mainly to celebrate the great philanthropist whose legacy they were seeking to develop.

Estella sat next to Hamish Macdonald, inquiring about his past and his views of his new position.

"I am very pleased indeed to find such a position in such a well-known practice. Mr. Pip and Mr. Wemmick have been very kind, helping me understand the vagaries of the English Bar as I was trained in Edinburgh."

"What kind of work do you prefer?

"Advocacy, defending the poor, but I am also fascinated by the possibilities the Trust has before it. In the slums of Glasgow I have seen such abysmal conditions for women, particularly women of the night. I don't know the extent of the problems in London, though I have heard some wicked stories about Mr. Gladstone's concerns for such, as they say, fallen women."

"We don't move in society, so please tell me."

"Oh, that he goes out at night to talk with such women, attempting to help them, and gossip suggests that he gets a stimulation from such encounters after which he assuages his guilt by whipping himself."

"What a wicked tale. How would he do such a thing?"

"No, I am serious, and apparently he does not attempt to disguise his nocturnal perambulations, though the flagellation story may be embellished."

He then spoke to Albert, sitting on her other side. "Albert, what are you going to study?"

"I'm really interested in art and I am to spend a day with Mr. Morris at Kelmscott, but my tutors will be for Literature, French, Classics and Mathematics, though my father also thinks I should study science. He has been interested in the work of Charles Darwin and the reports of the debate with that Bishop Wilberforce. The Gargerys I lived with were religious, and that is how I was brought up there."

"Och, you must get you a science tutor if you are to understand Mr. Darwin's views," said Hamish.

"That would be exciting, too," said Albert. "I want to be prepared to go to the new Art Institute in Kensington, when it opens."

Estella was slightly puzzled that Hamish took an interest in Albert; perhaps he was just being polite, but he was talking across her which she considered rude, though Hamish had been very civil with her. As lunch ended, a message came to say that the Unworthys were on the way. Young Pip and Susanna went home in a cab, and Albert walked home to Soho.

Old Pip had become a very tranquil man with age, tolerant of many things nowadays that might heretofore have upset him, even made him angry, as with the Unworthy's arrival at such short notice. On the way in a cab, Wemmick volunteered to have food and drink sent in for them which Old Pip and Estella thought desirable.

"You will come too, won't you, dear. Unworthy is an interesting specimen, your half-brother, though I think there is absolutely nothing observable in your physiognomies."

On arrival, Hamish disappeared into the back office for information about the Unworthy's investments. Satisfying himself that he knew enough to make conversation, he hurried back just as the family arrived in the outer office.

"Now, let us confront the Australians," said Old Pip.

The office which the Unworthys now entered would not have been familiar to Mr. Jaggers. The plaster casts were gone, the bookcases had been cleaned, and the law books dusted. The dirty walls had been painted pure white and there was a large dining table in the center with Old Pip's desk now under the window, as Jaggers' desk had been sold at auction.

"A hearty welcome to you again, Ezekiel. Let me introduce my wife, Estella. Mr. Wemmick, you know, and this is Mr. Macdonald, my junior partner."

"Gooday to you all. This place looks very different. This is my wife, Angharad, and this is our eldest daughter Gwyneth who is almost eleven. We have left the other four at the hotel with the maid."

"But, Estella," he said, moving toward her. "We share a father, I believe, which makes you my half-sister. Mind you, if you don't mind me saying so, I knew you were related to me because you are so beautiful."

"Oh, come, come, half-brother, you are a very handsome man, too."

Waiters then entered with food, roasted chicken, legs of lamb, pastries, and so forth. Wemmick was a silent observer in a corner of the room. Only the Unworthys were eating, as the hosts had just celebrated at *The Cheshire Cheese.*

At their end of the table Estella was conversing with Angharad, whose Welsh accent was not often heard in Little Britain.

"Well, this is very nice, in'it? To be honest, I was never in London before. When we married, we went straight after to the boat at Southampton, see. Terrible journey. I was sick all the time."

"So, where did you meet your husband?"

"Well, he came over for a bride, see. That was after he had been 'ere, looking for his father. He came to South Wales, really, to find himself a wife—and he found me! He said he'd come to South Wales because there's a New South Wales in Australia and he wanted to see the old one. My people are farmers down in Ogmore Vale, Glamorgan, and life is hard; they were glad to see me go, but they cried crocodile tears, I tell you. I loved Ezekiel at first sight, being young then: only sixteen. So strong and such fun. As I had grown up a farmer's daughter, when we got to Queensland, I could adapt easy, see."

She called to Ezekiel. "We've never looked back, have we, Ez-e?"

Then to Estella, "I call him Ez-e, because he's so easy. But here I am gabbing on. My mam says I'm real chopsy, talk the hind leg off a donkey, I do."

They continued chatting, though Estella was scarcely able to retain her civility in talking with this ebullient Welsh woman with her incessant talking, but they stopped to listen as the men's conversation got going.

"Thank you, sir, for your warm welcome, Pip. May I call you Pip?"

"Indeed, it is very good to see you again."

"Our sea-journey here was good. The report you sent on my shipping investments last year was most helpful. They're doing well, eh? Trade across the oceans is increasing. I now have another sheep farm. I have started planting sugar which will always be in demand. I am looking for partners here in England and I hope you will be an investor."

"Let me hear more about it. Sugar must be very different from sheep farming, if I understand it. You need a lot of laboring hands, don't you? Do you have that number around, or are there still some convicts willing to work on it? In Jamaica, from what I hear they were accustomed to using slaves on the sugar plantations."

Estella, Macdonald and Wemmick were listening intently.

"I started with this crop four years ago. We brought in labor from the Pacific Islands, you know, natives, darkies or whatever you call them."

"Brought in?"

Old Pip looked at Ezekiel quizzically, with raised eyebrows.

"I did not do this myself, of course, but a small company of white men, down-at-heel settlers, sometimes former convicts too, went to the Pacific Islands to recruit and they made it sound attractive, and, so they say, the darkies volunteered."

"Did these people go on your sole behalf, or are there other plantations needing labor?"

"Not just for me, but a group of us pioneer farmers paid them to do the recruiting."

"So the natives were never forced to come."

"Well," says Ezekiel, slowly and nodding and winking at Old Pip, "such a possibility can't be excluded, can it? Of course, we put up some huts for them, but once they were there, we didn't pay them at the rate they were offered. They are stuck with me," he says, laughing out loud.

"Hmm. Are there men and women, married couples?"

"To be sure, but we put the men in one hut and the women in the other, as couples make the others envious, and we need a docile labor force."

"I must confess, I don't like the sound of it. What's the difference between your labor and slave labor?"

"Well, I suppose, in a way, my workers are slaves," he replied with a cocky demeanor. "I can't afford to give them houses, though I feed them what they need. There's a lot of sickness among them, too, and I get a doctor in once a month. They are slaves, perhaps, but I don't own them."

"Are they free to come and go as they wish?"

"Put it like this: I would not stop them, but they are many miles from the sea, and they wouldn't have enough money. I don't keep them prisoners, but they don't leave either. They had to be brought in, as the Abbos wouldn't do the work."

"The Abbos? Do you mean the Aboriginal population who were there long before Captain Cook?"

"Yes, that's them, sullen lot they are. But ignore the workers. I hope you'll invest in Australian sugar. It's going to make a lot of money, I can tell."

"Ah, Ezekiel; thank you for your offer, but no. Slavery was abolished in this country many years ago. I regard it as thoroughly immoral to constrain a person against their will, unless, of course, they are criminals. It is certainly unchristian, though I don't hold any views on that score. I think you will find it difficult to attract investment from English capital."

Ezekiel raises his voice in anger: "You know, that's exactly the kind of hypocrisy you English are famous for. You have something like slavery in your factories and mines. I know you had five-year-old kids pulling carts in the mines. And don't you believe it. I'd bet there's plenty of investors who would not give a damn what I do with my workers as long as the dividends roll in."

"Maybe, but it is certainly not for me," said Old Pip, his voice rising.

"The difference, in response to your charge of hypocrisy, is that we are trying to eliminate such practices, not starting them. And we have long ago abolished child labor in the mines. But let us not argue further. Estella wants to join in."

Estella now joined her conversation with Angharad with Pip and Ezekiel listening, both simmering with anger.

"We have been listening to the gentlemen talking long enough. Angharad, what do you think of these natives you have on your plantation?"

"Ez-e does what he thinks best. I just run the house. But I don't like to see the bailiff beating the men with whips, certainly not in front of the children. I don't see why they do it."

"Oh, my dear," says Ezekiel, "you would not understand," at which she glared at her husband and stuck her tongue out at him.

"So, let me be clear about this," said Estella rising from her chair.

"Ezekiel, you employ workers who have been tricked into coming from their own islands many miles away. You don't treat them when they are ill. You don't let men and their wives be together. You whip them. You almost certainly don't feed them well. I expect you make them work from dawn to dusk in the heat, don't you? To me they are your slaves.

"Now, I want to be very clear. If you are not prepared to promise to stop this practice immediately and return your workers to their home islands, I wish to have nothing more whatsoever to do with you, half-brother or not. I have not seen slavery, but I have seen enough of inhumane treatment of others to know how it breaks a person's spirit, indeed their lives."

Ezekiel gets up, going red with anger, "I am sorry you take offence at sound business practice, ma'am. As you have made your position clear, I bid you Gooday. Come, Angharad, bring the child."

"Mr. Pip, I will be sending instructions to withdraw all my business from you."

"And Mr. Macdonald and I will be informing all the brokers we know that you are a slave-owner. As to the withdrawal of business, that will be most satisfactory."

Old Pip bowed as they left, Ezekiel still in a fury.

Old Pip and Estella moved to stand next to each other and held hands. Wemmick and Macdonald looked at them both fondly.

"I am so proud," said Wemmick. "It was a privilege to hear you both stand up for moral principle and English Law."

"Thank you, John. I appreciate your approval, but I am a little uncertain whether my husband feels the same, as he has lost some business."

"My dearest Estella, you humble me with the brilliance with which you exposed Mr. Unworthy for the serious faults in his character, his lust for gain over humanity, his dissembling when describing his workers and his own practice. Of course, his wife demonstrated their moral depravity when she said she didn't like the beating—in front of the children. As if the children were the only moral consideration in the treatment of these poor devils.

"I look forward to sharing this encounter with Young Pip. Maybe he will think better of us non-religious people, showing we can still have moral principle without a belief in God. Jaggers would have enjoyed this encounter, eh Wemmick? But how about you, Mr. Macdonald?"

"An important experience for me. But if I may say so without being impertinent, it is clearly a tragedy that Miss Estella is not permitted to join the English Bar. Her summary of the man's sins was quite exemplary."

"That is such a pretty compliment, Mr. Macdonald. I do like being flattered, don't I, Pip? What was that phrase country folks used in Kent, something about parsnips?"

Wemmick and Old Pip said in unison 'fine words butter no parsnips' and they all burst into laughter.

Like Old Pip and Estella, Susanna and Young Pip were starting to take a more informed interest in the politics of the nation. They were both anticipating the gradual emerging identity of a Liberal Party, as most of the cognoscenti thought Disraeli would lose an election, so that in 1868 Gladstone would form his first ministry and there would be a Liberal government. Electoral reform seemed imminent. For each couple, the serious work on the Trust might complement liberal domestic legislation.

It was the late Spring of 1867, and fortunately the weather was unseasonably warm. As the new chapel was nonconformist, Young Pip and Susanna had been to register their marriage at the Registry where their witnesses were Biddy and Harry, Old Pip, Estella and Albert, and all were able to walk to the Chapel nearby, Young Pip with a new fashionable blackthorn stick. The religious ceremony was conducted by Alice LeBone.

The couple emerged from the Chapel ready to get into her carriage for a ride to the reception for other guests in the garden at Gads Hill. Sir Charles and Lady Dickens were in town and sent their apologies. The Scots relations felt north Kent was decidedly out of the way for them to attend, but their gifts were munificent, especially from a Major Urchadan of the Gordon Highlanders.

Two carriages were drawn up, the second being for the witnesses.

"Thank you all for coming, family. Here is the other carriage waiting to take you to Gads Hill."

"Thank you, dear chap," said Old Pip, whose face seemed to have thinned with his illness, as yet undiagnosed, though he clutched his stomach once or twice, in palpable pain.

As Young Pip was about to join Estella in the carriage, a very disheveled man approached Young Pip who was at first startled.

"Don't you remember me, Pip? I saved you after you was wounded at Balaklava."

"Fletcher! Of course. My dear comrade, you don't look well, and, as you can see I am just married and off to our reception. I'd love to talk with you. Let me see—How would a fortnight hence do when I expect to be back here at the Chapel?"

"Congratulations, Pip, I knew you'd do well, if your wound healed." Then whispering to Pip, he said: "I am a bit skint at the moment and I wonder if you could help?"

"Wait."

Young Pip went to Estella as she was preparing to get into the second carriage and said quietly, "Estella, I wonder if you would lend me a sovereign—I have none on my person—and my old comrade-in-arms, Fletcher here, needs a loan. I will repay you of course."

Estella rustled in her purse and pulled out a small bag of sovereigns. She gave one to Young Pip who went back to Fletcher with the coin.

"Thank'ee, thank'ee Pip. The bairns and Nellie will be very grateful. We can eat today." He then ran away like the wind.

"That man saved my life, Susanna. After I was shot, he carried me from the battlefield. I am forever in his debt. He has fallen on hard times, it seems."

"He is the kind of poor person we should try to help, perhaps through the Trust you have mentioned, and it sounded as though he has a family too."

"We will meet with him when we come back from Edinburgh. Let me think. Did he say his wife was Nellie? I believe he did. Oh dear, what if it is the Nellie I encountered?

"When was that?"

"Joe, Biddy and I had come to Chatham for the first time and were quite frightened by the noise and the bustle, the drunks and the sailors. A young woman approached me. I was very innocent then. She was very young and pretty, as young as me, but she was a whore. I had no idea what she was offering. Fletcher said later he knew her, as I recall. I wonder if it is the same Nellie."

"Oh, my darling, that fits so well with my image of you as a young man—lovely and completely innocent. But if that is, so to speak, 'your' Nellie as well as 'your' Fletcher, all the more reason for us to help them."

"I agree, but we will see later."

XIX

Young Pip and Susanna arrived in the carriage, dismounted and began greeting their guests, most women with fashionable Victorian dresses and hats apart from one woman wearing very eccentric clothes for the period, more like that of a man, an artist presumably. Young men from the chapel were curious at the wealth on display. But there was no meal, merely a reception, so toasts followed quickly on the wedding party's arrival.

Old Pip mounted a small dais bearing the wedding cake.

"I find it difficult to control my emotion in proposing a toast to Susanna and Young Pip. Estella and I are thrilled by her intelligence and beauty, a perfect match for our dear Young Pip. I have known him since he was three years old, and he's now a man of rugged virtue, of great compassion, of fierce commitment to important causes and a man I regard as a war hero, which he, being self-effacing at times, constantly denies.

"Their marriage will, I am sure, be replete with goodness and adventure into significant attempts to diminish the poverty with which this rich and powerful nation is so afflicted.

"Ladies and gentlemen let us toast the bride and groom," at which the clink of crystal symbolized the traditional expression of goodwill.

"First," replied Young Pip, "our grateful thanks to Georgina Hogarth for hosting us here, and we are sorry Sir Charles and Lady Dickens are in London and unable to attend. We thank him most sincerely for the use of his garden. I will be brief, but I want to make publicly a commitment to my darling bride."

There was a robust round of applause and some cheers as he turned to Susanna.

"Susanna, it is customary, conventional and legal, though my uncle may correct me on that, for the husband in a marriage to see his wife as a junior partner, useful only for bearing his children. As you all know, as at present enacted, a man has full legal rights over his wife's property, which I hope we will see changed in our lifetime.

"I intend to break that law and custom and here and pledge that we will be equal partners in everything we do and in the control of all our assets, income and of course, our children. Everything will be ours.

"Susanna, I want you to hold me to that pledge."

She reached over to him to him, tears in her eyes, "My husband, you constantly astonish me with your goodness and love."

Gasps of astonishment from the audience at this extraordinary breach of the law and etiquette of marriage. Then loud applause, especially from the few women in attendance who had lost control of their dowries, and who began to discuss with each other the future of a law that might change this malignant practice.

The speeches over, Susanna moved to talk with Albert, Old Pip and Estella.

"Albert, I hear you have been helping the Semper House refurbishment and that you need an art tutor. We too will be thinking about buying a house in or near London and perhaps you will help with that, as I am sure it will need redecoration."

"Oh, and I'd be glad to help." Albert replied. "I must talk with my parents about it. But thank you very much indeed, you are most kind to invite me to help."

Susanna smiled broadly at him and moved on.

Estella whispered in Old Pip's ear: "So I am a parent now, not just your wife."

"He treasures you almost as much as I do."

The ceremonies over, Young Pip and Susanna prepared for their honeymoon visiting Scottish relatives.

⚜   ⚜   ⚜

After their return to London following six weeks away, they quickly decided it would be proper to visit Biddy and Harry after which they could begin a search for a house in Chelsea. Meantime they went to stay at Semper House. Old Pip was more cheerful and very delighted to see them.

"My expectations of you, my dear old chap, are coming into fruition. I am delighted we can get the Trust going, and now Susanna is a director, we have two formidable women's voices on our Board. I believe we shall do good work, and though I am not well enough to do much practically, I will be attentive to all our needs."

"Oh, Mr. Pip, how kind."

"Susanna, if I have told you once, I have told you a thousand times: Call me Pip. I know it is your husband's name, but neither of us will misunderstand the context. If you don't do this, oh, I don't know, I will ask the Board to remove you."

Everyone laughed delightedly because this was now a close family.

"Now I do hope you both will find a London house for purchase or rent. Weak though I am, Estella and I, being really country people, have been exploring. Tomorrow it's the British Museum. Perhaps you would care to accompany us? Albert will come too."

The following afternoon, the two couples with Albert were leaving the British Museum walking away from the Portico, all sharing their experiences. Susanna was particularly excited by the Elgin Marbles, but wished they were still at the Parthenon. Old Pip talked of seeing the Parthenon when he was in Athens but did not go there as it was an ammunition dump. Walking towards them as they leave was what seemed to be an old gentleman with a large black beard, deep in thought.

Young Pip looked at the man coming towards them.

"Karl, is that you?"

"*Gotten Himmel*, it's the young Preacher!" They shook hands vigorously.

"Karl, meet my bride, Susanna, my uncle Mr. Pirrip, his wife, Estella and his son, Albert."

"How good to meet the family. I meet zis young man in Salford, when I was with my friend Friedrich. We had very good discussions. I try to persuade him to start a revolution, but he is too much of a religious liberal."

"No longer a preacher, though. You have influenced me at least. I think that there are better ways of helping the poor than by saving their souls, but not, I still think, through revolution. But how come you are in London, particularly here; not plotting something, are you?"

"I find the Reading Room here is the only place I can get some peace to write, away from my family. My big book, *Das Kapital* is just published, and we need to get the Communist Party going strong—which I am sure you will join." He smiled engagingly.

"I'm afraid not. I doubt whether we will join your party, but we do discuss your Manifesto. If only you'd give up this revolution idea. Nonetheless, as I said, you have influenced my thinking and my future, and I am going to be administering a large wealthy Trust for the relief and education of the poor."

"Excellent: As long as they read the Manifesto and you train them in systems of revolution, eh?" Everyone laughed at this fantasy.

"How about your friend, Friedrich?"

"Oh, he went back to Germany some time ago but comes to London quite often. I have an idea he was disappointed in love when he was in Manchester, but who knows? He never talked to me about his love life. I am lucky to have a devoted wife and children.

"Good day to you all. I must get back to my writing. Come to our meetings."

"We might."

Marx walked up the steps to the Museum. Young Pip was quietly relieved that Marx did not know of Engels' rejection by Harriet.

"What a nice man, said Susanna. "Such a kind face."

"I always feel sorry for scholars like him," Estella added, "working away in their hovels or their libraries, writing books no one will read. What a way to spend one's life; who on earth will read a three-volume book about politics in German?"

"Maybe you're right," replied Young Pip, "but he is writing more about the economic situation of the classes, about the most serious social problem we face—the distance between the rich and the poor."

"Sounds far too ambitious to me," said Old Pip, ending the conversation with a dismissive grunt.

The summer of 1867 did not go well.

Hamish Macdonald had now been a junior for over two years and Wemmick was giving reports regularly to Old Pip about him, but his poor health prevented him from taking up many briefs, so he was continuing to hand them over and he had guided Macdonald from time and time, had seen him in court and given him advice on advocacy. They were colleagues, but not on the friendly terms Old Pip had developed with John Wemmick. Given the age difference, that was not surprising.

The amount of work in the practice had declined somewhat since Jaggers died, but the income remained stable and Macdonald was ready to build his own reputation anyway. Old Pip was confident in his choice, and a calm environment was what he hoped for.

However, Wemmick arrived one August afternoon at Semper House to report to Pip on Macdonald's progress. He knocked on the door and was let in by a maid, and then shown into the Morris-decorated sitting room where Pip was lying on a couch.

"Good morning, Mr. Pip. You don't look well, sir."

"No, John, and call me Pip from now on: We have known each other for what feels like generations. I am not well, and I fear that there is no cure for the ailment that I have. I am terribly fatigued; my head is sore, my stomach gives me pain, and I cannot see as well I used to.

"However, what of Macdonald? I must say his strong recommendations seem to have been justified. Although he is qualified at the Scottish Bar, the change does not seem to have been difficult. I must say, too, I liked his radicalism."

"Men from Scotland, others we've interviewed apart, always seem to be competent and confident. Just like Susanna, thoroughly capable. Indeed Macdonald is a first-class young man of exceptional industry, indeed an excellent junior. He has visited the new London prisons regularly and talks with some of your previous clients. He has performed well in court. He tells me of dire cases in Glasgow he has worked on. In sum, he relishes the kind of experience the practice has to offer."

"That is all very satisfactory, is it not, John?"

"Yes indeed, but I feel I must tell you of an incident which has me seriously worried about him. I do not wish to cause you any concern, but my conscience will not relent, so, without wishing to indulge it, I will tell of it."

"Pray, go on," said Old Pip, struggling to get up.

"You will be aware, I am sure, of the young criminal men in certain quarters of the city who, not to put too finer point on it, offer their bodies to other men. I was near Moorfields last week meeting an informant, and I saw Mr. Macdonald walking toward what has become known as Sodomites Walk. It was dark, so I was not convinced it was indeed he, though he has a distinctive gait.

"So, you will forgive me, Pip, but I had another of my informants track him two nights ago and indeed it was he. I should stress that I am told he did not engage with any of those criminal young men, although he did then enter a drinking establishment which such young men frequent. My informant tells me he left there alone after a half hour and made his way to his lodgings."

"Might he be talking with these young men as a matter for understanding the criminal mind, just as he has visited prisons?"

"That would be my earnest hope. But yesterday afternoon, he and I were discussing a case involving a young woman, and he ventured the remark that he was glad he had never had a romantic relationship with a woman—they were far too much trouble."

"We must wait and see, I suppose. I will not yet share this information with Estella or Young Pip. I must confess I have never to my certain knowledge met or even known of men with this particular complaint."

"Of course, it is criminal: Though thank goodness we stopped putting men to death for sodomy ten years ago. As Jaggers would have observed, that was a punishment which certainly did not fit the crime, if crime it truly is."

"But I think I must put the problem and the context to Mr. Macdonald, don't you?'

"It is a matter for your decision, Pip. Tell him you know of his outings and he may be mortally offended. Fail to warn him and he could be imprisoned and disbarred."

"I think I must risk the former. Ask him to come and see me directly, would you, John? As ever I am in your debt."

He coughed and fell back into his chair. An hour later Hamish Macdonald appeared at Semper House and was shown into the living room. He was a fine-featured young man, immaculately dressed. His main physical failing was a tendency to blink nervously, as he did now, in the presence of his senior with whom he had not had as much contact as he had expected—for obvious reasons. He was clearly well-educated with a real presence that suited him well in court.

"Ah, Hamish, how good of you to come. Do you feel completely settled after these two years or so?"

"Completely, thank you, sir, my lodgings are excellent. I hope I can sustain the excellence of the reputation Mr. Jaggers and yourself have established which, as I move around in the legal fraternity, is constantly remarked upon. It is an enormous privilege to work with you and to have such great expectations for the future."

"Oh, please do not use that expression, Mr. Macdonald, and it would take me hours to explain why. I am sure you will do well and more than well. But London must seem a strange place without your friends, eh?"

"I apologize for the expression, but och, yes, we were a very close group in Edinburgh, at school and then at the University."

"And, as I know from the lovely Susanna, your Scottish women are most attractive, eh?"

"I believe they have that reputation, sir, but we were too close a group to admit women into our company. None of us are married, or even engaged."

Old Pip pauses: "Hmm … I regret having to give you a warning, but I feel I must say this at the risk of offending you. It has come to my notice that you have frequented an area of the city in which there are criminal young men offering themselves for criminal practices. Am I right?"

Macdonald was shocked and he blushed deeply, replying sheepishly: "Yes, sir."

"While I cannot forbid you to do so, I must tell you this is exceptionally dangerous behavior. Were you to continue to engage in this behavior, publicly, you could be committing a criminal offence which would ruin your career, and almost inevitably see you behind bars.

"I suspect you are still ignorant of police attitudes and ways of dealing with such criminal behavior. I would be certain that within this group of young men there will be informers, men who are on a leash with the police, precisely to trap men like yourself. I am myself a liberal man, as is my wife. Individuals will love each other as did Socrates and many other Athenians, or David and Jonathan for that matter."

"My desires are what they are, sir, but I will take exceptional care in the future not to put myself or the reputation of the practice at risk. I grant you, Moorfields is a rum place. However, given my inclinations, I would like to find some way of helping these men: How? I have no idea—yet."

"That is a most interesting possibility. My wife has begun to work out how the Jaggers Trust can establish some way to help women in

a similar situation to those young men. I think that, if you are prepared to talk with my wife about this social problem, that would be
to your mutual advantage in the pursuit of solutions, permanent or
temporary.

"While I am completely ignorant of the matter, I am sure that,
as you establish yourself in London society, you will meet men of
your class who share your desires and will be as discreet as possible.
But if you were to seek to satisfy them in public in ways which open
yourself to great danger, your whole life and future will be at grave
risk."

"Thank you, sir, for your understanding and most helpful
advice. Perhaps I might talk with your wife about what might be
done soon. As to my desires, I suppose I am in truth conflicted. I
have grown up entirely in the company of men. My schooling, my
university experience, and my parents who, God bless them, have
tried to protect me from what they call 'the monstrous regiment
of women,' John Knox's famous phrase. I confess, then, that my
friendships are very intimate without being physical. I suppose I
simply lack experience of the company of women."

"On this, I cannot help you at all, I am afraid. No doubt there
are those who might help, but one obvious answer is for you to
spend more of your social time with the fairer sex to determine
which path of desire you will take. Please leave now as I must take
to my bed. I will ask Estella to meet with you."

Hamish left Old Pip intensely worried that his career might
already be jeopardized, but neither Young Pip, Susanna or Estella
as yet knew of this conversation.

Young Pip and Susanna soon made another duty visit to see Biddy
and Harry at the Cottage, though it was not a duty they resented. As
the trap arrived from the station, Young Pip said:

"I hope my mother will be very happy with Harry."

"Yes indeed, he seems a very stable and loving creature. I noticed how he looked at her at our wedding. He helped her into a chair too, for she must be near sixty."

"Yes, I think she is fifty-five."

They dismounted and Biddy came out to welcome them, telling Young Pip they had a visitor.

"Fletcher, what a surprise!" cried Young Pip. "How good to see you. How did you know I would be here? Of course, I must have told you once where I used to live. So you would try here if I wasn't at the Chapel? How straightforward. We have been in Scotland introducing me to Susanna's relations. We planned to come to Chatham to look for you this week, but here you are. But I am foolish. You have not met my bride, Susanna. Biddy here is my mother and Harry whom you've just met, is my new father-in-law. "

"How d'ye do, Pip, Mrs. Pip. I cannot tell you how much that sovereign meant to Nellie and the bairns. We'd had nothing to eat for four days and we were all starving, when I thought I'd come and look for you. I have since done a day at the dockyard a week, though the wolf is always prowling at our door."

"Come, let us sit together on the bench outside and you can tell me what has happened since we last met. Come, Susanna."

"Oh, Young Pip," said Biddy, "can we not all listen to your hero?"

"About the battle, what he did for me and his return, but nothing beyond that as we will need to talk privately."

Biddy brought Harry outside and Young Pip fetched a small bench from just outside the Forge.

"I am sure Pip will have told you how we was de-shoeing horses when the horse kicked, and Major Turner's pistol hit Pip in the ankle. I carried him up the hill, p'raps must have been a good two mile to the tents for the wounded as he couldn't walk, and he were only half-conscious, and his ankle was smashed and bleeding. They bandaged him, not very well, I thought, and then Major Turner wanted me back down the valley and I never saw no more of Pip till his wedding day. There was not much fighting for the Light Brigade after that battle.

"Anyways we just looked a'ter the horses that were left and a'ter a couple of months we was shipped home. It were a much easier journey 'cos it was winter, so, as it was cold, it were much easier on the horses, and the ship was emptier as it were for the Light Brigade only, and many of them were dead, so no strangers. I got back to Southampton and then got a boat to Chatham. I thought I was still under the Queen's shilling, but they said no. So, there I was with no work and hardly any money."

"Shameful after all you did for your country," Biddy exclaimed, "and they just throw you out."

"That's what I thought, though the wounded soldiers were in a much more terrible situation than me. Not much help, some with no limbs. At least, I had body and soul together."

"We will pray for you, my son," Harry interjected piously. "A very interesting story of heroism. My warm congratulations. You must have your private discussions now."

He took Biddy's hand and they went inside the cottage.

Young Pip stood leaning on his stick, looking very serious.

"So, you were then back in Chatham without work."

"Then I met my Nellie, again."

"Is this the Nellie I think it is?"

"Yes and I am not ashamed of her. I was only two days back from the war and our paths crossed in the street. Now, I had been with her, if you'se know what I mean, before we went off to sea. But there was more to it even then."

"Beggin' your pardon, Mrs. Pip, I don't know as to whether you should be hearing this."

"Nonsense, Fletch. I intensely dislike the notion that women are somehow too precious to hear how the world is with its evils such that women should be protected from knowledge of it. If I can hear about war, I do not need permission to learn of other distress that people endure."

"Go ahead," affirmed Young Pip.

"Well, she had a small room in a lodging house and the nasty landlord did not mind her comings and goings, though he had to be paid in kind, if you know what I mean."

"What kind of brute is that?" exclaimed Susanna.

"Exactly. She had a little money put by, and she took me in and stopped her whoring, at least for a while. But then the money got very short. I had no job, so she started again for about a month and that lasted three months. We was living together, so I was out of the house as needed. But I loved her then and I love her still. She's had such a terrible life, suffering in the worst way you can think of, abused by her father and her brother. Terrible, terrible."

Susanna began to weep, then stopped as if to stiffen herself to learn about such misery.

Fletcher continued: "But she and I got closer and then, long after her last do with a man, she was pregnant. I knows it were mine. That did it for both of us. She said she would do no more whoring, and I said I would support my family somehow. But never anything criminal. That worked for a while; I did have a job in the dockyard, and we moved away from that wicked landlord. Early this year, we had a second bairn right at the time they told me I was no longer needed at the dockyard. We've had to give up our lodging and beg. We thought of walking to London, but what good would that do us?"

"Where are the family now then? In Chatham?" asked Young Pip.

"They'se all hiding in the cemetery over there."

"Bless my soul," cried Susanna, now galvanized into action. "Go fetch them immediately," and she rushed into the cottage.

"Biddy, Biddy, we have four very hungry mouths to feed."

"Oh I've got plenty of pies and things laid by. I s'pose it's that young man and his family, right?"

"And I am sure you'll have some clothes of all sorts tucked away, haven't you?"

"I'll get what I have now in a minute."

Young Pip and Susanna looked anxiously for Fletcher and his family to emerge from the marsh.

"How did they get like this?" asked Susanna. "Clearly, responsibility for their situation falls not on your Nellie or on your Fletcher, but on the system, how things are. Much to talk about, but first things first, Pip, can we have them wash, I'm sure they'll need it?"

"I'm sure that's a good idea."

Fletcher and his family approached. Nellie was obviously pretty and had not lost her bloom, but her clothes were filthy and the children were ragged and under-nourished.

An hour or so later, after trying out garments from Biddy's wardrobe of old clothes for adults and children, Fletcher and his family were washed and eating voraciously at the table with Harry.

"Don't eat too fast, my friends," Harry said in an avuncular tone, "or you'll throw it back up again."

They all slowed down. Young Pip and Susanna watched as Biddy put more food on the table.

"Now," said Young Pip, "who are these two lovely children?"

"Here's Horatio after his father, proper little scamp he is," said Nellie, "and here's Victoria after you know who."

"They are really like both of you," said Young Pip, "but you won't remember me, of course."

"How could I firgit youse? Gorblimey, but no, this is polite company, so I won't say why."

She laughed and Young Pip, Susanna and Fletcher joined in.

"What's so funny?" asked Biddy.

"Nothing, Mother."

"But all that life is behind me, now I 'ave my Fletch" said Nellie, looking lovingly at her man, as the family rose from the table.

"I think the best way forward is this," said Young Pip. "You can all stay at *The Bargemen* for a week or so as our guests. That way, you can get some good food and some rest. Susanna and I will then work out some prospects for you all."

He turned to Fletcher: "My dear Fletch, how much do I owe you? Only my life, my comrade-in-arms." They threw their arms around each other.

He scribbled a note from a small pocketbook he retrieved from his waistcoat, using a small gold propelling pencil in the shape of an owl.

"I've never seen one of those," said Nellie.

"Oh it's a novelty given to me by one of Susanna's relatives as a present. Here is a note to the Landlord at the pub. Tell him Mr. Gargery will be by to see him. And here's another sovereign."

"I told you, Nellie, didn't I, what a good man this 'ere Pip is?"

"Thank'ee all very much. I don't know wot we'd 'ave done without you."

She burst into tears, almost howling with gratitude. Her children gathered round her skirts. Fletcher put his arms around her, and the family happily set out to walk to The Bargemen.

"It is such a treat to meet the young man who saved you, dear chap. I wish we could do something for him."

"We might, Biddy. Tell me, my dear, two matters. First, do Harry and you intend always to live here and not at Harry's cottage in All Hallows?

"Funny you should say that, dear boy. We was just talking about that the other day and thinking how much easier it would be for us to be in the village. My legs aren't getting any better, and there'd be lots of advantages, don't you agree, Harry?"

"Well, my dear," said Harry, "You know I'd always thought we should be in the village, us two old people," and he looked at the ceiling with a broad smile on his face, "in the twilight of our lives."

"Don't you talk like that, my Harry. We've got years ahead of us. But, why do you ask, Young Pip?"

"Let me ask the second question now. Do you get people stopping by asking if the Forge is open?"

"One or two a week, I s'pose."

"Oh my beloved Pip, you are a genius!" Susanna exclaimed.

"Harry," said Young Pip, "come and sit at the table here with Biddy and Susanna.

"Now, to you both, I have an idea. Yon Fletcher was trained as a blacksmith and he was with me as a farrier, and a very good one too. How about we lend them the Cottage when you both move to the Village? Meantime, he can begin to work the Forge and build his own business.

"You know of Mr. Jaggers' will, Biddy, because he left you some money. He also left a large amount of money in trust to aid the poor. We can use some of that to pay the rent on your cottage after you move. He will start up the Forge again. When he gets on his feet, then he can take over the rent. We'd have to seek the approval of the other trustees. But, what do you think?"

"I'd do anything for the young man in distress who saved my son," said Biddy, "I'd be happy not to have rent. It would be lovely to have the old fire lit and the anvil being banged. My Harry is a good Christian man, I know, and he will agree, won't you, dear?"

"I think it would not take us a week to move, Biddy: Let's do it and let this unfortunate family get on with their lives."

"We'll leave them enough furniture and pots. You know, my dear son, your father Joe—bless his memory—would be so thrilled. What a splendid plan, and I'll bet Susanna was behind it."

"What do you think, darling?"

"When a man like my husband has seen dire poverty in his work, and when he sees the opportunity to do good, he grabs it with both his strong arms."

XX

The arrangement went ahead. By Christmas 1867, Fletcher, Nellie, Horatio and Victoria were fully settled into the Cottage. Biddy left most of her furniture behind for, as she said, it was mostly Joe's and Young Pip would not want any of that old stuff.

The Trust had therefore approved the first decision in Young Pip's position as its Manager which included a one-year lease renewable, a good allowance of five pounds a month plus the rent payable to Biddy for the Cottage and the Forge together with the provision of a horse and cart, as Biddy needed hers. Josephine was sold. Customers who had known Joe came back as it became known across the County that the Gargery Forge was again open for business. Estella as Chair of the Trust was delighted by the arrangement, given her concern that the Trust should find ways to start spending money as their fiduciary responsibility.

During Spring of 1868, Susanna and Young Pip negotiated to buy a house in Chelsea at Cheyne Row, three houses down the street from the writer Thomas Carlyle. Young Pip was embarrassed by the amount of money paid from Susanna's income for the property, but he could hardly ask her to choose something inferior. Their first child was born a year to the day after their marriage, Lachlan Finlay Joseph Gargery.

Old Pip and Estella rode over from Numquam to see where Biddy was now living in Harry's cottage and deemed it delightful. It was close to the village, so she could walk there on market day. The following Friday they rode to the Fletchers to see how they were settled, which gave Estella the opportunity to ask Nellie if she would care to clean at Numquam occasionally. Old Pip had to go back to London, but Estella stayed on at Numquam to interview Nellie next day.

"How's your husband getting on at the Forge?"

"Oh, thank you, Miss, he's a changed man, he works so hard and he is so busy," she said, her Cockney accent still strong. "My bairns is lovely and getting so healthy as they play outdoors in the fresh air, not in some dirty London street."

"Splendid, Nellie, where did your family come from?"

"Aw, I came from Shoreditch, name of Mosscrop. My dad was a sailor, and I had an older brother, but they treated me somefink dreadful. My mother was a whore around the docks. I was on me tod most of the time. And when me mum died of some disease or 'uvver, I left London. I were twelve, but there was this fella in our building, an old man, who was coming to Chatham and he brought me. Nothing dirty about him."

"So before you met your husband, what did you do?"

"I thought I'd go into service when I got to Chatham, somewhere nice. I got a job as a skivvy in a house with a military recruiting man whose wife had just died. He seemed a nice enough fella at first. He comes to my room one night. I'd told him it was my thirteenth birthday, and he said he'd come to give me my present. Of course, I knew what he were a'ter as my father and brother had been there before."

"What did he do?"

"He tore off my clothes, so I was starkers. Oh ma'am, I don't want to tell everything, but he was very violent with my body. I had nowhere to go—I spent a lot of the time in my room locked up. Some nights he didn't come, it went on like that for, oh, I don't know, three month. One night, he told me to pack my bags though I didn't have any and to leave the house before he got up. He gave me two shilling, never paid me wages, not that they was much anyway. So I went on the game, as it was called."

"Oh, you poor child. How terrible."

"I'd got no reference from him, so I took the streets. I had to sleep rough for a while, before I could get another room. Only a very few men I had were violent and by then, I could see it coming, and I either showed them a knife or just refused them. But it was a terrible life."

"And how about Fletcher?"

"Oh, I was always sweet on 'im; he picked me up just before he went to war, so I gave myself to him for free. I longed to see him again, and when he saw me a year later, he just came out straight and said he loved me. So here we are. Him saving that Mr. Pip's life was his life saving too, as it's a help to get a fresh start in life, i'n it?

"Well, I am so very saddened by your experience, but will you come and work for me?"

"Oh, I'd love to."

"Right. I will pay you four shillings a week for you to take care of the house and keep it clean, and the silver will need to be kept polished. I will teach you how to do that. When we go to London, I will tell when we are coming back, so please to light the fires in advance."

"When shall I start?"

"Get settled in your cottage first, but, say, next week?"

"Oh, ma'am, you have all been so generous and helpful. I used to see that terrible man sometimes in Chatham, and he'd threaten me and said he'd tell everyone what a wicked girl I was. P'raps I don't need to be worried out here in the country."

"I hope not, but did you know that my mother was murdered in this garden by men wanting to catch up on her for her past?"

"Stone the crows! How terrible. We'll certainly be careful."

As Nellie left, Estella thought how strange it was that the young woman was not more frightened or shocked by being told of a murder in the garden. Yet perhaps her experience of life was that it was cheap and that there was nothing much to be upset about. It was if she felt that it was only murder, not some of the other evils inflicted on the poor and the criminal.

❧   ❧   ❧

Estella travelled back by train to London that night, arriving home well after dinner.

"Where are you, my dear?"

She walked upstairs hurriedly and saw him lying on the bed. "How are you? I stayed at Numquam only one night as I was so worried about you."

"Darling, I missed you. No, I feel very weak and very tired. I feel to be fading away, but how was your visit?"

"Excellent. The Fletchers are doing well. His smithing will thrive, I am sure. Nellie will keep our house immaculate and they are a changed family. I plan to have a long talk with her about her career as a prostitute as I see ways for the Trust to help. But, let me make you more comfortable."

She loosened his cravat, but did not undress him, throwing a blanket over him and adjusting a pillow.

"Thank you, my dear. I have avoided telling you till now. Wemmick is concerned about Macdonald as he is clearly more interested in men rather than women in terms of his desires, although he confessed he had never been in the company of women. He was seen frequenting an area where there are male prostitutes."

"Good heavens, I've never heard of that."

"Right; I have warned him of its dangers, of being disbarred, even sent to prison."

"Really? How strange. I thought this was possible when I was introduced to him."

"What do you mean, my dear?"

"It is very difficult to describe to a man. When a woman meets a man, any man, there is often a hidden mutual recognition, that some form of sexual intimacy might be possible. Of course, convention, lack of interest, age or even cowardice may eliminate the possibility.

But, when I met Hamish at lunch, then with the Unworthys, that recognition did not exist at all. I assumed therefrom that he would prefer men. Indeed, that lack of any potential intimate bond makes friendship with such a man much easier for a woman. Morris told me it was not an uncommon practice in artistic circles, particularly he said with Simeon Solomon, for instance."

"Huh. I have not heard of the gentleman."

"So, my dear, I really have no objections to men whatsoever doing what they want with other men, lovers or not. Fewer of them to hurt women. At that Cheshire Cheese lunch, I saw Hamish looking at Albert as he talked to him with an almost predatory eye. Probably nonsense, but, how can I put it. If Albert had been a beautiful girl and Hamish a lover of women, I would have said he found Albert very desirable."

"Goodness me, I am going to have a talk with Albert then, as, for all my warnings, Hamish might not be self-disciplined, and . Albert could be vulnerable."

"I will speak to Hamish, too. I now want to draw him in to develop proposals to the Trust for work with both male and female prostitutes. That will keep me very busy."

"That is very exciting for you, my dear," he said, gaining some energy.

"Work with Young Pip, get Macdonald involved, and focus on Moorfields where Wemmick had spotted him and perhaps the other areas you suggested, Shoreditch, was it? Do you know, I heard some gossip when I was last at my club that Gladstone was especially interested in prostitutes, as a phenomenon I assume, not as a customer."

Estella laughed: "Yes, Hamish told me about that at the lunch. Sound like malicious gossip to me. It certainly tests the imagination to think of him as a customer."

Estella took up the challenge and went to Little Britain.

"Mr. Macdonald," she said as she made herself comfortable in what used to be Jaggers office, "might you be interested in working with me on the Trust's Project on prostitution?"

"Indeed, I would."

"Mr. Pip and I are encouraged to do work with both women and men in this regard. But perhaps we should consider where to do this."

"I don't know London well, being a Scot, but a couple of areas come to mind, Clerkenwell and Shoreditch."

"Excellent; let us plan to conduct some interviews. Perhaps I should take the men and you the women."

"I'd prefer that, but what should we ask?"

"Leave that to me. I will consult with my house servant, Nellie Fletcher, who was a whore in Chatham."

"We need to have an office for the purpose," said Hamish, "with an eye to the administration of the work and perhaps a clerk to help us."

"How sensible. I will talk to Nellie soon and then we can make a start."

Their discussion concluded, Estella asked Hamish what he was working on.

"A terrible case," he said. "A three-year-old boy had been found dead in the back street of a tenement near Billingsgate. His father was in prison and his mother worked as a skivvy. There were four older children and suspicion had originally fallen on one of them, but then there was talk of a vagrant. But in the end I am appearing for this seven-year-old girl who clearly, I am afraid, murdered her young brother by strangulation."

"Oh, how shocking."

"Wemmick told me it was similar to a case years ago when Mr. Jaggers had a servant who had strangled a woman and later confessed to murdering her younger brother."

"I beg your pardon, what did Wemmick say?"

"He said this servant was convicted of strangling a woman but later told Jaggers she had also killed her young brother."

Estella flushed scarlet, got up from her chair and in a breaking voice said: "Where is Mr. Wemmick's office? I must speak with him directly."

Hamish escorted her through the outer office down a short corridor and knocked on a door. Estella went in.

"Estella, how good to see you. Can I help, what is the matter?" At which she burst into tears, howling with anger and grief.

"Did you tell Hamish my mother murdered her young brother?"

"Ah," said Wemmick. "Calm yourself. Did Molly not tell you about it?"

"No, she did not, I do not believe it. She would have told me. Does my husband know of this?"

"Yes, but we discussed it with Mr. Jaggers after you had left with Molly, and we decided you should not be told by us, assuming that Molly would tell you sooner or later."

"But how do you know this is true? I cannot believe either that she did it or that she did not tell me?"

"I was present many years ago, the first day after the court has consigned Molly to Mr. Jaggers and he asked her whether she had anything else to confess. If she concealed anything, he would throw her out in the street. So she told him."

"What did she say?"

"Are you sure you want to know?"

"Of course, I want to know, don't dissemble with me, John."

"She said she was so jealous of her younger brother and the love and affection showered on him by his mother and his father that, when looking after him one winter day, she locked him in a shed outside with hardly any clothes on and he was there about four hours.

"When their mother came back and found out, she was extremely angry, saying she was raising a she-devil for a daughter. But the boy soon was dead of pneumonia which broke her mother's heart and she died soon thereafter. That part I am sure you know and indeed the aftermath with her father."

"Why ever could she not tell me? Was the guilt and the shame simply too much to bear? She said once she could not tell me some things because she felt I would hate her, and I suspect she thought this would have been the last straw. But why has Pip never told me? I am going to have to take him to task on this."

"Do be careful, Estella. He is a sick man and his love for you is unbounded."

"That's as maybe but we have never ever had any secrets between us."

Estella left the office, getting more and more agitated. She could understand Molly not telling her, but why did Pip never say anything? She stormed into Semper House from the cab to find Old Pip lying was on a couch in the drawing room reading a brief.

"Where is Albert?" she asked.

"Upstairs, painting. What's wrong? Did Hamish upset you?"

"Why did you not tell me that my mother murdered her brother as well as that other woman? This piece of terrible knowledge you have hid from me all these years and one of the treasures of our marriage is that we have no secrets. I don't understand, Pip, how you could do such a thing?"

"How did you find out?"

"Hamish was telling me that he is handling a case of a girl killing her younger brother and then he told me this story about a servant of Jaggers that he heard from Wemmick, and I accosted him. He said you lawyers decided I should not be told. Why, Pip, why?"

"At the time Jaggers told me, Molly had just gone to live with you. We agreed to keep it secret as we thought it was in the best interests of both of you. It was really up to Molly to decide whether to tell you; not Jaggers, not Wemmick, not me.

"As your life with Molly proceeded so well, it never crossed my mind to tell you. It is not as if I thought about it at all, especially after we started living together. Was it not Molly's secret, not mine, to tell?"

"I am sorry; but I cannot accept that there has not been a time when you could have told me."

"But, be reasonable, my dear, when would you like to have been told? I could not tell you when she was alive for fear of interfering in your fragile relationship and perhaps creating a crisis or a breakdown. After she died, what would have been the point?"

"Surely you can see that it casts a quite new light on who my mother was, this woman I came to adore. I now have to see her as a double murderer; as a child she was manifestly evil. I am not sure at the end of the day whether she even regretted killing her rival.

"We had a brief discussion about it once and she admitted quite cheerfully that she would kill anyone who hurt me. But I am very much disappointed that you withheld this from me."

"I am deeply sorry about that, because I love you so much. But I have to ask you again; when, in these past few years, would you like to have been told?"

"I don't know, I don't know," said Estella, and she began to weep.

"Come here, my love. Maybe it is best that you found out by accident, years after Molly is gone. Let us suppose you had been told when you were living together. How would that have affected you both?

"Molly would probably have been wracked with guilt and shame and you would have been shocked to the core, probably finding it difficult to decide whether to forgive her, for she would have certainly asked for your forgiveness, would she not?

"Can you not see that your wonderful determination to rescue your mother from her criminal past, to educate her, to love her indeed, might have been perhaps damaged beyond repair, if I had told you? For you would then have lost confidence in Molly being able to be honest with you. For my part, I think her actions as a seven-year-old was an irrelevance to your life with her."

"I suppose so. I see your dilemma, but I can't help being upset."

"At me or at her?

"At her, of course. How can I be angry with you? She was the killer, after all."

"There seems to be no bottom to human vices and the depravity, and not limited to the poor: family conflicts, often the vice of greed. Lust, of course, jealousy, a catalogue of vices and human degradation.

"As I think about Molly and you, I see her total reformation built on the natural and the growing love of a daughter for her mother. That convinces me that all is never lost. We should seek to work with the poor from a viewpoint of forgiveness and restoration, not, as I have seen in the courts, revenge and punishment."

"How wise that is, my darling Pip," she said, putting her arms round him. "Indeed, there is work to do and Jaggers has given us the wherewithal which has sparked our best intentions."

Albert came into the room just as this conversation was ending and Estella went to her sitting room.

This revelation about Molly was a thunderbolt with which she needed to try to reconcile herself.

She sat in her armchair trying to remember how she felt when she told Old Pip she loved him. She now understood Miss Havisham and Molly as totally selfish women. Revenge on men and uncontrollable jealousy respectively had been the driving force of each, both emotions being venal in essence.

She knew she had put revenge behind her, and she remembered being jealous that day when she imagined Beatrice and Old Pip coupling together. Maybe envy, not jealousy for that would mean she felt she had a right to him.

No, that was not it at all, she mused, playing with the rings on her hands.

How could I have had a right to him when I spent my life holding him at a distance?

Why should I feel envious of him, or of them?

What exactly was the spark that changed my view of Pip? Was it really my mother's persuasion?

No, not really. True, perhaps, that Molly's chatter just gave me permission to love Pip as if I was countering Miss Havisham's rules.

Yet, she thought, living with my mother made me see myself as a different person.

How does that happen to anyone?

Perhaps, perhaps, she thought with a smile, she had always been more or less in love with Pip right from the very beginning when that urchin appeared at Miss Havisham's under instruction to play with her. For all her visible disdain for him, he was a distraction from Miss Havisham. She remembered how she had secretly admired his character in taking whatever that mad harridan would hand out, especially when she pestered him about her beauty.

I was just unable to tell him, as I simply did not know how, but I also did not know I was in love with him.

But how can one be in love but not know it?

Perhaps, the old story: She had never witnessed two people in love.

Then it dawned on her. You have to witness love and affection between others to feel it yourself. That is what living with parents demonstrate, even if they argue all the time, even if they come to hate each other. To her that was a closed book, apart from very dim memories of her infancy.

Say I had never met Molly. Would I have understood myself if my imagination had not been caught by seeing Beatrice lying on the chaise-longue? If that brief vision of this woman naked, moaning in ecstasy at Pip's hectic hurried body thrusting into her, had never occurred, I suppose I would have remained unchanged. My eyes and my body were opened so that, buried somewhere inside, I finally began to see that was what I had always wanted, but never recognized until that instant, for all the strange happenings between us and my rejection of him over many years.

And Molly, oh dear, what a poor creature she was. If I began to see myself differently, what of her? Did she see herself as a different person from being Jaggers' servant to being my mother on the day she was killed? Or was there still, underneath, a person ready to do evil if she wanted to, though living with me never gave her the opportunity. That woman, she concluded, was raw in character and a mystery.

Such a volume of thoughts occasioned a light sleep.

Downstairs, although Old Pip was tired, settled on the drawing room couch, he remembered that he needed to talk to Albert about Hamish. This was not an era in which genteel parents, fathers in particular, would talk about the physical side of affairs of the heart. However, Old Pip saw the need for this conversation in terms of a threat to his son and he was not sure how to approach it, but, in his mind, approach it he must.

"Albert, come here to me. Sit on the end of the couch."

"Yes, Father, but you don't look very well today."

"Oh, my illness comes and goes. No, I wanted to talk to you about Hamish. Now you know that men and women fall in love, marry, and express that love through physical contact, intercourse in a word. I assume you know that, don't you?"

"Yes, Father, of course. Like me, you were brought up in the country and I am sure dear Joe told you what was going on when you saw animals mating."

"Yes, he did," he said, laughing, "in his own inimitable way.

"Of course, of course, why would I ever wonder that you were not aware of that, and, that you will come to enjoy it? I hope greatly, as you grow older and marry a woman you love. But you have not been to school or mixed with other boys much so will not have picked up how such loving can be perverted."

"How so?

"Some men and some women love their own kind, not the other."

"What? Men and men, women and women? Coupling? Ugh, that is disgusting."

"No, my dear Albert. In ancient Greece, it was a commonplace that men would love men. They loved beauty and a beautiful boy was as lovable as a beautiful woman. And there are men today who, for whatever reason, do not look for intimacy with a woman, but with another man.

"The point here is love. If a person really loves another person, whoever they are, the fact of loving is a human treasure. We cannot dictate to other people and say you can't love this or that person. Of course, people often marry when they do not love each other, especially where money is at stake. Let me just say that Hamish is a man who loves other men. This is not something we want to tell the world. I just want you to know this, so that you can be on your guard."

"This knowledge will take me time as I like Hamish, and he was very friendly to me at that lunch."

"And that is good, provided you know his preference is for men, not women and he might think you were open to his affection. I doubt it, but I wanted you to know that. Now I must rest. My doctor said he would call later in the day with another man to try to decide what is wrong with me."

"Oh, Father, you have been so good to me: I hope your illness is able to be cured."

"We will see, won't we."

"Oh, I have intended to ask you; have you seen the house in Cheyne Row yet? Estella and I are going there soon to see what Young Pip and Susanna have acquired. Come with us?"

"I'd love to."

XXI

The visit was put off twice as Old Pip was unwell, but finally in June 1868, the three of them took a cab to Cheyne Row in Chelsea, a fashionable area of the fast-growing metropolis that was London, the Great Wen. It was only a short walk down the street to the Thames where Young Pip and Susanna regularly took an evening saunter with Lachlan to view boats plying up and down the river.

After the conducted tour of the house and almost excessive compliments had been showered on the young couple, Estella asked:

"So, Young Pip, are you finished being a preacher?"

"Fortunately, my replacement is in place and I am convinced that my new position as Manager of the Trust will enable me to help the poor, not by trying to save their souls, but in a much more practical way. That seems to me be God's work, too."

"I agree," interjected Susanna.

"As Young Pip knows, I am developing plans for work with Hamish and with Trust support," said Estella sitting close to Old Pip on the couch with her hand in his.

"Of what sort?"

"Well, Susanna, as women we know how our sex can be treated, no more so than those we call "fallen women." Prostitutes, poor souls, have to sell their bodies to stay alive and are often brutalized by the men who purchase their services.

"I had a long talk with Nellie Fletcher, whom you know, and her story is so shocking. But I have also been talking with Hamish

Macdonald, you know, the young lawyer at Little Britain. He is interested in helping young male prostitutes."

"Really? I'm afraid in my innocence, I did not know there were such people."

"Nor did I, Susanna. Perhaps as we will all be regularly in contact with him and we must be very discreet, but we should know that Hamish is a man who prefers men to women."

"Oh, goodness me," cried Young Pip, "what did you say? That is utterly against the laws of Nature and God's law. I find that absolutely abhorrent. Unlike the prostitutes, he is not so poor that he needs to sell himself to live. How could you have engaged such a man, Uncle?"

Old Pip roused himself from his chair where he had been listening to the conversation.

"My dear Young Pip, that is an interesting question. Had I known of this predilection would I have engaged him? Presumably it bears no relevance to his quality as a lawyer. What people do and whom they love is a matter for their private lives and conscience."

"I must object. You are a lawyer. He is a lawyer. That kind of behavior is against the law of the land."

"That is as may be, Young Pip, but we do not know whether he actually engages in acts which can be punished by law. For all we know, he looks at other men, but knows the penalties for satisfying his desires, so he abstains. His preferences may, how shall I put this, be thwarted by the law?"

"Let us think about this with great care, my darling," said Susanna, going to Young Pip and catching him by the arm and looking closely at his face.

"First, however much you and I may find the very thought of intimacy between two men abhorrent, the question is, notwithstanding the law, whether they should be free to do so."

"Perhaps, Young Pip," interjected Estella as gently as she could, "your revulsion is because you yourself could not even imagine that kind of relationship with another man?"

"Of course that is true, but only in part," said Young Pip. "I may have ceased to be a preacher, but I still believe the essential truth of the Garden of Eden, that God designed a world of a man and a woman which Christians down the ages have wrought into holy matrimony."

"Well, said Susanna, "I do agree with that as a religious belief. The difficulty is the extent to which a religion can impose its views on others.

"Put this kind of question. It seems probable that within a few years, there will some form of public education which all children must attend. Presumably there will be religious instruction. But is that to be the Protestant religion? Again, presumably so. But, if I were Jewish, should I not be free by having my child not attend such instruction? How about Catholic children? Or would you want to insist that your religion, which is the established one, be forced on children?"

"Of course not," he replied, "but I am not sure whether men loving each other and religious instruction in schools are on the same footing."

At this point, Old Pip chimed in: "This is such an interesting discussion. It has taken us away a little from the work of the Trust. What we seem to have are emerging proposals for helping in some as yet unspecified way those unfortunates who are female and male prostitutes."

"Correct," said Young Pip, "but is not the core of the challenge to find ways in which such people may earn money without going on the street? Say that the Trust, as the Peabody Trust is likely to do, builds housing, teaches such people to be builders, decorators, seamstresses, I don't know, but at the same time, trying to build a community."

"We need to have conversations with these men and women first, as Hamish and I are planning," said Estella, "and then select one or two to advise us. After all, we know nothing of their world. I am sure Nellie has much to offer, especially in terms of how she was trapped into that dreadful situation with the recruiting sergeant."

"My apologies," interrupted Young Pip, "but did you say recruiting sergeant, eh? In Chatham? That could be the one who recruited

Fletcher and me as farriers. I hope Nellie has kept that story from Fletch, or I'm sure he would try to kill him. Estella, please warn her about that."

"I have already done so but will do so again as soon as I see her."

"Well, recruiting sergeants apart, that is a beginning," said Old Pip, "but I think we are going to need political support, though I am ignorant of how that might be worked. And now I must return to Soho as I expect my doctor shortly."

On the way back in the carriage Old Pip dozed and Albert spoke to Estella:

"I think I understood most of that conversation, Estella, and I have been brought up by Joe and Biddy to be a religious person. But I do understand Susanna's argument that men should be free to be themselves and I don't think anyone should be forced to follow a religion of which they are not a part. The Vicar did not prevent my family from being Primitive Methodists, did he?"

"Indeed, I remember your father telling me about that," said Estella, "but your father and I have great difficulty with religious argument because neither of us believe in the picturesque side of it, you know, God making the world in six days and resting the seventh. But you must follow your own beliefs, as long as you take them out from time to time and examine them. That's what Susanna was talking about."

Soon after they got back to Semper House, Estella said, "Darling, I think I should make a start by talking to Nellie further. Might you be well enough to come to Numquam tomorrow?"

"I think not, my dear; you go but hurry back. It is so much quicker these days by the steam train. I do need to rest, I'm afraid."

As Christmas 1868 approached, the Fletchers had been taking a weekly trip to the Three Jolly Bargemen. The pub was its usual jolly self, undergoing constant improvements. Since that day when Young Pip asked Old Pip about his accent, the straw floors were now oak, the chairs were new, the settles had small cushions and Josiah had installed many candlestick holders, making the whole atmosphere feel different from those old days. Fletch was well known and liked in the village, largely because he had built an iron-work bench for the pub garden where folks could sit and drink in the summer.

The Fletchers were clustered together in their settle when Nellie suddenly hid her face, burying it in her husband's shoulder. Into the pub had come Whistler, the recruiting sergeant who had so brutalized her as a young woman.

"Fletch," she whispered, "we have to go. There's a man come in I don't want to see, an old customer I hated."

At first, Fletch's reaction was to confront the man but when she had pointed him out, he thought better of it. He recognized this huge man as the one who had recruited Young Pip and him as farriers. He didn't like him then and he didn't like him now. Unfortunately, there was no way out, except to pass him, standing at the bar, talking to Josiah.

Fletch quietly told the children to go first and wait outside and they were ignored as they walked slowly to the door, wondering what the fuss was about. Nevertheless, they did as they were told. But young Horatio brushed against Whistler in passing and he looked round, saying "Mind out, boy," and looking around for the parents who, he assumed, must be in the pub so that he could remonstrate with them. Then he spotted Fletch and recognized him as someone he had recruited. Their eyes caught each other and Fletch was hiding Nellie under coat.

"My wife's not well, Sergeant," he said as they passed.

"Oh, pardon me," said the Sergeant, and the two passed out of the door.

"I recruited that young man," he continued to Josiah. "I recall he was a farrier."

"Yes, that's right," said the landlord. "He's our blacksmith now, a fine man, a lovely wife, Nellie and two fine children."

"Did you say Nellie?"

"Yes indeed, they both came from Chatham two or three years back, took over from Joe Gargery who was killed in the dockyard, bless his soul."

"Oh, I knew her in Chatham, she was a whore."

"Don't you be talking about Nellie like that," said Josiah, "or leave my premises."

"You don't know nothing," said Whistler, draining his ale and leaving.

Josiah turned to his wife: "I hate all soldiers, you know, how dare he say that about Nellie? She's a little sweetheart with those lovely kids. She works over at that big house, Numquam, too. They wouldn't hire her if she was what she said she was."

"Trouble with those types is that they're too big for their boots," said his wife. "Sailors I like," she said laughing, "but those jumped-up soldiers. Dreadful."

Whistler had not left, however, knowing they would talk about him and hoping to find out where Nellie lived. He had listened at a slightly open window and discovered Nellie worked at Estella's house so he made it his business to find out where that was and when she was there. He remembered her little body and how much he enjoyed himself with her, and he thought he might try that again if he could catch her away from her husband.

So Whistler was often seen around All Hallows on his horse, supposedly on recruiting business, and it did not take him long to discover where Numquam House was.

Estella had not been there recently as she was preoccupied with Old Pip, but she arrived one afternoon in her carriage with her maid. Whistler saw the carriage driving down toward the house, and who should arrive in a cart at the same time but Nellie. I can bide my time, he thought, as he rode away.

"I must again warn you, Nellie," said Estella when she got into the house, "that recruiting sergeant you told me about could be a threat to you."

"Oh, I know, Miss Estella, he came in the Bargemen a week or so ago when me and Fletch and the kids were there. I am sure he'd have recognized me, though we didn't talk."

"So Fletch knows about him and you?"

"Yes, ma'am, with our pasts we daren't have no secrets."

"Well, you must be careful. Men like that are very dangerous. But I want to talk to you about your life. We now have money to work with women in Shoreditch and Clerkenwell. What would be the best way to help them?"

"Oh, I don't know, Miss."

"Well, put yourself back there, what would you have wanted if, say, I'd come up to you in the street and said what can I do for you, money no object."

"I was first of all terrified I'd get a disease, as I'd seen women I knew when my mother was on the game in London, with syphilis and all kind of other things."

"So, medical help would be a priority."

"Yeah, and a place they could go, as they can't afford doctors, and doctors that do work with 'em usually want payment in kind, if you know what I mean, so they are just as bad if not worse, and I'd bet some of them are not really doctors."

"I can see that would be a necessity."

"Most of 'em have nowhere to live; I mean, properly. They have a room with a bed, of course, which the landlord will charge a boatload of money, always in cash. So they need a room of their own. They pays their landlord most of what they earn on the street, unless they's married, then it goes to the husband.

"Like me mum many of them were married, sent out my dad on the street when he was broke, then he took 'er money and then went out and drank it, coming home in a dreadful state. I don't know what you do about that. But I'd say maybe for every tart I knew, one in every three was married to a man who was a right bastard."

"And what about their customers?"

"Oh, dearie me. All sorts, young and old, rich and poor, brutal and gentle, mad and sensitive: every sort of man, really—what's the rhyme: tinker, tailor, soldier, sailor, rich man poor man, beggar man, thief?"

"We will talk again, but I think we will start with medicines and homes."

"Cor, you don't know how much good that could do. I 'spects some women will want to leave their husbands, too."

"Wouldn't that be a good thing!"

Back in Chelsea in the dying days of 1868, Susanna was good health, and their mutual delight in each other seemed to be getting deeper roots as the months passed.

And yet. When a couple begin their lives together caught in a maelstrom of romantic love, they are prone to continue the style and tempo of romance into their day-to-day conversation. That fosters pretensions, as if one or the other conversant is play-acting the romantic lover. That pretense shields them from the reality of their present and from any depth of disagreement, and it can eventually prove their undoing. Romantic love can thus undermine conflict, real or imagined. As they came down to their breakfast, Young Pip was an ardent romantic, and Susanna responded, though some her terse remarks indicated her dissatisfaction with the style.

"Ah, breakfast! What is more wonderful than sitting with my lovely wife, radiant with another baby growing inside her, strong and loving, and here is our little Lachlan, now able to sit in his special chair," he said, tickling Lachlan under the chin.

"Oh Pip, sitting at the breakfast table with my devoted husband is a blissful contentment. In a few years' time, we will be sitting round a table like this with our bairns around us, as we Scots like to say."

"How many, I wonder? Four? Six? You have shown how much stronger you are than poor Beatrice, Old Pip's first wife. She had only one living child, Albert, out of four pregnancies."

"I didn't recall that; how terribly sad."

"Yes, it was, but that will not be your way.

"Oh no, my darling," said Pip, changing the subject. "It is wonderful that we can find shared endeavors and the Jaggers Trust will provide serious and challenging work for us. Hamish and Estella will be working on a very important project, too, whatever my views of the boundaries God has set for us by making man and woman the only proper relationship."

"The spiritual problem for us will be to avoid patronizing," remarked Susanna.

Here Young Pip started to sound particularly unctuous.

"I always loved the description of Christ washing a man's feet. We should be thankful that, with God's grace, it is not us on the street or with perverted desires. You and I must find our own cause, too. Perhaps it will be in education, though I confess still to being tempted by Africa. But, did you not enjoy that talk last night by Mr. Mill on the subjection of women? I'd like to have more conversations with him."

"A good idea, but you preceded him, of course, at our wedding with your pledge to me. How gracious you have been. It really is something we will need to work on throughout our lives, trying to get women treated properly, owning their own property and, even, voting in elections."

"For me, the most important part of our life together is that we share our financial assets, not just because yours are much greater than mine."

He laughs and smiles at her. "If we do that, and we may even disagree at times, we will have the strongest bedrock for our union, apart from our love. I suppose that is easier for me to undertake being brought up as a poor country boy. It is the so-called gentlemen who insist on owning dowries."

"Surely, my dear, the money is not our bedrock; our love is."

"You are right, of course. I am going too far, conscious of the imbalance of our financial contributions to our marriage."

Susanna then brought this syrupy conversation to an abrupt confrontation with reality.

"Do not be foolish about this, Pip. I happen to have money. That is all," she said firmly.

Young Pip, however, wanted to be serious but was still trapped in this romantic framework.

"You are right, of course, my darling. Karl convinced me that the basis to all human social existence is how property is distributed and who has rights over it. That is certainly true when we look at other couples where the husband dictates, gives his wife an allowance, makes the eldest son the heir and so on. I'd like to feel we distribute what we will have when the time comes equally to our children."

"But that might be neither fair nor sensible," said Susanna, struggling now to converse sincerely, without the romantic gloss, and trying to coax Young Pip back to earth.

"I think those with the ability, the talent and indeed the wealth should give to those in need, which is what we have been doing with the Fletcher family."

"That is a splendid elucidation of where we stand, my dear Susanna. But I did mean it when I said that your property does not and should not transfer to me as of right when we married. Mr. Mill mentioned that as a possible area for legislation, and we need election ballots to be secret to remove corruption. But, yes, of course, we are in love with each other as human beings, not connected just by our pocketbooks."

To some degree, to lace conversations with protestations of romantic love gives a man additional power because his partner feels obliged to accept his directions. To protest them might be read as implying that love is on the wane or being withdrawn. Women can thus easily succumb, frustrated in their attempts to speak their mind.

Only Susanna is aware that they must find their way through this trap.

Elsie, the maid, entered with the mail on a silver platter, and handed it all to Young Pip as the master of the house.

"In future, Elsie, please give my wife her mail and give mine to me. By the by, can you read and write?"

"Oh, no, sir, there wasn't no school where I came from."

"Should we not find a tutor for Elsie, Pip, and the other two servants to help them learn to read and write?"

"Of course."

"Oh, thank you ma'am, but I am not clever enough for readin' and writin'."

"Stuff and nonsense, Elsie: You'll be doing both before next Valentine's Day so you can send out your Valentines."

Elsie left, blushing deeply, but returned almost immediately with two copies of *The Daily Telegraph*, giving one to Susanna first, then one to Young Pip. Susanna was reading her mail first.

"Nothing much to date: Hamish's mother, whom I have met only once, is writing to know how he is faring. I suppose it is not odd that we don't see him at all."

"Oh, listen to this, Susanna, how nice of him: Fletcher has written to thank us and begs us to visit when we are Numquam. His writing is about like mine when I was in Malta, but I get the gist."

"Have we heard from Semper House?"

"No. I think we must go there today or tomorrow as I begin to fear for Pip's health and I know of his anxiety about the practice."

"Not to worry, my dear, I am sure Wemmick has settled him into the Jaggers mold."

They continued to read their newspapers, when Pip asked, now in a serious tone:

"Why did Mr. Mill not mention this the other night, my dear, for there is a report here that Parliament is now considering this bill to start some kind of public education for every child, led by the admirable Mr. Forster? I recall your cleverly mentioning its desirability recently.

"Most people in Parliament except some diehard Tories believe that to be a good thing. Of course, it won't affect Elsie and the others as they are not children. But now this word conscience is everywhere. My life has been changed by that word ever since Old Pip talked to me on the marshes."

"I certainly think we need a system of education for all children," said Susanna, "but explain the proposals to me, as we have briefly discussed."

"I don't think I am saying more than you said the other day, Susanna, when we were discussing Hamish and his perversion.

"The idea of a universal system of public education is to replace these charity and church schools; it has been under discussion for some time, and the Liberal Party is keen on having children go to school for five, perhaps six years, starting when they are five. Now the powers-that-be, that is, the Church of England, want all children to have a religious education—that is, to have some instruction in the Bible and the Protestant Religion.

"For every child?"

"Yes. We would be very upset if our children were to be instructed in a faith we do not share, would we not?"

Reading on, he said, "Well, well; they are talking about a Conscience Clause in any the bill which would allow parents of children to remove their children from the religious part of their education if they were not Christians. I must say, I never thought I would hear the word conscience mentioned in politics."

"So we must refer to the problem as one of conscience, not practical politics, eh? I cannot fathom the self-righteousness of those who would deny parents that right, Pip. Just seems politically sensible. Our children will have the religious education we want for them, although we are going to have to decide ourselves what that amounts to."

"Yes, we will, as our beautiful boy Lachlan grows up."

"You are a Methodist, and I am a Presbyterian. It is this freedom matter once again. We are also going to have to decide about whether to send them away to school, not to Eton or some barbaric place like that, but, say, to the school the Methodists opened near Bath, Kingswood, I believe it is called."

"That's true, but that is not a matter for today, dearest. We will reach a sensible accommodation, my darling. The joy of having children shall not be sacrificed on the altar of religious perfectionism,"

Young Pip pronounced with a degree of unction which Susanna found distasteful.

As she walked into Numquam House that afternoon for her quick visit, Estella had grown very uneasy about this soldier who had so brutalized Nellie and had turned up again in the Bargemen. She urged Nellie to be careful and was told that Fletch knew the whole story which was a relief.

She immediately returned to London to hear from Old Pip what the doctors had said. She walked into the drawing room, going straight across to her husband, bending down to kiss him, and waving Young Pip on with his pompous style of talk about politics. Albert was listening intently.

"On the political front," said Young Pip, "I hope to be impressed, now we have the government we need, with the progress Mr. Gladstone will make on several items of importance. Although the Liberal Party is new, we plan to join and perhaps help with some organizing of the poor to influence the Party. Of course there have been Whigs for decades, but this new party seems to me a sensible development."

"That all sounds admirable, my dears," said Old Pip, now sitting with Estella, quietly listening, "but, with regret, I need your attention."

"I have told Estella a week or so ago, but my doctor confirmed yesterday that I probably have only a maximum of a few months to live, maybe much less. He has detected a growth in my abdomen which, though it is still small, is almost certainly a cancer. It is this tumor that is giving me pain and the lassitude I feel."

"Can nothing be done?" asked Susanna.

"It appears not, given my general health. I could go through the rigorous process of having the tumor cut out, but these surgical possibilities are quite dangerous, not because the surgeons don't know their craft, but because it is apparently difficult to create the conditions which will obviate infections thereafter.

"The surgery taken by itself would not kill me outright. My doctor has consulted with others and advises that, while one or two surgeons do remove cancerous growths, patients rarely survive, mostly for hygienic reasons."

"But if you have only a few months," said Young Pip, "why not risk the surgery? "

At this point Susanna interjected.

"Wait. Let me think. I have to recall something very important about this problem. I remember on our honeymoon visit to Scotland hearing a doctor friend speak of the work of a scientist called Joseph Lister who had managed to prevent the infections that come with surgery. I cannot remember the detail, I'm afraid, but I will find out promptly.

"Lister worked at Glasgow Royal Infirmary, I think, so you might go there rather than stay in London for surgery to remove the tumor. But I am going ahead of myself. This discussion came about because we were discussing the plight of the poor in Glasgow and my friend said Lister was trying to diminish different practices, such as amputation, by using some liquid to prevent gangrene. Surely, you remember that, don't you Pip?"

"Where were we?"

"We went see these friends in Princes Street, you remember surely."

"Oh, that's right, but I spent the evening listening to that Presbyterian minister, unable to get a word in edgeways."

"This sounds to be a real possibility," said Estella, "Susanna, will you write to your friend immediately and if surgery is a possibility, we could go to Glasgow for it. But Pip must decide, must you not, darling?"

"Let me think; this is all so sudden, a dim light of possibility. My doctors said it was very likely I would die of the infection. But if that likelihood is substantially reduced, then it makes sense to take up the opportunity."

"Oh, my dear old chap, you can't leave us, we all depend on you. Losing Joe was bad enough, but you too?"

"I will write post-haste this afternoon. But I am deeply saddened by your news, for you have been so kind and loving to us," continued Susanna.

"Dear Old Pip, we must get all the ideas you have for the Trust down on paper and ready to implement. In case."

"Very practical, my dear. I don't have any in particular, but I like the idea of a school.

"I must rest now."

It took only a week for Susanna to receive a letter from her friend, James Dunwoodie, a doctor with that fine Scottish name with its origins in the Lowlands. He had made inquiries at the Infirmary and found that Old Pip could indeed have an operation to remove the tumor there in the next few weeks. He had talked with a surgeon, Dr. Cameron, through a mutual acquaintance, who was using Professor Lister's methods which included the use of a carbolic to kill infections in wounds with startling positive results. Young Pip took a cab immediately to Semper House with the news.

"I think we should go, my dear," said Estella. "You are obviously within a few months of death with that tumor playing around in your abdomen doing whatever tumors do. I will accompany you, of course, and we will stay there after the operation and return to Numquam for your convalescence."

"I do agree," murmured Old Pip. "Fortunately, we can travel by steam train and probably by a direct line. I have nothing to lose, have I, and as Joe would have said, this will be a lark."

"Hardly a lark, darling, when your life is at stake."

"Would you like me to come as well?" asked Young Pip.

"Certainly not, your Susanna needs you. But Albert will come to see something of Scotland, if nothing else, and we might have to away for some time."

Later that day Old Pip was asleep and Estella left her sitting room and went to find Albert.

She got up from her chair and walked down to the studio.

"Albert, come here a moment. You seem to be very busy these days. What are you working on?"

"A scene in Gerrard Street at the moment."

"We must go to Glasgow in January. You know, don't you, that there is a real possibility that having this operation in Glasgow may not succeed and that your father may die."

"I know, and I am frightened."

"Me too, I cannot envisage life without Pip, after these last fifteen years which had proved so life enhancing for me and, I think, for him, too.

"But you, my dear boy, you are so much like your father even in his mannerisms though you spent so much time with the Gargerys. You are almost fifteen, and your tutors have taught you well; you clearly have some talent in painting, and I am glad you have a proper studio here."

"I am trying not to think about it, Estella. But, if it happens, we will have each other, won't we?

She put her arms around him lovingly, murmuring "always."

XXII

Old Pip and Estella arrived in Glasgow after a long, tiring jour-ney and found a comfortable hotel in Sauchiehall Street. It was a very cold day in January 1869 and Old Pip was doing very poorly. Estella made sure he was comfortable, and the following morning in pouring rain she called on Dr. Dunwoodie as arranged. He was immaculately dressed, with fine slim hands and a long dark face not typical of the Scots. He was younger than Young Pip, but clearly a highly intelligent man, as one might expect of a friend of Susanna's. His stone house, typical of that era, had a consulting room attached to it, and it was there that Estella investigated the possibilities of Old Pip's surgery.

"I'm delighted to meet you, Mrs. Pirrip. Susanna's family and mine have always been quite close, though since her parents died in that terrible storm, we have seen much less of her."

"Indeed," replied Estella, "she is a real treasure, a modern woman too with extensive knowledge and a heart of gold, and so well suited to my husband's nephew. But, Doctor, tell me of these new practices which might help my husband."

"Medical men have become increasingly effective as surgeons; we know how to cut off limbs and cut out lumps from the human body. Since the seventeenth century doctors have known about the major cause of all illness, the presence of what are called bacteria, discovered long ago by a Dutchman. He noted that bacteria are all around us, on us, everywhere, some not so dangerous, to put the matter simply.

"So, in principle, we know what can cause disease and how these micro-organisms, to use the medical term, are everywhere. But, undesirable ones get into wounds and create the havoc of infection, damaging and weakening blood vessels, organs and the like.

"Professor Lister, up at the University and the Infirmary here, last year tested a very strong carbolic to kill off these bacteria. Instead of amputating a leg with gangrene, for instance, he treated it with this carbolic, and the need to amputate receded as the leg gradually healed. One or two surgeons here have used it in internal surgery, and it has worked. Patients lived. Of course, because a lump is removed does not guarantee that the disease like cancer which caused the tumor has been halted. But it would give relief, at least for a period."

"That is most interesting and helpful for us. My husband is so ill I am sure he would be ready to undergo surgery and this treatment of Lister's."

"Very well. I assume you have hotel accommodation here in Glasgow? Please have your husband come to meet me at the Infirmary tomorrow morning at ten o'clock and ask for me. Dr. Cameron, a very skilled surgeon, will do the operation, and I will help if needed. We will not expect your husband to be conscious, of course, and will use chloroform very carefully so he feels nothing.

"We have a private room where your husband can be kept apart from other patients. We are even washing bedlinen and the floors nowadays with carbolic. But this is still an experiment, so there are no guarantees. Your husband is a very courageous man."

Estella returned to the hotel very hopeful and found Old Pip also in much better spirits.

"You seem more cheerful this morning, my dear."

"Yes, I am. I am relieved to be able to do something to try to prolong my life, though I am not sanguine about the surgery."

"As I understand it, you won't know much about it as they will use chloroform while they remove the offending object."

"Don't talk about it; let us just hope that this new plan to combat these bacteria, or whatever they are called, is effective."

The day after that conversation Old Pip and Estella went to meet Dr. Finlay Cameron at the Infirmary. He was a man obviously in the prime of his career; tall, angular, also with beautiful hands, which Estella noticed with pleasure, just as she had noticed Dunwoodie's. These would be the human implements that would work their magic inside her husband's body. She wondered vaguely whether the Camerons massacred by the Macdonalds in 1692 had hands like these.

However, Cameron was very direct as he spoke with Old Pip.

"Well, sir, let me first examine you. I need to see what ails you, and I am told you have a tumorous lump in your abdomen."

Old Pip took off his frock coat, vest and shirt, then undid his trousers to allow Cameron access, and laid down on the medical bed."

"Ay, yes," said Cameron as he probed Old Pip's stomach, "ay yes, I see. Here it is."

Old Pip winced in pain and Estella put her gloved hand to her mouth.

"That's good. Let me tell you, Mr. Pip, as I believe you are known; I have cut out some lumps of this kind before, and I am sure it is what is making you feel so ill, fatigued, pained and so on.

"But your lump is, as it happens, easily accessible, not like some I have seen which are so far inside that excision is impossible in the state of our present knowledge. I will make an incision here," and he pointed to Old Pip's stomach just around the lump.

"I will open you up and cut out as much of it as I can. By the feel of it, I think I will get it all. You will bleed a lot, I am sure. Afterwards, these are the rules.

"Number one: Lay absolutely quiet for at least 24, probably 48 hours to allow your body to create the blood you have lost. When I say quiet, I mean as absolutely still as you can. A nurse will give you a sip of water, no more. No food for 48 hours."

"How about infection?" asked Estella.

"I was coming to that. Everything in the room, including my hands, all the instruments will be immersed in carbolic before use.

"Number two: No visitors until I am satisfied the wound is free of infection.

"Number three: No clothes until we are sure there is no infection."

"Number four: Do not return to London or Kent until I say so.

"Thank you for taking all these precautions, doctor, which I hope will be successful. My confidence in you is strong indeed, as I feel so ill."

"We know very little about these cancers, Mr. Pip, and we have no idea whether there are other tumors lurking around your body. For you should be aware that once a person's body becomes cancerous, most of the time, the disease is there somewhere and will strike again.

"Come tomorrow at eight o'clock, sir, and say goodbye to your wife for two days. Then a month or so resting here before I let you go home."

Albert did not come to the Infirmary, choosing to wander up Sauchiehall Street looking in the windows of stores. In the window of a small bookshop, he saw a copy of John Ruskin's *Modern Painters*, and he had just enough money with him to purchase it.

The following day Albert and Estella went nervously to the Infirmary with Old Pip. Both of them thought he would get better. Estella was to receive bulletins by going to the Infirmary to meet Dr. Cameron and later the nurses who were attending him. They wished Old Pip good fortune and watched him with a nurse walk slowly down a tiled corridor and into a room at the end. They then turned around, arm in arm, and took a cab back to the hotel.

Estella realized that she might have seen him seen Pip alive for that last time. Controlling her tears, she wondered whether that happening would bring back that appalling sense of gloom which had pervaded her life, a sense she had not had since Pip suggested she went to see Jaggers all those years ago. But she resolved to expect the best of Dr. Cameron. Away from the familiars of her usual day, she went to the hotel to begin to prepare letters to Young Pip and Biddy to let them know how Old Pip was progressing.

The following afternoon, Old Pip lay in a stupor as the chloroform began to relax its grip and his lungs started to inhale the fresh air of the hospital room. As it did so, the pain in his stomach intensified and a nurse gave him a little laudanum to hold the pain at bay. He had begun to return to consciousness as Dr. Cameron came in to visit him, dressed in a white coat and mask. The stink of carbolic was everywhere.

"Are you awake, Mr. Pip?"

"I think so," said Old Pip.

"I have good news for you. I cut out a large tumor nestling alongside your stomach and it came away quite cleanly, leaving no pieces of it behind. Now, we are being very cautious to try to keep you free from infection. If you start a fever, then that would be one sign of an infection, but so far, so good."

"Thank you, Cameron. I'm in your hands."

As Cameron left, Old Pip felt an immense relief that he was at least alive. Running helter-skelter through his head were images of his past life, starting with Magwitch jumping out at him, but then a hotchpotch of memories, of Joe and Biddy, and of the activities of his wife, his son, his friends and colleagues.

He could only imagine Estella as she now is, as beautiful as she ever was, he thought, a soft smile coming to his lips as he drifted into sleep. She came to the Infirmary just as Cameron had completed seeing other patients, and saw how diligent, caring men, dedicated to progress, were not like London doctors content to rely on traditional methods without experiment. She went to Cameron's office and asked his clerk-nurse if it was possible to see him.

"Come in," said Dr. Cameron from within, "come in, Mrs. Pip."

"Thank you, indeed," said Estella.

"Now I have tentative good news for you. I saw your husband a half an hour or so ago. He is recovering well, crucially without a fever. I was able to take out his tumor, about the size of a golf ball."

"What size is that?"

"Oh, I always forget, you English don't play golf, do you. It's our game in Scotland, and everyone plays who can get out on a course. Anyway," he said, circling his thumb and forefinger, "it was about that size."

"Really, that big? What did you do with it?"

"The golf ball or the tumor?" He asked, laughing. "I jest. The tumor is of great interest to us, in fact. We are a scientific establishment, not just a hospital. So, that tumor has gone to one of our laboratories and our scientists will dissect it, test it, try things out on it. It may well be in use for a year or two, one way or the other."

"Let us assume, Dr. Cameron, that he does not succumb to infection. Will it really be a long time that you will you want him under observation here?"

"At least a month until I am sure the wound has closed. We clean it up regularly, usually four times a day while he is in hospital. We don't know, you see, where all these dangerous bacteria are. Then a month resting here before he can travel, in your hotel if that is convenient."

"And if he survives, can we assume he is free of cancer?"

"I'm afraid not, and we do not know why. As I told your husband, cancer is like an evil jack-in-a-box; it pops up when you least expect it, often nastier than the first time. If he does recover from this surgery, he will almost certainly resume his healthy life. But if later he begins to show signs of fatigue or pain, cancer will have reared its ugly head again, and it could be anywhere and everywhere in his body. That would almost certainly be fatal."

"Thank you, doctor. I will visit each day until I can take him to the hotel, and then probably to our country house in Kent to convalesce. You will let me know your fees before we go, and I will give you a banker's draft."

"Thank you. Indeed, if at all possible, when you both leave, do take him straight to your house in Kent to avoid the world of noxious evil bacteria prevalent in a big city. Don't be in a hurry as, however hard you try, there are always infections waiting for the intrepid out there."

❧ ❧ ❧

Unlike Glasgow where the rain was relentless, it was a fine day in early February in All Hallows. After that meeting at the Three Jolly Bargemen when the family encountered Whistler, Fletch and Nellie had both decided they would always conceal small knives in their clothes, lest there be any attempt on either of them by Whistler. Nellie was on tenterhooks to learn about Mr. Pip's surgery, but there was no message.

Fletch had decided to find out more about Whistler and rode over one morning to see Josiah Steppings at the Bargemen. They both agreed the man was a bastard, that he was a nuisance with women in the pub and Fletch confided in Josiah that Nellie had been a servant in his house.

"Our worry," Fletch concluded, "is that he might be after Nellie, or me, or both of us."

"Soldiers that's been in India or foreign parts get to think they can use women any ways they want. They're like cancers in society; they need to be removed. But you get any trouble, just let me know and I'll come over with one or two of the young men and confront him."

Fletch returned to the cottage and told Nellie what Josiah had said about him coming to help if needed. He put his arms around her and said she must be careful, and she kissed him and said she would, especially when she went over to Numquam. He then added that he would accompany her when she went there, and he'd find odd jobs to do for Estella.

But evil was stalking Numquam House. It was a grey Friday afternoon three weeks later.

Whistler crept around the perimeter noticing that there was no carriage, only a cart outside, for Nellie had received a letter telling her to expect Estella and Old Pip within a week, and she was there to get the house in order. He had been watching the place for several days.

He craved to have his way with her, for through the perspective of his lust, he created a tale, a creature of his fevered imagination. Nellie had spurned him and disappeared, abandoning him, yet now she was back, a temptress, pining for him, so she deserved what was coming to her for her sins against him. She wanted him to savage her, the bitch, and now that was again within his reach.

He told himself he must not kill her as that would mean trouble, yet no one would care for a former whore who was beaten and assaulted. Afterwards he thought he might not be satisfied, so he wondered whether he should not kidnap her and lock her in his house so he could use her whenever he wanted.

What right did that farrier have to her, anyway? She was *his* slut and his power would overwhelm her. He had surveyed the house when it was unoccupied, looking in windows, getting to know the layout without breaking in which would arouse suspicion. He left his horse tied to a tree in the lane outside, and now from the outskirts, hurried quickly through the grounds, being careful not to be seen as he peered in the windows.

His excitement intensified. For there, polishing the silver in the dining room was Nellie in her apron, her hair tied in a bun, her neck visible, and her arms bare as she worked on the candelabra. He would rip those garments off her in a second. He snorted like a boar about to cover a pig. He was right too, he found, as he reached the kitchen door. She'd left it unlocked for him to come to her. She wanted him.

He walked stealthily and very slowly through the kitchen to the dining room. Intent on the dining room door, he did not notice Fletch in the scullery off the kitchen, quietly repairing a broken stool. Fletch had heard the kitchen door open, so he fell dead quiet, knowing it was an intruder, probably Whistler. He could hear Nellie singing quietly to herself in the dining room. Whistler's shadow passed the scullery door on his way to the dining room, so Fletch drew his knife and followed as silently as Whistler was doing.

"Ah, my Nellie," said Whistler, with a hoarse low grunt as he entered the room, "are you ready to give old Whistler what you owe him?"

She was on the other side of the dining table and she turned round as she heard his voice, sure that her dear Fletch would be there to protect her. Indeed he was, appearing behind Whistler, putting his finger to his lips to indicate she should not yell or scream.

"Well, are you going to let me have my way with you or do I have to force you?"

"This ain't your house, Whistler, be gone," she said with admirable presence of mind.

"No, but your body's mine, isn't it, my love?" as he started to move around the table.

"Not bleeding likely," she said, standing her ground.

"Oh, yes it is." As he lunged towards her, Fletch moved up like lightning and plunged his knife up into Whistler's right arm just above his elbow, withdrew it and then stabbed his left shoulder. Whistler howled in anger, but with such pain he sat down hard on a dining chair, blood coursing from his wounds. Nellie came up to him with her knife as he sat there moaning and drove her knife into the slight hollow beneath his right knee. Whistler was screaming with pain and was so shocked he could not move.

"Go and fetch Josiah, Nellie, I'll keep watch on him."

She fled to the front door, rushed to their cart and drove like a mad thing the mile to The Bargemen, returning in only a few minutes with Josiah and young Tom Friendly who had been enjoying a drink at the time. Josiah took command.

"Well, well, well, Sergeant Whistler. Now we will just have to bind your wounds and take you off to the constables in Chatham, won't we?"

Whistler growled and leapt from his chair at Nellie, gripping her round the throat. Josiah and Tom tried to pull him off, but he was immensely strong. She quickly lost consciousness with his iron grip. Fletch wasted no time and plunged his knife into Whistler's neck. Blood spurted from the wound, all over Nellie and Fletch. He died in a few seconds, the blood from his jugular artery running copiously over Estella's Turkish carpet as his body crashed to the floor, releasing his grip on Nellie.

"Keep calm, everyone," said Josiah. "Good man, Fletch. We will need to call the constables. You'll both have to tell the beak what happened as the bastard is dead."

Nellie coughed and spluttered as she recovered from the assault. Fletch was holding her tight as he stared with disgust at the body.

Leaving the body, the four of them returned to the Bargemen, and word was sent to the constables who came to the pub first. Nellie and Fletch then accompanied them to Numquam to see Whistler's body. They had listened carefully to the story from Josiah and Tom Friendly, and then they asked Fletch and Nellie questions too, after which the pair returned to the cottage to get different clothes, soaked as they were with Whistler's blood. Fletch burnt them in his furnace.

Fletch thought the constables would be anxious to get them to a jail, but they were biding their time. No jail, just appear before the beak soon, they said. Then they explained how much time they had spent trying to catch Whistler in the act of raping young women, one of whom had died recently from her injuries. Over the past few months they had had six such women tell them of his lawlessness. Nevertheless, the constables were bound to charge Fletch and Nellie.

Josiah knew that Old Pip was a lawyer and he told Fletch and Nellie that the beak could be a cruel man. So they sent an urgent message to Old Pip in London, but, of course, he was in Glasgow. Nevertheless, Wemmick read the messages on the Monday morning, realizing that the two would face charges in the court on Tuesday as justices of the peace in country courts did not sit on a Monday.

So Hamish and he went post-haste by train to All Hallows to defend the couple. Fletch briefed them on the full story on the Monday evening, and Josiah, Tom, Fletch and Nellie all appeared at the Magistrates Court the next day. The magistrate was Lord Maidstone, a brusque country squire, bald, fat and very curmudgeonly.

The constables in turn gave a brief account of what happened, the charge being manslaughter. However, their evidence was very sympathetic to the Fletchers and they described Whistler as a rapist and a killer, anticipating a dismissal from the magistrate.

"Good God, man," Maidstone said to the final witness, "here is a soldier of the Queen stabbed to death by these two persons and you are asking me not to commit them for trial? What do these two have to say for themselves, eh?"

Hamish got up and told Maidstone he was representing the Fletchers.

"Ah, a London lawyer, and a Scot to boot. Get on with it, Mr. Macdonald, we have not got all day."

Hamish was brilliant. He called Josiah and Tom Friendly as witnesses first, aware that the Fletchers, Nellie in particular, might not impress this beak. From these witnesses, he elicited a picture of a violent man, bent on revenge on a defenseless woman, who had threatened the Fletchers, had stalked Nellie to Numquam House, who had plotted to rape and even kill or kidnap her, but had been forestalled by a loving husband determined to protect his wife from such villainy. He then called back the senior constable to tell of their search for Whistler for his behavior in Chatham. But the examination of Josiah was a key, as he was able to describe Whistler as a drunken villain of great strength who, even with small cuts on his arms and his knee, was within a few seconds of killing Mrs. Fletcher by strangulation.

"Never in my career, my lord," concluded Hamish, "have I come across such a clear case of justifiable homicide in self-defense, and I would ask your Lordship not to send for trial these two loving parents and upstanding members of the community, one of whom is the sole blacksmith able to shoe horses in his neighborhood. I ask that they be bound over to keep the peace for one year."

Lord Maidstone then pontificated about justifiable homicide, self-defense and all that. He wanted the notoriety of being the magistrate who started the process whereby two young lovers went to the gallows. That would be in the newspapers. Here was an achievement that had eluded him after thirty years on the bench, occupied as he was with vagrants, small-town thieves and occasional civil disputes.

Restraining him, however, was the thought that the loss of a blacksmith would be a dire event, in fact a punishment on the community. He was mindful, as he said, that his own blacksmith had left his employ to work in the Chatham docks and he had to have his stablemaster taking horses to be shod in the village near his estate. Indeed he said so:

"I am of a mind to let a judge and jury decide this case, but the involuntary loss of a blacksmith is too much for the community to bear. I accept the advice of counsel. Mr. and Mrs. Fletcher, I am binding you over to keep the peace for five years. Court adjourned."

"You should be very pleased with that result, Mr. Macdonald," said Wemmick as they came out of the courthouse in Chatham.

""I am, I am indeed," said Hamish.

"Well, I fink it's a right liberty," said Nellie. "He was trying to kill me, the bastard."

"I know, Mrs. Fletcher, and I sympathize," said Hamish, "but the best is the enemy of the good."

"What's that supposed to mean, when it's at home?"

"It means, quite simply, that you and your husband are much better off than you would be if the nincompoop magistrate had sent you to the Assizes for trial, when goodness know what might have followed."

"He's right, Nell," said Fletch, "trial or not trial, I've never killed a man before and it makes me feel right weird."

"You will get over it," said Wemmick. "He was in the act of killing your wife, remember."

"Good luck to you both, now," said Hamish.

"Oh, Mr. Macdonald and Mr. Wemmick," said Fletch with his arms around his wife. "We don't know what we would have done without you. You was great in there, Mr. M., really great. I wish I had your gift of the gab."

"It has been a pleasure to see justice done," said Hamish.

"Bringing villains to justice is our trade," said Wemmick, "though in this case, you did it for us, we had just to clear it up with the Law. Mr. Macdonald and I must walk over there to the station for the train back to London."

They all shook hands, though much to Hamish's surprise, Nellie threw her arms around his neck and kissed him fervently, weeping with thanks as she did so.

Both Wemmick and Macdonald felt this was a day well spent, but they talked more on the train about what might happen if Old Pip was unable to return to the practice.

The Fletchers took the cart the eleven miles to All Hallows and on to Numquam House first. They had not had time to clear up the mess of Whistler's blood on Estella's wonderful carpet. They laid it out on the grass shortly and washed it as best they could. They returned it to the gardener's shed to await Mrs. Pip's instruction. The body had already been removed.

Nellie was in tears several times during the next day, recalling the feeling of the knife in her hand and the fearsome grip around her neck and then blood, blood, blood everywhere. Had they been religious Christians, they would have had a priest of some kind to counsel them. Nellie longed for Mrs. Pip to return for her to share her anxiety and distress. She did not have to wait long. Word reached her that Mr. and Mrs. Pip would be arriving at Numquam in two days.

Young Pip and Susanna had also received word that Mr. Pip had recovered well enough to travel home to Numquam, not to London. This new couple was settling into the beginnings of a political life. The year before the 1868 election, a constituency of Chelsea had been created and the member of Parliament was a baronet, Sir Charles Dilke, whom Young Pip had voted for as a liberal. Attractive to Young Pip and Susanna were the young Dilke's radical views.

As Young Pip had joined the Party, women being excluded, he was invited to meet his MP at political meetings in the Chelsea neighborhood, specifically on education, at various times in the spring of 1870. Dilke was impressed by the vigor of his speaking at such meetings, and Susanna and he were invited to social gatherings, though they thought his attacks on monarchy unimpressive. After Dilke had made an unseemly bad-mannered approach to Susanna at one of these gatherings, they turned their attentions elsewhere, specifically to their neighboring constituency MP for Westminster, Mr. John Stuart Mill.

In the fourth year of her marriage to Young Pip, it seemed to Susanna that it was astoundingly successful. Conversation was now on an even keel, the romantic claptrap subdued. She loved her home, its situation and decoration. The substantial library and the piano from her parents' house were now in the assigned downstairs room. They had called in at Gads Hill, and Miss Hogarth was very friendly. Yet, it was her pride that was both her main asset and her weakness: proud of being Scot, proud of being a woman, a wife, soon to be a mother again but proud of her looks and her intellect.

She was fascinated by ideas, as she had told Pip when they first met. She tried Browning but found *The Ring and The Book*, well, boring. She had just completed *Adam Bede* in the year 1859 when Marian Evans revealed that she was the author and was using the nom-de-plume George Eliot. This was a revelation of intense excitement to Susanna, and she connected Mill's as yet unpublished ideas about women to the story of persecution in a small town which forms part of that novel. Her financial and intellectual independence was now critical to who she was.

One afternoon, she read Tennyson's *Charge of the Light Brigade* which Young Pip, buried in Salford at the time of its publication, had never heard of.

She read it to him, and he was moved.

"It does capture the thunder of horses' hooves very well, but it is so difficult to match the horror of the day to the verse."

"I can believe that," she said. "It is totally beyond my comprehension what you suffered, my dear.

"As I have thought about it since, I am more than ever convinced that God does not want us to kill each other, even though he seems to take sides a lot in the Old Testament. You see, I think all the war indicates is men's stupidity, arrogance and greed. That leads to such extraordinary catastrophes as that cavalry charge. Yet men like this Lord Cardigan seem to have no sense of shame or guilt at the damage they cause, I am sure.

"Indeed, the more I read," she continued, "the more I am discovering how where power is unequal, whether in larger matters like warfare or in small matters like a household, there will almost inevitably be animosities leading to violence. Almost every book I read contains descriptions of power or protest against an illegitimate power, like that of men over women."

"I do follow you in this, my dear, and that is why it is useful to hear Mr. Mill. You are quite the political radical and literary enthusiast. Don't stop, will you?"

"No, I am being enriched in every way."

They went the following day to another of Mill's meetings where he discussed the position of women to which he now added the proposition that they should be able to vote, a very radical suggestion.

After their disagreement about Hamish Macdonald's proclivities, the topic had not been raised between them again until they went again to a meeting of Liberal Party members, some twenty in number, addressed by Mill, once again, on the subjection of women. While several husbands in the audience were without their wives, there were several young couples, like Young Pip and Susanna.

The discussion had turned not to questions of whether women should vote, but as to how it might become law. Dr. Harold Griffin set out the reactionary views of women as too emotional and so on, but he was ignored. Susanna, however, whose outspoken radicalism was becoming familiar beyond her family, asked Mill whether his view about a free man would extend to a man who loved other men.

After a stunned silence at the question, a lively debate began in which Young Pip and Susanna were on opposite sides. Mill said that, for his part, he believed the question was a matter of convention, but that should not be an obstacle. Young Pip was adamant throughout, as were many in the audience, that this behavior was forbidden in the Scriptures, an argument which carried no weight with the atheist Mill.

They returned home, both agreeing to differ, conscious that further ferment on the matter would not be conducive to their mutual happiness.

XXIII

However, the debate between Young Pip and Susanna flared up again in the following days, constituting a quite serious argument, unhampered by the tissues of romantic love. They went to bed one night both seething with anger at the other and entrenched in the rightness of their own position such that they arrived at the breakfast table the following morning still sore from the argument.

Susanna decided this was not worth their distress and when she came into the breakfast room, she went straight to her husband and put her arms around him, and they kissed affectionately. Lachlan was sent to breakfast with cook in the kitchen. But it would not go away.

"I suppose," said Young Pip when they began to eat, "that we may have a major difference in that religious belief has a different place in your life from mine."

"Perhaps," Susanna replied, "it may depend on whether we treat the Bible as a text which tells us what to do, which is in many cases ambiguous, or, whether we take New Testament Christian precepts, such as loving your neighbor, and work out their application to our lives."

"Perhaps we can just beg to differ, provided we don't press too much."

"I don't agree, if you mean we are to go our own ways with regard to religion and to major questions, like who can love whom."

"You sound angry," said Young Pip, "but there is really no need."

"I am angry. You sound so patronizing. If I were a man, you'd be arguing fiercely all day about any number of things, this matter in particular, but you seem to want to keep me quiet with this agreeing-to-disagree nonsense. Expressly, you said you wanted a partnership and we are going to argue about matters, especially matters of conscience, not just hide them under the table."

"Is this the discussion about Hamish Macdonald all over again? I cannot alter my beliefs on such a matter. Having a conscience is about holding to beliefs, not merely about how one acts."

"But you are now shifting the discussion. I understand well your position on men like Macdonald. I may not agree, but it is only one matter of your beliefs. But we moved on to the general question of our differences, large or small, about religion in general. These are extremely important matters as we bring up our children which force us to think very carefully indeed about them and how we teach them."

"I do agree with that, and I do see what you mean about being patronizing, and it was not my intention at all."

"I know, but men just get into the habit of wanting control of some kind over every matter. When you say, let's just agree to disagree, you are implying that if you wait long enough my disagreement will disappear."

"Not at all, that is not what I anticipate."

"But you do want to postpone the argument, not prolong it, don't you?"

"Yes, I suppose so."

"But what if I want to continue the discussion? I cannot do that without your participation, can I?"

There was then that uncomfortable silence where both parties are holding their ground, as if they are generals considering their strategy. Inside each of them was a rehearsal of their own righteousness and a certainty of the other's mistakes, foibles, faults, weaknesses, and intransigence. Elsie came in to clear the table and was embarrassed by the quiet where usually there was laughter and argument.

The longer the silence lasted, the more difficult it was to break. Mutual recrimination was the *sotto voce* conversation. Susanna was calmer than Young Pip, so she took the initiative in breaking it, which was seen as a recognition of defeat by him, but of common sense by her. A complete change of topic she deemed essential.

"From her letters, Estella says Old Pip will be convalescing at Numquam. Why don't we go and see your mother and Harry and perhaps the Fletchers, too? A time out of London will do us good. We can stay at the Blue Boar."

Young Pip grudgingly concurred, so she rose from the table and put her arms round him again.

"Dunna let's fight," she said, in a broad Scottish brogue.

She now recognized, however, that in addition to couching argument in the frame of romantic love, this other tactic of agreeing to disagree lent additional power in the armory of a man's control over his wife.

Yet early in May they went to Kent.

"Oh, how wonderful," cried Biddy as she came out of her new home to greet them, tears streaming down her face.

"How healthy you look, Susanna."

Young Pip greeted his mother very warmly and kept his arms around her.

Harry greeted them too, saying: "Oh, you couldn't be a nicer surprise. But where's the baby?"

"Oh yes," said Susanna. "We've left Lachlan behind with the nurse as we came up in part to pay our respects to Sir Charles as his coffin was being taken down to Westminster Abbey."

"Yes, I read about that. But tell me, how are things with you two?

"Excellent," said Young Pip, "we have a house in Chelsea which you must come and visit now there are trains to London."

"Yes, we are very pleased with it," said Susanna, "but we've been married long enough now to have some fierce arguments."

"Now, you two be careful," said Biddy. "You are very strong people, both of you. Arguments always need to be made up when you're married, or they rankle. And, let me give you advice from an old married-twice woman. Never let teasing the other one become a habit, especially a loving tease, which can quickly become a serious criticism, and that then spells trouble, it does."

Young Pip and Susanna looked at each other, neither willing to open up discussion on their marriage.

"Mother, you are so wise."

"Biddy," said Susanna, "I have had no mother to guide me in my marriage, but I so appreciate what you have just said. Young Pip and I will follow your precepts, won't we, darling?"

"Of course. By the way, Harry, do you see the Fletchers? I assume they are all settled and doing well as I have heard nothing."

"You didn't hear?"

"No, what happened?"

"Let me put something on the table and we'll explain," said Biddy.

Susanna and Young Pip then sat listening the story about Whistler in utter astonishment. After lunch was finished, and the story had sunk in, Susanna said:

"We should go and visit them while we are here, Pip. Maybe we can offer some comfort."

"Yes, Biddy, we will stop at the Blue Boar for two nights, which will give us plenty of time with the Fletchers tomorrow."

Fletcher was banging away on his anvil when the trap arrived carrying Young Pip and Susanna. They stayed outside the cottage and Fletch came out rubbing his hands on a cloth. Horatio was watching his father and Victoria was in the kitchen with Nellie.

"How good to see you both—my hands are dirty, so I won't shake yours," he said. "Have you been with Biddy?"

"Yes, and we heard the story about Whistler from them, so we wondered whether we could help you both?"

Nellie came out to greet them with Victoria.

"Lovely to see you. Yes, Mr. Pip, you can help us, as you used to be a preacher, didn't you? We've been so upset at what happened. I mean, between us, we killed a man."

"You could talk with Alice LeBone, a preacher in Chatham," said Young Pip.

"But he's been too busy at his anvil and I'm struggling to keep up."

"Yes," said Fletch. "As you know, like you I've seen a lot of death and destruction, but never done it meself, have I? I mean, he was a real brute and he did try to kill Nellie. But we can't get over it."

"Come, let's go inside and talk about it," said Young Pip.

"When I was worried about going off to fight, we had a long discussion, Joe, Biddy, me and Preacher Whitehouse. On one side there was God and the rules about not killing. On the other side there was Britannia, the country telling us it was our duty. Now, our duty was to go to war, but only if we thought the cause was just. That is, God would be on our side, even though we were killing other people. Well, not me or Fletch, because we just looked after the horses, but we were a part of it all.

"Now, you see, you both are in the same kind of situation. On the one hand, you hate the very idea of killing someone, probably because, deep down, you've a conscience, a voice inside you which may well be the quiet voice of God whispering "Thou Shalt not Kill." But then on the other side, there's this evil man, not only well known for his evil deeds, but he tries to kill Nellie.

"Let me tell you. I think the God I worship would say that you were right, that you had to stop him. When the verdict was justifiable homicide, I want you to think that God Himself would also think you were justified."

"Oh," cried Nellie, weeping buckets, "that is such a comfort."

"Yes," cried Fletch, equally moved, "Now we can put it all behind us."

"I think Pip is right, too," added Susanna. "Put it like this. Although there is the commandment, what would anyone have done in your situation? Everyone, everyone should protect their loved ones. And I don't think it would be any different if Whistler had been an upright citizen. His other behavior doesn't matter."

"Well," said Fletch, "I think we should go and talk with Preacher Alice, anyway. Neither of us grew up religious, and we should investigate."

"Yes," said Susanna, "but please also see that your guilty feelings about killing him came from somewhere other than a religion. You are, in the proper sense, good people."

Young Pip and Susanna were moved by their visit to Kent and they sat on the train, hand in hand. They did not converse much, but they enjoyed each other that night in a welter of mutual forgiveness and passion.

The return from Glasgow had been uneventful. They were able to secure a first-class carriage to themselves to London, crossing in a cab to Victoria Station, and arriving at Numquam House very weary after such a long journey. Estella was confounded by the absence of the dining room carpet which was beautiful and expensive, and thought it must have been stolen, but Nellie was due the next morning and would no doubt explain.

The next morning, Nellie arrived to tell the whole of the Whistler saga, including the court, during which both Estella and Albert, with Old Pip lying on a settee, listened with open mouths, horrified that a killing had taken place in their dining-room. Nellie then burst into tears, helpless with guilt about the killing.

"Are you a religious person?" asked Estella.

"No, ma'am, but I sometimes wish I were. I need to pray for things."

"Now then, cheer up, all is not lost. Young Pip has told us of the time when he was a preacher in Chatham and there is a woman preacher there, called Alice something."

"LeBone," said Old Pip.

"That's right, Alice LeBone: She is in the Methodist chapel there. Why don't you and Fletch go and talk to her and mention Young Pip who has been so kind to you?"

"We will, we will. We saw him the other day and he suggested that too. But he was a great comfort, saying God would think we was justified, and," said the ever-practical Nellie, "just so as you know, the dining room carpet's in the shed. Fletch and me washed it best we could, but I don't fink you'se should bring it back in here. Can I get the gardener to burn it?"

"Please do, Nellie, and we'll get a new one when we are next in London."

"Is there something about this house?" Estella wondered. "First Molly, then Whistler?"

"Not at all," said Old Pip. "We should certainly not let the demise of this reprobate Whistler distract us from the loveliness of this house. It was coincidence that it happened here and thank goodness, Nellie, that your husband was hiding here too."

"Yes, we planned that, but, excuse me, sir," Nellie asked Old Pip, "are you recovered?"

"Thank you, Nellie, I am still weak even two months after the operation, but I do feel immense benefit from the surgery, and we hope that will continue and I will be back to work within the month, and we will go back to Soho."

"That's wonderful. Someone up there," she said, pointing upwards, "looking after you, eh?"

"Maybe; maybe."

The return to the office in June was like a Roman triumph. Everyone in Little Britain, Wemmick, Macdonald, the clerks and the servants, were delighted to see Old Pip return. He was briefed on all the cases Macdonald had handled and was mightily pleased to read letters of thanks for Hamish's work, even a small note from Judge Marcus, extolling his advocacy. Hamish was also delighted that Estella was back in town.

A meeting of the two of them with Young Pip as the Trust Manager had been arranged and took place the following month in Little Britain.

"After my last conversation with Nellie, there seem to be two primary areas to consider: medical help and housing for prostitutes."

"I agree," said Hamish, "but the men I have spoken with need employment."

"That is true of the women, too."

Young Pip said that he had been thinking about how the Trust might be managed, specifically with regard to accommodation. His primary concern was that the Trust needed to move out of Little Britain for its own offices and he was prepared to ask the Trustees, with Courtisone's agreement, of course, that they purchase or build a large building in either Shoreditch or Clerkenwell and let rooms and offices be there as well as making it their location. If not, then they should lease offices.

From these discussions, accommodation would be needed for the doctors they would need to employ in a clinic, and Hamish suggested that a property be acquired to house those women and men in special distress. Estella now saw that the plight of some of these women was like Nellie's mother, whose husband forced her out on the streets. That was a topic she would raise with Nellie when next in Kent.

The meeting ended with responsibilities for finding accommodation assigned to Young Pip, as manager. Hamish would search out doctors who might be available, though he thought it better to appoint a person full-time, perhaps even with a nurse. Estella would probe with Nellie how marriages worked where the woman was a prostitute.

Hamish, with Old Pip's advice ringing in his ears, would get some information of the backgrounds of male prostitutes in terms of their family life, if there was one, and how a young man came into this sordid occupation.

Albert came to Little Britain looking for his father two days later, as he had seemed a little unwell that morning and he planned to escort his father home, although Old Pip had barely resumed his full-time responsibilities, and was in court. Albert was now almost nineteen years old in the flush of becoming an adult and taking seriously his art studies in Kensington with a particular focus on painting landscapes. He had become a handsome youth, tall, with dark, almost black hair, deep brown eyes and was very well dressed. He asked the clerk in the outer office where his father was just as Hamish came in from another court.

"Albert, how good to see you. Can we help?"

"I was looking for my father, as he seemed a bit unwell this morning."

"Well, why not wait here with me and chat until he returns from court which should be, let me see," and pulling out his pocket watch, "in a half hour."

They went into Hamish's office and sat down.

"How are your studies going?"

"Very well indeed. I love painting landscapes, but yesterday we had to start drawing the upper body of a man they called a model. I was not good at it, but the tutor said we must know how to draw a man's muscles and his limbs in shadow and light."

"That sounds very exciting," said Hamish, "I think men can be very beautiful, don't you?"

"Yes, I suppose so; this was a young man and he obviously enjoyed being watched and drawn. He had this slight smile on his face as if he was offering something to us. I could not work it out and in fact it distracted me from drawing his limbs. He caught my eye once or twice which was embarrassing."

"Why embarrassing? He obviously liked you and your looks."

"Do you prefer men to women?" Albert said directly.

Hamish blushed deeply, wondering how on earth Albert would know of his lusts, and answered carefully:

"Yes. I am unsure whether I was just born with this preference or it somehow came upon me through my upbringing. I know that

I have never actually wanted a woman, but then, I have never really had much to do with them."

"Never? Oh, you must meet some. I am finding life very interesting at the School. I have led a very sheltered upbringing, having never been to a school before. I am there in a group of men and women my age, and while I am not shy, I find conversations very difficult. But I look at one or two men I'd like to be friends with and the same with one or two women, especially those that are attractive to me."

"But why these men and not the others? Is it their talent, their intellect or their looks that attract you to them?"

"I don't know. For the women, I like them for different reasons; one because her laugh is pretty, another because she has the most wonderful complexion with a couple of little dimples on her cheeks."

"You see, for me, I have been accustomed to look at the men like that, or rather I would look at that first. Admiration of their talent or intellect would come after. I suppose that might be true of women of my age too, if I knew any."

"How do you cope, Hamish, when the law forbids you to want this, and you a lawyer?"

"I don't cope. I am a bundle of contradictions. I am condemned to seeking out only the company of men and having to stop myself going further than acquaintance with another man. Of course, I could do what I know some men do, that is, marry, have children, but seek out the love of another man or other men. I would not be averse to coupling with a woman for the sake of getting children, but it would be an act without passion, I think, not that I have tried it."

"Would that not be more complicated? I mean, you are picturing yourself in a situation without love. But it need not be like that."

"Probably, but if I could find a woman who understood me and my passions, maybe that would work, perhaps if she were open to loving women."

"Oh, my goodness, how can you think of such a thing?"

"With my desires, the search for happiness is a constant."

As this conversation ended and Albert left, Hamish sat in his chair musing over Albert, but he had to control himself and, with a long sigh, returned to his briefs. Nevertheless, he was now open to the possibility that he had put himself in his own trap.

If Old Pip or Estella had heard that conversation, they would have been mightily pleased. As it was, Albert told them about it at dinner and they looked at each with great satisfaction. After Albert left for his studio. Estella asked:

"Yet why do we look at Albert that way, wanting the love of a good woman for him? We both believe strongly that everyone should be free to love whom they want."

"Social convention obviously plays a part, but I know I want him to have the love of a woman like we love each other."

The summer and autumn of 1869 passed. Young Pip and Susanna's second son was born in late June, the gap between Lachlan and his brother being fourteen months. The baby was to be blessed with the name Malcolm Harold Philip, nothing more, nothing less, which would make him the third living Pip. Susanna gave birth for the second time confidently and easily, which delighted Old Pip greatly as every birth he knew of brought Beatrice to mind.

This birth calmed that household down, love replacing conflict, with Young Pip now firmly recognizing his wife's intellectual power and she controlling her desire to complete with the man who was her heart and soul. Both wanted their marriage to succeed, but even wondering about it might herald an uncertain future.

Old Pip was subject to irregular bouts of pain, though he believed he was better, yet Estella began to confront the fact that Old Pip would not recover.

The surgery had simply given him an additional few months.

So she decided to hold a house party at Numquam in November on St. Andrew's Day as an early Christmas celebration, though without gifts.

And so it was. Albert was thrilled by his status as the oldest child. Young Pip, Susanna and their two children were comfortably accommodated in the house. Hamish was delighted with the date, the celebration of Scotland's patron saint, though he would go up to Scotland for Hogmanay in Edinburgh when the time came. Biddy and Harry arrived with Fletcher and Nellie after they had had a celebration at the Bargemen.

Estella had gone the whole hog and the house was alive with candles, two decorated trees, with presents and cards for everyone, early though it was. The infamous dining room had been cleaned and repainted from ceiling to floor to wipe away any stains of the Whistler incident, and no one remarked on it.

Estella hired a cook and two maids and there was a feast that would have made Parson Woodforde envious. Wine was plentiful, but no one misbehaved. It was as if some magic had appeared in a room which had known such terror. Then there were games which all the children bar Baby Malcolm reveled in. Carols were sung, for Susanna was a competent pianist, a talent which Estella envied and was determined to learn.

Old Pip tinkled a glass after the dessert and said how blessed they all were, for love and friendship. He introduced the silver loving cup found in a cupboard in the Soho house, obviously a relic of Jaggers' ancestors and taught everyone the ritual. Nellie wept, as was her wont, when her emotions were taxed.

"Where were we all ten years ago?" said Young Pip.

"Shut your eyes and think about that."

Everyone did and each of them told of their 1859 Christmas, which unleashed a flood mutual and individual memories. As that ended, in a sonorous baritone, Fletch began to sing that old love song 'Drink to me only with thine eyes' and all the adults joined in, but so quietly that the younger children were almost asleep.

"That was so beautiful," said Susanna. "It reminds me of a scene in a George Eliot novel I read once."

"Me too," said Young Pip. "I heard it sung by a sailor when we were on board the *Majestic*; no, it wasn't a sailor; it was Fletch himself who sang it there, was it not, old comrade? Yes, right there, in the middle of the Mediterranean. Where did you learn it?"

"I think my mother used to sing it," said Fletch, "when she wanted me to sleep."

"I sang it to Joe early in our romance," said Biddy, "and then he tried to sing it, but you know what his singing was like," and those who knew him smiled at the memory.

Old Pip and Estella looked lovingly at each other and sang from memory the second verse, getting most of the words right. After which, there was a loving silence, punctuated only by the sweet noises of children sleeping. Those who needed to went home, and those who did not went to bed.

Old Pip and Estella had to return to London in December as both had commitments, and Old Pip managed the journey and seemed healthy enough. They spent Christmas Day alone with Albert at Semper House, which was now as perfect as Estella could make it, especially with its fine Christmas tree in the hallway. By the turn of the year, he was again unwell.

One January morning he did not stir, and she left him to sleep and went downstairs as Young Pip and Susanna had come to see him, and they were playing with their children and Albert was drawing them with a very fine pencil.

He came down later, dressed, but said he felt his end was near. Estella helped him to their drawing room settee as the morning sun was streaming through its window. She loosened his cravat once more and threw a blanket over him, propping him up with a couple of pillows.

Young Pip and Susanna decided to stay a while to see how Old Pip fared. Young Pip went out for a walk by himself, knowing his uncle was at death's door. He remembered those days when Old Pip told him his story and had urged him to follow his conscience. He thought, as he wandered in the streets, how limited his attempts at good expectations had been.

To be sure he had been a modestly good preacher. He thought of Harriet and how delightful her company was, without stress, without conflict and images of her body flashed before his mind and his desire was momentarily re-kindled. His recent arguments with Susanna were showing to him a side of her that he did not appreciate.

He was a confused and troubled man, and uncertain whether he should not return to preaching, for his faith had started to waver, partly through all those around him, Biddy excepted, who seemed to be seeing the world through secular eyes. Perhaps he was a weak man after all: What exactly were these good expectations urged on him by his lovely uncle, now dying?

Young Pip and Susanna left, but returned the following day, the Feast of the Epiphany 1870, as Susanna was later to remember. Old Pip had not improved, but he had managed once again to struggle downstairs to lie in the drawing room on the settee and Estella comforted him.

Albert went over to talk to them both.

"Father, what can I do for you?" said Albert.

"Read me the morning news, my son, please."

"There is an article looking back at the year, father. The Education Act is mentioned and plans for a Married Woman's Property Act."

"Oh, yes, that is so important," said Old Pip, now struggling for breath.

"When Young Pip got married, you know, he said his wife's property would be hers, and also that they would share everything. Of course, I never took over Estella's property, did I, darling? But now, I fear you will soon have mine. I am feeling so ill. Dr. Cameron said there might be other cancers in my body, and I have begun to feel such intense pain this morning."

"Oh, my dear Albert, come closer, I fear the worst," he said as Estella came into the room.

"Albert," said Estella with what strength she could muster, "can you fetch Young Pip and Susanna from the Library and ask them to come in here, please?"

Young Pip and Susanna followed Albert back into the room. Albert was trying to be strong as he anticipated the death of his father, something not possible for him when they were in Glasgow. He had calmed down and sat by his father on the settee, sobbing occasionally.

Old Pip was slumped, slack-mouthed, deep into the cushions.

They all looked at him carefully, now obviously a dying man. Estella knelt by him, stroking his head, and Albert reached out to hold his father's hand. Young Pip looked very sorrowful, Susanna wept quietly, and then Old Pip spoke hoarsely and with tears in his eyes.

"Oh, I am glad my loved ones are all here. Oh, my dear son, my Albert," he groaned, "look after Estella and become a great painter."

"I will try. I lost Joe and now I am losing you, my father and my hero. How I will I survive?"

"You will; you will, my son. Rely on Estella and Young Pip for advice and help and I am sure they will give it to you."

"Indeed, we will," Young Pip avowed, "Indeed we will."

"Young Pip, tell your mother when I'm gone how much I have cherished her friendship, and you, my dear old chap, keep up the good expectations."

"Susanna, my dear, love your man and help him, I know you will."

"And now, my darling Estella, the time has come."

"What a life we have had together." He paused and groaned slightly.

"If it had not been for Abel, I would not have become a gentleman."

Then, his voice weakening,

"If it had not been for Miss Havisham, I would never have met you."

Now his voice had dropped to a whisper. "Two very odd and dangerous people, really, but they were the instruments that led us to each other. Eventually."

"And then Molly, poor dear Molly, who convinced you that you could love me."

Then, his voice weakening to a whisper, "How grateful I am that you love me."

Estella moved closer to him, kissing his forehead and cheeks. Albert kissed his hand. Young Pip and Susanna were wrapped in each other's arms, watching him gradually leave this world.

There was silence for several minutes, apart from the quiet weeping, as he settled gradually into unconsciousness.

Estella wept, cradling Old Pip, and said: "Dearest Pip, my love. How I have loved you!"

Then Old Pip started up suddenly from her arms, staring into the distance, and, in a firm voice, said:

"What love, eh, Joe?" and collapsed into Estella's arms, dead.

END

Appendix A: Afterword:
Dickensian Themes in a
Contemporary Light

Great Expectations is an autobiographical tale with Pip, a child of the Kentish marshland, telling of how he grew from longing to enjoyment and on to disillusionment over his life up to his mid-thirties. The novel has attracted continuing detailed analysis and literary critique from its first publication in 1860 and has spawned several iterations in film and television. Pip describes his complex relationships in these three phases, and Dickens gives us such intriguing characters as the convict Abel Magwitch, the bizarre Miss Havisham, the domineering lawyer Mr. Jaggers, but also rich and complex relationships, such as that Pip has with Joe Gargery, the blacksmith and also with Estella, Miss Havisham's ward.

At the end of the novel, Dickens tantalizes us with ambiguity in this relationship between Pip and Estella, and he introduces a young Pip, age three, the son of Joe and his wife Biddy Gargery. A sequel beckons: What happened then? This narrative has followed the fortunes of these six characters and introduced several others in a Dickensian tradition. 1840 is thought to be the date at the conclusion of the novel, so the tale has moved from there up to the death of Pip in 1870.

The formidable Dickensian theme of how to help the poor runs through his tale. The politics of reforming Poor Laws and Workhouses, Chartism as well as the abolition of slavery manifest how men's consciences could be stirred to improve the lot of the poor, especially the helpless victims of the Industrial and Agricultural Revolutions. For Dickens, it is partly a matter of the law, partly the generosity of individuals whose moral conscience is well grounded, but rarely in religion, and partly through religious organizations they endow. Dickens was described by Robert Browning as an enlightened Unitarian, but clerical characters in his books are rarely if ever treated with sympathy. Scrooge, in *A Christmas Carol*, meets three ghosts, but they are not the Father, the Son and the Holy Spirit. Across the century, three approaches to the lot of the poor were politically dominant.

First, there was the traditional political activity of Parliamentary legislation, in addition to such philanthropists as Octavia Hill who worked to improve housing and living conditions. Yet there were also politicians and lawyers exemplified by Mr. Jaggers, who tried to keep the poor out of jail or from being transported, a punishment he regarded as savage, especially for children. He sees himself in Dickens' novel as having saved Estella from the grim fate awaiting the children of the poor by making her Miss Havisham's ward, but also saving her mother, a convicted killer whom he then protected as his servant. Jaggers was not a sentimental man but a man with something of a moral conscience interpreted through the law.

Second, however, Dickens does not take account of the impulse embodied in the work of John and Charles Wesley, ordained ministers of the Church of England, who founded Methodism as a gospel of perfection, different from the original sin doctrines of the Established Church, but also open to man, woman and child. This was the antithesis of ecclesiastical class attitudes, notwithstanding the work of Christian Socialists such as Charles Kingsley and F. D. Maurice. The Wesley brothers' movement spawned more radical offshoots, particularly Primitive Methodism, which, in this book, attracts the Gargery family and Young Pip in particular. 'Save your soul' then was religion's advice to the poor.

But Nonconformity not only provided a spiritual basis for reformers, it brought with it the urgent perennial question: what would God want me to do? For poor illiterate people with little intellectual independence, facing such a question opened their minds to the possibilities of thought and action beyond the acceptance of the customs of their station in life. War for them became a personal matter of conscience, not a political matter of grim acceptance. It is no accident that the steady stream of reforming ideas in the 19th Century was supported by individuals not merely having a direct line to God but through their sense that their lives might be different.

The third approach was avowedly political, with roots in English Chartism, the French Revolution and subsequent revolutions in Europe. While social changes implemented by politics were engendered through liberalism in a general sense, the clearest definition of the revolutionary tradition is in the Communist Manifesto, where Karl Marx, using Engels' analysis of working conditions in England, created a theory of the class struggle that led to advocacy of an organized proletariat engaged in civic revolution. Gladstonian liberalism was a gradualist, not a revolutionary, political movement and Marxist ideas influenced the emergence of an organized proletariat in the Trade Union Movement and the Labor Party.

Each of these approaches is favored or entertained by one or more of the characters in this story and each raises matters of conscience for them. However, the active conscience is deeply connected to the Dickensian themes of shame, remorse and guilt. How far a child understands what he has been told about conscience illuminates the question of when and how it begins to flower in a human being; whether it is the outcome of how a child is brought up, or whether, like a sense of fairness, it is somehow innate. If innate, of course, it can still be burnt out or destroyed by others. We might wonder what Estella's moral sensibilities were before she became a ward, or whether Miss Havisham in her final days had her upbringing of Estella on her conscience.

To forgive Miss Havisham is a challenge, but perhaps not if we imagine how she might have been brought up before the tragedy of her engagement. It is hard to view her as having no conscience at all before the overwhelming pain she felt at being jilted. If she simply went mad, conscience would be irrelevant; disturbed perhaps yes; mad, no. After all, she was kind to Old Pip and to Joe by paying for Pip's Articles. Yet even there, we might suspect her motives, for if Pip is defined as a blacksmith, he can never be a suitor for Estella's hand, doomed to live in torment until his adoration of Estella wanes. The vagaries of conscience remind us of our status as moral beings which Dickens frequently appeals to in the creation of such characters as Tim in *A Christmas Carol*, Spike in *Nicholas Nickleby* or Laura in *Hard Times*, yet without a religious base.

Conscience implies a constant preparedness to reflect on thought and action. For instance, Jaggers does not seem to be a compassionate man, nor a man of conscience except where the minutiae of law are concerned. In this novel the question of conscience was raised for Jaggers in somewhat spectacular form with considerable impact on his view of himself. Indeed, there is always the possibility of a man changing his life's direction, which Dickens illustrates so beautifully in the character of Scrooge. Old Pip's crisis of conscience, on the other hand, stems from that period as a gentleman in which he disdained intimacy with his childhood friend, Joe Gargery.

Serious self-oriented reflection is critical to any man or woman experiencing such a dramatic change in their behavior and attitudes, a fact not to be ignored by anyone who advocates reforming the character of others. That the term was a central part of mid-Victorian life is visible in what was known as the Conscience Clause of the 1867 Education Act whereby parents could opt their children out of religious instruction if they did not share official religious doctrines.

Finally, throughout this novel, two contemporary socio-political issues are explored. The influence of religion has already been noted for its absence in Dickens' work, and for its power in enabling people to ask questions of their lot, albeit in addressing what God would want us to do. In our generation, this has far too frequently been interpreted by the hidebound limitations of the Biblical text, rather than by indulging in the free will of thought which God may be said to want us to enjoy.

The second is feminism in its most general terms. For these Victorians matters of property rights and intellectual independence, and the emerging questions of voting became paramount. The Married Women's Property Acts of 1870 and 1882 in the United Kingdom were the result of earnest conversation and debate for many years before. In 1870, women were able to keep money they earned and in 1882 the principle was extended to all property, including dowries which so possessed matters of the heart in Jane Austen's novels. There were exceptions. When Old Pip married Estella, he would not have presumed to control her wealth.

It is not unreasonable to suppose that this quest for a woman's independence was to be found in matters of sexual attraction. The narrative of prudish Victorian morality with standards set by the Monarch is drastically undermined by the awful facts of prostitution. With sensitivity to property questions came the sense that women were being set free to indulge their passions, notwithstanding that this will have been rare as a matter of fact. Indeed, we know of several lesbian relationships as Emma Donoghue's book, *We are Michael Field*, reveals.

Early in the century, Mary Woolstencraft had written trenchantly on women's rights and modeled what became known as free love. Mid-century, John Stuart Mill wrote an essay on the subjection of woman, in line both with his work on liberty and his unconventional relationship with Harriet Taylor. Moreover throughout the century, women novelists and poets such as George Eliot and Elizabeth Barrett Browning became central to literary culture, often exploring the psychology and status of their heroines.

Dickens' life embodies the contradictions in Victorian morality. Happily married at first, in mid-life he takes a mistress. Yet his novels rarely if ever tread that particular ground, more's the pity. We do not need to regard a woman who becomes the mistress of any man as an object of pity, rather than she chooses to occupy that position without being seen as succumbing to male power. Indeed the empowerment of women is such a significant theme in thinking about Victorian life and culture and it is worth the attempt to view it through a contemporary lens as has been in this fictional form.

Appendix B: Contextual Notes.

The *Great Expectations* novel ends in 1840, as determined by one scholar. This work mentions several factual events to provide context.

The village is named throughout as *All Hallows*, the real village nearest to the location of the Forge. It has an ancient church and a pub, *The Rose and Crown* which is named *The Three Jolly Bargemen*, following Dickens. *The Blue Boar Inn* in Rochester, Kent was demolished in 1975 but opened its doors in 1820. In this story, it is a coaching inn on the Rochester-Chatham road nearest the village. The train service to Chatham from London began in the 1850s with Chatham Station being opened in 1858.

Primitive Methodism had a small following in Chatham in the 1830s, and there was a woman preacher. It grew for several decades with a social basis among the poorer members of society, who appreciated both its content, which included perfection and sanctification, as well as salvation and sinners. Its style was direct, spontaneous and passionate. Itinerant preachers were its central feature as with Methodism itself, and this offended Anglican clergy who felt a parish was their rightful domain.

The Chatham Dockyard was a famous shipbuilding dock for over 400 years. All ships named are taken from historical records, including the HMS *Majestic* as a troop ship to the Crimea and passengers ships. Wemmick and Old Pip discuss the well-known sinking of the HMS *Birkenhead* in terms of its evacuation and of marine insurance as an investment: Likewise the sinking of the RMS *Tayleur* which foundered off the Irish coast on her maiden voyage.

The chapter recalling conditions in the Crimea is based on G. W. E. Russell's dispatches to *The Times of London.*

Engels and Marx frequented The Crescent public house in Salford near where Engels was part-owner of a family mill. Marx wrote much of *Das Kapital* in the Reading Room at the British Museum.

Sicily suffered freakish weather in 1852 when two tornadoes hit the island together with considerable loss of life, accounting for the deaths of Susanna's parents.

Sixty thousand people were "recruited" from the Pacific Islands to work on sugar plantations in Queensland in the mid 19th Century, many of them as slaves. John Oxley was a pioneer in Queensland and Macarthur was responsible for the initiation of sheep farming.

Young Pip's letter from the Crimea is a reproduction of a letter sent home by a soldier and is preserved in the Imperial War Museum.

Joseph Lister followed Louis Pasteur on bacteria and developed the use of carbolic acid to treat infections, initially gangrene. He was a professor at Glasgow University, working in the Royal Infirmary in the mid-century.

APPENDIX C: CHARACTERS

(* indicates from *Great Expectations*)

*Old Pip (Philip Pirrip):   1805:   born. Died 1870.
                            Married: i) 1847. Beatrice
                                Pocket d. 1853.
                            ii) 1855. Estella Havisham/
                                Magwitch. February.

Beatrice Pirrip (née Pocket):   1821:   born. Died 1854.
                                1847:   Married: August: to
                                        Young Pip.
                                1848/1850: 2 miscarriages.
                                1852: Albert Joe born. August.
                                1854: 3rd miscarriage and dies.
                                July.

*Estella Havisham/Magwitch: 1804:   born.
                              1846:   Spring, Molly and
                                      Estella reconciliation.
                              1847:   Move to Numquam
                                      house. October.
                              1852:   Molly's murder and
                                      funeral. July.
                              1855:   Married to Old Pip.

*Young Pip (Pip Gargery):   1837:   born. Married,
                                    1865, to Susanna
                                    Urchadan.
                            1847:   May: Converted by
                                    Preacher Whitehouse.

	1853:	Recruited as a farrier.
	1854:	March. Crimea. Wounded Battle of Balaklava. October.
	1855:	Returns from the Crimea.
	1856:	Training as Preacher. Itinerant Preaching.
	1857:	Goes to Salford: Affair with Harriet Middleham.
	1865:	Marriage to Susanna Urchadan.
	1867:	Manager/Director of the Jaggers Trust.
Susanna Urchadan:	1835:	born. Married to Young Pip, 1867, April.
	1868:	House in Chelsea. Birth of Lachlan Finlay Joseph Gargery.
Harriet Middleham:	1838:	born. Affair with Young Pip, 1857.
*Joe Gargery:	1795:	born. Married to Biddy, 1835.
	1851:	Moves to Chatham for dockyard work.
	1853:	Launch of HMS *Majestic*: returns to Forge.
	1861:	Killed in dockyard accident in accident. January.

*Biddy Gargery:	1815:	born. Married: i) Joe Gargery, 1835. ii) Harry Shoreham, 1866.
Albert Joe Pirrip:	1853:	born. February: Son of Old Pip and Beatrice.
	1854:	Lives with Joe and Biddy.
	1864:	Moves to live with Pip and Estella.
*Molly (Magwitch):	1790:	born.
	1814:	Convicted of murder. 1815 – 1847: Jaggers' servant.
	1846:	Reconciliation with Estella.
	1851:	Murdered. Funeral at All Hallows Church.
Ezekiel Unworthy:	1835:	born: Son of Abel Magwitch and Sally Unworthy.
Angharad Unworthy (nee Evans):		born 1836, married 1854 to Ezekiel.
*Mr. Jaggers:	1784:	born. Dies, 1864.
	1821:	Benefactor visit to Pip.
	1847:	Invites Pip to join his practice.
	1864:	Retires July. 1865 dies. April. His will sets up The Jaggers Trust.
*John Wemmick:	1805:	born. Senior Clerk to Jaggers. Discovers Molly's

		Murderers, October 1852.
Horatio Fletcher:	1837:	born. Young Pip's farrier companion in Chatham and the Crimea.
	1854:	Meets Young Pip.
	1867:	Takes over the Gargery Forge.
	1869:	Kills Whistler.
Nellie Fletcher:	1850:	Born. Young Whore in Chatham, later Fletcher's wife.
	1868:	Assists Estella with Prostitution Project.
	1869:	Attacked by Whistler, March.
Hamish Macdonald:	1841:	Born.
	1865:	Junior Lawyer to Old Pip: Appointed March.

*Abel Magwitch: Old Pip's benefactor. Molly's common law husband.

	1820:	Captured and transported.
	1820 – 1835:	Farming sheep in Queensland.
	1835:	Revealed as Pip's benefactor, Dies in prison.

Secondary characters:

Preacher Jeremiah Whitehouse:	Chatham Chapel
Herbert & Clara Pocket:	Old Pip's friends.
Mary Magdalena Burns:	Young Irish woman in Salford.

Annie Smith:	A beggar widow.
Friedrich Engels and Karl Marx.	
Mary:	Jaggers' house servant.
Harry Shoreham:	Biddy's second husband.
Reverend Claud Windnortham:	The Vicar of All Hallows.
Algernon and Sybilla Pocket:	Parents of Beatrice.
Adam Thistlewood:	Estella's gardener.
Josiah Steppings:	Landlord (wife Jezzy) The Three Jolly Bargemen.
Thomas Mistyfield:	Dockyard agent.
Alice LeBone:	Chatham Preacher.
Jonah Steppings:	Landlord of *The Blue Boar Inn*.
Recruiting Sergeant Whistler.	
The Primitive Methodist Elder in Salford.	
Dr James Dunwoodie:	Doctor in Glasgow.
Dr. Finlay Cameron:	Surgeon, Glasgow Royal Infirmary.
Lord Maidstone, J.P.	

Other mentioned characters

Georgiana Gargery:	Joe's first wife.
Sam and Mary Friendly:	Customers at the Three Jolly Bargemen
Tom and Mary Butterworth	
Miss Havisham	
Cecilia Turnington:	Beatrice's Bridesmaid
Jack and Billy Compeyson:	Two villains
Corporal Dereham:	Assistant to Sergeant Whistler
Elsie:	a midwife.
Gladys:	a midwife.
Farrier-Major Turner	
Lord Cardigan	
Herbert Buzza:	Stables Owner in All Hallows.
Mr. Hector Bristle:	Gatekeeper at Chatham Dockyard,

Printed in Great Britain
by Amazon